WHERE THE DEAD GO

SARAH BAILEY

T0363527

ALLEN&UNWIN
SYDNEY·MELBOURNE·AUCKLAND·LONDON

This edition published in 2020
First published in 2019

Allen & Unwin
83 Alexander Street
Crows Nest NSW 2065
Australia
Phone: (61 2) 8425 0100
Email: info@allenandunwin.com
Web: www.allenandunwin.com

 A catalogue record for this
book is available from the
National Library of Australia

ISBN 978 1 76087 805 4

Set in Minion Pro by Midland Typesetters, Australia
Printed in Australia by Pegasus Media & Logistics

10 9 8 7

'Every bit as addictive and suspenseful as *The Dark Lake* . . . Sarah Bailey's writing is both keenly insightful and wholly engrossing, weaving intriguing and multi-layered plots combined with complicated and compelling characters.' *The Booktopian*

'Bailey's writing is sharp, her sense of place harrowing, and her mystery intriguing. A great read for anyone who likes complex characters and gritty crime.' *Glam Adelaide*

'If you're a fan of quintessential Australian crime fiction, you must read *Into the Night* . . . Sarah Bailey shows us that she is a force to be reckoned with in the Australian crime field.' Mrs B's Book Reviews

'An excellent follow-up to *The Dark Lake* . . . sets a new bar for psychological thrillers.' Blue Wolf Reviews

'Gemma's prickliness matches perfectly with a city alive on the page—one both recognisable and horrifying to local Readings customers who traipse the streets where blood is spattered in these pages. This is a gritty metropolitan police procedural that shows Bailey is only getting better.' Readings

'Dark, gritty, teeming with atmosphere, *Into the Night* is police procedural crime fiction at its very best.' Theresa Smith Writes

PRAISE FOR *THE DARK LAKE*

'*The Dark Lake* is a thrilling psychological police procedural as well as a leap into the mind of a woman engulfed with guilt.' *New York Journal of Books*

'*The Dark Lake* hooked me from page one! Sarah Bailey combines the very best elements in this stunning debut thriller—a troubled detective still trying to find her way as a female investigator, a small town haunted by secrets both past and present, and a beautiful victim whose unsettling allure appears to be her biggest asset and largest downfall. With clever twists and all-too-human characters, this book will keep you racing toward the end.' Lisa Gardner, #1 *New York Times* bestselling author of *Right Behind You* and *Find Her*

'This polished debut is a winner from the first page.' *Daily Telegraph*

'I read *The Dark Lake* in one sitting, it's that good. A crime thriller that seizes you from the first page and slowly draws you into a web of deception and long buried secrets. Beautifully written, compulsively readable, and highly recommended.' Douglas Preston, #1 *New York Times* bestselling author of *The Lost City of the Monkey God* and co-author of the bestselling Pendergast series

'An addictive and thoroughly entertaining read.' *Weekly Review*

'Debut author Sarah Bailey depicts both the landscape and Gemma's state of mind vividly, bringing into focus the intensity of Gemma's physical and emotional pain and her increasing discontent. *The Dark Lake* adds to the trend of haunting, rural Australian crime fiction, and provides a welcome addition to the genre for those left bereft after finishing Jane Harper's *The Dry*.' *Books + Publishing*

'*The Dark Lake* is an absolutely stunning debut. This is such a beautifully written and utterly absorbing read, it's hard to believe that it's the author's first novel. I love to get my hands on a good character-driven murder mystery—especially one with a complex protagonist and a plot that keeps me guessing. *The Dark Lake* delivers all of this and more. The characters and relationships portrayed are so intricate and messy and real . . . it was a real struggle for me to put this book down.' Sarah McDuling, Booktopia

'. . . a page-turner that's both tense and thought provoking.' *Publishers Weekly*

'*The Dark Lake* by Sarah Bailey is a brooding, suspenseful and explosive debut that will grip you from the first page to the last.' *New Idea*

'A compelling debut.' *Booklist*

'I raced through this deliciously complicated, mesmerising debut at warp speed. Sarah Bailey's *The Dark Lake* is sure to keep readers awake far too late into the night.' Karen Dionne, author *The Marsh King's Daughter*

'Enthralling . . . Bailey uses solid character development and superior storytelling, rather than violence, to fuel *The Dark Lake*, and she is off to an excellent start in this launch of a series.' Oline Cogdill, Associated Press

Sarah Bailey is a Melbourne-based writer with a background in advertising and communications. She has two children and is currently the Managing Partner of advertising agency VMLY&R in Melbourne. Over the past five years she has written a number of short stories and opinion pieces. Her first novel, the bestselling *The Dark Lake*, was published in 2017, followed by *Into the Night* in 2018. *Where the Dead Go* is her third novel in the Detective Gemma Woodstock series.

*For my mum and dad, who filled our house with books
and, as a result, filled my head with ideas*

Sunday, 10 April
12.21 am

The girl pushes blindly through the wall of trees, tripping over her feet. The crash still rings in her ears and joins the uneven rhythm of her breathing. She pauses, momentarily overwhelmed as she stands in the darkness. Then she yanks her phone from her pocket, waking the screen and pressing buttons until a fresh rush of anger surges through her. She shoves it back.

What's the point of calling him? What more is there to say?

There's a low rumble nearby before the road lights up like a runway, and two giant beams bear down on the asphalt. She scrambles backwards to the safety of the thick shrubbery. A truck thunders past, rattling the bones of the earth. The world is cast back into darkness, and she wrenches strands of her long hair free from twigs and branches, stepping back onto the road and running toward a distant street lamp.

Mannequins leer from their glass cages, and cartoon signs seem to have an underlying sinister tone. Even though it's still warm, the girl hugs her hands around her torso, desperately wishing she was wearing a jacket.

Snap.

She stiffens. Was that the sound of someone treading on a stick?

Without stopping to look, the girl veers off the main street and darts to the small path leading to the beach. Blood pounds through her veins. Sweat and make-up mingle with her tears.

Stop crying. Stop being so pathetic.

Deep down she knows where she's headed and swallows past the shame. But it's not like she planned for the night to work out like this, for any of this to happen.

Underfoot, the grainy dirt turns to sand and the tunnel of trees opens onto the curve of the bay. The moon hangs above the ocean, a giant white orb that spotlights the tips of the waves.

A stitch stabs at her side, and she bends over to catch her breath. Pushing her fingers against her belly in an effort to ease the pain, she stumbles along the edge of the sand past the car park.

A sob escapes her throat and she hastily blocks out the scenes from earlier. Arguments echo in her head, the words chasing each other until she's crying again. His touch lingers on her skin, and regret overwhelms her. She lost her mind for a moment back there.

On the left she reaches a worn wooden fence, and beyond that the soft glow of the service station. She looks up along the shore to where the jagged cliffs mark the end of town. She looks back toward the shop; she desperately needs some water.

A low voice threads past the pulsing in her brain. She whips around, eyes huge and heart hammering.

Nothing. Just the wind ruffling the dry grass and the rhythmic hum of the sea kissing the shore.

She eases the gate open and steps onto the cracked asphalt.

That's when she sees them: two shadowy figures huddled in the far corner of the car park, next to the open boot of a vehicle.

Her eyes adjust enough for the twosome to be recognisable, for her to make out what is happening.

Betrayal smacks her hard in the face and, to her horror, she whimpers.

The shadows freeze.

Her feet are balls of concrete, rooted to the ground.

Tree leaves swish gently, waves crash against sand.

One of the figures breaks away, takes a step toward her. 'Hello, Abbey,' he says. He tilts his head kindly, but there's malice in his gaze. 'You're out late.'

She tightens her grip on her phone and fumbles backwards, gasping, falling. Her wrists buckle as she hits the ground, but she barely registers the pain. 'No!' she yells, scrambling to her feet.

'Come on, don't be like that.' He walks quicker now.

She staggers away from the beach toward the shops. Her veins become ice tunnels, jarring against the heat of her blood.

Another voice yells her name, high and desperate.

There's a sharp metallic clatter as something hits the ground. Her phone, dropped from her shaky fingers.

He kicks it along and picks it up. He laughs.

No, no, no.

Desperate, she scans the empty street. The artificial light from the service station reaches around a large vehicle parked near the bowsers but there's no way she can get there before he reaches her. She knows how strong he is, and she doesn't know how far he'll go. What he is capable of.

She doesn't even think to scream. Her only thought is to run.

His footsteps are loud behind her as she propels herself forward, struggling to breathe while dread threatens to choke her.

The sporadic cries of her name are lost in the dance of the wind.

FIRST DAY MISSING

Sunday, 10 April
7.42 am

Dot Clark eases herself out of bed, grunting with the effort. Daniel is already up. Dot squeezes her eyes shut and says a brief prayer, the fear she felt last night as raw as the bruises on her shoulder. Hopefully he's on the back porch sleeping off his hangover. He sits out there in the early hours sometimes when it's particularly hot, legs spread and belly bulging like a scantily clad Father Christmas. The bugs never bother him, not even the mosquitoes. Dot wonders if his temper makes his blood taste nasty.

He was especially bad last night, worse than usual, and the stink of booze distilled through his leather-thick skin still perfumes the air.

Dot pulls her stringy hair into a low ponytail and swaps her thin nightie for a faded sundress. She throws the sheet across the bed and fluffs the limp pillowcases, the movement causing a little jolt of pain to charge through her. Sections of her rib cage are dark purple and throb unprovoked. She puts her hands on her hips, already exhausted. Despite her solid sleep, the events of last night have left her completely drained.

She feels an unexpected rage toward both of them: Daniel's a human landmine, unpredictable and vicious, but Abbey always seems so intent on setting him off. She crossed a line last night—they will all pay for that.

Dot wheezes through a few breaths as her anger fades to a familiar hopelessness. She shuffles to the end of the bed. She hates this house but she especially hates this bed; she hates the ugly wooden headboard and the rock-hard mattress with its stubborn sweat stains. Odd, then, that all she wants to do after getting up every morning is to crawl back onto the grotty slab and close her eyes again.

She limps slightly as she approaches the boys' room, her knee still aching from her fall last weekend; Daniel pushed her down the three stairs to the backyard.

Chris and Wayne's curtains are drawn but the day is determinedly muscling in, giving the wooden room a rosy glow. Tentative sunlight reveals the ancient fan in the corner, stoically shifting stale air from one spot to another. Their floor is littered with things: clothes, books, papers, gadgets, trinkets. Dot remembers them as little boys, always with objects in their hands or mouths, bashing, chewing or picking them apart.

Not like Abbey. Dot's daughter would sit for hours just staring out the window or drawing shapes in the dirt with a stick.

Boys are busy, Dot's mother used to say with a bored shrug. *They can't bloody sit still—they're too scared to, it'll mean they have to think.*

Dot's twin sons are certainly not busy right now; they are asleep, naked but for underpants. Chris is on his front, his legs spread wide, the balls of his dirt-stained feet facing the ceiling. Wayne is a long soft curve, his heavy brows two sharp lines above his spray of dark lashes. They are just starting to show signs of manhood, a thought that prompts both fear and relief.

She doesn't like to think about the inevitable: the fact that one day, they will all leave. Escape. Abbey's bedroom door is wide open, and so are her curtains, the small room awash with clean white light. As always it is rigidly neat. Daniel finds it maddening: just one more thing he can't lash out at her about. Dot's eyes scan the photos on the desk then drift to the denim jacket lying across the bottom of the bed, the covers under it smooth, the faded blue pillowcase undented at the opposite end.

A loose knot of worry that has been forming in Dot's gut pulls tight. She bends at the middle, pressing her hand to the grubby wall, and wheezes again before spluttering through a few asthmatic coughs.

Her legs are shaky as she makes her way slowly down the stairs.

Daniel is in the kitchen, dressed in a blue singlet and faded jeans. His bronzed face shines with sweat. Despite the extra weight, he looks remarkably similar to the teenager she once swooned over. If she's completely honest, a certain look from him can still make her insides lurch with desire, her body somehow immune to the years of pain and suffering.

Daniel's eyes are fixed on the mug of tea in front of him. The tea bag hangs out the side, wetness edging along the string to the label. She gets a whiff of the fat from last night's sausages. Flies buzz above the stack of dishes in the sink, and the sound fills Dot's head.

'She's not here,' Daniel says, the husky rumble of his voice joining the hum of the flies.

'Oh,' says Dot, trying her hardest to think around the noise, to think of something to say. She clasps then unclasps her hands, before gripping them together again. She swallows. Cold beads of perspiration erupt from her pores.

'I'm going to bloody kill him!' roars Daniel. Tea sloshes everywhere as he slams his fists on the table.

SECOND DAY MISSING

Monday, 11 April
8.14 am

Scott slipped away to wherever the dead go in the early hours of Wednesday morning. Three months to the day he was diagnosed with the illness that ravaged his body, trapped his mind and stole his future.

The illness that drove a stake through our normal.

The hospital called me just after 10 pm last Tuesday, minutes after Ben had finally fallen asleep and just as I was fixing myself an extra-large whisky. Doctor Dave's soothing voice informed me Scott had slipped into a coma; after resisting death so stubbornly, he was now catapulting toward it. Jodie had asked Dave to call me, and he was of the view we should come now, if this was what we wanted.

Dad and Rebecca decided not to go, so it was just Ben and I who stepped out into the night. The wind roused the gum trees above the carport and they spritzed eucalyptus into the air as I bundled Ben into Rebecca's Volvo. Shutting his door gently, I looked to the ceiling of silver stars and breathed shakily through my fear.

I steered us through Smithson's dark streets, gripping my son's hand across the console, unable to speak. This thing that was about to happen seemed so impossible, no words made sense.

The hospital glowed eerily and was set to a soundtrack of electronic beeps, expensive machines grimly breathing life into fading humans. I can barely remember guiding Ben through the white corridors, only the harsh smell of disinfectant and the occasional sympathetic look from a nurse.

Jodie was breastfeeding Annabel when we reached Scott's room, her free hand gripping Scott's left one, pain etched so deeply into her expression that I wanted to scream. I can't remember ever feeling so helpless.

But Ben, our little boy, was astoundingly fearless, laying his head on the pillow next to Scott's face and stroking his cheek with his hand. 'It's me, Dad,' he said softly. 'I'm here.'

I hung back, hand glued to the doorframe, my chest compressing violently. The ghost of the conversation Scott and I'd had only days earlier taunted me. This was it, I realised. Everything we'd talked about started now.

After a few minutes, Jodie gave me a pointed look. She sniffed and stood, clutching Annabel to her chest as she moved to the corner of the room.

My turn.

I picked up Scott's free hand, still warm from Jodie's touch. A hand that until recently had been so capable. So strong. I squeezed gently, looking across his chest to our son. Ben's eyes were like green marbles, his mouth moving in a silent one-way conversation with his dad.

The bed shuddered with Scott's scratchy breaths. My throat swelled as I closed my eyes and said a final goodbye, said sorry, and made silent promises I hoped like hell I could keep.

My relationship with death is solid. We go way back. We were initially introduced through my mum, who died of an aneurism when I was fourteen, and again a few years later when my first serious boyfriend, Jacob Mason, committed suicide. As a detective I've touched death with my bare hands. I've circled it, smelled it and looked it straight in the eye. I know it's never far away. I spend a lot of my life thinking about it, talking about it, even expecting it—and when you confront something over and over, your brain eventually relaxes around it.

Perhaps this is why I'm so surprised that Scott's death has rattled me so badly. I'm a shuddery, miserable mess, even though I absolutely can't be. Every sobering thought of my fatherless son, poor widowed Jodie and blissfully clueless baby Annabel is a stabbing reminder that I have no right to grieve. In life, I treated Scott like a toy I'd grown tired of. I expected so much of him while he expected so little of me. Now, years of regret have surfaced with astounding force. I keep replaying our final conversations in my mind, his words gnawing at my heart. I was terrified of him dying, but now he's gone I'm really scared.

Both Mum and Jacob were snatched away, leaving me devastated but stinging with the absolute certainty they had vanished from this world, despite how desperately I wanted them to come back. In contrast, I feel Scott everywhere. He's watching me curl around Ben at night, our faces soaked with tears. He's listening as I try to reason with Ben, who has declared he won't go back to school or respond to his friends' clumsy messages. Scott's also listening as I stumble through conversations with his brother, and as I try and fail to say the right thing to Jodie.

I'm stuck in a bizarre limbo between the life I had in Sydney and this life—back in my home town, but with everything broken and unfamiliar.

With Scott's widowed mother too unwell to travel and no other relatives coming from afar, the funeral is arranged at lightning speed.
Jodie and Scott confirmed the details over the past few weeks, so it's
just a matter of going through the motions on the conveyor belt of
grief. And there seems to be no shortage of people to tell us what
needs to happen next.

I'm grateful to be propelled forward, reluctant to do anything
but practical, physical tasks, knowing the mental part of this will
be the most difficult. Impossible. Establishing a new life, forming a
new plan. In many ways I'm desperate to remain in this holding
pattern where the expectations are low. On the other hand, the
endless time to think, in the fishbowl that is Smithson, is making
me go completely insane.

On the morning of the funeral, Ben and I barely speak. I shower
and pull on a black dress, one I packed with Scott's funeral in mind.
Then I comb out my thick hair and twist it into a low bun, before
helping Ben into his new suit, purchased only two days ago.

'Buy him a new suit for the funeral, Gemma,' Scott said to me,
around the time his skin lost the last of its tan. 'I don't want him
in the same suit he wore to my wedding.'

I snip off the tags and help Ben gel his hair. Cupping his face in
my hands, I stare into his eyes, giving him a firm nod as my jaw
wobbles dangerously. He swallows hard and nods back.

We can do this, but only just.

The sunlight is a cheerful yellow and I fish around in my
handbag for my sunglasses but can't find them. Ben and I clamber
into the back seat of Dad's Toyota Hilux, which makes me feel like
a child. Dad's profile is solemn as he turns the key. He has combed
his grey hair flat, and the woody smell of his aftershave permeates
the confined space, making my eyes water. Rebecca sits ramrod
straight, her ash bob weighted down by hairspray. A string of fat

pearls circles her neck. Every few minutes she dabs at her eyes with a floral-print hanky.

Peak hour in Smithson has nothing on the madness of Sydney traffic. A modest line of vehicles falls into a convoy, starting and stopping to the beat of the traffic lights. We pass the supermarket, the library, the tattoo parlour. On both sides of the street, kids in school uniform brave the new week in little clusters, giant backpacks bobbing above their small heads. Women push prams, their lycra-clad legs pumping energetically, sunglasses masking their lack of sleep. Older couples walk dogs.

We see it all but absorb none of it. We are not part of that world today.

My phone vibrates with a message from Mac.

Thinking of you and Ben. I really wish you had let me come to support you. I love you, call me later.

I picture him pacing the small home office in our apartment, a worried expression on his chiselled face; his kind eyes, his thick blond-grey hair that I love to grab onto when we're kissing. Tears blur my vision as I tap out a reply and slide my phone into my purse. I miss him, but I was right in not letting him come. Mac doesn't have a place in today's narrative and I want to avoid the pointless mental loop of bemoaning how cruelly our life together has been disrupted. There's plenty of time for that tomorrow, and all the days beyond.

Cheerful rays of morning sun stream through the car windows as the familiar strains of the ABC Radio news sting roll through the car. The bulletin is spearheaded by a breaking homicide in Fairhaven, a beach town north of Byron Bay. A seventeen-year-old male has been beaten to death in his home, and police are appealing for anyone with information to come forward. They are also seeking information about a missing teenage girl, known to the slain boy, who was last seen at a house party on Saturday night.

The words 'missing teenage girl' turn my blood to ice. Around six months ago I worked an investigation that all but broke me, arguably the lowest point of my career. A game of cat and mouse that played with my emotions, made me question my instincts and tossed me between hope and dread, until I was forced to let go of the last shred of faith I had in humanity.

Nicki Mara had brought Mac and I together, and in the end she almost tore us apart.

I grip Ben's hand as we near the church. In spite of the circumstances, my mind begins to riff off the sketchy details in the news report. Were the dead boy and the missing girl a couple? Friends? Are the two incidents linked? Is the girl still alive? Could she have murdered him?

My train of thought is interrupted by Dad clearing his throat and flicking off the radio, no doubt deciding we already have enough death and tragedy to deal with today.

The funeral is unbearable. Ben is like a statue beside me. Jodie weeps loudly a little further along the pew, while baby Annabel's happy gurgles break every heart in the church. It's hot and stuffy and I worry first that I will be sick, and then that I will faint. An oversized version of Scott watches me serenely from the easel beside his coffin, almost as if he is waiting for me to fuck up.

The burial is brief. Scott is lowered into the gaping hole in Smithson's church graveyard to a soundtrack of muffled crying and shaky breaths. The minister says something about the earth and Scott's soul, and then it's over. He's gone, just like that.

At the wake, I endure excruciating small talk for what feels like hours but is in fact only twenty minutes. Finally escaping to the kitchen at the back of the church hall, I fill a glass with water and knock it back in two large gulps before refilling it to take to Ben. As I walk away from the sink, exhaustion hits me like a gunshot, sharp through my brain, energy flowing out of me so quickly I worry I'll collapse. I want to be anywhere but here.

Josie Pritchard bustles in, an empty plastic tray in her hands, and gives me an efficient once-over that somehow feels both maternal and cool. 'How are you holding up, dear?' When she opens the oven, I can feel the heat from where I'm standing. She pulls out the tray and plonks it on top of the cold hotplates, then starts picking up the steaming pastries with her bare hands.

'I'm okay,' I say, which is a lie but one I know everyone around here is keen for me to keep telling, especially today.

'Terribly sad for your little mite, all this,' she says absently, arranging the flaking squares in neat rows on two long plates. 'Especially seeing as he was so happy about finally having a sibling! And poor Jodie, god bless her.'

I don't reply, muttering a sound that hopefully passes as polite agreement before I head back into the main room and walk briskly to the outside area. No one knows what to do with me. I'm not Scott's girlfriend, not his widow, not even his ex-wife. But I'm hardly just an acquaintance. My presence feels like a glitch, a contagious awkwardness.

I spot my best friend, Candy Fyfe, across the faded green lawn. She's a beacon of colour in the sea of black mourners, her lilac dress stretching over her huge pregnant belly. I pause abruptly when I realise she is talking to Jodie.

I'm fighting a strong impulse to throw a tantrum. A giant messy number. I want to beat at the ground with my fists. Roar into the dirt. I want someone to tell me what to do. What the fuck do I do now?

My old boss Ken Jones, 'Jonesy', is on the phone in the shade of the church hall, his spare hand holding a paper plate stacked high with club sandwiches and cake. The creases in his forehead deepen. It must be a work call.

I join Dad and Rebecca, who are talking to Jack Grace, one of Scott's long-time work friends.

'God, this is awful, huh?' he says to me.

I nod, another wave of hopelessness threatening to drown me.

'When are you heading back to Sydney?' he asks.

Everyone's eyes are on me as goose pimples pepper my arms. 'I don't know yet. We need to work out whether Ben will live in Sydney with me, or whether I'll, um, move back here for a while.'

Dad's eyes remain fixed to the ground during this exchange, and Jack looks between us in surprise. 'Oh, so you're going to have custody of Ben? I figured he'd keep living with Jodie.' Jack shakes his head. 'Wow, that's massive.'

'Excuse me,' I say, tripping slightly as I make a beeline for the trestle tables.

Jonesy strides toward me, his large frame stretching the seams of his dark suit. 'Woodstock, how are you holding up?'

I snap back into focus and serve him my standard line. 'I'm fine.'

'No, you're not,' he barks, placing a hand on my shoulder.

I shrug through fresh tears and throw a hand across my eyes to block out the glare. Where are my bloody sunglasses? I grind my jaw and shift my weight from leg to leg, the rarely worn high heels pinching at my ankles. I'm doing everything I can to avoid going to pieces, but I'm not sure it's going to be enough. I miss Mac. I miss Sydney. I miss how everything was before Scott's goddamn phone call.

Jonesy hustles me sideways, out of the sun. I spot Ben standing with Jodie. His hair gel has fallen out and dark locks drift into his eyes. He doesn't look eight; he looks like a toddler.

'Is something going on?' I ask Jonesy. 'I saw you on the phone before.'

'What? Oh yes.' He stuffs a triangle of chicken sandwich in his mouth and skilfully manages to talk around it. 'There's been a homicide in a coastal town near Byron Bay and they're looking for a stand-in—the local inspector had a car accident yesterday, if you can believe it. I know him, actually, we did some training together years ago. Anyway, the regional chief called—Tran, I think her name is. She asked me to go but I told her I've got an internal investigation starting tomorrow, and there's no way I can leave the squad unsupervised anyway. Bloody useless, half of them.'

On the other side of the lawn, Jodie has her hands on Ben's shoulders, and someone leans forward to hug her. My little boy disappears into a swirl of black fabric. I look down at the grass, where cake crumbs are crowd-surfing along a mob of ants.

I look up at Jonesy as my heartbeat accelerates to a gallop. 'I'll do it. I'll go.'

Monday, 11 April
11.52 am

I don't realise I've spoken out loud until I see Jonesy's confused expression. 'You?'

'Yes. I could go. I could do it. I *want* to do it.'

Jonesy's hairline gleams with sweat, and he almost drops his paper plate as he mops at it with a serviette. 'What about Ben?'

'I'll take him. He hates being here at the moment anyway. Maybe a change of scenery will do us both good. Do you think they have holiday programs up there? That's what he normally does when school's not on. Or I'll get a nanny—if he comes to Sydney with me, I'll need to do that anyway.'

Jonesy looks at me doubtfully. 'Are you serious, Gemma? I know the last few weeks have been really tough on you, and today's obviously very difficult, but I really think—'

'I'm totally serious. Let me speak to Ben, and then you can call the chief back and tell her I'll come. I can't stay here anyway, it's killing me.'

———

Someone has moved the photo of Scott to the rear of the hall, and people have formed a line to say goodbye to Jodie and offer their final condolences. Soon, I assume they will slink away to drink heavily and reflect on the tragedy of a young life cut short.

After tugging Ben away from where he's standing with Rebecca, I quickly explain the situation in Fairhaven.

He doesn't hesitate. 'I want to come with you.'

'Are you sure?' I say, holding his chin and looking into his eyes.

He nods vigorously. 'I don't want to stay here.'

I walk back over to Rebecca.

'Gemma, you can't just leave,' she says, her grey eyes alarmed. 'You need to talk to your dad.'

But the desire to escape is coursing through me. 'No, we have to get going,' I say.

She desperately scans the crowd. 'Please let me find Ned first.'

I call to her over my shoulder while I walk with Ben across the grass. 'I'll talk to Dad at home. We have to pack.' I bundle Ben into one of the taxis lining the street outside the church, squeezing his hand as I tip my head back against the car seat.

Feeling nervous, I call the number Jonesy gave me.

Chief Inspector Celia Tran's voice is clipped and businesslike. 'So, Ken would have told you we're dealing with a homicide and a missing person, but we're not sure at this stage if they are linked.'

'How did the boy die?' I ask.

'Beaten to death in his garage,' she replies. 'Head injuries.'

'No weapon?'

'We're still looking.'

I nod, trying to imagine a teenage girl beating a teenage boy to death.

'Does the girl have any history of running away?' I ask.

'No,' says Tran, 'but her family situation is extremely volatile. To be honest, I was pretty sure we were looking at a runaway or perhaps a suicide until we got the call about Rick this morning. Now I'm not sure what to think.'

Déjà vu has me flailing as if I'm falling, even though my feet are still flat on the ground. The seeds of doubt that lodged inside me during the Mara case are back.

'Do either of them have known drug links?'

'It's a pretty clean town these days,' she replies, a hint of pride in her voice. 'We had an ice issue across the region a few years back, but all of the squads from Byron to Fairhaven have worked hard to drive it out of the community. The new hospital in Fairhaven has helped, and there was some government funding as well. There's still a lot of low-grade marijuana use, but that doesn't cause too many problems. The party drugs are normally brought in by the backpackers and tend to be seasonal. We watch it over summer, but it's pretty tame.'

What she's describing sounds similar to Smithson, except I know from talking to Jonesy that ice remains a big issue.

'I'm keen to get on top of everything asap,' I say.

'I'll send you what we have so far, which obviously isn't much.' She pauses. 'You'll need to hit the ground running, I'm afraid. It's a small town and there will be a lot of pressure to assure everyone they're safe.'

Blood pounds through my head. 'No problem. I'll read as much as I can on the plane.'

'Good. Well, you're certainly getting me out of a bind. The local CI says there's no way the team up here can manage something like this. Now, I've just checked—I can get you and your son on a 1.30 pm flight from Gowran, if that's doable?'

I glance sideways at Ben, then at the clock on the taxi's dash. 'We'll be there.'

'Okay, good. We won't move the body until you arrive, so let me know if you're delayed.'

———

'Gemma, this is ridiculous.' Dad stands in the guestroom doorway while I shove clothes and toiletries into my suitcase. 'Ben needs to be with family right now.'

I spin around. 'No, he needs to be with me. But not here. We need to get out of here.'

The toe of my workboot peeks out from under the bed. I add it to a growing mountain of items on the ugly apricot armchair.

My phone pings with emails that I know are from Inspector Tran: case notes, accommodation details, paperwork.

'What does Mac say about all this?' says Dad stiffly.

I feel a sharp stab of guilt as I push strands of hair from my sweaty face. 'He thinks I should do whatever feels right,' I snap. 'He trusts me.'

'And Jodie?'

'I haven't spoken to her yet, but I don't need her permission. We've agreed Ben is staying with me for now. I'll call her later.'

Dad closes his eyes and his face tics with frustration. 'Gemma, can you at least stop and think about this? Sleep on it. This isn't a good time to make hasty decisions.'

'For god's sake, Dad, I need to get to the crime scene today. The flight is booked.' I push my weight against my overflowing suitcase, tugging the zip around the bulging sections. I turn back to face him. 'Look, I know you're worried but me sitting around here isn't really achieving anything. And it's not like Ben is missing class for the next two weeks—the holidays start on Thursday.'

Rebecca appears in the doorway, her gaze flicking nervously between the two of us. 'Maybe some time away from Smithson is a good idea, Ned.'

Dad throws his hands up in the air. 'What, it's a good idea to drag a grieving little kid to some strange place while his mother loses herself in a murder investigation? Are you crazy?'

'I just meant,' Rebecca says, fidgeting with her hanky, 'I can see how being here might be difficult for Gemma and Ben right now. Nothing about any of this is easy.'

Surprised, I throw a grateful look her way. 'Rebecca's right.'

He opens his mouth before simply closing it again, shaking his head. 'It's Easter this weekend.'

'Who fucking cares? It's not like we're going to be celebrating anyway.'

'Gemma!'

'I'm sorry, Dad, but I need to do this.'

An old memory drifts into my consciousness, of Dad and me going through the motions of Christmas a few weeks after Mum died, the excruciating pain of pretending the familiar routine would make us feel better.

Dad gives me a long look, the heat of his anger cooling into sadness. 'I'm not going to tell you what to do, Gemma—lord knows I haven't bothered doing that for years—but I want it known that I think this is an incredibly stupid idea.'

'Thanks, Dad,' I say sarcastically. 'I appreciate your support.' I push past him to grab Ben's suitcase.

He follows me up the hall. 'Surely you realise things are different now? It's not all about you anymore. You don't have the luxury of assuming Ben is okay and that someone else is looking out for him.'

My face flushes violently and I clench my teeth trying to keep the venom from my words. 'I'm very aware that Ben is my son and it's my job to look after him. And that's what I'm trying to do. But I can't be here right now. I just can't.'

Dad sighs. 'Well, I guess you have some thinking to do, my girl. This is Ben's home. He has family here. People who love him. And, frankly, he is the priority, not you.' Dad adds quietly, 'What would Scott think?'

Fury hits me, followed by a gut-punch of guilt, but I don't want to fight with Dad anymore; I don't have the energy. I take in his fallen face, riddled with creases and sunspots. Had he wanted to leave Smithson after Mum died? Had he felt compelled to start over somewhere else? I can easily summon Dad's drawn expression and empty stares, but that's all. Despite my grief and confusion, the agony of being alive after Mum was gone, I never considered we'd do anything but soldier on in Smithson.

I fill my lungs with air and try to calm down. 'It's only for a little while. I need time to think, and I can't do that here. Plus, I'm better when I'm working, you know that.' I pluck Ben's T-shirts, shorts and underwear from the sofa bed in the study and push them into his backpack.

'Gemma, I know you love Ben. You just need to remember that he needs you like he's never needed you before.' Dad's voice shakes. 'You just better bloody make sure you're there for him.'

Candy and I are standing outside the security checkpoint at the airport waiting for Ben, who is buying a packet of chips. I catch my reflection in a shop mirror. I'm a head shorter than Candy and I look almost childlike next to her. My long dark hair is held back from my face with the cheap sunglasses I just bought from the chemist but my ponytail is a messy mane down my back. The skin on my arms and face is pale and there are dark rings under my green eyes. Not only do I feel unfit but I look it too—the recent pause in my exercise routine is obvious in the roundness of my figure.

'Thanks for driving us,' I say.

'No problem,' says Candy evenly. She's still wearing her funeral attire but has added a denim jacket. She shifts her weight to her other hip and clutches at her huge stomach. 'I mean, I get it. A boy is dead, a girl is missing, probably dead, and you're like a bee to honey, you totally get off on that stuff.'

'Candy!'

'Don't worry, I get off on it too.'

Ben returns and I pull him into a hug, the chip packet rustling between us. 'All okay?'

He nods. 'Can I have your phone?'

'Ten minutes,' I say, handing it over.

'And I don't think you're running away,' continues Candy, her gaze fixed on Ben.

'I didn't say I was.'

'I mean, you already did that ages ago.'

'*Candy!*'

'I'm just mucking around.' She tips her neck hard to the right, wincing. 'What did Mac say?'

'I'm going to call him later.'

She folds her arms over her bump and purses her lips. 'You haven't told him yet?'

I don't reply.

'Jesus, Gemma,' she mutters.

'Mac will understand,' I say, even though I'm not sure he will. 'He knows I'm not ready to bring Ben to Sydney. I need time to think about what we're going to do.'

Candy fills her cheeks with air, then huffs it out. 'Well, I can see how some people might think going from your ex-partner's funeral to some tin-pot surf town to solve a homicide is weird. But you *are* weird. And I get that you need a bit of time out from good old Shit Town. *Plus*, you're a workaholic so you're going cuckoo not having a case. This way you get to kill a few birds with one stone.' She yawns widely. 'Sorry, I'm knackered. Anyway, who cares what anyone thinks? You're in mourning—you can act as weird as you like.'

'Thanks, Candy.' I give her a hug, breathing in her citrus perfume.

'Don't thank me.' She talks into my hair. 'Just make sure you come back with a plan. It's fine to be in freefall for a little while, but your kid needs to know where his life is heading. Or at least where he's going to live.'

Her comment burns. I essentially deactivated my parenting licence four years ago, and I know it. I played an active support role, cheering enthusiastically from the sidelines, but was more than happy to let Scott drive. And now I'm in the driver's seat of a speeding car with faulty brakes, a white-knuckled Ben beside me.

When our flight is called over the speaker system, I gesture for Ben.

'I plan to come back with a plan,' I say softly.

Candy gives me a long, hard stare. 'Good.' She looks over at the airport restaurant and clutches her belly again. 'Shit, what a day. Don't tell anyone but I'm going to have a wine.'

Monday, 11 April
2.03 pm

The flight is brief, barely thirty minutes. Ben draws a picture of a dragon on the back of a sick bag while I review the case notes Tran sent through on my tiny phone screen.

Rattling around in my head is the phone call I had with Jodie before we took off. She was irritated about our sudden departure, but she was also exhausted, and I got the feeling that part of her felt relieved I was removing myself from her life, even if only temporarily.

'It's not like you called to ask me, Gemma,' she snapped. 'I didn't even know where you and Ben went after the funeral.'

'It all happened really quickly,' I said.

She just sighed and asked to speak to Ben.

I bristle as I recall her parting words. 'Ben obviously has everything he needs here, Gemma, so if it all gets too much for you he can just come home.'

I give his leg a quick squeeze and train my eyes back to my screen. There's barely any information on the murdered boy yet, just basic details. Richard 'Rick' Fletcher, seventeen years old. Both parents are still alive and together, and he has an older brother,

Aiden, and an older sister, Belinda. Rick's lived in Fairhaven his whole life. He dropped out of school at the end of Year Eleven and very recently became a self-employed landscaper. No priors, nothing to suggest he would wind up dead in his carport one Monday morning.

The report on the missing girl isn't much more substantial: she's younger than Rick, just fifteen, and in Year Ten at Fairhaven High. A family file is included: her father is a suspected serial domestic abuser, but no charges have been laid against him since the late 1980s when he was arrested for a drunken bar fight that left a man permanently disfigured. The Fairhaven police are frequently called out to the Clark home by concerned neighbours but Daniel's wife, Dorothy, refuses to press charges and denies her husband is abusive. I shift in my seat and wriggle my toes. It's not much of a stretch for abuse to escalate into murder, particularly if Abbey was starting to assert her independence.

I feel a familiar bubble of apprehension as I click on a photo of Rick Fletcher. Seeing a victim always sears a homicide onto my soul; there's no going back once they have a face. Blond, tan and with a friendly smile, Rick could easily star in a tourism ad for a quintessential Australian beach holiday. What a waste.

Next I click on a photo of Abbey Clark. Goose bumps break out on my arms and legs. She looks so much like Nicki Mara. The same wavy brown hair, similar pretty features. I am catapulted back to the brightly lit case room, Nicki's face smiling down at me from the photo board as I tried to make sense of her disappearance.

I fight the urge to stand up and demand the plane turn around. Even though rationally I know this case is different, that Abbey is not Nicki, it doesn't stop the dread. The steady pulse of doubt. Ben is still sketching on the sick bag next to me, and the plane hums along. Tiny white spots flood my vision. My heart still racing, I count to ten. I close Abbey's photo and start to read the case notes.

Abbey's father reported her missing just after 10 am yesterday. He said he'd woken up a few hours earlier to discover she hadn't returned the previous evening, then immediately driven around to Rick Fletcher's house, searching for her there. Apparently Daniel was convinced that Rick was responsible for her disappearance.

On Saturday night she'd attended a large house party, and several witnesses say she seemed fine—although later in the evening, she reportedly had a heated argument with Rick. When Tran interviewed Rick on Sunday, he admitted he and Abbey had recently broken up and said they'd argued because he thought she was flirting with another guy at the party, which he felt was disrespectful. Rick claimed he'd seen Abbey leave the party alone on her bike about half an hour later, just before 11.30 pm.

My forehead creases as I read the next section of the missing person file. At about 11.45 pm, Abbey went to the Fairhaven Police Station claiming her bike had been stolen from the party. The constable on duty, Kai Lane, wrote up the report, then a local resident rang to complain about the noise at the house party. Lane called the CI and arranged to meet him there before offering Abbey a lift home, which she declined.

She hasn't been seen since. Her bank accounts haven't been touched. Her phone went off the grid around midnight; its last tracked location is central Fairhaven, so I make a note to ask Tran about CCTV in the area.

It also seems like the cops only did a cursory search of the Clarks' house on Sunday. As far as they could tell, Abbey hadn't been home, but maybe they missed something. The squad in Fairhaven is unlikely to be very experienced and detectives have their biases too; maybe they assumed that Abbey was just passed out at a friend's place or wanted some time out.

I tap my pen against the fold-out plane table. Despite the misery of the morning, my brain is clicking into gear for the first time in weeks. It grips around the facts of the case, trying to arrange the sequence of events. If something did happen to Abbey Clark, then Rick Fletcher is surely suspect number one—a recent break-up, a fiery clash an hour before she disappeared.

Or was it the other way around? Was Abbey furious enough at him to go into hiding and then strike out a few days later?

I scroll forward a few pages to the summary of the statement Rick gave on Sunday. In her report, Constable Edwina de Luca describes him as 'devastated'. He said he left the party and went to meet his sister and her friends on the beach where they were having a drunken gathering: not the most airtight of alibis. He was on foot; he could have easily encountered Abbey, disposed of her and still gone to the beach party so the others could vouch for him. But why? Humiliation about the break-up? A sense of betrayal?

I click back on Abbey's file. What does the stolen bike mean? Perhaps it wasn't really stolen. Or if it was, then why did Rick say he saw her leave the party on it? He might have misremembered because he was drunk, but it seems like a strange thing to conjure up. Maybe Abbey claimed the bike was stolen as part of a ruse to cover up her plan to disappear. I make another note to review how far she could get on her bike at night without being spotted.

My mind wanders to all the heated exchanges Mac and I had about Nicki Mara. We profiled her endlessly, talking late into the night, long after Owen and the rest of the team had gone home.

After a few weeks, our heated conversations shifted to the pub opposite the station. Tucked away in a private booth, we downed beers as we debated the hidden clues in Nicki's phone records and WhatsApp messages. I felt like I knew her intimately: her ongoing issues with her mother, the jealousy she felt toward her older sister, her fondness for her dad. Her propensity to take party drugs, her history of mental illness. I got so deep into her head I couldn't see straight. My instincts were shot. Mac, on the other hand, kept his distance. He could see things I couldn't.

I'm well aware Nicki's case has made me a little gun-shy, scared to fix onto a solution too quickly. I've been second-guessing myself, then second-guessing my second guesses, terrified my assumptions could compromise a solve—or even a life.

I don't know where Abbey sits on the scale yet, but I do know most runaway kids don't bail in the middle of the night, especially if they're on their own. Especially not if they're from a coastal town that has few options for an exit strategy. No buses, no trains, not even a taxi service. I make another note to look into her finances. Nothing about this seems planned, but if it turns out she was stock-piling money then that might suggest otherwise.

A voice comes over the loudspeaker informing us we're ten minutes from landing, so we need to stow our large electronic devices. I snap my laptop shut and glance at Ben. His expression is unreadable as he stares at the back of the seat in front of him.

I still can't quite believe I'm doing this. My insides twist tight. I'm increasingly aware this might be the most foolish decision I've ever made.

We disembark and collect our luggage, my corporate suitcase like a sore thumb among the colourful beach bags. I look at our fellow travellers—shedding jackets, putting on hats and pausing to apply sunscreen, they chat excitedly about ocean conditions and bushwalks, in between bemoaning their pale skin. I loop an arm around Ben and give him a reassuring squeeze.

Rental car keys in hand, we leave the small terminal and are immediately engulfed by hot, damp air. Perspiration rallies on my skin and I lick my lips. I can taste the sea.

Ben points at a sign with the hire car brand on it. 'This way, Mum.' We find our car, and I set the GPS to the address Tran gave me. The case has already wormed its way into my brain. I'm still trying to plot out the sequence of events: a missing girl, a dead boy, both of their lives about to be torn open and picked over like a Christmas turkey.

Ben fiddles with the window controls and switches songs on the radio, his movements jerky.

'Are you alright, baby?'

He shrugs. 'Yep.'

'I know this is pretty strange. If you change your mind about wanting to be here, or if you want to go home, you just need to tell me, okay?'

'You hate Smithson,' he says.

Heat rises up my neck, onto my face. 'That's not true.'

'It's okay, I hate it too.'

'Ben, come on. Smithson is your home.'

He shrugs. 'Everything is different now. Dad's dead, and we're living at Grandad's.' His voice wobbles dangerously. 'No one knows what to say to me. I don't want to go back to school after the holidays, it was bad enough when Dad was sick. Can't I just come and live in Sydney with you?'

Despite the sun streaming in through the windows, I start to shake as if I have chills. He's saying what I want to hear, but I can also hear the pain in his voice.

The road stretches out in front of us, a black line disappearing into the green corridor. What was I thinking coming here?

'You might feel differently after a few days,' I say feebly.

He pouts and slumps back against the seat. 'You don't want me to come to Sydney.'

'That is absolutely not true, Ben. I just think we need time to decide what's going to be best for you.'

He pulls off his cap and wipes his nose with the back of his hand. Tilting his chin, he looks at me defiantly. His expression jolts a memory of Scott and me watching him as a baby, only a few days old, sleeping in his cot. *He has the same face shape as you*, Scott said dreamily, tracing Ben's jaw, his voice cracking with emotion as he put his arm around me and pushed my chin skyward, smiling. *But hopefully not your stubbornness.*

I remember how hard school was after Mum died. The stares. The whispered conversations that stopped every time I rounded a corner. My heart breaks for that version of me, and it breaks for Ben.

'I know it's hard, sweetheart. Your friends care about you so much but they don't know what to say to you. They don't want to upset you. But it will get easier, I promise.'

He doesn't speak for a few moments but I sense his limbs relax, the anger fading. Or perhaps he's just exhausted.

'Is the missing girl dead?'

His bluntness makes me baulk. 'She might be,' I admit, 'but I hope not. Either way, her family really want to know what happened to her. *I* want to know what happened to her.'

He nods but keeps his lips pressed together.

Frustration swells in my chest and I try to breathe around it, gripping the steering wheel and focusing on the road. I know he's hurting. I just wish I knew what to say.

My personal phone rings: Jonesy. Glancing at Ben, I put a head-phone in my ear and answer it.

'Are you there yet?' His gruff voice sounds faraway.

'Yes. We're on the way to the scene.'

'Christ,' he breathes. 'Okay, so I made some calls. I think I mentioned that the bloke who had the car accident is an old mate of mine? Chief Inspector Tommy Gordon. Anyway, his wife, Vanessa, is a retired schoolteacher and she's offered to have Ben during the day while you're in Fairhaven. She's already looking after a little boy for the school holidays, so she says it's no trouble. She's a good person, Gemma.'

'That sounds great,' I say, surprised to find my eyes welling up.

'Yeah. She said she can meet you tonight—you know, so you can make sure it's all okay. I'll send you her number now so you can give her a call later and sort it out.'

'Thanks, Jonesy. I really appreciate it.'

He snorts. 'I'm still not sure about this, but I guess that ship has sailed. Just be bloody careful up there and keep me posted.'

'I will.'

I tell Ben about Jonesy's babysitting plan as our rented Toyota tunnels through vibrant green passages littered with leaves. The sky above us is sapphire blue, the sun a blazing white circle. Scott's funeral seems like a lifetime ago.

After about fifteen minutes we pass a large road sign that reads *Welcome to Fairhaven! Population 4080*, with a faded cartoon sun positioned above the text alongside what appear to be two bullet holes. The speed limit drops as the road begins to curve, and abruptly the world to our right falls away, revealing a sharp decline to the sea. Ben strains against his seatbelt to get a better look. A small yacht drifts into the shimmering path that the sun has etched onto the water. We descend past several postcard-perfect lookout points and a few gravity-defying houses before driving onto flat land. The odd home appears on the left, then we're closing in on an abandoned-looking hardware store and a run of shops.

One sign points to the Fairhaven Caravan Park and another to the lighthouse.

We reach the main street, where the lightly salted air is suddenly weighed down with a thick mossy scent. Ben wrinkles his nose as we pass a faded plastic playground, then a bed and breakfast with an enormous orange cat asleep on the front step.

Up ahead beside the road, an A4 sheet of paper is taped crookedly to the wall of a Telstra phone booth. The smiling face of Abbey Clark flutters in the breeze, *MISSING* printed in large type above her head. Clusters of people are bunched sporadically along the street, wide eyes indicating they know death has struck nearby.

'Okay, we're close,' I murmur. The GPS leads me through more turns until we reach a street lined with modest houses, and it's clear we've arrived. An ambulance is reverse-parked in a driveway to the right of a single-storey weatherboard residence. Police tape loops the carport, and a small crowd of shell-shocked neighbours have gathered under the shade of a gum across the road.

I pull up behind a marked cop car just as my personal phone starts ringing again: Mac. The third time he's called since this morning. I let it ring out before I turn it off and put it in the glove box.

A young police officer is pacing the lawn while talking on his phone, the light blue of his badge indicating he's a constable. Two paramedics sip bottled water and chat quietly near the letterbox.

'Wait here for a sec,' I say to Ben, who is looking past me up the driveway.

It's hotter than I realised, and the relentless cries of the cicadas needle at my brain, reigniting the headache I've had off and on for weeks. I nod at the constable and walk over to the paramedics, a middle-aged man and a younger woman with blonde streaks through her dark hair. I show them my badge and introduce myself.

'I have my son with me,' I say. 'He's eight, and I couldn't get anyone to mind him at late notice. Would you be able to watch him for a bit? Just while I'm briefed on the case.'

'No problem, I know what it's like juggling kids,' says the man. 'We actually just got here but apparently the coroner is running late so we won't be moving the body for a while.'

I get Ben from the car and leave him with Andy, who immediately embarks on an enthusiastic tour of his ambulance. I watch them for a moment and then, satisfied, turn toward the house.

A tall Eurasian woman appears in the doorway dressed in full scrubs. She yanks off her gauzy hood as she marches toward me, revealing a face dotted with dark freckles beneath a sleek black bob streaked with grey. 'Gemma?' She snaps off her right glove and sticks out her hand.

'Chief Inspector Tran.' My arm tenses at her firm grip.

'I'm glad you're here,' she says solemnly. 'Come on, put on some scrubs and let's get you a look at him.'

Monday, 11 April
2.59 pm

Rick Fletcher is crumpled on the concrete floor of his garage next to his white ute, the driver's door wide open, his shoulder-length blond hair splayed out around his face. Full rigor mortis is yet to kick in, and his features look slack and dumb, his limbs flopping drunkenly from his torso. Congealed blood cakes the wound on his temple, tinting the crown of his head a dark red. His navy eyes are frozen open and seem to watch me watching him.

'We think he was attacked just after 6 am.' Tran's dark eyes jerk to Rick's body and then drift back to me. 'He was due to start a landscaping job today about twenty minutes from here and told the client he'd be there at 6.30 am. We still can't find a weapon, but clearly he was hit with something sizeable. Possibly one of his own tools.' She gestures to an impressive array of gardening instruments hanging on the wall. 'We're not sure what's missing and I can't see any splinters. It definitely wasn't a gunshot—there'd be more mess.'

'Who found him?' I ask.

'A next-door neighbour, Bruce Piper.' She points to the cream-coloured bungalow on the other side of the garage. 'Says he thought he heard something when he first got up. When he was pulling out to go to work, he noticed Rick's car door open and just said he had a funny feeling about it. He found Rick and called the station just after 7 am.'

'He's not a suspect?'

Tran scrunches up her nose. 'I don't think so. He was pretty shaken up and said all the right things. He's known Rick since he was a kid, said this used to be the family home.'

I bend down to study Rick's hands. They're badly callused, and his left index finger has a cut on it that looks old.

'I think he was hit from behind.' I rock onto the balls of my feet. 'The way his hair is all gathered like that at the back makes me think there's another wound there. My guess is the first blow put him on his knees, then he was hit again here before he bled out.' I point to his head. 'Maybe several times. That makes sense in terms of how he's positioned.'

Tran nods, though seems reluctant to comment and instead says, 'The coroner will be here soon. He's coming from a farming accident a few hours away. Same as the forensic team.'

I step out of the garage and look along the front of the house. 'You said this used to be the family home? Did Rick Fletcher live here alone? He's only seventeen, right?'

'His twenty-year-old brother lives here too, but he's not around at the moment. We're trying to track him down. The neighbour, Bruce Piper, said their parents semi-retired last year and live a little further down the coast. I sent Edwina de Luca and Damon Grange there this morning to do the death knock and ask some questions—they're the two other constables in Tommy's squad. Kai Lane's out front.'

'I read the notes on the way here. Abbey Clark and Fletcher were a couple.'

'Yes. Apparently it was quite a serious relationship until last week.' Tran looks at her watch and frowns. 'God, it's already past three.' She glances back at Rick's body briefly and says, 'Let's grab Lane, then I'll run you through everything. I can't stay much longer, we've got our own dramas in Byron today.' She grimaces. 'I can't see anyone getting much of an Easter break this year.'

I push the hood of my scrubs down and quickly check on Ben. He's sitting on the portable bed in the ambulance, talking to Andy.

'All okay?' I ask Ben, who nods.

'We're having a good old chat,' says Andy.

'Okay, well, we're just going to run through a few things inside and then we'll go to the hotel. Sound okay, Ben?'

'Yep, I'm fine, Mum.' His face is serious but all traces of the tension from the car trip are gone.

'Come get me if you need me,' I say to Andy, who gives me a discreet thumbs-up. Thank god he's on duty today.

A white Mazda pulls up behind the ambulance as Tran and I step onto the grass. A skinny man in faded tan cords and a sky-blue T-shirt pushes out of the passenger door and walks confidently up the driveway. 'Inspector Tran! Do you suspect Abigail Clark for the murder of Rick Fletcher, or are you treating these incidents as separate?' He doesn't remove his aviators but holds his phone out and appears to take a few snaps of the house and the garage.

'It's still no comment, Simon,' snaps Tran, balling her fists before muttering, 'I thought you went home.'

'Nah, I want to talk to the new blood here.' He turns his focus on me. 'Simon Charleston, *Byron Bay News*. You must be the new detective from Sydney. Can you confirm that this is the residence of Rick Fletcher, boyfriend of Abbey Clark, missing since Saturday night?'

Tran's nostrils flare. 'I mean it, Simon. Get out of here or I'll have you for trespassing. That goes for all of you.' She glares at the other journalists and photographers who are keeping a surprisingly respectful distance on the nature strip.

'Sorry, sorry.' Simon pushes his sunglasses into his curly hair and looks sheepish. Little flecks of light dance in his grey eyes. 'Just letting you know I'll be right here if you decide to comment.' He makes his way back to his car, craning his neck to see past the ambulance.

I exchange a look with the baby-faced cop on the lawn as Tran mutters under her breath, motioning for both of us to join her on the front porch. 'Here.' She hands the man a set of scrubs. 'Gemma, this is Constable Kai Lane. He's been with the Fairhaven squad for just over a year. Kai, you obviously know about Detective Woodstock already.'

Lane attempts an odd greeting that involves him tipping his upper body forward as he pulls on his scrubs. He almost loses his balance. 'Sorry.' He steadies himself, clearing his throat nervously. 'It's really great to meet you, Detective Woodstock.'

I nod. 'Yes, you too.'

I recognise his name from Abbey's file. He was the constable on duty when she reported the bike stolen after the party. Apart from the healthy flush of thick stubble across his jaw, Lane could easily pass as a high school student. One of his front teeth is slightly crooked, and his generous mop of brown hair makes me think of Ben.

Tran opens the front door and swishes down the narrow hallway in her booties. 'Let me show you Fletcher's room first, then we can talk.'

Inside, the steady tick of a clock gives the house a hollow feeling. We pass a wide archway that leads to a kitchen and, beyond that, a lounge. The kitchen is neat except for a scatter of dishes on the bench. A plastic milk bottle pokes its head out from the sink. I imagine Rick making himself breakfast here this morning, having no idea it was the last thing he would ever do.

In the lounge, a trio of surfboards lean against the wall behind a worn armchair. On the opposite wall, a huge television hangs above a tatty couch. The floor is half-covered by a light-brown shagpile rug.

Up ahead Lane ducks comically to avoid hitting his head on a dangling light shade as he trails behind Tran. She pauses and gestures for us to enter the bedroom at the end of the hallway.

It's been ransacked. The linen has been ripped from the bed, and clothes spill from the wardrobe across the carpet, mixing with the contents of an upturned bin. A surfboard has been knocked sideways against a desk, and a glossy guitar has a nasty crack across its neck. An empty whisky bottle lies on its side next to the bed. I notice a pink skirt in the tangle on the floor.

Several photos of Rick and Abbey are stuck to the far wall. In every single one, the girl's face has been coloured in with black permanent marker, dozens of scribbled circles that seem to blur into one the longer I look at them.

'Whoa.' Lane's face is close and his warm, mint-scented breath brushes my cheek. He surveys the mess, wide-eyed.

'Do we think Rick Fletcher did that?' I tip my head toward the photos. 'How angry was he about the break-up?'

Tran is still behind us in the hallway. She stabs at her phone. 'He admitted things had turned nasty between them when we interviewed him yesterday. It's possible he defaced the photos, but I find it strange he'd trash his own room. The photos certainly weren't like this on Sunday afternoon.'

I step around a pair of shoes to get a better look at the bizarre mural. Against the medley of beach backdrops, Rick is either grinning or intentionally looking sultry. It's clear that he and Abbey were very comfortable with each other; in several shots it's hard to know where her honeyed limbs end and his begin.

Him dead, her missing.

'It's pretty sinister, blacking out her face like that,' I say. 'And it looks fairly precise, not like it was done in a drunken frenzy—though I guess it's hard to be sure.'

Tran's eyes flick over the photos again. 'Rick wasn't very mature,' she says finally. 'He was struggling with his emotions when we spoke to him.'

Tran's right: the defacing of Abbey's image could be incredibly dark or just the childish reaction of a hurting teenager.

I nudge a scrap of paper with my mesh-covered foot. Three mobile numbers are scrawled on it, and I pull out my phone to take a photo.

Tran's phone buzzes with a series of messages. 'Forensics are thirty minutes away.' Her fingers fly across her phone. 'I've put in a call for some extra manpower—you're obviously going to need it.'

I'm surprised at her no-nonsense manner. I'd expected someone running a regional squad to be a bit more relaxed—more like Jonesy. I wonder whether she's overcompensating; I can't imagine her pathway to chief inspector was an easy one.

'How many FTEs will we get?' I ask as we head back into the lounge.

'I'm trying for three extra bodies, maybe four. We absolutely need the station to run twenty-four seven for the foreseeable future, and there will be some community pressure to run patrols until the killer is caught.'

'I have some questions about the case notes you sent me,' I say.

The three of us form a little huddle in the kitchen.

'Go ahead,' says Tran, folding her arms.

'The missing bike makes no sense to me. I mean for starters, either she was lying about leaving the party on her bike or Fletcher

lied about seeing her with it. I just can't work out why either way.'
I turn to Lane. 'You were on duty when she came in?'

He nods. 'We get a bit of theft around here so it didn't seem strange at the time, but it obviously does now.'

'How did she seem when she came in?' I ask.

Lane becomes a little flustered, his smooth cheeks turning red, and I'm reminded of his youth and inexperience; I hope the rest of the local team aren't so nervous around me. 'Abbey was upset about her bike. She said it was a Christmas gift from her father and she was worried about his reaction.'

'Daniel Clark, yes, I saw the DV summary. Is he abusive toward Abbey?'

'We're sure he is,' says Lane. 'But we could never convince her to make a statement. Daniel's been beating his wife, Dot, for years. Tommy Gordon, that's our CI, he's tried to talk to Dot about making a statement a bunch of times, but she's too scared, I guess.'

'That's a fairly common scenario,' I say.

'Especially around here,' says Tran. 'DV goes through the roof in summer, then again in winter when the work dries up.'

If Rick is suspect number one in Abbey's disappearance, then her father is surely suspect number two.

'Has her bike turned up?' I ask.

Lane shakes his head. 'We have no idea where it is.'

'So unless it's with Abbey, it sounds like it really was stolen?' I look between them.

Lane shrugs. 'That's likely.'

I'm trying to get it all straight in my head. 'And she refused a lift home from the police station even though it was almost midnight?'

He opens his mouth to reply just as someone starts screaming in the front yard.

Monday, 11 April
4.06 pm

A young man is wrestling with the paramedics at the end of the driveway. Veins ripple grotesquely on his tan arms as Andy struggles to restrain him. I rush over to the ambulance and find Ben kneeling on the portable bed, peering out the side window at the commotion.

'Stay here, okay?'

He nods, his eyes huge.

The reporter who Tran dressed down earlier, Simon Charleston, stands in the open door of his car, filming the scene with his phone.

'Let me in!' screams the young man.

For a moment I wonder if Rick has somehow come back to life, so similar is this man to the dead body lying on the garage floor. But then I notice the spray of tattoos on his neck, see that the blond hair is straight and not wavy. Behind the ambulance I notice a shiny black ute parked sloppily in the driveway.

Tran walks purposefully over to the man. 'Aiden Fletcher? I'm Chief Inspector Celia Tran. Please come with me.'

The man eyes her warily, but he calms somewhat. Andy slowly releases his grip.

'I live here!'

Tran nods.

'What's happened to Rick? Tell me!'

'Please, come with me.' Her arm loops firmly around his waist as she leads him to the far corner of the yard, away from his brother's bloody corpse and Simon's phone. 'Some police officers are with your parents now at their house.'

Aiden lets out a low moan. 'Is he dead? Oh god, no.'

Tran's voice remains robotic. 'Aiden, I'm afraid your brother was attacked this morning and his injuries were fatal.'

Aiden crumples to the ground and begins to rock back and forth, glancing from the garage to the house, squinting into the sunlight. 'I knew it,' he whispers, before giving way to sobs.

What on earth does he mean by that?

'Aiden.' I sink down next to him. 'Do you have any idea who could have attacked Rick?'

He keeps making those tortured moans.

'Aiden?'

He turns to me as if waking from a deep sleep, his pupils shrinking into focus, spittle hovering on his lips. 'This is all my fault.'

Aiden sits across from me, his head in his hands. After his outburst I herded him away from the journos into the backyard and directed him to a rickety outdoor setting.

Tran stomps after us muttering about Simon Charleston with Lane trailing behind.

'Aiden, I'm really sorry about your brother,' I say.

He doesn't reply but I recognise the tremors of shock.

'Aiden, what did you mean before when—?'

His head jerks up and he groans, smacking his hands hard against his face. 'Oh god! I can't believe this.' His face is patchy with uneven whiskers, his eyes dull and bloodshot. 'When?' he whispers.

'Around six this morning. We think he was on his way to work.'

Aiden descends into sobs again. 'Oh god, oh god.'

I lean forward and put a hand on his shoulder. 'When was the last time you saw him?'

'Last week. I've been away since Thursday, but we hang out all the time.' He rides the wave of another sob. 'This is going to kill my parents, you know.' His face collapses as he shakes his head in disbelief, saliva forming silvery strings between his lips.

'When did you last have contact with Rick?' I say gently.

'What? Um, yesterday. He told me about Abbey going AWOL on Sunday, then he called me again last night after her dad had come round here again.'

'Daniel Clark came here last night?'

Aiden sniffs and swipes at his nostrils, leaving a trail of snot along his wrist. 'Yeah. He reckoned Rick knew where Abbey was, but he didn't. I swear to god he didn't.'

'What did Rick say to you about Abbey disappearing?'

'Just that he was worried. I mean, I know they'd just broken up, but he was crazy about her. They would have got back together.'

I think about the black marks all over her smiling face on Rick's bedroom wall. Did Daniel Clark see them? Could that have convinced him Rick had harmed his daughter?

'Aiden, did you ever witness any violence between Abbey and your brother?'

He emits a shuddery breath. 'No, no way. He was so into her. He was worried she was seeing someone else, but I told him it was all in his head. Abbey's a good chick.'

'Why did Rick think she was cheating on him?'

His right heel starts to tic uncontrollably. 'I dunno. He just said she was acting weird lately.'

Something is ducking and weaving in the darkest corners of my mind, but I can't seem to catch it. 'Can you think of anyone who'd want to hurt your brother, Aiden?'

'No, *no*. Oh god, I really just can't get my head around this.'

'Aiden, why did you say this is all your fault?'

'What?'

'On the lawn before? What did you mean?'

He opens his legs wide and presses his elbows against his knees, head down. 'I don't know. I don't know what the fuck I'm saying.' He begins to cry again, and Tran and I exchange glances. We're clearly not going to get more out of him right now.

'Do you want us to contact your parents, Aiden?' asks Tran. 'We can get an officer to drive you to their house?'

'No. No.' He reels forward but manages to stay on his feet, wiping tears into his mottled cheeks.

'We know today has been a terrible shock,' I say, 'but we'll need to speak with you again soon. We need your help to find out who did this to Rick.'

Aiden moans and manically shuffles in a circle, his hands still gripping his face. 'Can I go inside?'

'Not right now, I'm afraid,' says Tran. 'But if there's anything you need, I might be able to get it for you.'

Grabbing fistfuls of blond hair, he stares at the house hopelessly.

'Aiden?'

'I just need to be with my family.' He stumbles forward and then bolts to the narrow grass corridor that leads to the front yard. There's a slight delay as we scramble to follow him.

Upon seeing Aiden, the journos come to life, tossing water bottles to the ground and flicking on their phones and video cameras.

He jumps in his ute and reverses at speed in a wide arc, almost clipping the front of Simon Charleston's Mazda.

'Hey!' Simon shouts, running half-heartedly across the lawn.

Aiden looks possessed as he pitches the car forward and takes off down the street. The reporters buzz like flies in his wake.

From the other direction comes the forensic van, causing the crowd of neighbours to fragment as it pulls up at the kerb. A Jack Russell breaks away from the group and races across the lawn, dragging its leash on the ground. The dog makes a beeline for Simon, yapping at his heels while he tries to talk on his phone.

Tran purses her lips as she surveys the chaotic scene.

'I think Aiden knows something,' I say. 'Did you hear him say it was his fault?'

'Maybe. But I think he's probably just in shock. You can speak to him again tomorrow or Wednesday.' Tran's cheekbones jut away from her face as if to accentuate her point. I struggle to guess her age. Her skin is luminous, but has the tell-tale tightness of Botox.

Leaving Lane to guard the property, Tran and I walk over to greet the three male techs who emerge from their van.

'Locating the weapon is priority number one, but I want the house, garage and yard swept for any traces of drugs,' I say as we gather in the shade of the carport. 'And we need all electronic devices bagged and sent to the lab as soon as possible. I also want the photos in the bedroom dusted for prints—someone has scribbled over the missing girl's face with what looks like permanent marker.'

'We can test the ink,' offers the youngest-looking tech. 'It might give an indication of when they were drawn on.'

The techs pull on their white suits and gloves and head into the house, just as two more cars park at the end of the driveway. A middle-aged bald man virtually falls out of a Nissan Pathfinder and huffs toward us. 'Hi, Celia,' he wheezes at Tran, then turns to me. 'Mick Lamb, I'm the regional coroner.' He sticks out a sweaty hand. 'My air con packed it in halfway here,' he offers by way of apology. 'So, I hear we've got a deceased kid with head injuries?'

I glance at Tran, who has returned her attention to her ever-vibrating phone.

'That's right. He's through there.' I indicate the garage. 'I'm particularly keen on understanding what type of weapon you think was used and also whether you think a teenage girl could have inflicted the injuries.'

'Sure, okay.' Mick Lamb's breath is slowly returning to a normal pace. 'That likely won't be clear until we do the full autopsy, but I can give you an opinion later once I've had a look.' He circles Fletcher's body, looking solemn, then collects his kit and gets settled in the garage.

Lane has switched places with one of the fill-in constables Tran requested, Tim Mayfair, a stocky pale man with bright red hair and a high-pitched voice. He chats calmly to the distraught locals on the street, while Lane, Tran and I regroup near the front door to complete our case handover.

'Okay, so,' Tran begins, 'Lamb thinks that Fletcher's autopsy will be on Wednesday.' She squints against the afternoon sun as she scrolls through her phone. 'There was already pressure to clear the backlog before Easter but I've made it clear we need this done urgently.' Now she's looking anxious. 'Right, I've got about ten minutes. Is there anything else you want to go over?'

I work through my list of questions from the plane. 'Do we have any CCTV footage? Is there likely to be anything from Saturday night or this morning?'

'We were in the process of securing council footage when this all blew up, but we don't expect to get much,' replies Tran.

'There's barely anything,' adds Lane. 'We keep hearing rumours of new cameras going in but nothing happens. I don't think there's any funding.'

Tran shoots him an irritated glance.

'Besides Daniel and Abbey, who else is on your list?' I ask her.

'A few of the kids at the party said a guy was hassling Abbey,' says Tran, her eyes back on her phone, 'but we haven't been able to ID him. You should get access to her social accounts and phone records later tonight or tomorrow, so hopefully something turns up on those.'

I feel the all-too-familiar smack of invisible brick walls. Most homicide cases are really about juggling resources, working out what to spend time on and what to ignore. Clearly this will be no different.

'Okay, last question,' I say. 'Were the kids at the party boozed or on drugs?'

'Not that any of them will admit. You'd think the whole party was powered by a couple of mid-strength six-packs they found in the kitchen cupboard.' Tran laughs wryly. 'I really have to go. The others can keep filling you in. My squad is having its own dramas and I need to be there.'

'No problem.'

I'm actually desperate for Tran to leave; I want her out of the way so I can take the disparate case threads and start to weave them together, but part of me feels rusty and nervous.

'Just a heads-up,' says Tran, 'you'll need to manage Daniel Clark carefully, Gemma. He isn't a fan of the police force, and I don't want to get tripped up by some bogus complaint. I suggest you go see him first thing, introduce yourself, and question him and his wife about Rick.'

'Sure, no problem.'

'Oh, and one other thing I forgot to mention,' says Tran, suddenly looking sheepish. 'Rick called the station last night to say he wanted to tell us something.'

'What was it?'

Tran hesitates. 'We don't have any idea. After Abbey was reported missing I planned to run the station twenty-four seven, but I couldn't get anyone in overnight and everyone on staff had already worked all day yesterday, so I stayed as late as I could, around 11 pm. Rick's call went to the station voice bank, but I hadn't linked it properly to my phone. By the time the message was picked up this morning, I was already here looking at his body.'

Monday, 11 April
5.28 pm

Tran gives us a final cursory nod and stalks off to her car, her fingers still dancing across her phone. She clearly feels guilty that she didn't receive Rick's call on Sunday night. I watch as one of the techs inspects a pair of sneakers near the front door. I would feel bad too—hearing what Rick had to say might have saved his life.

I turn to Lane, who appears a little wide-eyed. I wonder whether he's ever worked a homicide before. 'I want to have a case meeting tomorrow at the station before I visit the Clarks. Can you tell the others to be there at eight-thirty?'

'Yes, of course.'

'Can you also send me the voice file of Fletcher's phone call to the station, along with the footage of his interview yesterday?'

'Yes, I'll do it right away.' Lane attempts a relaxed smile. 'What a day, huh?'

'I expect there might be a few more like this headed our way.'

He swallows and looks over to the garage, the occasional camera flash illuminating the dark rectangle of the door. Then he subtly squares his shoulders and clenches his jaw. In spite of everything,

I smile; his boyish enthusiasm is endearing. I tell him to get a good night's sleep, then slide on my new sunglasses.

I'm conscious of Simon Charleston watching me as I walk across the lawn.

'Mum,' says Ben loudly, stepping out from the open doors of the ambulance, 'is the man in the garage dead?'

———

'I think that's our hotel.' Ben points to a two-storey wooden building a few hundred metres in front of us. *THE PARROT* is spelled out in gold lettering along the top.

'Sure is.' I force some cheer into my voice. 'Good spotting.'

The reception area is about as far from a beach house as you can get, with textured wallpaper and classic upholstered furniture. A huge photo of a macaw soaring through the air hangs behind the desk.

'Hello!' booms a loud voice. A man with thick copper-coloured hair and a broad smile appears at the top of the staircase and makes his way toward us. 'Now let me guess—Detective Sergeant Woodstock and Master Ben? Am I right?' His thick Irish accent turns his greeting to music.

'Yes,' I say, as Ben nods.

'Well, welcome to Fairhaven and specifically to my fine establishment. I'm Cameron O'Donnell. But my close friends and enemies call me Cam.' He leans across the counter to shake our hands, his enthusiasm almost childlike. 'I've got you in number nine, the ground-floor room on the far corner. You'll love it. There's a nice view of the beach from the bedroom, which comes free of charge.'

He's a smoker, I can smell it on his breath. He doesn't wear a wedding ring. The edge of a black tattoo peeks out from the sleeve of his shirt. He's incredibly attractive, his boyish good looks paired with a muscular physique.

He taps a sequence of keys on the computer. 'Okay, here you are. Right, so it looks like the boys and girls in blue are kindly picking up your bill. I just need you to sign a few things for me and then you're all set. And I'll grab you some food vouchers for the pub, my treat.'

'We're going there for dinner tonight,' says Ben.

'I know.' Cam winks at him. 'A little bird told me.'

Suddenly wary, I sign the forms hastily.

Cam hands over my keys before pulling a container of fish food from behind the desk. 'Here, mate, do you want to feed Paddy?' He points to the tank on the other side of the room, where a bloated red-and-white goldfish floats listlessly between weeds and plastic turrets. 'Not too much. Just a pinch.' As Ben trots off, Cam leans against the desk and gives me a conspiratorial look, his face grim. 'I heard about Rick Fletcher. I just can't believe it.'

The bloody scene from the garage bubbles up in my mind.

'Yes, it's always difficult, especially when a victim is so young.'

'Was he shot? That's what I heard. I mean, what the hell?' Cam shakes his head in disbelief. 'It's Fairhaven, not some dodgy suburb in Limerick.'

'I really can't comment.'

'No, of course not. Sorry.' Cam sighs and rubs his eyes. 'He worked here, you know. Until about a month ago. I can picture him in the kitchen, mucking around with the staff . . . god, he was just a kid.' With a sad smile, Cam adds, 'I guess you deal with this kind of stuff all the time, but I'm just finding it hard to get my head around.'

Ben returns the fish food and starts plucking fliers from the Fairhaven information display under the macaw photo.

'It doesn't really get easier.' I remain impassive while Cam struggles with his emotions. 'Do you know Rick's girlfriend, Abbey Clark?'

Cam sighs and blinks, clearly trying to pull himself together. 'A little. Fairhaven isn't a big place, especially during off-peak. She came into the restaurant with her friends sometimes, and I see her about the place. She works at the supermarket. Seems like a nice girl.' He spins a pen around in his fingers. 'But the Clarks aren't regulars here or anything like that. Daniel, her dad, comes in occasionally and drinks too much, but as long as he keeps to himself I figure it's better than him causing trouble somewhere else. Everyone knows what he's like at home. It's very sad.' Cam grimaces. 'Most of the lads I spoke to about Rick today reckon Daniel probably had something to do with what happened. He's like a walking grenade—he completely lost it yesterday when the search for Abbey was called off. He was telling anyone who'd listen that Rick knew where she was.'

I nod. 'And how long did Rick work here?'

'About a year, I think, waiting tables. A month or so ago he left to focus on setting up his landscape business. I was sad to see him go, but at least it was for a good reason.' Cam shakes his head and pinches the bridge of his nose. 'You know, I heard he broke up with Abbey. One of the other kids working here told me that. I know they were having troubles.'

'What kind of troubles?'

Smiling, Cam shrugs. 'Just teenage stuff. Rick was always complaining she was moody. I told him to give her a break, seeing as she obviously had it pretty tough at home. Then a little while back he got it in his head she was cheating on him, but who knows? I lose track with those kids.' He laughs, clearly trying to lift the mood. 'It's like musical chairs sometimes.'

I wonder if Abbey really was involved with someone else. Rick might have just been paranoid—but if he was right, we urgently need to locate the mystery person and question them.

I ask, 'Did Rick cause you any trouble while he was working here?'

Cam looks thoughtful. 'Rick's a good kid. Was. Had a bit of a short fuse sometimes, and every now and then he'd get a bit worked up about something, but he was a good worker. Like I said, I was sad to see him go.'

'Did you know his brother Aiden?'

'Only to say hello to. Nice guy. He's a bit older than Rick, I think.'

Next to me Ben starts to fidget. He tugs at my hand, and I run it through his hair.

'Can we go, Mum?'

'Sorry, mate, I've been hogging your mum,' says Cam, leaning forward to give Ben a playful nudge on the shoulder. He grins, revealing two rows of perfect teeth. 'Please go and settle in. I know you're not exactly here for a relaxing break, but I hope you enjoy your stay, Detective.'

'Gemma, please.'

'Sure,' Cam says agreeably, rocking from his heels to the balls of his feet. 'Gemma.' He switches his attention to Ben. 'You've got Vanessa Gordon looking after you while your mum's working—right, buddy?'

Ben nods. He seems slightly in awe of Cam.

'Well, you are a lucky man. She's the best.'

I feel a flicker of concern. 'How did you know Vanessa's looking after Ben?'

Cam smiles again, his face creasing attractively. 'It's been a big couple of days in Fairhaven, Gemma. First Abbey goes missing, then Tommy Gordon has his accident, and now of course there's what happened today, but your arrival hasn't gone unnoticed. You're headline news.'

I hold up the room keys and find myself returning his smile. 'Well, thanks. I guess we'll see you around.'

'No worries. I live upstairs so I'm always around.'

I feel oddly reluctant to leave the old-fashioned room, but I pull my gaze from Cam and hustle Ben through the door.

A square of light hits Cam's face, turning his blue eyes neon. 'I'm working the bar tonight,' he calls after us, his accent curling the words. 'Come find me and I'll shout you a drink. You deserve one after today.'

Monday, 11 April
5.57 pm

Our room is surprisingly spacious, almost as big as my old apartment. I quickly tour the kitchenette, lounge, bathroom and bedroom, wondering how long we'll be here. I catch my reflection in the bathroom mirror; I look pale and dishevelled. I wash off my make-up, wondering how the fuck we ended up here.

After we've showered and unpacked, I realise I'm starving. But I also feel bloated, so the idea of eating isn't as appealing as it should be. Ben is watching TV, momentarily distracted enough by the bogus plot to be free of his crushing pain. I fold my lips around my teeth, trying not to cry again. I feel so overwhelmed by what's ahead of us, namely helping Ben face the horror of grief, knowing better than anyone that it doesn't pass, it's simply something you absorb over time until it becomes part of you.

And for me, beyond this emotional rollercoaster is the brutality of the admin. The paperwork. The grown-up conversations and difficult decisions. Dealing with Jodie. Working out where to live. Determining how much of my old life I get to keep.

My blood pressure drops and the floor tilts. I curl up on the double bed, counting the dots that form a swirling pattern on the bedspread. Reaching one hundred, I breathe out.

I text Jodie, letting her know we're fine. I send the same message to Dad, then I call Vanessa Gordon.

'Hello!' Her voice is rich and melodic. 'I know the circumstances are awful, but I'm looking forward to meeting you and Ben tonight.' We chat politely for a few minutes and arrange a time to meet at the pub. 'I'll be wearing purple,' she says, laughing.

I lie back against the pillow and stare at the ceiling. I can't put it off any longer.

I call Mac on FaceTime. 'Hey, it's me.'

'Hey.' His worried face appears on my screen. 'I was just about to message you. How are you holding up? Did today go okay?'

I can't see the rest of the room, but I know there will be half a cup of tepid tea somewhere on his desk, and Arthur will be curled up nearby, purring loudly.

'The funeral was horrible, obviously.' I force a cough. 'But, um, I'm actually working a case now.'

Mac's features tense. 'What?'

I fill him in on Jonesy's call from Tran, the quick decision to come here and the drama at the crime scene.

'Do you really think this is a good idea right now?' he says stiffly.

His light brown eyes are solemn behind his black-rimmed glasses, and his hair is more ruffled than usual, making me think of the last time I ran my hands through it. He's wearing one of his expensive blue-checked shirts—I always joke they are his version of a police uniform, because he has at least six that are almost identical and never works without wearing one, even if he's working from home. He was wearing one of those shirts when I met him.

I heard about Mac when I first moved to Sydney: the former psychologist and lawyer who had switched to the police force in his mid-thirties, quickly making a name for himself as a formidable detective before escaping to the world of academia at the age of forty-three.

A few years ago the commissioner lured him back to consult on complex homicides and cold cases, an appointment that paid off. Mac helped to put away some of the most notorious killers in the state. I'd occasionally caught a glimpse of him in large briefings or on the news. And I'd watched a couple of his lectures online, compelled by the rich tone of his voice and the unique way he talked about police work. He spoke of it as an art, a complicated dance. He likened interviewing a suspect to a song, the verses always softly leading back to the key question. The way he described what I had spent my adult life doing was incredibly validating. It was exactly what I had always felt about being a detective but could never articulate.

About three months after I arrived in Sydney, Mac was present-ing a lecture to senior detectives about the approach he'd taken to solve his past few cases. I missed the first five minutes of his pres-entation because I mixed up the conference room number, and I ended up running from one end of the university campus to the other. I burst into the theatrette, nodding an apology as the sea of eyes turned on me, and scurried up toward the back row, my new silk blouse sticking unflatteringly to my clammy skin.

'You're actually just in time for the audience participation,' Mac boomed.

It took me a second to realise he was talking to me. Unsure what to do, I reached my seat but remained standing while my stomach dropped to the floor.

'I was just talking about the importance of personal vulnerabil-ity in this line of work,' he said, locking eyes with me. I searched for a trace of humour in his gaze but found none. 'Would you like to share a time in your career when you felt vulnerable?'

Mortified, I stood there as perspiration trickled down my back. 'Um, right now?'

Everyone laughed, and I sat down, studiously avoiding eye contact for the rest of his lecture.

After that I noticed Mac everywhere at work. Leaning against the back wall in my case briefings, his hands locked together in front of him, his eyes closed. And in the corridors at the Harbourside squad rooms. His demeanour belied his sharp mind, and I came to learn it only worked at one speed: turbo. Until Nicki he was only peripherally involved in my cases; even so, he'd send me emails after a briefing to suggest new angles and reference old cases. His ability to think laterally and with such empathy was very attractive. I found his quiet energy magnetic, and I wanted to impress him before I knew him.

But I had no idea what was ahead of us as he spoke in the lecture theatrette that day. I just knew the bolt of electricity that ran up my arm when he shook my hand afterwards was unusual—after three years of shying away from anything remotely romantic, something had shifted. I liked this clever, handsome older man.

That handshake took place less than four months before Nicki Mara went missing. Less than ten months ago. I find it almost impossible to think I didn't even know Mac a year ago, but it suddenly feels like those two strangers in the theatrette are characters in a movie. Innocent versions of ourselves blessed with witty lines and brewing chemistry. There was a lightness to our intensity. Now I feel a heaviness every time we interact and I know I'm pulling Mac down with me.

'Gemma, did you hear what I said?' He sounds uncharacteristically annoyed. 'I'm really not sure if you working a missing persons case is a great idea right now.'

Mac is the only person who knows just how much Nicki's case rocked me. At first I was grateful to have someone I could be completely honest with, someone who would follow me into the pit of despair and pull me out, but lately this has started to feel like something he has over me. A piece of information that has stolen my usual hiding places.

'I think it's fine,' I say, irritated.

Mac takes off his glasses to rub his eyes. 'We may have to agree to disagree on that. Where exactly are you?'

'Fairhaven, a tourist town about forty minutes north of Byron Bay. It over-indexes on surfing and dolphins, apparently.'

He sniffs and moves his hand, offering me a brief glimpse of our study in Glebe. The corner of Mac's favourite oil painting—a Paris street scene—and the rows of books on the oak bookshelf. A vase full of pens. 'I know Fairhaven. I assisted on an inquest there years ago. A young couple went missing. In the end, the coroner ruled the man killed his girlfriend and then did a runner. It was a bit of a mess, if I remember right. Retracted witness statements and compromised evidence.'

'Really?' I say, making a mental note to look into it later. 'You probably know the chief, then. I think the same guy's been here forever.'

'His name was Gordon,' says Mac predictably. He has an incredible memory.

Neither of us speak for a moment, and the high-pitched chatter from Ben's TV show is all I can hear.

'We're going to grab a pub dinner soon,' I say, filling the silence. 'It's part of the hotel.'

Mac sighs. 'I don't really know what to say, Gem. I was so worried about you today, and I really wanted to be there—and now I find out you've gone to the middle of nowhere to run a missing person case.'

'And a homicide.'

Mac doesn't even roll his eyes. 'Gemma,' he admonishes.

This is what our relationship is: me pushing and him pulling me back. I think back to all those late nights we spent together, our heads bent close as we pored over dead end after dead end trying to find a thread, something to grab onto that would lead us to Nicki. I fell in love with him then, marvelling at his calm and wisdom. But it's all changed now. Even Mac can't help me navigate this post-Scott world; I need to do it on my own.

'This girl isn't Nicki, Gemma.'

'I'm not an idiot, Mac.'

He tries a different tack. 'Do you really think dragging Ben up there with you is a good idea? Couldn't he stay with Jodie?'

'No.'

Mac's gaze is unrelenting. 'Don't use him to prove a point, Gemma. Take it from someone who knows, it doesn't work.'

Mac has two adult children and a frosty relationship with his ex-wife. A self-diagnosed workaholic, he believes the intensity and ambition that initially attracted her to him were ultimately what drove her away. His daughter, Molly, lives in Sydney and they're on good terms, but his interactions with his UK-based son, Billy, are always complicated. *We have more baggage than an A380*, Mac is fond of saying.

'I'm not trying to prove anything,' I snap. 'I'm just trying to think, and I can't do it in Smithson with everyone breathing down my neck.'

My anger flames skyward before fizzling into a smoking grey heap.

'How is Ben?' Mac says quietly, and I can almost feel his hand stroking the side of my face.

'I have no idea,' I admit. 'He's talking. He's sad. He's angry. All the standard stuff.'

We settle into another uncharacteristic silence.

'I have to jump on a briefing call shortly,' Mac says, reluctantly.

A wave of longing hits me hard. I think back to the last time we were together, five weeks ago, me pressing against him in Dad's guest-room, terrified that everything happening around us was causing the precious thing we'd nurtured to die and rot. I wanted so badly to get lost in the moment, I wanted Mac too, but I couldn't seem to block out all the noise. Lying in the dark afterwards, our heart-beats slowing to normal speed, we made the decision to cancel our holiday—what would have been my first trip overseas—agreeing there will be a more suitable time for an European adventure in the future. But if I'm honest, we haven't just postponed the holiday; our entire relationship feels like it's on hold.

The first few times we were together were so intense, the intimacy almost shocking, but now I feel numb. I'm not sure what's real anymore.

'You're working a new case?' I say.

'Yeah. A cold case. An accidental fire that killed two people. One of your guys got a deathbed tip-off it was actually arson.' He pauses. 'I saw Owen yesterday. He said to say hi to you. He's hating working with Jock, you know—he's desperate to have you back.'

I shift sideways so I can see Ben. He's still curled on the lounge, his chin on his bent knees as he stares at the TV.

'Yeah, well,' I say. 'Owen will be fine.'

'I'm pretty desperate to have you back too, Gemma,' Mac says. 'Realistically, when do you think you can come home?'

I don't reply. The faint jerk of a water pipe vibrates through the shared wall as someone turns on the shower.

Swallowing a sob, I angle the phone away, trying desperately not to lose control. We'd only been seeing each other for a month when Mac suggested I give notice on my tiny apartment in Forest

Lodge and move my small jumble of earthly possessions into his tiny terrace in Glebe. He was as keen as I was nervous to formally merge our lives, and comfortable enough with the notion to tell me so. And despite my doubts, it had been great. We never formed the tight Venn diagram that Scott and Jodie had created with Ben; we remained separate circles enjoying a parallel orbit, our lives harmonising slowly but surely. The last few weeks have left me feeling cheated, and deep down I'm certain our interrupted happiness is some kind of karmic punishment.

'Sorry,' I say, realigning the phone and clearing my throat. 'I just don't know. I don't want Ben to feel like I'm trying to force my life onto him. He's confused enough.'

Mac clears his throat. 'Yes, I understand that. But at some point, you will need to decide what you're going to do. This case might buy you a week or two of thinking time but, regardless, surely staying in Smithson isn't really an option long-term, is it?'

Despite the sun streaming through the window, an icy chill rushes my body. I just want to sleep for a million years. My eyes fill as I look at Mac's concerned face, which momentarily morphs into Scott's.

A ringing noise shrieks in my ears, and I direct my eyes back to the dots on the bedspread. 'I don't think there are any good options right now,' I whisper, ending the call.

Monday, 11 April
6.24 pm

The sky blushes a deep rose as I pull the hotel door shut and take Ben's hand in mine. Speaking to Mac has made me feel untethered and slightly dangerous. On the other side of the building a gentle buzz drifts from the groups of people who stand talking and smoking outside the restaurant entrance. Most are tourists: the distinctive clip of their European accents is a dead giveaway, paired with their ferocious sunburn. The women wear an informal holiday uniform of flowing strappy dresses or dolphin-print tank singlets; garments I noticed on the sale rack at the surf shop we drove past earlier. Sunbakers are still dotted along the curve of the beach, and several fishermen are stationed on the pier; onlookers whoop and clap as one of them stands up to reel in a catch. Even though I've spent the past few weeks recalibrating to Smithson, swapping the concrete and noise of Sydney for fresh air and long grass, Fairhaven feels like another step closer to nature altogether. Here nothing separates the town from the vastness of the ocean, and I feel the prickle of my own mortality more acutely than normal.

The hot air inside the pub gropes at our bare skin like a drunken man. Jimmy Barnes screams at us from the speakers, while a hearty blend of beer, sweat and animal fat clogs my nostrils. A glittering chandelier hangs in the centre of the dining room and the carpet is a vivid emerald. A garish parrot mural covers the main wall and, in my mind's eye, Scott's funeral, the argument with Dad, Rick Fletcher's broken face and Mac's disappointment all pile on as well, forming the strangest of montages.

I reel a little from the onslaught.

The front bar is full of families, the local alcoholics have commandeered the stools and, from the sound of it, the backpackers are out in the beer garden. Several of the journos who were at Rick's house are seated at a large table in the corner chatting boisterously, relieved to be back in their natural environment. I spot Simon Charleston pressed against the far wall trying to have a phone conversation.

Several people have the pinched look of shock, and there's an undercurrent of fear. This is a town on alert.

I steer Ben through the boisterous crowd. 'This way.'

Cam grins at us from the bar, and I return his wave before grabbing a table for two in the main section. Almost immediately, a basket of defrosted herb bread and a jug of water is plonked in between us. 'Thanks,' I say to the waiter's retreating ponytail.

Ben rocks backwards on the already precarious stool and looks around, taking in the room.

'Hey,' I say, 'so I know it's been a crazy day. Are you doing okay?' I hate how formal I sound, like a clueless guidance counsellor in a TV movie. And I can feel Scott rolling his eyes at me. *For god's sake, Gemma, just talk to him. It's not that hard.*

Ben shrugs.

'I'm sorry I took you to that house today. Things were moving really quickly but it wasn't ideal.'

'Why did someone kill that man?'

Rick Fletcher was less than ten years older than Ben. But even though Rick's tan skin was still flawless and his body yet to complete its transition to adulthood, he certainly was more man than boy. Looking at Ben's narrow shoulders and the soft curves of his face, I have an urge to wrap him up and hide him away so he remains frozen in childhood forever.

'I don't know yet. People do a lot of things that don't make sense.'

The lead singer in the cover band starts smacking a tambourine against his thigh, and for a few moments Ben watches him, barely blinking. Then he says, 'That man knew the girl who is missing. I heard you and Cam talking about it.'

I'm startled that he's picking up so much. 'Yes, they were friends.'

'Do you think he did something bad to her?'

'Come on, Ben, I don't want you thinking about this stuff. It's my job to worry about it.'

'Dad always said your job's dangerous.'

The world tilts again, and I press my heels into the bar stool. 'It can be, but I'm very careful.'

We both watch the band for a few minutes. More than anything I want to step into Ben's head and read his thoughts. Make sure he is okay and rewire him if necessary.

'I know you're going to miss Dad like crazy.'

His head bobs but he doesn't reply.

'Are you glad we came here?' I venture.

He kicks the table leg and stares moodily across the room. 'It's way better than being in Smithson.'

'Well, I don't know about that but I'm hoping a change of scenery will do us both good.' I immediately realise I said the same thing to Jonesy—maybe I just have to keep repeating it and I'll believe it.

'Do you get to make the other cops here do all the work because you're the boss?' asks Ben.

I smile. 'Sort of.' I squeeze his hand across the table. Despite the physical distance that has often come between us, some instinctive force has always helped us fit together after time apart. I'm worried about how it's going to work if I'm always around, but I'm even more fearful of the alternative. Oddly, the possibility I could be completely erased seems real in a way it never did when Scott was alive. Although he wasn't always my biggest fan, he supported my role as Ben's mother despite our non-traditional custody arrangement.

'Bread?' I wrinkle my nose and offer Ben the basket.

'Excuse me? Hello.' An athletic-looking woman has stopped at our table and is staring intently at me. Her leathery skin is taut across her nose and cheekbones. 'I don't want to interrupt your meal,' she says loudly, her face inches from mine, 'but I wanted to introduce myself. You're Gemma, I'm Tara Sheffield.' Her voice drops dramatically. 'I know you're here because of Rick's murder. I googled you. That's how I knew what you looked like.'

'Hello,' I stammer. She is the kind of woman I find incredibly intimidating, so harshly groomed she's more mannequin than human.

After an awkward pause, I hold out my hand. She laughs and shakes it. I'm mesmerised by her hot-pink nails, which she keeps raking through her jet-black hair. 'I just cannot believe what happened to the Fletcher boy. What a tragedy.' She moves her hand in a lazy sign of the cross; she points in the vicinity of her temple then back to her chest, and flicks her index finger toward each collarbone. 'Of course you can't tell me anything. I know all about that, living with a doctor.' She rolls her eyes. 'Privacy is a total buzzword in our house.'

'Yes,' I say, swallowing.

'I'm Vanessa Gordon's friend, by the way. I'm here with my family, over there.' She points to a table of olive-skinned kids and an athletic-looking bald man. 'That's my husband, Eric. He heads up the hospital here. He often has quite a lot to do with the cops, so you'll probably cross paths, you know how it goes.'

Eric gives me a friendly smile, and I nod in response.

'And how are *you*?' Tara bends her knees to level with Ben, arranging her face in a way that indicates she knows about Scott.

'Good, thank you,' says Ben.

'That's the way,' she trills. '*Adorable.*' She grabs my hand as if we are old friends.

Ben takes a large sip of water, his eyes locked on Tara.

I clear my throat awkwardly, desperate to offer up a safe topic.

Tara beams at us, unperturbed. 'I know you're here to work but I hope you get to enjoy Fairhaven regardless. I run the beauty salon on Church Street, the big one on the corner. It's pink, you can't miss it. You'll have to pop in for a treatment.' Her gaze sweeps my messy ponytail and hours-old make-up. 'Only if you have time, of course.' Then she leans closer to me and whispers, 'Do you think she's still alive? Abbey, I mean.'

'I'm sorry, Tara, I really can't discuss it.'

Her eyes are darting from one side of the room to the other. 'Normally I would assume she's done a runner. There's always so much drama with teenage girls, and she doesn't have a good home life to start with. No stability. My eldest is the year below her in school, so you hear the talk, they're always bitching and gossiping, you know how it is.' She props her hand on her hip and sighs. 'But her father is such bad news, I just can't help thinking . . . well, it doesn't bear to say it out loud, does it? I used to say to Eric that Daniel was born evil, you know how some people just are? His folks were the same. Real bad seeds. Anyway, I know that's what everyone's thinking. And now he's gone and done the same to her boyfriend. The poor loves.'

'I really can't discuss it,' I repeat, trying to keep my expression friendly and jerking my head in Ben's direction, hoping she'll get the message.

'Of course.' She zips her lips with her fingers before blurting out, 'It's just that really, nothing bad has happened here for years. Not since those other kids disappeared—which was absolutely terrible, believe me. The boy, Greg, used to work here, you know. Lovely kid. He served us drinks all the time and seemed nice enough, but I guess you never know what's really going on under the surface. I tell you, it was all anyone talked about for years.' She pauses and then whispers, 'Sally's mother still comes into the salon sometimes. She looks dreadful, I have to say, the whole thing really aged her, she's so drawn in the face.'

I realise Tara must be talking about the same case Mac mentioned on the phone earlier.

'Anyway,' continues Tara, even louder than before, 'now all of a sudden we've got teenagers being bashed and killed, and predators on the beach photographing our children. Someone even broke into our salon, can you believe it? There's no cash there, it was just pure destruction. Honestly, I told Tommy just last week that he needs to think about doing patrols like they do in the city.' She thrusts out a hip and examines her nails. 'I'm sure it's expensive, but you have to nip these things in the bud, don't you?'

I jump in as she takes a breath. 'Well, thanks for saying hi.'

Tara is holding up her hand as if to silence me. 'Anyway, I've nattered on for way too long. I'll get out of your hair. Good luck. And don't forget to come into the salon—my treat.'

Ben watches as Tara trots away. 'That lady had a really loud voice.'

'I think she was just trying to be friendly.'

Cam ambles over from behind the bar, throwing Ben a wink. He rests his forearms on the table and says conspiratorially, 'I notice you met the welcoming committee.'

'Um, yeah.'

He laughs. 'Tara's an acquired taste, but she means well.' From his pocket he pulls out a flat metal token, which he hands to Ben. 'Maybe you'd like to have a go at that game over there later?' It's an arcade classic. 'You can take a shot at beating my top score while I have a drink with your mum.' Cam looks at me pointedly, and a shiver darts through me.

Ben's eyes shine. 'Cool. Thank you.'

'Who says city kids don't have any manners?' Cam laughs. I don't bother to correct him.

He takes our orders and heads back to the bar. Ben and I chat fairly steadily, keeping to safe subjects like sport and his classroom teacher. The steady rumble of conversation in the room spurs us along. Glancing over toward Cam, I notice Kai Lane at the bar with a pretty blonde, her waist-length dreadlocks piled on top of her head like a beehive. He doesn't see me, but I notice him manoeuvre his hand into the waistband of her skin-tight red skirt as he kisses her neck. It makes me remember my first boyfriend, Jacob, how we were always touching each other, and I have a flash of nostalgia for that time of my life.

We're just finishing our meals when Vanessa sends me a text saying she's on her way.

A few minutes later, Ben looks expectantly at the side entrance. 'I think that's her.'

I follow his gaze to see a woman in the doorway flashing a smile and waving at various people around the pub. Spying us, she thrusts a hand skyward as if she's trying to get picked from an audience to join an onstage skit. Despite her long grey hair she looks a lot younger than the fifty-plus years I've estimated she must be. Her bright purple shirt is tie-dyed and blurs into a muddy vortex at her stomach. A faded denim skirt brushes her tan thighs. 'Gemma?'

'Yes. Vanessa?'

'And you must be Ben!' she exclaims, beaming at him.

Ben smiles back and I can tell he likes her.

'Welcome.' She turns to me, her eyes full of concern. 'So how are you guys doing? I know you've had quite the day.'

There is something about this simple question, something so appealing about her kind motherly voice, that almost breaks me. I'm tempted to fold myself into her lap and let her hold me while I cry.

'Thanks for coming to meet with us,' I say instead, forcing a smile and wiping my clammy hand discreetly on my jeans before holding it out to her.

'A handshake!' She grips my fingers, seeming delighted. 'Very formal. You'll be good for the team here, they could use a bit of polish. I'm Vanessa, obviously—Ness, if you like.'

'Hello,' Ben says, sitting up straight. His green eyes shimmer in the dim light and he bites his lip as if he's nervous.

Vanessa bends down so she's level with him. 'I know about your dad, and I know things seem impossible right now. They will probably feel that way for a while. But while you're with me, you just do whatever you need to do and we'll make everything work around that, okay?' She pulls out her phone and scrolls to a photo. 'This is my dog, Inka. She's a Hungarian vizsla. You'll get to meet her tomorrow. She's pretty excited about having another new playmate.'

Ben nods, his eyes glued to the dog. I know Scott had been planning on getting him one for his birthday in July; he has been begging for a pet for ages.

Vanessa straightens up and gestures for a waiter. 'On me,' she insists after she orders us house white wine.

'I should be buying you a drink,' I say. 'You're doing me a massive favour looking after Ben.'

She waves the hours of child care away. 'Don't be silly. It's like I told Ken, I'm really looking forward to it. I love kids. Plus I'd go crazy with just Tommy and me at the house all the time.'

Ben asks if he can go play the pinball machine with Cam's token.

'Just come straight back when you're done.'

Vanessa and I watch him make his way across the room. 'What a lovely little boy, Gemma.' She turns back to face me. 'I couldn't believe the news about Rick Fletcher. It's just terrible.'

'How is your husband's recovery going?' I say.

'Oh, he'll be fine, but he's not the best patient and he's still in a lot of pain. I keep reminding him he's actually very lucky. He's pretty frustrated, of course, especially with all that's going on around here. I know deep down he's glad you can help—of course, there's a part of him that's desperate to be involved.' She gives a lighthearted laugh. 'But he can't work at the moment, so he needs to get over it.'

This seems like a loaded comment, but our wines arrive and then Vanessa starts chatting enthusiastically about Fairhaven's natural attractions. 'Anyway,' she concludes, 'despite what happened today it really is a nice little town. I'm sure you'll slot right in.'

We agree that I'll bring Ben to her house at eight tomorrow morning.

'Our place is only a couple of k's up the road,' she says. 'And the police station is less than five minutes from our place.' She smiles. 'You'll soon discover that everything in Fairhaven is pretty close.' Tilting her head, she squints at me. 'Are you sure you're okay?'

'Just a bit tired,' I admit.

'Well, I'd say get some sleep, but I know what you cops are like.' She pauses and seems to hesitate before saying, 'Take care, Gemma, okay?'

Emotion surges in my chest again as she gives me a sad smile and heads off to say goodnight to Ben. On the way out she stops by Tara's table, and they talk animatedly for several minutes. Tara's husband rolls his eyes; he catches me looking and smiles sheepishly.

Cam gestures to me as I pass the bar on the way to drag Ben from his game.

'Gemma Woodstock! Ready for that drink?' Cam's accent sounds even more distinctive now, after Vanessa's rounded vowels.

'Thanks, but I might pass. I need to get Ben to bed.'

I look over to the pinball machine but can't see Ben. My heart begins to race. 'Where is he?'

'Who?'

'Ben!' I'm frantically scanning the crowded room.

'Um.' Cam squints and looks left to right. His face relaxes. 'He's over there.'

My head jerks to where Cam's pointing. Ben is standing in the corner of the room talking to Simon Charleston.

Monday, 11 April
8.23 pm

'Excuse me, but what the hell are you doing?' I say, pushing past several groups of people.

Simon looks up with a smile. 'Hello, Detective Woodstock. Ben and I were just having a chat.'

'Well, don't,' I snap, pulling Ben away.

Tara glances over with interest and says something to Eric as I herd Ben back toward the bar. 'What did he say to you, Ben?'

My son shoots me a look like I've lost my mind. 'Nothing. He was just asking about school and whether we've ever been here before.'

'I don't want you talking to people you don't know,' I say.

'Like Vanessa?'

'People *I* don't know you're talking to,' I clarify.

'Everything okay?' says Cam when we reach the bar.

'Fine.' I glance over at Simon, who is typing on his MacBook.

Cam nods good-naturedly and waves at someone leaving. 'Good to hear. Sure you don't want that drink?' He drops his voice to a stage whisper. 'I might be able to rustle up an ice cream if you're lucky.'

Ben looks at me hopefully.

'Alright,' I say, smiling. 'I guess it's not that late. I'll have a beer—just a middy, please.'

A waitress brings over a chocolate ice-cream cone for Ben, and Cam pours me a beer.

'How long have you lived here, Cam?' I ask.

His eyes widen in pretend shock and he exaggerates his accent as he says, 'What? You mean, you don't think I was born here?'

'It is my strong investigative opinion that you were not.'

'Wow, you're good.' He smiles warmly. 'I came here for a week about fifteen years ago.'

'Did you fall in love with the climate?'

'A woman, actually. But the climate was appealing too, and, as it turns out, more stable.'

I laugh.

He takes a drinks order and sets about making a complicated cocktail at breakneck speed. My tired eyes relax as they follow his movements.

'My family is very academic,' he says. 'I completed one year of a medical degree myself, actually, and my three brothers seem to be addicted to putting letters after their names.' He gestures at our bustling surrounds and laughs. 'They are very confused about all this.'

'Do they all still live in Ireland?'

'I have a brother in Sydney. He has a wife and a bunch of kids, all my brothers do.' Cam winks. 'Again, I'm the black sheep.'

'I'm sure they're very impressed with what you've built here. I mean, who wouldn't be?'

Cam's face dimples in boyish pride, and he finishes the cocktail with a flourish. 'You can come back any time with that kind of comment.'

Several patrons are jostling for his attention, so we say goodbye. I leave through the side entrance to avoid Simon. It's still warm and the ocean breeze swirls around us as we head to our room. It feels nice to be in our own space again. I let Ben watch the tail end of a kids' movie while I unpack the last of our things before herding him through his nightly ritual and into the single bed. His eyes droop when I kiss him goodnight and pull a sheet up to his chin.

He buried his father today, I think, as I look at his perfect face.

Flicking off the main light switch, I snap on the bedside table lamp and change into an old T-shirt. I crawl in between the clean white sheets on the double bed and log online, spreading out the case-file notes Tran gave me. Several emails appear in my inbox: as well as the files from Lane, I've been sent access to Abbey's social media accounts. The top half of my face feels heavy as I flick through several photos of her and some friends. She definitely looks like Nicki, but not as much as in that first photo I saw. Waves of Abbey's long dark hair are honey-tinted, and her smooth olive skin is scattered with pretty freckles. The seriousness of her golden-brown stare in several shots makes her appear a lot older than fifteen. I read through a few pages of her online conversations, recent comments and friends, her little world coming to life in front of me. She loves art, dolphins and music. She's worried about the planet. She's never left Fairhaven. I check her messages, mainly just links sent from friends to news articles, blogs and YouTube videos, and a few birthday party invites. There's nothing to suggest bullying or depression or thoughts of suicide, not that I'm willing to rule it out but, still, there are no obvious red flags. There aren't any messages from Rick—they must have communicated via text, Snapchat or WhatsApp.

But there are two messages from someone called Robert Weston, both sent in the past three weeks. The first one reads:

Hi! It was great to meet you today. I hope you don't mind me contacting you on here but I asked around and got your name ☺ You are so pretty. Hopefully see you again soon. Rob.

Abbey didn't reply to this message, but that didn't deter Robert from sending another, on Wednesday last week.

Hi again. I hope you are having a great week. Wondering whether your going to the house party on Friday night? Me and my mates keep hearing about it. Would be great to see you there. I'd love to have a proper chat to you. R

Abbey replied on Friday morning:

Hi. Yep, I'm definitely going. See you there! Abbey.

I click through to Robert Weston's profile page. The settings are private but a few images can be viewed. His profile photo is of a giant dead fish; the hands that grip it are strong and pale. The other two photos are of landscapes. He's from the UK but clearly he's in Australia now: the recently uploaded photos are all beach shots. None feature people. I tap my finger to my mouth, thinking. It's interesting that Abbey replied to him the morning after her alleged break-up with Rick. I read over Robert's messages again. He and Abbey clearly met, but I can't tell whether they saw each other again after he sent the first message. Her response is friendly, but it hardly seems like they were romantically involved despite Robert's attempt at charm.

I jot down the mobile number linked to his Facebook account and yawn deeply, trying to stay awake.

My mind drifts to what Mac said about the Fairhaven inquest he consulted on years ago, the same one Tara mentioned. I do a Google search and dozens of articles appear, most of them with Simon Charleston's by-line. I click on the piece he wrote two days after the young couple, Gregory Ng and Sally Luther, went missing.

The photo used at the top of the article could have been pulled from a fashion shoot. Greg's arm is hooked around Sally's shoulders, there's a beer in his hand, and he is smiling, his glossy dark hair spiked upward, his tanned skin clear and glowing. Sally's blonde head tilts at the camera, her collarbones exposed and angular, her smile both wholesome and seductive. They ooze health and youth.

They weren't together the night they disappeared. It was a Sunday, and Sally had dinner at her sister Evelyn's place and helped her organise some last-minute things for her wedding the following weekend. Just before 10 pm, Evelyn walked Sally to her car at the end of the short driveway and she drove off. Evelyn Luther didn't ask her sister where she was going, but only because she assumed Sally would head to their family home where Evelyn had lived until three months prior. Sally's car was out the front of the house the following morning, just like it always was, but her parents were in Sydney with some relatives who had come to Australia for the wedding, so it's unclear if she ever went inside that night.

Greg worked an eight-hour shift at the pub like he always did on Sundays. It was a quiet night and they closed up around 10 pm. Sally and Greg didn't speak on the phone that Sunday, though he texted her at 10.13 pm to say he was closing up at the pub. He said goodnight and told her he loved her. She never replied. The other two staff members clocked off, and Greg stayed to complete the clean-up and close. Cam is quoted as saying he was in the kitchen when he heard Greg call out that he was heading off. Cam replied with a goodnight and thought nothing of it—until the next day, when he realised almost eight hundred dollars was missing from the till.

By then Sally and Greg were both gone. His car was gone too, fuelling the rumours they had eloped in the middle of the night. Sally's family have never given up hope of finding their daughter, offering a substantial monetary reward for information on her whereabouts.

I read about the inquest, which was held almost two years later, then I close the article and do a fresh search for Simon Charleston.

A few head shots appear, along with his latest piece: 'Tragedy Strikes Sleepy Beach Town Once Again' screams the headline. There's a photo of me standing on Rick Fletcher's lawn talking to Lane, the ambulance behind us in the driveway. 'DS Woodstock flew in to lead the case,' reads the caption.

I close the laptop and tune in to the low hoot of a nearby owl as I think about Sally and Greg, two souls who have never been able to rest, their memories tainted with doubt. My thoughts turn to Abbey, the natural comparison to Greg and Sally making her seem even more like a kid. If she died on Saturday night, she will have started to rot into the ground. I picture her bloodied and crying, buried alive. I see her abandoned in the bush, praying to be found. I see Nicki Mara. I squeeze my eyes shut. No. I can't let Nicki into this; I can't let my guilt cloud my thinking. Abbey deserves more than that.

There's another possibility, of course: that Abbey is a killer. Mick Lamb wouldn't rule it out following his initial review. I glance back at her photo. It doesn't seem possible.

I don't remember dozing off, but when I wake an hour later the lamp is still on, the case files are splayed across the sheets to my left, and to my right is Ben, his small body shaped to the curve of my spine, his skinny arm tight around my waist.

THIRD DAY MISSING

Tuesday, 12 April
5.12 am

I toss and turn all night, finally giving up on sleep when daylight muscles in around the blinds. I lie looking at the ceiling for a few minutes, my eyes grainy and sore, and wonder how Rick Fletcher's parents are coping today; they've woken up to a new reality, a world without their son.

I push the covers away, careful not to disturb Ben.

I cry in the shower as I wash my hair using the miniature bottles of coconut shampoo and conditioner from the bathroom cupboard. Clad in a towel, I go back to the kitchenette where I tap out a brief email to Jonesy and flick a text to Dad. Through the kitchen window the sea glitters like a field of sapphires. The fishermen are back, and several surfers bob in the white froth a little further along the beach. My mother loved swimming in the ocean; I remember her talking passionately about it. I've always been a strong swimmer and since moving to Sydney I regularly swim laps at the local pool, an activity strongly encouraged by my psychologist, but the few times I ventured into the open water I disliked not being able to see below the surface.

Feeling vaguely unwell, I make myself a midnight-black instant coffee and continue to review the case notes, trying to commit the facts to memory.

Abbey has a savings account, and like clockwork she withdraws the four hundred and twenty dollars she is paid every fortnight from a company called Fresh Holdings. That aligns with what Cam mentioned about her working at the local supermarket. I tap my pen against the coffee mug. It would be good to know what she was spending her money on. Perhaps she's been giving money to her parents, as the Clarks certainly fall into the category of the working poor. Their home was purchased over fifteen years ago and is in Daniel's name but has a long history of missed payments and is currently in arrears. Dorothy works casually at the caravan park as a cleaner, but Daniel lost his job a few months ago when the mechanic closed down, and is now receiving a benefit payment.

I wonder if he's been tempted to supplement his income by becoming involved in something illegal. If that's the case, Abbey or Rick may have stumbled upon it. That's partly what happened with Nicki. Or maybe Abbey was just the messed-up teenager I had diagnosed Nicki as: a young girl who was overwhelmed and snapped. No note has turned up, but there's nothing to suggest this isn't a suicide. Although her online interactions appear lighthearted enough, I know full well darkness can be hidden and resilience doesn't always turn up when you most need it.

I'm trying to summon the particular flavour of complexity that comes with being fifteen. I knew it then and I absolutely know it now: teenagers are terrifyingly impulsive and skilful at making hasty decisions with horrific consequences. I've had the misfortune of standing next to many fit, strong young bodies that oozed with health before a misjudged party trick or ambitious sporting feat turned them grey and cold. Beautiful brains broken by reckless drug taking or a thoughtless punch. It's a cruel truth that vitality gifts the young an otherworldly confidence at the exact moment their emotions rob them of sound judgement. Their desire to punish can be brutal, with suicide, drug use and theft the key weapons in their arsenal. Disappearing into thin air is another appealing option to a teenage brain, a seemingly reasonable reaction to whatever injustice they are facing—but I still doubt that Abbey ran off in the middle of the night with only the clothes on her back.

I flick back to the disturbances at the Clark house. They sound depressingly similar: neighbours called the police, worried about the safety of Dorothy Clark and her children due to the sounds of Daniel's fury. A local constable was dispatched; upon arrival, an eerily calm Daniel assured them everything was fine.

A traumatised-looking Dot agreed, and the children, including Abbey, remained silent.

This scenario has played out three times since Christmas. I read on and note that Daniel lost his job in mid-December. Idle hands are never good but, in my experience, when they belong to someone with a tendency toward violence, it's even more important they are occupied.

Ben appears in the doorway, his hair standing on end. 'Hi, Mum.'

'Hi, baby.' I pull him into a tight hug. 'Sleep okay?'

He nods and I make him a bowl of cornflakes that he carefully carries to the coffee table.

My limbs protest as I stretch my arms toward the ceiling. I really need to go for a run, though there's no way that's going to happen today.

Mac hovers around me like a caffeine craving I haven't sated, but since our phone call something has hardened in me, grim and cold. Our relationship has always had an unusual rhythm; his wisdom tilts the balance of power ever so slightly, causing me to overcompensate with youthful passion. But last night's conversation drifted into unchartered territory—a clear paternal vibe snuck in. I felt his judgement and, perhaps even worse, his doubt in me. I thought the bond we'd formed during the Mara case was indestructible, but maybe something built on so much chaos was destined to crumble. He was my rock during that madness and in its aftermath, but now he feels more like a weight. Our life together feels so far away, as though all that happiness belongs to someone else. I can see how it might be easier to take Ben and just slip away, leave the loose ends loose and simply start over. It's not like I haven't done it before.

Scott's death hits me fresh and hard, and I close my eyes and clutch the back of a chair. *He's gone, gone forever*, I remind myself for the hundredth time. Funny how the mere existence of some people can be so reassuring. Scott and I weren't in contact often—before his illness we only spoke about once or twice a month—but I always knew he was there and I could count on him. That Ben could count on him. With the momentum from the funeral gone, my loneliness is intense.

Taking a deep breath, I unfold the A3 map of Fairhaven that Tran gave me. The Clark house is circled, as is another address where I assume the house party took place on Saturday night. I find the Fletcher brothers' house too and draw a ring around it. The tiny sliver of bush behind the Clark house that was searched on Sunday afternoon is highlighted, as is a short strip on the two front beaches, the Parrot Bay lookout and the pier. Beyond that, there are acres of wild bushland. Stretches of sand dunes and endless sea.

She could be anywhere.

My thoughts lurch from the case back to Mac. My desire for the past few months to be erased creeps in until I want to scream.

It's not even seven and I'm exhausted. I fetch some clothes for Ben, who has a shower and then gets dressed while he watches cartoons.

Still wrapped in my towel, I plug my headphones into my laptop and open the files Lane sent me. After a click, a young male voice fills my ears. 'Hello? This is Rick. Rick Fletcher. Look, I need your help. There's something I want to talk to you about. To the cops, I mean. It's, um, important. I should've said something today but I guess I just panicked. Can, um, can someone call me back? Or should I come to the station tomorrow morning? Sorry, but look, thanks. Um, you have my number.'

Rick's voice is unexpectedly androgynous, without the masculine timbre I expected. He sounds scared and desperate. When Tran told me about Rick's call yesterday, I got the impression that she thought he was calling to confess something, but listening to it now I think his message sounds more like a cry for help.

I load the video file next. A small room comes into focus. Rick is seated at a grey table with two glasses of water on it, and the camera is angled toward him. Alive, he's as attractive as I suspected.

Tran's voice comes through the speaker with trademark curtness. 'As I explained earlier, we are very concerned about the wellbeing of Abbey Clark. Do you have any idea where she is?'

Rick's arms remain firmly crossed, his eyes on the table. 'No.'

'She never mentioned anything to you about leaving town? Even just going away for a few days?'

Rick tosses his neck back to shift his blond hair from his face. 'She always talked about leaving Fairhaven after school finishes, but that was years away.'

'Her family say you two have been in a relationship for over a year. How serious was it?'

A flash of malice crosses Rick's face as he leans forward. '*I* was serious about it. I dunno about her—she's been hot and cold on me since Christmas.'

'That must have been frustrating,' says Tran, attempting empathy.

'She dumped me on Thursday. I picked her up from school like usual and she just said it was over.' The veins on Rick's neck strain as his breath comes out in short puffs. 'I said "whatever", I couldn't be bothered with the whole thing anymore anyway. And I told her I knew she'd been hooking up with someone else.'

'What made you think that?'

He shrugs. 'Dunno, just had a feeling.'

'Did you ask her about it?'

'Yeah. She said she wasn't.'

'Did you argue about it?'

He slumps back in his chair. 'Not then. I just dropped her at work and went for a surf. I was pissed, but I couldn't see the point of talking about it.'

'Did you speak to her after that?'

Pushing his finger along a dark scuff mark on the table, he says, 'I sent her some texts on Friday. Probably shouldn't have—I just didn't get what was going on. She didn't even give a proper reason for breaking up with me, just said we'd "grown apart" or some shit. She just didn't want to tell me the truth.'

'You were angry,' says Tran.

Rick meets her gaze. 'Yeah, I thought she was cheating on me. The break-up didn't make any sense and she was all weird about it.'

'Was your relationship sexual?'

He laughs nervously and crosses his arms again. 'I'm not talking to you about that.'

'Abbey is fifteen,' continues Tran. 'She's still a minor. You're two years older—if you were sleeping together, technically you were breaking the law.'

Rick's eyes widen. 'I never did anything she wasn't into. I swear.'

I can tell Tran is satisfied she has regained the upper hand. 'Okay. So she broke up with you on Thursday and you didn't know why. You sent some texts on Friday. Did she explain herself after that?'

'Nah, just wrote some shit back to me about us not being right together anymore,' he mumbles.

'Did you go to the house party on Firestone Drive on Saturday?'

He nods. 'Everyone went.'

'Did you speak with Abbey there?'

'I got stuck into her. She was all over some guy—dunno who, probably her new boyfriend. I hated that she was acting like that in front of me. Told her I thought she was being a bitch.'

'You confronted her about the other guy?'

'Yeah. She said he was hitting on her and she barely knew him. She started saying all this stuff about how sorry she was we'd split, like crying and whatever, and that she felt bad but things had changed.'

'But you didn't know what she was referring to?'

Rick's eyes drop to his hands, which twist in front of him. 'No idea.'

'What happened after that?'

'I hung out with my friends, had more drinks. Then Bel called me, she's my sister, and said I should come to the beach with a bunch of her friends. I went round the side of the house so I could hear her better, and I saw Abbey leaving.'

'Around what time was this?'

'Eleven-thirty, I think.'

'Where was she going?'

'Dunno. She just got on her bike and took off.'

'Alone?'

'Yeah, she was by herself.'

'What about the guy she'd been talking to? Any idea where he was?'

Rick shrugs. 'Reckon he was still inside, but I dunno.'

Tran shifts forward. 'And Abbey was definitely on her bike?'

'Yeah.'

'It's really important, Rick—I need you to be sure.'

'I told you, she got her bike from across the road and she left.'

'Which way?'

'Back toward town. I figured she was going home. Her dad wouldn't have let her stay out after midnight. She was barely allowed to do anything—he's a total prick.'

'Did you follow her?'

'No!'

'Bump into her later?'

Rick's face flushes. 'It's her dad you should be talking to. *He's* the psycho. Do you know the kind of shit he does to her and her mum? It's bullshit.' Rick pulls up the sleeve of his T-shirt to reveal a purple bruise. 'Look what he did to me this morning. He's fucking crazy.'

Tran frowns. 'Daniel Clark did that?'

Rick runs a hand through his hair, clearly agitated. 'Yeah, he came to my house and almost kicked the bloody door down. He kept saying Abbey was there—he searched the whole bloody house even though I told him she wasn't.'

'Daniel Clark is certainly part of our ongoing investigation,' says Tran, 'but right now we want to speak to you. This would be a very good time to tell us if you know anything that will help us track down Abbey.'

'I already told you I don't.'

'You definitely don't know where she is?'

'No!' His voice breaks. 'I haven't seen her since Saturday night.'

'At the party?'

Rick's eyes remain downcast. 'Yeah.'

'Did you have any theories about someone else she might have been seeing romantically?'

'Not really. I don't reckon it was anyone from school, but who knows? Maybe some tourist?'

'Where do you think Abbey is, Rick?'

When he lifts his head, his eyes are bloodshot, obviously on the brink of tears. 'Don't know,' he croaks, 'honestly I don't. But I shouldn't have fought with her like that.' He pauses and wipes his eyes, rakes a hand through his hair. 'I upset her, I know. Maybe it made her do something stupid.'

'Did she ever give you any reason to think she was suicidal?'

'Not really, but she wasn't herself these past few weeks. I guess anything could've tipped her over the edge.' Rick bites his lip. 'I called her a slut. I was being a prick but she was flirting with that guy and, I dunno, I guess I lost it for a minute.'

A car engine comes to life outside, jerking me back to the present. Rick's angst swirls around me, his regret palpable. I swallow the last of my cold coffee, trying to shake off the heavy feeling.

I dress quickly and then call the mobile number for Robert Weston that I scrawled in my notebook last night. It rings out and beeps. Unsure if it's a voicemail recording, I leave a message asking for my call to be returned. Then I glance at the time— we need to get moving. 'Hey, Ben, brush your teeth and get your shoes and socks on, we've got to go.' I shove the case folder into my bag and give myself a quick once-over in the mirror. Neat white shirt and tailored pants. Hair tied back, minimal make-up. A dark circle under each eye and impractical winter boots.

At least I look professional.

Ben turns off the TV as I open the door.

I gasp before I register what I'm seeing, my hand slapping hard against my open mouth.

Curled on the concrete stoop is a large possum lying in a pool of blood, its neck so deeply cut that its head has come away from its body.

Tuesday, 12 April
7.48 am

'What is it, Mum?'

I slam the door shut and step backwards, shooing Ben into the lounge room. My teeth crack against each other and I taste vomit.

'Mum?'

'It's nothing. I just remembered I need to make a phone call before we go.' I walk into the kitchenette, a hand on my churning stomach. 'Why don't you pop the TV back on, okay?' Forcing a smile, I rustle through one of the drawers trying to find the guest book. All I can see is the demented grin of the dead possum, its row of jagged teeth, the horrible red mess of insides spilling from its throat.

I find the book and call the reception number.

'The Parrot Hotel, this is Cam.'

'Cam, it's Gemma Woodstock. I need your help with something.'

'Gemma!' His voice is warm. 'Of course. What's going on?'

I bite my lip, trying not to cry. 'Can you come to my room, please? You'll see what I mean.'

Ben is on the couch oblivious to my panic, lost to the TV again.

'Just wait here okay, sweetheart?' I say, and he grunts.

When I open the door again, I'm half expecting the possum to be gone, but it's still there. Several ants are marching toward the bloody puddle. I snap a few photos with my phone.

Cam appears around the far end of the building, his tan face cheerful as he lumbers over. 'Detective Woodstock, what seems to be the trouble? Oh.' He slows as he approaches our doorstep, eyes widening. 'What's this? Who did this?'

'I don't know. It was here when we went to leave this morning.'

Cam swallows, his Adam's apple bobbing madly. 'Where's Ben?'

'Inside. He hasn't seen it, and I want to keep it that way.'

'Okay.' Cam grips his jaw and briefly closes his eyes. 'Wait here. I'll get something to cover it.'

'A garbage bag,' I say automatically. 'A brand new one. I've taken photos, but I think I should call someone in from forensics to test it.'

'Of course.' He turns to go but swings around again. 'This is . . . Fuck, are you alright, Gemma?'

I nod, the stone in my core hardening even more. 'I'm fine.' I attempt a laugh. 'Someone around here clearly thinks they're the Aussie version of Don Corleone.'

Cam just gives me a worried look.

I wait next to the dead possum, Ben's cartoons audible through the thin door. The sun has pushed between the clouds, beaming down hot and hard. I feel exposed, as if I'm standing on stage under a spotlight. I know I need to call Tran, call Vanessa, call the team at the station, but I feel numb.

My phone beeps with a message from Owen Thurston. I've worked with him on every case I've been assigned in Sydney so far. He's probably the best partner I've ever had; he is extremely conservative, more librarian than cop, but he's shrewd and funny and incredibly kind. He's divorced and childless, and I've been told he's bisexual but it's not something we've ever discussed. We're close while knowing very little about each other's personal lives.

Owen's text tells me that a key witness in the case we were working when I left Sydney has turned up dead, executed at point-blank range in his driveway, his wife and kids less than five metres away.

I'm standing in the sun, my back to the possum, as I scroll through the cast of faces I've been intimate with for the best part of this year, trying to work out who could have pulled off a kill like that. I feel stuck between two worlds, dizzy and impotent, unable to do either version of my life properly. I reply to Owen that I'll call him later.

Cam reappears holding a roll of garbage bags and two bricks. 'Here, I think this will work.'

I help him unfold the sheet, and we lay it lightly over the possum just as my phone starts to ring.

A young couple emerge from their hotel room a few doors up, chatting excitedly about their plans for the day. The man lifts his hand in a friendly wave. 'Morning!'

'Morning,' Cam manages, kneeling down and pinning each side of the plastic to the ground with a brick.

I realise my phone is still ringing. It's Jodie, probably wanting to speak to Ben. I switch it to silent.

'Take it,' says Cam. 'I'll wait here.'

I nod, but then the world tilts. Clenching my feet, I press my heels into the ground. I need to get it together.

I cross the road and pace the empty block next to the service station. Everything is racing: my pulse, my thoughts, my breathing. I exhale slowly, trying to walk through the panic, trying to ignore the growing sense that coming here was a big mistake.

The sun beams down, and I fix my eyes to the ground, shielding them with my hand as I ignore the missed call message from Jodie and dial Tran's number.

Weeds, cigarette butts, ants, bits of plastic. A nail.

My call goes straight to voicemail. 'Hi, Inspector Tran,' I stammer, 'this is Detective Woodstock. Gemma.'

And then I see the blood.

Tuesday, 12 April
8.17 am

Vanessa pulls into the hotel car park and rushes over to us, her long peasant skirt flying behind her.

I press send on a text to Lane, telling him I'll be late to the case meeting.

'Thanks for coming,' I say to Vanessa in a low voice. 'Ben's inside.'

'Of course,' she murmurs, her eyes glued to the plastic sheet outside the door.

I steer Ben swiftly past the possum, bundling him into Vanessa's jeep. 'The front step broke so Cam's just helping us fix it.' I keep my voice light. 'I'll come get you from Vanessa's house later, just like we planned.'

His mint-green stare bores into mine, but he simply nods and does up his seatbelt. I give him a kiss and push the door shut, letting out a breath I didn't know I was holding.

'Oh, Gemma, this is so awful.' Vanessa wrings her hands. 'Are you alright?'

'Absolutely fine,' I say firmly. 'I'm sure it's just a prank that went a bit too far. I don't want Ben to think anything is wrong, okay? I'll be in touch later. Call me if you need to.'

Vanessa glances at Cam. He's pacing up and down the concrete path outside my hotel room, smoking and talking on the phone. The crease between her eyes deepens. 'You can't stay here, Gemma. Not after this.'

The tech van that came to Rick's house yesterday drives into the car park. A trickle of sweat runs between my shoulderblades. 'I've got to go. We'll talk about it later.'

Vanessa visibly pulls herself together and climbs into her car, a big smile on her face as she turns to say something to Ben. I wave them off and head over to speak to Jason, one of the three techs I met yesterday.

'It's definitely blood, but it obviously might just be from an animal,' I tell Jason as we cross the road. I point out the large patch of rust-red on the uneven asphalt.

He circles the area and bends to peer at it. 'Yep. I don't think there was a body here though.'

'No.' It's not like blood patterns I've seen following a fatal gunshot or stab wound, and there's not enough for someone to have bled out here, but it's a decent amount. Maybe this is where the possum met its gruesome fate? Or maybe it was just the scene of a clumsy pub fight.

Or maybe Abbey was attacked here.

'It hasn't rained since Friday, so there's a chance it's from the weekend,' I say. 'What do you think you'll be able to tell me?'

Jason clicks his tongue. 'Whether it's human. DNA, obviously, which hopefully we can match. And possibly how old it is, though that will just be a ballpark. Some of the guys in the office might be able to hypothesise on the injury and give you a couple of scenarios.' He stands up and grimaces as his knees buckle. 'Let me get it sealed off and take some snaps.'

'We need to search the surrounding area.' I put my hands on my hips and squint into the bushland. 'Can you arrange that?'

Jason whistles through his teeth. 'I'll call my boss but I'm not sure of your chances. You might be better off speaking to the fireys.' He glances over at the servo. 'I need a coffee.'

'There's something else I need you to look at first,' I say.

Jason jerks to a stop when he sees the possum. 'Pow,' he exclaims, 'fucking brutal.' He hooks a thumb toward the door. 'And this is your room?'

I nod.

'Jeez.' He seems impressed and makes another clicking sound; he's like a one-man sound system.

'Jason, I don't want a word about this to anyone, okay?'

'Absolutely, goes without saying.'

Cam ends his call and joins us, eyebrows drawn together with worry.

'Are you okay to stay here for a little while?' I ask him. 'Jason might need your help keeping people out of his way until the other tech gets here.'

Cam nods. 'No dramas, Gemma. I've got someone covering the front desk all morning.' He looks over the road where he must have seen me and Jason examining the blood. 'Did you find something else?'

'What's that vacant block used for?' I ask.

'Nothing, just dead land. Sometimes people park there in summer if the front car park is full. I don't even know who owns it—the council, I guess.'

I notice a sticker on my hotel room's window that claims 24-hour CCTV monitoring, but when I scan the length of the building I can't see any cameras. I ask Cam, 'Do you have security footage along here?'

'No, only at the entrance to the pub and in the lobby.' He seems a bit embarrassed.

'We need everything you have,' I say, 'from Saturday night to this morning. And I need a list of all the guests who stayed here during that timeframe. Oh, and I need you to ask your staff if they noticed anything suspicious last night—but don't mention the possum. We have to keep it contained, okay?'

'Sure, absolutely.'

Jason returns to his van to get his equipment. A light breeze tousles the gum trees, scattering stray gumnuts across the asphalt. Was someone following us yesterday, waiting to see which room we were staying in? Watching us come back from dinner?

'Thanks, Cam,' I say, with a tight smile. 'I've got to go.'

He stares at me with concern. 'Look, Gemma, I don't even know what to say. I'm really sorry about this, especially with Ben being here. Are you sure you're alright?'

'I'm totally fine.' I shrug. 'Like I said, it's just a sick joke. I'll talk to you later.'

I get into my muggy rental and find myself back in Scott's hospital room.

His face blends into the white pillow as he stares at the ceiling.

'I won't be going back to Sydney straight away,' I repeat. 'I don't know how long I'll stay here but it will be a while.'

Scott makes a rasping sound and coughs out my name. 'Gemma.'

'Yes,' I whisper, my voice dangerously close to breaking.

'You don't have to give up your whole life. I wasn't even sure you would come here.'

A stabbing pain erupts in my chest. 'I never considered not coming.'

'He has Jodie,' murmurs Scott. 'He has a family.'

'He has me,' I say.

Scott turns toward me but his brown eyes look cloudy. I don't think he can see me.

'Look after yourself, Gem.'

'I will look after Ben,' I say, tentatively squeezing his hand.

He closes his eyes, exhausted. 'No. Look after *yourself*. Ben loves you so much, Gemma. I don't want him worrying about you.'

The last word fades into the relentless beeps of the hospital machines and my fingers shake as I plug the address of the police station into the GPS.

Tuesday, 12 April
8.49 am

Fairhaven Police Station resembles a large toilet block: a squat square of bricks painted a garish aqua with rusted bars crisscrossing small glass windows. A concrete ramp leads to a homely wire door. Jutting out of the left wall is a standard-issue New South Wales Police sign, which looks like a formal postage stamp on an outrageous postcard. Residential homes are positioned to the left of the station, and on the right are two storage sheds, their concrete bases extending past the corrugated-iron walls. Everything has been touched by the invisible tentacles of the sea, salt damage having eaten away at the wooden window frames and ravaged the paint. Even the shrubs, optimistically planted moat-like around the buildings, flatten toward the car park, relenting to the pressure of the ocean breeze.

A handful of journos are parked on the street outside the station. Simon Charleston is there with his aviators on, leaning casually against his car bonnet. As I drive past he waves at me and makes a phone-call gesture.

Two older model squad vehicles are in the small car park, and a motorcycle is propped in front of a shed. I take the second-last spot closest to the entrance. While getting out, I tug discreetly at the armpits of my shirt. The air is rich with birdsong as I walk up the ramp, ignoring the frenzied questions from the journalists. At the front desk sits a middle-aged man with an impressive shock of grey hair. The size of the text on his name badge has been reduced due to the length of his name: Constable Noah Kingston-Ford.

'Good morning,' he says cheerfully. 'What can I do for you?'

'Detective Sergeant Gemma Woodstock.' I offer my hand.

'Oh jeez, sorry, I didn't realise you were you. I'm normally stationed at Evans Head but apparently I'm here until at least Easter. De Luca's shown me the ropes, and I've got a whole lot here to keep me busy. I'm told a Kylie Crossin will step in for me at 5 pm.' He jerks his thumb at a mound of paperwork. 'But sing out if you need anything else in the meantime.'

'I'm glad you can help us.'

'Me too. It certainly sounds like you'll have your hands full.'

He answers the phone and scribbles notes on a pad that I can see is already covered with his writing, the name 'Fletcher' scrawled several times.

When I look around, I can't help comparing the tight space to the bustling reception area in Sydney's Harbourside squad rooms. Even Smithson's police station is at least three times bigger than this. I'm struck by the thought I might not be able to do this again, to shrink my universe after so many years in a metro squad. I feel a pang of longing for Owen and our team. I miss the sleek case rooms and my neat office. I even miss Marie, our moody boss. I miss the gritty mayhem of Sydney, the colour, the noise, the chaos. I miss my old life.

I shake my head, trying to ward off a full-blown tumble into despair.

Noah's smile indicates the caller is settling in for a story, so I smile back and head into the main office. Three heads whip around as I enter.

On top of a desk in the middle of the room, a young woman sits holding a folder. Her dark hair is cut into a feathery shag, tendrils curling around the collar of her uniform. Her eyes are a stormy grey, and the fingers that grip the folder are long and fine. Lane and another constable are seated on office chairs in front of her.

'Morning,' says Lane, standing up.

The woman slides cat-like from the table, while the other cop jumps to his feet with a nervous smile.

Lane squares his shoulders. 'Guys, this is Detective Sergeant Woodstock.' He turns to indicate the others. 'This is Constable Edwina de Luca and Probationary Constable Damon Grange.'

The woman eyes me coolly, angling one of her hips to the side. 'Hello.'

Grange bounces over to me, and I'm surprised to see that he's my height; he must have only just scraped into the academy. He has oddly long eyelashes and an extremely round face.

He nods his bald head up and down. 'Really pleased to meet you, Detective. What a day yesterday was, huh?' He rocks back on his heels, arms swinging as his nervous smile turns conspiratorial, directed at all three of us.

The room dips into silence.

'I'm really sorry I'm late,' I say. 'This morning has been surprisingly eventful.'

De Luca arches a perfect eyebrow.

'Everything alright?' asks Lane.

'I had to get the forensic team over to the vacant lot next to the service station. I found some blood on the ground.'

Three pairs of eyes widen in unison.

'It hasn't rained since last week,' says de Luca. 'That blood could be Abbey Clark's.'

'Yes, I wondered the same. The techs are going over it now, but we might have to wait a few days for anything concrete.' I decide not to mention the possum, at least not until I've spoken to Tran. 'I want to arrange for the bushland around the servo to be searched. Can you help arrange something similar to what took place on Sunday?'

De Luca nods and picks up a phone.

I grab a glass of water and my laptop and a notebook, mentally ticking off all the things we need to do.

With a shrug, de Luca hangs up. 'All sorted. The regional firemen are going to send a dozen people there in the next twenty minutes.'

'Okay, great.' I clap my hands together. Something about de Luca's tone feels hostile, but I tell myself I'm imagining it. 'Let's quickly catch up so we can get moving.' I peer into a dark room on the right of the building. 'We'll go in here.' I snap the lights on. The stuffy room contains six mismatched office chairs, a tape recorder and an ancient TV on wheels.

'There's no fan.' De Luca glides in behind me and takes a seat at the head of the table.

I spend the next few minutes wrestling with the window until it finally pops open. 'Right.' I take a seat at the opposite end of the table. Grange and Lane are sitting on either side of de Luca, their laptops open in front of them. Nerves turn my stomach. 'Firstly, I want to say I'm looking forward to working with you all, and I appreciate that this is an unusual situation.'

The boys' expressions remain friendly, but de Luca gazes at the door behind me.

'I also want to remind you that we're investigating a serious homicide, possibly two, and we need to keep things tight. I'll be asking a lot of you all, and I need you to let me know if anything I ask you to do is unclear. Okay?'

They reply in murmurs and nods.

'Good.'

I turn to de Luca. 'How were Rick's parents yesterday?' The soothing calm of procedure kicks in—I know how to do this.

'Not good.' Her full lips barely seem to move. 'Their neighbours were there when we arrived, which ended up being a good thing, otherwise I'm not sure we could have left them. Especially the father.'

'He was a mess,' pipes up Grange. 'Crying and barely able to talk. It was really sad.'

'Did the brother turn up when you were there? Aiden?'

'No.' De Luca shakes her head. 'We came back here to write up our notes.'

'Do you suspect the Fletchers know anything about what happened to Rick?'

'They just said he'd seemed so happy lately and was excited about his landscaping business,' says Grange.

'They're doing the official ID this morning,' says de Luca, 'after Lamb cleans up the body. I was thinking we'd let them do that and then speak to them again tomorrow. They really weren't in a position to be very helpful yesterday. We barely got the chance to ask them about Abbey.'

De Luca's voice has an appealing cadence to it, a quiet assertiveness.

I try not to show I'm annoyed—I would have liked to have spoken to Rick's parents yesterday. Despite their primal emotions, people are less reserved when they are fresh in grief; they reveal things more freely. In my experience, time often gives loved ones a chance to decide what information is best withheld.

'Okay, that works,' I say. 'We definitely need to understand Rick's relationship with Abbey and his other friends. And whether he was in financial trouble or taking drugs.'

The three young officers stare at me.

'I have several questions that I think should form the backbone of our investigation,' I say, 'but take me through where you're at and then we'll plan out the next forty-eight hours.'

De Luca gets to her feet in one clean movement and gives the slightest of shrugs. She walks to the far side of the room and picks up a large pin board, flipping it to reveal photos of Abbey Clark, along with a map and several printouts that look to be phone records and bank statements. De Luca rests it on the table and remains standing behind it. 'This is where we were at on Sunday night.'

There's something of a challenge in her tone, a defiance, as if I've already questioned her ability, but I simply nod and look at her expectantly.

She runs through Abbey's known movements and ends with her rejecting Lane's offer of a ride home. 'Both parents admit Abbey argued with her father before she went out. Daniel claims the tension on Saturday night centred around the fact he wanted her home by midnight, which she felt was unreasonable. And he expressed his dislike of Rick Fletcher, apparently an ongoing source of animosity between them.'

'But Abbey broke up with Rick last Thursday, right?'

De Luca takes a moment to respond, as if my question is an inconvenient disruption. 'That's what Rick told us. A few texts between them on Friday seem to confirm this, although I wouldn't call them definitive. Some kids from the party told us they argued about breaking up.' De Luca arches an eyebrow at me as if to confirm whether her answer is satisfactory.

'So Abbey didn't tell her parents that they split up?'

'Apparently not.'

'Do we know if Rick and Abbey's relationship was volatile prior to last week? Had they broken up before?'

'Not as far as we know.' She clears her throat delicately. 'We don't know who the guy Rick mentioned Abbey was flirting with is, but one kid from the party said she thinks he might be staying at the caravan park. We haven't had a chance to follow that up yet.'

'I reviewed her Facebook messages last night,' I say and flip a page in my notebook. 'A Robert Weston had been in contact with her recently and alluded to a real-life meeting they'd had. He's from the UK but I'm not sure if he's moved here or just travelling.'

De Luca makes a note in her book. 'Could it be a fake account?'

'It's locked but has several hundred friends, so I think it's legit. This morning I called the mobile number listed and left a message asking Robert to call. Here,' I find the number and pass it to her, 'dig up what you can on him. And see if you can track the phone.'

She nods.

'How many kids from the party have you spoken to so far?' I ask all three officers.

'Probably about seven, but at least sixty kids were there,' says Grange. 'The majority were locals from the high school but there were several out-of-towners as well. We've formed a list that we were going to start working through.'

'We need to move pretty quickly—it's school holidays from this week, so I expect a lot of them will be heading away with their families.'

De Luca keeps her eyes on the pin board and continues as if I haven't spoken. 'Abbey Clark's phone hasn't been used since Saturday night, and it was switched off or disabled approximately thirty minutes after she left the police station. Earlier in the night she called a friend from the party and sent a text to another friend, but there was nothing out of the ordinary. And she had no phone contact with Fletcher either before or after the party.' De Luca pauses, then lifts her eyes to the room, regarding us in turn. 'From her phone records, it's clear her relationship with Fletcher was sexual and fairly volatile, especially lately. They had several arguments over text last month and they exchanged several explicit images last year, but nothing like that recently.'

'Right,' I say, already feeling impatient. I get to my feet. 'I want to be clear that we have two key objectives. We need to find Abbey Clark. While I appreciate there's a possibility she was involved in Fletcher's murder, there is every chance she wasn't, and that she is alive and out there somewhere. If that's the case, we are running out of time, so I want to proceed with a sense of urgency. We don't have the resources to conduct a broad search, which means we need to be focused. Our other task is to determine who killed Rick Fletcher. The timing and proximity would suggest these cases are linked, and we will certainly conduct them in tandem, but please don't let this limit your thinking. As far as I'm concerned the field is wide open. No theory is off the table at this point.'

I walk over to the pin board, looking at a photo of Abbey.

'Lane, I'd like you to get Bruce Piper's formal statement and follow up with Fletcher's other neighbours. Can you also talk to the forensic team and get the key take-outs of their crime-scene report? Once they're done with the blood this morning they will be at the Fletcher brothers' house all day. Mick Lamb said he won't have much for us until the autopsy on Wednesday.'

'No problem,' Lane says.

'Good. Grange, please pull as much security footage as you can find from Saturday night and Monday morning. I know it's limited but I want council footage, private cameras, dash cams—whatever you can get. I've already spoken to Cam O'Donnell at The Parrot, and he's sending through his records asap. The clue to the entire case could be sitting on a tape somewhere and I don't enjoy that kind of irony. And can you speak to the caravan park and get a full guest list from them? I want to know everyone who was there on Saturday plus anyone who has checked out since. Same goes for other hotels and Airbnb rentals in the area.'

Grange's tongue pokes out the side of his mouth as he takes notes. 'Yep, yep,' he mutters.

I turn to de Luca. Her pretty face remains impassive. 'I want you to come to the Clarks' with me, then help me map out a clear timeline of Abbey's movements on Saturday night.'

'I was going to continue interviewing the kids from the party,' she says curtly.

'This is more important.'

She purses her lips. 'Fine.'

Heat rises up my neck. I don't know what her problem is but I have zero time for it.

I grab a piece of blank paper from the far end of the table and start jotting down points as I say them aloud. 'I want you to keep the following in mind. Firstly, we need to locate the man who was hassling Abbey at the party. Maybe it was Robert Weston, maybe someone staying at the caravan park. Either way we need to track Robert down. Let's get the caravan park manager to help us out. Secondly, I want to know what Abbey was spending her money on. She was earning at least four hundred dollars a fortnight and withdrawing it almost immediately. Thirdly, I want to know more about her mental health. Was there any indication she was suicidal? Who was she close to? Did she confide in anybody? We need to know if anyone noticed anything else about her that night, such as who she was speaking to and any details about her behaviour. I also want to locate that bike. If it was stolen then who took it?

The family doesn't have much money, so I'm thinking it wasn't worth a lot—does that mean it was taken for some other reason? And what made her feel compelled to report it in the middle of the night?' I turn to Lane. 'I assume there is footage of her coming to the station on Saturday? I'd like to see it.' I put the lid of the pen back on, then stretch out my back. As I straighten up, I say, 'I'm still struggling to understand why she didn't let you drive her home.'

Lane nods, moistening his full lips. 'I just should have insisted,' he says quietly. 'I should have said it was non-negotiable.'

He looks forlorn, and I feel a flicker of sympathy. The game of 'what if' is a dangerous one in our world. So many wrong turns are served up to us, inevitably we end up down a dead end at some point. The sooner we reverse out of there, the better. Guilt is a sure-fire ticket to nowhere.

'I suspect a lot was going on in her head that we are not aware of.'

'I'll send you the station footage,' he says, turning back to his computer.

I pin my list of questions to the board and grab another bit of paper. 'We need to speak with her employers and co-workers at the supermarket. Same with Rick—did he work with anyone? And what about the other adults in their lives? Teachers? Relatives?'

'Abbey's teachers wouldn't know what went on at the party,' says Grange doubtfully.

'She might have confided in someone about things that were happening in her life. It's not uncommon for victims of domestic abuse to turn to an adult outside the home.'

The back of my neck burns hot again. Somewhere in the room a fly buzzes sporadically, like a lawnmower that won't start.

'I just need you all to keep an eye out for anything that doesn't add up. We can't afford to waste time.' I stifle a sigh, knowing my role as cheerleader is critical at this point. 'We can do this. Stay in touch during the day, and report back to me no later than five. Any questions?' I look around the small room.

Lane clears his throat. 'I was just wondering about our shifts. I know Tran organised the extra resources but how will that work? Will we still do any night shifts? I'm happy to if you need extra cover.'

'No, I want the four of us to work as a team during the day. The station will run twenty-four seven until further notice, but the others can take care of the night shifts and we'll also have one extra resource between 7.30 am and 4 pm to look after the everyday jobs and do some patrol shifts. I don't know how the weekend will work yet, but I advise you warn your loved ones now that you might need to postpone your Easter celebrations this year.'

When Lane nods, my mind jumps back to seeing him at the pub, watching his hand down the back of that woman's skirt.

'Okay, same time, same place tomorrow morning unless you hear from me.'

Lane and Grange get to their feet and gather their things.

'Okay if we leave in ten?' I ask de Luca.

'Sure.' She hugs the folder to her chest, then says, 'Lane? Can I just quickly chat to you?'

'Sure,' he says agreeably and falls into step beside her.

I use the bathroom and apply some sunscreen to my face. The sickly sweet smell makes me feel sick.

'Bye,' says Grange, scurrying off self-importantly.

'Bye,' I reply.

The door to the other meeting room is still closed, and I can hear the faint murmur of Lane and de Luca's conversation. I look back at the head shots of Rick and Abbey. Young, beautiful people who likely had no idea their photos would end up on the wall of a police station.

Realising I've left my sunglasses in the car, I head back out the front. The exposed line of skin on my scalp immediately starts to burn, and then of course my phone rings.

Tran.

'Sorry, Gemma, I've been tied up in meetings all morning. Is everything okay?'

I tell her about the possum and the blood in the vacant lot. 'We've got the local fire department helping out with a field search of the area.'

She doesn't reply straight away. I walk around the back of the building to evade the sweltering journos.

'I wish you had contacted me about that. I don't like owing favours.'

'Sorry,' I say, taken aback. 'Things are moving pretty quickly here.'

'Yes, well next time run it past me.' She pauses. 'I'm not going to jump to any conclusions about the origin of the blood,' she says carefully, 'but I don't like this possum business.'

'I'm not taking that seriously,' I lie. 'It was a bit of a shock but it's probably just kids mucking around.'

'I don't like it, Gemma. I think we should consider moving you.'

'I really don't think that's necessary.'

Tran sighs. 'Let me speak to my boss. I'll call you back later.' She pauses, then says, 'Gemma, now is the time to say if you want out. I know you have your son with you and things are . . . difficult.'

I pull my collar away from my clammy skin. Could I leave? Pretend this never happened? Forget about Rick Fletcher and Abbey Clark and take Ben back to Smithson and . . . what? What then?

'I came here to run a murder and missing person investigation, and that hasn't changed,' I say with more conviction than I feel.

'Good,' replies Tran, blunt as ever. 'I'd be pretty screwed if you pulled out now.'

I walk back around to the car park, causing the journos to stand to attention. Then the wire front door swings open and de Luca glides down the ramp. 'We just got a call from Georgina Fletcher,' she says to me quietly. 'Aiden has disappeared.'

A pair of kookaburras begin to cackle loudly from a nearby tree.

Tuesday, 12 April
9.35 am

De Luca drives like she talks, all fluid movements and measured turns. The air con blasts into my face, and the sweaty patches on my shirt have turned to ice. Goose bumps rise on my arms and I cross them hoping she won't notice. She seems completely unaffected by the temperature, both outside and inside the car, her ivory skin still clear and luminous, her carefully made-up eyes unsmudged.

I make calls from the passenger seat. Aiden allegedly left voluntarily; he told his parents he wanted to be alone for a while and took off in his van. If it wasn't for his alibi—his car was clocked by a toll point early on Monday morning as it drove from Sydney and his credit card has been used there all week—I'd have him as a suspect in Rick's murder, but I still feel uneasy.

I recall the desperation in Rick's voice message and wonder if Aiden is in the same boat. I don't doubt his grief, but either way he knows something and we need to track him down. I put out an alert on his car, and request monitoring of his phone and bank accounts. His parents aren't aware of a girlfriend, but Grange is working through his known contacts, friends and workmates. Frustrated, I lean back heavily in the car seat, squeezing my eyes open and shut. Right now we can't do much more in regard to locating Aiden except wait.

I glance sideways at de Luca. 'What did you think of Rick's reaction to Abbey being missing?'

She looks surprised. 'Me?'

'Yes. Did he seem shocked? Guilty?'

'Daniel Clark went to Rick's house as soon as he realised Abbey hadn't come home, so we weren't the ones to tell him. Daniel said he thought Abbey might have stayed there because of the argument they had the night before. Rick told us he woke up to Daniel screaming and banging on his front door. Apparently he turned the house upside down looking for her.'

I wonder if Daniel Clark's frantic search was born out of desperate concern for his daughter's safety or was intended as a dramatic demonstration of parental care when the suspicion inevitably turned on him.

'We didn't speak to Rick until around 11 am, after we'd been at the Clarks'. I thought he seemed pretty rattled.'

'Rattled in the sense his ex-girlfriend was missing and her crazy father had just ripped through his house trying to find her, or rattled because maybe he lost his temper the night before and accidentally killed her?'

De Luca's jaw ripples. 'I don't know, but he seemed genuinely upset.' She flicks on the indicator and executes a smooth turn. 'And we know he tried to call her several times after Daniel left his house, which suggests he was genuinely worried.'

'Maybe.' I've worked hundreds of crimes where people have placed calls to make themselves appear ignorant of the truth. 'If only it was easier to tell the difference between guilt and grief.'

De Luca shrugs. 'I guess.'

'Clearly the photos of Abbey were fine on Sunday?'

'Yes,' she says. 'They must have been vandalised sometime between Sunday afternoon and when Rick was found on Monday morning.'

I think of the empty bottle of Jack Daniel's on his bedroom floor. Maybe he got so drunk and angry on Sunday night that blacking out Abbey's face seemed like a good idea. But then I think about his voice message—he didn't sound drunk at all.

'Did you grow up here?' I ask de Luca, deliberately switching gears.

'I've lived here since I was twenty.'

'Right.'

The police car rattles along, a sporadic *tick-tick-tick* coming from the engine. The carpet at my feet is worn fuzz and there is a rip in the pleather upholstery. We pass a strip of matching double-storey holiday homes, brightly coloured towels draped over the balcony railings. De Luca pauses the car at an informal crossing spot and a blur of skateboarders zip past. A fish-and-chip shop on my left has a giant plastic octopus hovering above the open door, and next to it there's a laundromat called Play, Wash, Repeat. Over the road, a busy cafe spills out onto the footpath; patrons chat to each other across small tables as they attempt to keep toddlers and dogs under control. There's a surf shop, a supermarket, a large newsagent, and a bookstore with a table of bonsais and succulents out the front.

I notice several teenagers huddling in small groups, clearly upset. The shock of Rick's murder has given way to sadness.

I shift my gaze to de Luca. There's something decidedly impenetrable about her, and I try to break through again. 'When did Inspector Gordon have his accident?'

'Once we established Abbey was missing, we organised emergency services to help out with a basic search of the bushland around her house and near the house party, but Tommy had a meeting with the regional team about increased budgets. The state minister was flying in, so it was a big deal. I guess that's why Tommy went even with all that was going on.'

The houses we're passing now look distinctly less opulent. Several broken-down cars are on display in the front yards.

'That's a lot to deal with in one day.'

'It was fine.' She shrugs dismissively and adjusts the air-con vent.

Puzzled, I try yet again. 'You've attended a few DV calls at the Clark house, right? I saw one of your reports.'

'Sure have. Not as many as Tommy and the boys—I don't tend to work the night shifts. Tommy doesn't like women doing those, and that seems to be Daniel's primary problem time.'

'I used to work a lot of DV cases in my home town,' I say. 'They can be really frustrating.'

'I mean, why would he stop, I guess?' She laughs sarcastically, her voice rising. 'Dot's never going to say anything, and without her pressing charges no one can touch him.'

De Luca's outburst seems to surprise her as much as it does me, and for the next few moments we just listen to the ticking motor, her breathing fast and hard.

'What about Abbey's brothers?' I say tentatively. 'They're twins, right?'

'I don't think he touches them. They've never been treated for any injuries. They're still young though, so who knows? I don't think he started knocking Abbey around until she was a teenager.'

I know this pattern so well I could draw it in my sleep. A male abuser often focuses his anger on the females in the household, especially once they hit puberty, blaming his violence on perceived sexual promiscuity. Other males in the household might be spared the physical attacks but are forced to bear witness to their mother and sisters being treated like property, forever skewing their views on the role of women and the entitlement of men.

De Luca continues, 'I could tell Abbey wanted to come forward but I guess she figured it wasn't worth the risk if he didn't get put away. She was worried about her mother.' A bitterness has crept into de Luca's voice, and her fingers curl around the steering wheel.

Before I can reply, we turn into a jellybean-shaped court.

'We're here,' she announces flatly, parking at the top of the curve.

The Clark house is the epitome of a renovator's delight. For some reason it has me conjuring up the nursery rhyme about the old lady who lives in a shoe. Muddy brown, it leans slightly to the left. The exposed roof of the lower level is tin, with the second storey set back several metres and erupting out of the middle like a wart. The two levels are completely mismatched. A deceased tree takes up most of the front lawn, its branches scratching at the house. Insects bleat like a faulty smoke alarm, and I smack my arm to dislodge a feasting mosquito.

'Is it this way?' I gesture to the left. I can't see a front door.

'Over here,' says de Luca, walking to the far right of the house. An old Ford is parked in the driveway and I count three deflated footballs in the weedy garden beds.

Along the side of the house the paint is peeling so badly it looks like someone has been scraping it off. A top-floor window is open and thin curtains shift in the breeze. De Luca knocks firmly on the glass panel of a cracked wooden door.

A heavyset woman appears, with bloodshot eyes and a worried expression. She fumbles around for a few moments, struggling with the lock. Finally the key turns and she shuffles out onto the step, a plump hand wedged over her eyes. Her posture has the beginnings of a hunchback, and her dark brown hair is frizzy, forming a messy halo. Her broad cheeks are pebbled with freckles and pigmentation.

'Hi, Dot,' says de Luca.

I hold out my hand. 'Mrs Clark? I'm Detective Sergeant Woodstock.'

Dot allows me to shake her hand. 'Yes. That other woman rang and told us you were coming.' She nervously smooths the front of her faded sundress, then fondles one of the oversized buttons. 'Have you found Abbey?'

'Can we come in, Mrs Clark?' I say, feeling both self-conscious and hot in my corporate shirt and tailored pants.

She drops her hand to her waist and disappears into the house, leaving the door gaping open. I exchange a look with de Luca. From her expression, I garner this is a standard greeting.

The walls are bare and dark, the skirting boards etched with grime. In the kitchen heavy curtains are bunched at either side of the narrow window above the sink. The cupboards and benches are made of wood, and there's a table with six chairs scattered around it, a wooden fruit bowl at its centre. A trio of flies hover around its shrivelled contents; a sweet turning-to-sour smell fills my nostrils.

In the adjacent room two identical young boys are sprawled on the couch, their faces lit by screens.

'I'll get Daniel.' Dot shuffles through another doorway, and I take the opportunity to go into the lounge. De Luca remains in the kitchen.

'Hi, boys,' I say.

'Hi,' they chorus, barely looking up.

I introduce myself and they confirm which is Wayne and which is Chris. They have Abbey's eyes, but their faces are rounder and their messy brown hair is without the rose-gold tint. Their innocent faces effectively conceal the damage that no doubt lies underneath.

'We're trying to find your sister,' I say, kneeling at their level. 'You haven't heard from her, have you?'

They shake their heads.

'And you have no idea where she is? She never said anything about going away somewhere?'

More headshaking.

'I said she might still be at the party,' Chris says, 'but Mum said she went somewhere else.' He kicks at his brother, who smacks his bare leg in response.

Wayne speaks, unperturbed by their minor tussle. 'Mum says Abbey'll come back soon but we don't have to go to school this week because everyone's still looking for her.'

'Were you both here on Saturday night?'

They nod. 'I had a bad dream,' pipes up Chris. 'It woke me up in the middle of the night.'

I lean a little closer to him. 'Did you hear anything when you woke up?'

He bites his lip, his eyes still on his device. 'I don't think so. Maybe there was a noise outside but it was probably just a possum. They're always on our roof—Dad hates them.'

I am momentarily thrown by this. 'Does your dad ever catch them? Does he have a cage for them?'

Wayne giggles. 'No.'

I smile and nod, thinking that this doesn't mean Daniel didn't leave the early morning surprise on my hotel doorstep. 'So, Chris, do you know about what time you woke up that night?'

'Um.' He scrunches up his eyes and nose. 'I could hear birds so I guess it was almost morning?'

I watch as his little face relaxes back into a video-game trance.

'What about yesterday morning? Were your mum and dad both here then?'

'Dad was outside, I think,' says Wayne. 'He works on engines in the yard.'

I hear footsteps on the floorboards and draw myself back up. 'We're just going to speak to your mum and dad for a bit, okay?'

They nod in unison again, clearly unfazed by my presence.

I return to the kitchen just as a man enters from the opposite end. Daniel Clark is wide and tan, each shoulder almost brushing the edges of the narrow doorframe. His features are attractive: smooth skin and thick dark hair shaved close to his head. He carries a bit of extra weight around the middle but the ghost of an athlete lingers. His chest rises and falls rapidly as his dark eyes settle on me. Dot trails behind him looking more like his mother than his wife.

'You're the woman cop from the city,' he says.

'Detective Sergeant Woodstock. You must be Daniel Clark.' I step forward to shake his hand.

He looks from me to de Luca and back again. A slow sarcastic smile creeps across his face as he firmly grips my hand. A dark energy swirls around me—he's like a laced cocktail.

'Is there some kind of discrimination against male cops these days? Do I need to start a petition?'

'Chief Inspector Gordon is taking personal leave, so I am in charge of your daughter's case.'

'Yeah, I know all about Tommy's accident.' He grabs his elbows and rocks back on his heels. 'Very unfortunate.'

'Mr Clark, can we perhaps sit down?'

He yanks a chair out from the table and sits down heavily on it, legs spread wide. He doesn't break his stare as I take a seat, de Luca and Dot following my lead. Then Daniel turns his head toward the lounge. 'Boys! Outside!'

A moment later the twins charge past the table. Daniel looks at me and blinks expectantly. 'I'm guessing you haven't found my daughter yet?'

'No, we haven't located Abbey. But we do have some more questions for you both.'

Daniel drums his fingers on the table, irritated. 'Go on, get cracking.'

'Where were you yesterday morning, Mr Clark?'

Dot's head jerks up.

'*Yesterday* morning? I was here. Like every morning. Why?'

'Were you both here yesterday morning?' I say, turning to Dot.

'Yes,' says Daniel. 'Why are you asking about yesterday? You do realise Abbey went missing on Saturday night?'

'There was an incident yesterday morning involving Rick Fletcher. I'm surprised you haven't heard about it. It's been on the news.'

'Don't watch the news,' says Daniel. 'Waste of time.'

Looking around the dour kitchen, I suspect it's unlikely the Clarks have friends over to gossip with either.

'That kid is a piece of shit,' adds Daniel. 'I'm not surprised he's in some kind of trouble. I told Abbey to stay away from him, but she wouldn't listen. She never bloody listens.'

'What made you feel that way about Rick Fletcher, Mr Clark?' says de Luca.

Daniel turns to her and shrugs. 'Just a bad feeling. And it turns out I was right. He went and did something to Abbey, didn't he?'

We let this accusation hang in the air for a few seconds before I say, 'Did you ever witness Rick being violent toward your daughter, Mr Clark?'

'Well, they never stuck around here, did they? But I know what he's about.' Daniel leans forward, resting his forearms on the table. 'I'm telling you, he knows where Abbey is.'

I fight the urge to glance at de Luca. I can't work out if Daniel really doesn't know about Rick's murder or if he's an incredible actor.

'I understand you've been threatening Rick, Mr Clark. That you went to his house on Sunday night and harassed him on the phone.'

Daniel's eyes burn with anger. 'We had words. Someone has to bloody try to find my daughter, seeing as you lot are barely lifting a finger.'

'Rick Fletcher was found dead at his home yesterday.'

In my peripheral vision I see Dot's eyes bulge open and her mouth form a circle.

Daniel sits back heavily, appearing genuinely surprised. 'Dead how?'

'He was attacked.'

Dot is crying silently. Daniel flicks the back of his hand along his nostrils and sniffs. 'Well, like I said, he was bad news. He must have been mixing with some bad people.'

'You really hadn't heard anything about it?'

'Nope.'

Dot's lips move as if she is talking to herself and I think she might be praying.

'We've been wondering whether someone attacked Rick because they thought he had something to do with Abbey disappearing,' I say.

Daniel crosses his arms. 'It's possible, I guess.'

'Mr Clark, I'd like to reconfirm that you didn't leave the house yesterday morning?'

He rolls his eyes. 'I didn't touch him. Had plenty of opportunity if I'd wanted to.'

I turn to Dot. 'Mrs Clark, can you please confirm you were both here yesterday morning between five and seven?'

'Yes.' She chews her lip and bobs her head.

I lean back against the chair and it creaks loudly. 'As a result of what happened we are obviously running two investigations, and we're trying to determine if your daughter's disappearance is linked to the attack on Rick Fletcher. We may have more questions for you as we work through the information.'

A dark flush creeps up Daniel's neck. 'I don't like the idea you'll be focusing on what happened to him and ignoring Abbey. You haven't even issued an amber alert.' He says this with the naive indignation of someone who has been given a piece of information to weaponise, despite not understanding its context.

'Mr Clark, I can assure you we're working hard to find your daughter. An amber alert is not appropriate for this situation but we're taking her disappearance very seriously.' As I give my little speech I'm transported to the Maras' kitchen. Its white tiles and marble benchtops were a world away from this dingy cave, but Abbey's parents' expressions are exactly the same as the ones Deirdre and Lucas Mara had worn the first time I went to their house.

Daniel grunts and mutters under his breath.

'Had Abbey seemed herself lately?' I direct this question to Dot, who immediately defers to Daniel.

'Oh, yes,' she murmurs absently.

'Abbey was *fine*,' spits Daniel, pitching forward. 'I know what you're getting at, but she hasn't run off or done anything stupid. Either that Fletcher kid did something to her or some other piece of shit did. Whatever happened, you better bloody find her.'

'We still need to speak with a lot of people.' I push away from the table and stand up, keen to put some distance between myself and Daniel Clark. 'I'd like to look in her room, please.'

Daniel cocks his head at de Luca. 'The other lot already did that on Sunday.'

'I would like to have a look as well.'

He shoves his chair back, causing wood to screech against wood. 'You can waste time poking around in her room again, pretending to know this and that, but then I want you out of here.' Leaning forward menacingly, his palms on the table, he adds, 'It's unbeliev-able, really—you cops are always sticking your noses in our business when it's not welcome, and then when we actually need you, you're fucking hopeless.' He kicks the chair out of the way and yanks a cigarette from a pack in his jeans pocket. Dot flinches as he stalks past her.

The back door bangs loudly against the side of the house, making Dot and I jump, while de Luca just raises an eyebrow.

'Don't bother coming back here unless you're bringing my daughter home,' Daniel snarls over his shoulder.

Tuesday, 12 April
10.03 am

Abbey's room is small and exceptionally neat. The single bed is made, and a laundry basket in the corner is half full of clothes. There's no desk, but sagging shelves hold a few books, an empty glass full of dried wildflowers and several loose sheets of paper. On the wall is a landscape watercolour with Abbey's name spelled out in stylised font, a stunning mix of feathers and scales, animals writhing and wrestling, faces peering out from the dips and curves. Several other pencil sketches, some clearly unfinished, are attached to the wall with Blu Tack.

Dozens of photos are stuck along the front of the shelves. Some are copies of the ones that were in Rick's bedroom, while others are of Abbey with female friends. There's a photo of her brothers but none of her parents.

De Luca stands in the doorway, arms folded. 'What are you looking for?'

Through the window I can see Daniel in the narrow backyard. He's squatting on a patch of faded grass next to a motorbike and fiddling with one of the parts, a trail of smoke coming from the side of his mouth.

'Daniel seemed surprised when we told them Fletcher was dead,' I say, still watching him.

De Luca snorts. 'The man is pretty experienced at covering his tracks. You should see him when we come here on DV calls. The lies pour out of him like honey.'

I appreciate what she's saying, but I saw real shock in Daniel's face. Still, I have been fooled before; Nicki's father Lucas had me completely fooled. Some people are so good at lying they could throw their hat into the ring for an Oscar.

'So, what are you looking for?' de Luca repeats.

'I'm not sure yet,' I reply.

I approach the cupboard with apprehension. The evidence I found in Nicki's wardrobe was when the problems really started for me.

Nicki had been missing for six days when I searched her room. After an argument with her mother on a Friday evening after school, and some confusion about where she was staying on the weekend, two days had passed before Deirdre reported her missing. Messages sent from her phone on the Sunday and a photo uploaded to her social accounts after that had further confused the timeline.

Another thirty-six hours went by before we made it official, issuing a media release. We may as well have thrown a grenade to them, that's how spectacularly it exploded. A beautiful young white girl from a wealthy background, who happened to be a talented gymnast, was missing, feared dead. It was a media wet dream.

I had a bad feeling about it from the start. The first time we went to the house, the day Nicki was reported missing, we did our best to navigate Deirdre's hysteria and unearth some facts. Three days later when it seemed like Nicki might not be a simple runaway, the forensic team went through the house. The techs found nothing to suggest there had been any foul play on the premises, and Mac and I spent another few hours arguing about whether her parents were involved in whatever happened to her. I thought no; he thought maybe.

Both our theories were turned on their heads when Susie, a remarkably articulate heroin addict, stormed into the station six days after Nicki was last seen, sniffing theatrically and demanding to speak to the 'detective in change of the missing rich girl'.

'That stuck-up princess is completely fine,' Susie announced to everyone in the waiting room, after I came out to talk to her. 'I saw her with my very own eyes. And I have a photo.' She pulled out a new model iPhone and showed us a dark picture of a retreating figure on a generic streetscape, a figure that did look very much like Nicki Mara.

Susie claimed she'd met Nicki the night before.

'She was just sitting in the drainpipe that I normally base at, like she owned the place,' said Susie. 'She was bragging about running away. She said she thought it was funny how everyone reckons she was dead. She reckoned she was going to head up north and change her name, start a business or something.'

Owen questioned Susie as I sat there silently raging. I'd barely slept since Nicki went missing and had been more convinced than the others on the case that she was murdered.

A few hours later, Deirdre Mara sobbed on her crisp white sofa opposite me after I relayed Susie's story. 'I don't believe it.'

'I want to look in Nicki's bedroom,' I told her. 'Will you show me?'

She nodded and led me to the rear of the house, past Lucas who sat at the kitchen table staring into space. The whole place had a slightly disturbed vibe to it, lingering currents of tension in the air. I watched the back of Deirdre's head, trying to resolve the nasty and petty woman Nicki described in the messages to her friends with this kind and broken one.

'This is her room,' said Deirdre, a damp hanky pressed to her red nose.

I found the photos in Nicki's desk cupboard, wedged down the back of the bottom drawer and resting on the carpet. Twenty-four prints of her naked body twisted into various positions, her dark eyes inviting under her thick lashes.

I felt betrayed. Foolish. I still can't quite explain why, but until that moment Nicki had been an innocent, someone I'd thought had met with the most fatal of bad luck. I hadn't given Susie's story much credence but I'm ashamed to say those photos altered my perspective. I judged Nicki, and she shifted in my psyche from a pure victim to a murkier category, a complicated Lolita-esque archetype I found much more challenging to get a handle on.

Of course, the rollercoaster continued. Two weeks later, Susie confessed to fabricating her encounter with Nicki for a cash payment, the request coming from a man she said approached her in the street.

Blinking back to the present, I pull open Abbey's wardrobe door to reveal a modest collection of clothes—mainly surf-wear— hanging neatly on the rail. A pair of ripped jeans and a few T-shirts and singlet tops are folded in a wire-drawer inset. Six shoes are in neat pairs on the wardrobe floor. None of the items look expensive.

I stand back and survey the small space. 'It doesn't seem like Abbey was spending her wages on clothes.'

Two plain calico bags sit on the cupboard floor next to the shoes. One contains bathers and a beach towel, and the other has three sketchbooks, two are A3 and one is A4. I flip through them, impressed by some of the drawings. Abbey has a good eye, especially for birds and animals.

The third sketchbook turns out to be one of her school note-books. There are several pages of assignment plans and class notes interspersed with half-finished sketches and a few passages of prose. I flip to the reverse of the book and find a few to-do lists and a jumble of loose notes.

'What is it?' de Luca asks.

'About as close to a diary as we're going to get, I think.'

I check under the mattress and under the bed, feel around in the wardrobe beneath the clothes, then reach up to run my hand over the top of the wardrobe. I check inside an empty suitcase, shoving my hands into the front and side pockets but find nothing else.

When we come downstairs, Dot is still sitting at the kitchen table. 'Did you find anything?'

I indicate the calico bag on my shoulder. 'Just a few sketchbooks. Would you mind if we take them?'

She shifts her gaze toward the window and says nervously, 'Can't see why not.'

'That painting in her room is beautiful,' I say. 'Is it Abbey's work?'

Dot's voice becomes strained. 'She's always drawing. That and playing music. She plays the flute. Dan hates her playing here 'cause of the noise, but one of her schoolteachers lets her practise there. She's a nice lady.' Dot's anxious gaze darts to the window again as she grips the back of the chair. A large tear escapes her eye and runs down her cheek.

'Dot,' I say, 'it's really important you're certain your husband didn't leave the house at any point yesterday morning?'

Outside Daniel starts swearing, and there's a staccato *bang-bang*, metal on metal. In the lounge one of the boys yells out, 'Suck it, I killed you. My turn!' The other cries, 'Get off me!'

Dot's face turns impassive and she looks toward the window. 'He was here. Now he's not working, he's here most of the time.'

The kitchen tap drips, marking the seconds.

'And you're sure you don't know where she is?'

Dot meets my gaze this time. 'No.'

As we stare at each other, I wonder whether everything would have been different if I had pushed Lucas Mara that little bit harder, if I hadn't been so goddamn blind to what was going on.

'Well, we'll be in touch. Please contact us if you hear from Abbey or you think of anything else that might help us find her, okay?'

Dot nods slowly, and we see ourselves out.

We emerge blinking at the sunlight.

'Was there ever any indication that Rick was violent toward Abbey?' I ask de Luca.

She pauses and turns to face me. 'You think what Daniel said in there is true? Come on.'

I raise my eyebrows, surprised at her dismissive tone. 'One violent man doesn't write off the possibility of another. Abbey wouldn't be the first person to grow up in an abusive household and end up in an abusive relationship.'

De Luca brushes back her feathery fringe. 'There was nothing to suggest anything like that. Rick Fletcher wasn't on our radar.'

I fall into line beside her. 'Which neighbours have you spoken to?' I ask as we reach the car.

'Of the house party?'

'No, here.' I gesture to our surrounds.

'I don't think that's happened yet.'

I smother a sigh and glance at my watch. 'Well, no time like the present. Let's see if they have a different view of what happened on Saturday night or of Daniel's movements yesterday morning.' My phone rings. 'Hang on,' I say to de Luca as I walk a few metres into the middle of the road. It's Tran.

'Any sign of Aiden?' I ask her.

'Nothing yet. At least, no phone or bank activity.'

'Damn it. We really need to speak with him. I'm absolutely convinced he knows who attacked Rick—he said it was all his fault.'

'Gemma, I'm moving you out of the hotel,' says Tran. 'I know you're happy to stay, and maybe the dead possum was just the work of some bored kid. But the director doesn't want you staying there. Especially not with your son.'

I fight the urge to stamp my foot. 'Fine. I'm happy to relocate if everyone would prefer.'

'Good. Vanessa Gordon has suggested you stay at her place. It makes sense, seeing as she is looking after Ben anyway. It will give you a bit more flexibility—which, frankly, I think you're going to need.'

Although the thought of camping out in someone's home again hardly fills me with joy, I figure being close to Tommy can't hurt case-wise. Plus, I can tell that Tran isn't going to budge.

'I think it's completely unnecessary but it sounds like it's non-negotiable. I'll call Vanessa about it later.'

'Gemma,' says Tran, but I cut her off by hanging up.

I march back past de Luca, trying to arrange my features in a pleasant expression but failing miserably. 'Come on.'

It seems three other houses are situated on the court, though it's hard to be sure because their gardens and nature strips are so overgrown. I knock on the front door of the nearest house. A painfully skinny woman with bleached hair and features arranged in the centre of her face peers out at us. 'What do you want?' she barks.

Fifteen minutes later Jacqui Cobb, 'nee Dawson', is holding court at her stained laminate kitchen table, flicking ash from the end of her cigarette as she launches into further analysis of Daniel and Dot's doomed union.

'Poor Dot,' she says. 'Poor stupid Dot. I've known her since we were kids, you know. Dan too, but I had the good sense to stay well away from him. We all told Dot he was bad news, but she wouldn't listen. No siree.'

'What was wrong with Daniel?' I say.

'He's an angry bastard,' Jacqui says bluntly, one hand tucked into the opposite armpit, the other hand scratching her head, the cigarette smoke drifting into her scraggly ponytail. She takes a deep drag then coughs the smoke out in a series of sharp puffs. She looks at us as if she's bestowing precious intel, her voice a little lower. 'His old man used to beat the living shit out of him, that's what my mother told me. He killed himself when we were in high school, his dad did. Shot himself in the head.'

De Luca shifts uncomfortably in her chair.

Jacqui continues, her voice slightly dreamy now, 'I remember 'cause it was the same day I crashed my dad's car into the fence.' She lights another cigarette. 'Daniel Clark could be a charmer though, and he was always nice to look at. Has a lovely smile when he can be bothered to use it. Dot was desperate for a boyfriend and she was a goner over him from the get-go. To be fair, Dan absolutely adored her back then, and she fell for it hook, line and sinker. Dot's mother had a lot to say about it. I remember her screaming at Dot to stay away from him. She must turn in her grave knowing what he's like now. I'm not sure Dot's ever been with anyone else.' Jacqui shudders. 'God, can you imagine?'

I begin to steer her away from memory lane and ask her about Saturday night.

'Dan definitely went off about something. He was ranting and raving like no one's business. And bashing that bloody plank of wood against the clothesline.'

I raise my eyebrows. 'Is that something he does often?'

'Yeah. He generally calms down after a few minutes but it makes a racket, I tell you. I've called you lot heaps of times about it.'

'But you didn't call on Saturday?' de Luca asks.

'Didn't see the point. I figured JC would probably call.' She points past my head. 'He's in number three.'

'What was Daniel yelling about?' I ask.

Jacqui sucks hard on the cigarette, eyes closed. 'I was having a beer on the back porch, guess that must have been around seven-thirty. That's when my son called—he's always wanting money, he lives in Brisbane but just lost his job again, poor bugger. That's when I heard the yelling start up. Even Matty could hear that bastard down the phone line.'

'Could you make out what Daniel was saying?' presses de Luca.

'Nah, but it was him and Abbey arguing as per usual. Dot was there too—I heard her crying, telling them both to stop. She hates it when they fight.' Jacqui wrinkles her nose, rubs her wrist along the bottom of it and sniffs loudly. 'He called her a slut, I heard that. But he does that a lot. He's always saying it to Dot as well, which is weird cause she definitely isn't.'

I recall Dot's empty gaze when we left her house and think about how long her short life has probably felt.

'Jacqui, do you feel like things have been getting worse lately? Like Daniel's been angrier than usual?'

She narrows her eyes, clearly considering. 'Maybe. He's been yelling a lot more out in the yard and banging that bloody clothes-line. And he's always fighting with Abbey about something. She's a smart girl, despite everything. I reckon that probably pisses him off.'

'How did the argument end on Saturday?' asks de Luca.

Jacqui kills her cigarette and toys with the packet, passing it back and forth between each hand. 'Matty and I hung up, and I refilled the bird feeder so I could keep listening to the carry-on from over the fence.' She lifts the cigarette packet to her mouth and purses her lips to pluck out another smoke. 'Abbey said something like, *I don't care what you say!* And there was a sound like a slap. And then Dan called her a bitch. He said it a few times. Dot cried out again for them to stop. I wondered if maybe Abbey'd hit him—that's the impression I got, but she'd be brave to do that, wouldn't she? I saw her a few minutes later zooming past on her bike, all dolled up, heading out to that party, I suppose. She has the most beautiful hair, god love her.'

Jacqui waves a waft of smoke from her eyes and tugs on her own pitiful ponytail. 'I hope Daniel didn't do something to her. I've always said the man needs to be locked away before he does real damage.'

'You didn't see him leave the house after that?'

'No, but my room's at the back, and my ex used to say I sleep like a log.' Jacqui pauses, scrunching up her face. 'A car stopped at the end of the street at some point. I got up to go to the loo and heard it, just idling. It only had its parkers on, which I thought was weird.' She holds up her hands. 'I didn't see it, so there's no point asking me what type of car it was.'

'But you say the headlights were off?'

'Yep.'

'What time was that, Jacqui?'

She squints at me. 'Just after one in the morning? I thought it was late for someone to be dropping Abbey home. I'm pretty sure I heard the car drive off again a few minutes later.'

De Luca's gaze is on the floor.

'Jacqui, were you home yesterday morning?'

She nods.

'What time did you get up?'

'Oh, well now, it probably wasn't until about seven. I'm usually up a bit earlier but I had a few wines after dinner and needed my beauty sleep.' She pats her face and laughs.

'Did you see any cars coming or going after you got up?' asks de Luca.

'Don't reckon so. Apart from you two arriving, that's been it over these past few days. It's not exactly main street out here.'

'Thanks for talking to us, Jacqui,' I say, standing up. 'Please call if you think of anything else, okay?'

'I know where to find you,' she says cheerfully. 'I used to be up at the cop shop all the time with my ex.'

She swivels the cigarette into the crowded ashtray and walks us out, her narrow hips creaking.

'It's a shame really,' she says thoughtfully. 'Dot and I were great mates. She used to pop in here when Abbey was little, and we'd watch her tear around the yard. But then Dot had the twins. These days I barely see her unless she's on the way to clean the rentals at the caravan park. If I'm out front I give her a wave and say hello, but we don't have much to talk about. My useless husband ran off with some tart a few years ago, thank goodness, but poor Dot seems to be stuck with hers.'

Tuesday, 12 April
11.22 am

De Luca and I knock on the door of the house opposite Jacqui's, rousing a weedy young man called Leo from bed. He's so stoned he can barely string a sentence together amid his dog's incessant barking. After establishing that Leo was away on the weekend and asleep all yesterday morning, we make a hasty retreat, the pungent smell following us up the driveway.

A heavily tattooed man in his late fifties answers the door at the remaining house. 'JC,' he says, thrusting out his hand with a wide grin, 'just like the lord.'

He tells us he was at the Parrot Hotel until roughly 10 pm on Saturday before he walked home. He didn't hear anything during the night, and he only found out Abbey was missing on Sunday afternoon when the street filled up for the search.

'I often see Dot crying.' JC shakes his head, his colourful arms crossed over his bulging belly. 'She's always coming down the street crying with her cleaning bucket, him still yelling at her from the house.' JC chews a nail and sighs. 'I'm old enough to remember her crying as she pushed her babies in a pram. Nothing changes—Daniel's as slippery as an eel, and Dot's too scared to say anything.'

'Did you see any cars coming or going yesterday morning?'

'No, can't say I noticed anything. But I'm out in the back garden a lot of the time so probably I'm not much help to you.' He gives us a canny look. 'Is this about that young boy that died? I heard about that.'

We thank him and leave.

De Luca calls Grange from the car while I stand on the street in front of the Clark house and call Lane.

'Hey, Gemma.'

'Yes, hi.' It takes me a moment to process his casual tone. 'Did the techs find anything?'

'Yep, a wad of cash in a biscuit tin.'

I try not to leap to conclusions. 'How much?'

'Almost six grand. That could mean Rick was involved in something off the books, right?'

'It screams of drugs but it could be anything. Stolen goods perhaps or maybe just cash in hand jobs. And it might be Aiden's cash. It was pretty hard to get a read on him yesterday. Can you review both of their finances and see if things line up?'

'Can do.' Lane sounds out of breath, as if he's walking. 'It's gotta be dodgy—they wouldn't have that kind of money lying around if it wasn't suss.'

'Maybe.' I think of the look Aiden cast at the house yesterday and wonder if he knew about the money. 'Was there anything else?'

'A few old phones stashed around the place but no SIMs.'

'That's pretty standard. Fingerprints?'

'Dunno, they've dusted everything but they said it wasn't looking positive, so I guess we'll have to wait. They said there weren't any prints on the ruined photos and they don't think they can tell us anything else.'

'That's interesting. If Rick did it, surely there'd be prints.'

'I guess so.' Lane sounds distracted.

I picture the phone numbers I saw on the floor in Rick's bedroom. 'Lane, I took a photo of a piece of paper with phone numbers on it in Rick's bedroom. I assume it's still there but I'll text it to you just in case. Can you make sure all phone numbers from the house are recorded and that we work through the contacts? That goes for all the phones. I want to know everyone Rick had contact with over the past few months.'

'Yep, no worries.'

'Still no sign of a weapon?' I ask.

'No weapon.'

'What about Bruce Piper, did you take his statement?'

'Uh-huh. He checks out. I spoke to the other neighbours too. One lady reckons she heard something yesterday morning, but she assumed it was a TV. Another neighbour, at the end of the street, got up early to let his dog out for a piss and reckons he saw someone walking on the other side of the street just before six.'

'Any chance of an ID?'

'Nah, the guy was wearing a hoodie. He's sure it was a male though.'

'Alright. I know Damon was going to chase up footage but I doubt he'll get to it because he's following up Aiden's contacts. Can you double-check there are no cameras in the streets around the Fletcher brothers' place that might have captured something?'

'No problems. Are you and de Luca still at the Clarks'?'

'We're about to head off. We just spoke to the three neighbours. One of them reckons there was a car in the street early Sunday morning.'

'Really? Could they ID it?'

'Unfortunately not. We don't know if it's linked, but it's something to go on at least. I can't imagine someone would just randomly park here in the middle of the night. But perhaps they saw Abbey walking home and snatched her.'

'Jeez. Yeah, maybe.' Lane trails off, then asks, 'Did Dot say Daniel was home when Rick was attacked?'

'Yes, apparently as far as she knows he was here.'

'Bloody typical.' Lane hangs up.

The dial tone rings in my ear as I glare at my phone before shoving it in my pocket. Tommy Gordon must run a pretty casual ship, and I think I'm going to need a little bit more respect for hierarchy if this team will work the way I want it to.

I can see that de Luca is still on the phone, so I quickly call Vanessa. She answers out of breath. 'Hi, Gemma. Don't worry, everything is fine here.'

'Ben's okay?'

'He's fine. He's really hit it off with Charlie. They're playing outside right now. Do you want to speak with him?'

'No, that's okay. Just tell him I say hi.'

'Celia said you were happy to stay with us. I'm so glad, Gemma— I really think that with what happened at the hotel this morning, it's a good idea.'

I feel a flash of irritation. 'I think it's an overreaction but I appreciate it. I'll try to be back by six. Can you let Ben know, please?'

De Luca is drafting an email on her phone when I get into the car. 'The fireys didn't find anything,' she says. 'They only searched the immediate area but there was an accident on the highway.'

I clip in my seatbelt. 'Yeah, well, we don't even know if it's her blood.' One of the Clark twins darts across their front lawn. 'Any updates from Damon?'

'None of Aiden's friends have heard from him. Apparently he's between jobs and was planning to work with Rick for a while but his old boss hasn't heard from him either.'

I grimace in frustration: the last thing we need is another missing young person, willing or otherwise.

'What about the caravan park? Did the manager get us a guest list? Is Robert Weston there?'

She continues typing on her phone. 'Kate Morse said there was no Robert Weston registered to stay. But she only takes the details of those paying for a room, so he could be in one of the twin shares. Apparently something's wrong with the sewerage system at the caravan park, and Kate was in the middle of trying to sort it out and couldn't send through the list.'

'But we need it.'

'Yes, I know,' de Luca says stiffly. 'Kate told Grange she'd try to get it to him tonight.'

I laugh incredulously. 'Did he make it clear it was urgent? Does this woman realise we're investigating a murder?'

De Luca presses send with a flourish and faces me. On the crook of her elbow I spot a pinched scar; someone extinguished a cigarette there a long time ago. Further up her arm, under the fold of her blue shirt, is the edge of a similar scar. Her crystal eyes shimmer against her dark lashes as she shifts her arm away. 'I don't know exactly what Grange said, but Kate told him she'll send everything through.'

'Okay,' I say, breaking the stare. 'Well, let's hope so. We need to get on top of it.'

She starts the car and the air con whirs to life; I turn it down a few notches. De Luca's grip is firm on the wheel. I still feel ridiculously tired, and for the second time today a thought begins to take shape in my consciousness and then promptly disappears.

As we drive out of the court, I spot a white Mazda parked on the adjoining street. The driver's window is down. Simon Charleston smiles and waves at me as we pass.

'Do you know him?' I ask de Luca.

'That reporter? Yeah, a bit. He's alright. He's definitely not as bad as some.'

I look at her, surprised at this unexpected diplomacy.

'So where do you want to start?' she says. 'At the house party?' Her tone remains short; every word out of her mouth is strained.

I ignore her tone. 'Yep, let's start at the house party, then go to the police station and head to the vacant lot. I want to time and map out Abbey's likely route on Saturday night.'

De Luca releases a long breath and eases the car right at the real estate agent. We pass a small high school, an oval and a kitsch outdoor pool complete with a dated Coca-Cola sign.

'Is that Abbey's school?' I ask.

De Luca nods.

We drive for another ten minutes, passing sweet-looking houses and nature strips bursting with native flowers, before turning onto a wide residential street and pulling up in between two driveways. A few houses down a man is washing his car, large headphones clamped over his ears.

'This is where the party happened,' says de Luca. 'The Kinlons live here—obviously the parents were away on Saturday. We've interviewed the sisters, Maggie and Beth, but they aren't particularly close to Abbey and don't remember her leaving. They don't think they even spoke to her, though they saw her in the kitchen early in the night.'

Today the house and yard are silent, but it's easy to envisage it crawling with teenagers.

'Come on.' I undo my seatbelt.

De Luca turns off the car and I get out, overwhelmed once again by the trill of insects. The heat hovers above the ground, swamp-like.

'Is that where Abbey said her bike was stolen from?' I point to the other side of the road.

'Yep. She told Lane she left it next to a tree opposite the house. About a metre off the road.'

I move to point at the passage on the left side of the house. 'And Rick said he was on the phone over there at the time Abbey left, right?'

'Uh-huh. We checked his phone records—his sister, Belinda, called him just before eleven-thirty, so that adds up.'

'Why do you think he'd lie about the bike?'

Her smooth brow furrows slightly. 'Sorry?'

'One of them is lying. Rick either saw her leaving on it or he didn't. Let's start with him. Give me a theory.'

For the first time today, de Luca seems unsure. 'He wanted us to think Abbey wasn't on foot.'

I look down the length of road. 'Okay, why?'

She frowns. 'I don't know.'

'What if he was the one who took her bike? We know they argued. Maybe he snuck out the front and hid it somewhere. Then, the next morning when her dad was banging on his door and screaming that she was missing, Rick decided to lie about it.'

De Luca looks sceptical. 'Then where is it?'

'I have no idea. Maybe he stashed it somewhere or chucked it over a cliff.' I pause, thinking it wouldn't be too hard to throw a body from one either.

'Rick obviously had something to get off his chest when he called the station. Maybe this was it?'

'Maybe. Hang on.' I pick up the case file, pulling out the map of Fairhaven. 'So, let's say Abbey was lying and she left the party on her bike. Does that line up better with the timing?'

'She got to the station at around 11.45 pm,' says de Luca. 'We don't know exactly what time Rick saw her leave here, apparently when he was on the phone. I think the call with his sister began at 11.24 pm and went for about three minutes.'

'That's a pretty tight window.' I look back at the map. 'Could she have walked from here to the police station in that time?'

De Luca goes quiet for a moment. 'Yes, if she cut through the bush track.'

'Up there?' I point to a strip of greenery at the end of the street.

She nods. 'That's part of the area that was searched on Sunday morning. Once of the theories was that Abbey might have come back to the party after she left the police station.'

'Show me.'

The cicadas are almost deafening as we walk to the top of the narrow nature reserve. A thin uneven path snakes through the trees, littered with stones and gum leaves.

'This takes you straight through to the street parallel to the station. If she went this way on foot, she could easily have got there in fifteen minutes.'

I take in the wild tangle of bush. 'But do you think she'd walk down here alone at night?'

'I wouldn't,' says de Luca. 'There's no lights and there'd be animals everywhere. Spiders.' She squints into the sun. 'But Abbey fought with Rick. And she might have been drunk and feeling more reckless.'

I cast my mind back to house parties in high school. Nights were a blur until an adult appeared and forced a sharp snag of lucidity. Important life-changing moments happened without any fanfare. Things seemed critical and terribly trivial all at once. They were like stage plays: a giant thundering rollercoaster of emotions over the space of a few hours. Back then, it felt like everything important existed in a small fenced backyard beneath the stars.

'So it's possible she was telling the truth, discovered her bike was missing and went straight to the station on foot using this shortcut. But it's also possible she rode her bike on the road.'

De Luca gives me a cautious nod.

'Either way we can deduce that she didn't muck around—she came straight from the party.'

'Do you think there was time for her to run into someone and for them to take her bike?' says de Luca doubtfully.

I head back toward the car. 'It's possible but it seems unlikely. And if that happened then why would she lie to Lane and say it was taken from the party?' My stomach rolls uncomfortably, desperate for food. 'Maybe she was embarrassed to say what really happened? Or scared to?' Possible scenarios jostle for position in my mind. 'But if she *was* scared then she wouldn't have rejected a lift home. That doesn't make sense.'

De Luca simply blinks. 'Where to now?'

'Let's go past the station. We need to take the most direct route, the one you think it's most likely Abbey took if she was on her bike. Then we'll go to where the blood was found.'

As we pull away from the kerb, I notice a teenage girl in one of the second-storey windows. We lock eyes as she drags a brush through her long brown hair.

De Luca weaves us expertly down the streets: right, left, left, right. 'The path comes out there.' She points to the other end of the tree tunnel. We drive another few hundred metres and pull up outside the police station.

'So whether on foot or on her bike,' I say, 'she came from that direction.'

De Luca nods.

'Right, so she comes along here, out of breath either from walking or riding. She's possibly had some kind of confrontation and maybe her bike was taken from her.' I lean down to adjust my sock, which is wet with cooling perspiration. 'So let's think about it. Why would she lie? Maybe she threatened someone with going to the police. Maybe she made up the stolen bike story because someone was watching her and she wanted them to think she was reporting something else. She could be the one who stashed it.'

'But then it's like you said, why would she decline a lift home if she was scared?'

I tip my head back against the seat and tap it gently. 'Rick might have followed her from the party. All we know is that he told his sister he'd come to her beach gathering and that he was there at some point until the early hours when he went home. None of the times are clear, and everyone at the beach was drunk. What if Abbey and Rick did meet, and they argued again?'

De Luca's lips open in a soft pout. 'Then who killed Rick?'

'Someone who knew what he'd done? Rick was suspicious that she was seeing someone else, right?'

'That's what he said, but there's no evidence of it. No calls, messages or emails. Nothing.'

'Still, it's not unheard of for someone to run a relationship off the grid, especially when they're cheating. Maybe she was involved with someone and they felt threatened by Rick. And obviously Daniel Clark is a known risk. Dot's assurance he was at home isn't exactly what I'd consider a solid alibi, and that goes for both Saturday night and yesterday morning.' I watch as a tiny blue wren darts from one tree to another, performing a flirty little dance. 'Daniel himself admits Abbey's curfew was midnight, and we know she was still at the police station at midnight. What if Daniel woke up, realised his daughter wasn't home and went out looking for her? Maybe he came across her walking home and lost it—bike or no bike, it doesn't really matter.'

'Or maybe,' says de Luca, 'some random kid stole her bike from the party. It might not be relevant at all.'

I take a swig of water, which only makes my stomach growl more. 'True, though I always treat coincidences with extreme caution.'

De Luca's warmth vanishes. 'Do you want to go to the lot now?'

'Yes, please. And again, we want to take the most obvious route.'

We drive a few hundred metres, then turn right. Another few hundred metres takes us to the intersection leading to the main street. A homemade sign hangs in a shop window spruiking music lessons for people of all ages, and another boasts of the best pizza in town. Several gloomy-looking dogs are tethered to street signs and bike racks. Near the corner we pass a giant pink shopfront that must be Tara's beauty salon. Two tradesmen are manoeuvring a big sheet of glass into a vertical position. The gold lettering on the pub's roof glints sharply in the sun. A strip of beach is visible through the gate, afternoon revellers lying in rows on colourful towels, their feet pointed toward the ocean.

We pull up next to the uneven block of asphalt that Cam called 'dead land'. Grass pushes through cracks, and the bordering shrubs shine with discarded beer cans. The fire crew and techs are long gone; the block is empty. De Luca stares at the rust-coloured stain circled by a faded loop of chalk.

'Is the service station open twenty-four hours?' I say, looking over at it.

'It is on weekends.'

'Let's go find out if anyone saw anything.'

Tuesday, 12 April
3.13 pm

A skinny teen with bad skin is behind the counter. He clicks desperately at his laptop touchpad when we enter, then does a terrible job of looking nonchalant. His name is Kevin and, as luck would have it, he worked the Saturday night shift.

'Do you know Abbey Clark?' I ask him.

He swallows nervously. 'No. But I know she's missing. She was going out with Rick Fletcher. I used to play footy with him, years ago. I can't believe what happened to him. My girlfriend is completely freaking out.'

I can't imagine Kevin on the footy field unless perhaps as a referee, but I push on. I pull up a picture of Abbey on my phone and show him. 'Did you see this girl on Saturday night?'

'No, nope. Definitely not.' His voice lifts an octave and he coughs to hide it.

'Rick Fletcher?'

'No, he didn't come in here.'

'You're mainly behind the counter all the time, right, Kevin?'

'Ah, yep, yep.'

'Great. I might just duck around there if that's okay with you?'

I walk past the display of chips and chocolate bars and wait for him to unlock the door. He snaps his laptop shut and hovers anxiously while I sit on his chair. I have a direct line of sight to the section of the block where the bloodstain is.

'Did you see anyone hanging around over there on Saturday night?' I ask, pointing at the block.

'Um, no.' Kevin scratches his head in a disturbingly manic way. 'But wait—on Saturday the tanker was parked there.'

'What do you mean?' I notice that de Luca is scanning the shop for security cameras.

'The guy from the fuel company came to do a fuel transfer. It all gets pumped into these giant underground storage vats.'

'What time was this?'

'Um, probably about seven that night, I reckon. He signed in and got it going. Takes a few hours. He stayed in town overnight and parked his tank along there.' Kevin holds out his scrawny arm. 'I'd gone before he left in the morning.'

'What time did your shift end?'

'Six am,' says Kevin.

'We'll need his name,' I say.

'Ah, sure. Guess that's cool. Or maybe I should check with the manager?'

'We need to speak to your management about getting their security tapes anyway,' says de Luca, appearing back at the counter. 'We'll mention you gave us his name then.'

'Okay, yep, great. I'll, ah, just go grab the logbook.'

As we step back into the heat, de Luca tells me that she'll follow up with the tank driver.

'That would be great,' I say, pleased at her initiative.

Standing alongside the bloodstain again, I find myself praying it is Abbey's. At least then we'd have something concrete. I turn in a slow circle, visualising the tanker. If it is her blood, then what was she doing here? The missing pieces of the timeline are driving me crazy. Why did she refuse a lift home? Had Lane made it sound like a hassle, or was she planning to meet someone? The hypothetical jealous rival, perhaps.

Even if it is hers, the blood could have appeared in the car park any time from midnight until dawn, so maybe we're thinking about this all wrong. Maybe she went somewhere after she left the police station and was heading home in the early hours of the morning when something happened to her.

After reviewing the map from the car, I conclude that walking along the main street isn't the most direct path to the Clarks' from the station, though it probably would have felt the safest to Abbey at that time of night. But it was definitely the straightest path to Rick's place. Was that where she was going? Had they spoken when she was leaving the party and made a plan to meet up? Was she planning to meet him on the beach with the others? Abbey could have gone to Rick's place and waited for him. But then what about the car that Jacqui Cobb heard idling near her house? Maybe that was Daniel heading out to find his wayward daughter. Or coming home from looking for her?

Two teenage girls, arms looped, walk toward the pub car park. One is clutching a flimsy bouquet of white daisies. They have clearly both been crying.

Please let us find her, I think. *The last thing I need right now is a loose end. Or another dead body.*

'What?' De Luca is peering at me curiously.

I must have spoken out loud.

'Nothing,' I say, stifling a yawn. My back is killing me and I'm so past being hungry that I feel sick. Plus, the thought of having to make small talk with the Gordons tonight is excruciating. I just want to crawl into bed.

De Luca hangs up and walks over to me. 'I left a message,' she says. 'If he doesn't get back to me I'll call the company.'

'Has Daniel's car been searched?' I say.

'No, I'm sure it hasn't been.'

'I'd like to run forensics on it. Obviously Abbey's DNA will be all over it, but if there are any traces of blood we'll have a lot more to go on than we do now. It's possible something will turn up at the Fletcher brothers' place. I just want to get as much forensics done as we can while the techs are around. At the moment it's like Abbey disappeared off the face of the earth. Even if she was attacked here, it's most likely her body was moved somewhere else by car. There wasn't that much blood.'

'Sure,' de Luca says smoothly. 'I'll get onto it.'

'Let's call it a day,' I say.

She clicks on her seatbelt in response.

'Do you live far from the station?'

'I live with my girlfriend on the west side of town.' Those grey eyes settle on me again as if daring me to comment. I feel off kilter, not quite sure whether I'm misreading her or not.

'That's great,' I say awkwardly.

As she starts the car, her mouth tugs into a smile. I get the sense she is enjoying my discomfort.

'Where do you want to go?' she asks politely. 'I know you're staying at The Parrot but your car's at the station, right?'

'How does everyone know where I'm staying?'

She shrugs. 'Tran mentioned it.'

'Well, actually, I'm not staying there anymore. I do need to get my car, though, so the station is great, thanks.' I try to relax into the curves of the road but feel increasingly unwell.

'Where are you staying now?' de Luca asks.

'Um, at the Gordons' actually.'

She swings around for a second in surprise before focusing intently back on the road. 'At Tommy's?'

'Yes,' I manage through my carsickness. 'Everyone just thought it would be easier. Vanessa is looking after my son while I'm working.'

We turn into the small gravel car park and I pray I won't be sick. De Luca pulls the handbrake skyward. 'Well, see you in the morning.' She leans forward and turns the air con back up again.

'See you,' I mutter.

A few moments later her car reverses in a sweeping arc and propels forward, leaving me in a cloud of grey dust. I beep the hire car open and all but collapse into the driver's seat, panting in the hot air. I'm about to start the car when I notice a piece of paper wedged in between the wiper blades. Taking a deep breath, I clamber out of the car to retrieve it.

It's Simon Charleston's business card. Scrawled on the reverse: *DS Woodstock, we need to talk. Call me!*

I get back in the car and sit there until the air con kicks into gear, hoping the sick feeling will pass. De Luca has really gotten under my skin, and as I'm mid-fantasy about dressing her down, I remember where I have seen the name Aiden Fletcher before.

Tuesday, 12 April
5.46 pm

All traces of the possum and blood are gone as Cam helps me carry
my small collection of luggage from room nine at the Parrot Hotel
to my hire car. Pushing the boot shut, he steps toward me, his hands
on his hips. 'I feel like I need to apologise again.'

'Thanks, Cam, but please don't stress. Truthfully, I've got bigger
things to worry about right now than a dead animal.'

'Yeah.' He lights a cigarette and sucks on it hungrily, lifting his
hand to greet someone at the other end of the car park. 'Everything
really hit me today. I think it hit everyone. My staff are in a bad way.
I just keep thinking about Rick, the poor guy. I knew Daniel Clark
had painted a target on his back, but still.'

I make a non-committal sound and get in the car, trying not
to cough as the smoke from his cigarette wafts past my nostrils.
'Thanks for your help today, Cam. I really appreciate it.'

His blue eyes lock on mine. 'It was the least I could do. I don't
know what's going on around here, but I hate that you feel you have
to leave.'

'Boss's orders,' I joke, but it comes out flat. I give him a tight
smile and throw the car into gear.

Before I put my foot on the accelerator, Cam leans in at the window. 'Hang on.' He tugs a piece of folded paper from his pocket. 'It's the guest list from last night.'

'Thanks.'

'No worries. And hey, it probably goes without saying, but anything you want at the pub is on the house as long as you're here, okay?'

I can feel the heat radiating from his tan forearm and find myself avoiding his eyes.

'That's not necessary, but thanks.' My heart racing, I exit the car park. I use the hands-free to call Mac but he doesn't answer. I dial Owen's number instead. 'Owen, it's me.'

'Gemma! Hang on for a sec, hang on.' I have a rush of emotion at the sound of his voice. 'Sorry, G,' he says, 'goodness, what a week. How are you? How's your son?'

'He's okay. You know, doing as well as can be expected.'

'Mac told me about the gig in Fairhaven and then I read up on the homicide. How's that going?'

I give Owen the run-down on Abbey and Rick, then find myself telling him about the possum. 'But please, Owen, don't mention it to Mac. He'll just worry and I really don't need that right now.'

Owen breathes out through his teeth. 'I won't say anything but holy shit, Gemma, that sounds bad. So what, you're staying with the local CI now?'

'Yeah. It's certainly not my preference but I don't really have a choice. Tran put her foot down. My old boss from Smithson knows Tommy, so I'm sure it will be okay. I'll be working most of the time anyway.'

'Well, I wish you'd hurry up and come back home. I'm having to play nice with the other kids and it's not nearly as much fun.'

I laugh. 'Owen, you always play nice with everyone.'

'I try but,' his voice drops to a whisper, 'Jock the Jerk is especially maddening.'

I roll my eyes. Jock Canterbury is a complete dickhead and Owen is the only person who bothers trying to be nice to him. No one else calls him Jock the Jerk—to them he's Jock the Cock.

'Don't laugh, Gem, I'm with him all week. I can only think the lord is testing me.'

'Oh, Owen, you'll be okay. Think of the upside, you'll know at least fifty more filthy jokes by the end of the week.'

Owen groans. 'Just get a solve up there and come home, okay? Realistically, when do you think you'll be back?'

The vice tightens on my chest again. I still can't see how Sydney is going to work with Ben but I hate the thought of never working with Owen again.

'I need your help with something,' I say, ignoring his question. 'The kid who died yesterday lived with his brother, Aiden Fletcher.'

'Okay.'

'I'm pretty sure there was an Aiden Fletcher in the mix with that drug murder case Jock worked late last year, do you remember? The one where the guy shot himself but Jock thought it seemed suspicious. I think the kid who died tried to contact Fletcher the day before or something?'

'Vaguely. Maybe.'

'I'm sure,' I say. 'Jock was going on about a drug ring up and down the coast and complaining about the resources because he didn't have budget to travel. I remember the names because I was going to help out with some interviews but then it went nowhere.'

I can tell Owen is thumbing through his mental filing cabinet. 'Oh yeah, I remember Jock whingeing about it.'

'Well, anyway, this Aiden kid in Fairhaven said some stuff at my crime scene that seemed strange and now he's taken off. Plus the forensic guys found a decent amount of cash at his house, the one he shared with his murdered brother. I'm thinking drugs.'

'But surely his brother's murder is linked to the missing girl-friend?' says Owen.

'I'm wondering whether all three of them got involved in some-thing that spiralled out of control. Whoever attacked Rick wasn't mucking around—it was almost like a hit.'

'What do you need?'

'Can you ask Jock about Aiden Fletcher? And send me the file? I'll have a dig through and see what comes up.'

'You could have just called Jock direct, you know.'

'I know.'

Owen laughs. 'Take care, Gem. I'll speak to you tomorrow.'

I pull up in front of the Gordons', jerking the handbrake into position. I briefly consider calling Jodie back but decide I don't have the energy. Remembering the guest list Cam gave me, I take it out to have a quick look. There are only eighteen rooms, and four have been vacant since the weekend. One name jumps out at me: Simon Charleston.

I survey the house, a rustic weatherboard. Flowers and tree branches reach toward the walls as if they're trying to reclaim it back to the wild. The front door is wide open; to its right is a long timber bench seat with a crocheted cushion, and to its left a row of small elegant trees in stylish planters. I haul myself out of the car, and almost immediately a large terracotta-coloured dog is at my heels, teeth exposed, its tongue a slobbery flag.

'Inka!' Vanessa rushes toward us, grabbing the animal's furry face in one hand and laughing as it licks her chin. 'Sorry about that. She's been worked up all day because of the kids.' Vanessa holds out her arm above Inka's head. 'Sit.' Satisfied with the dog's response, Vanessa says, 'Let me help you with your things.'

She plucks Ben's suitcase from the boot and charges up the wooden steps of the wide porch, into an airy hallway. I follow with my cumbersome suitcase.

'Hi, Mum.' Ben barrels toward me with another little boy, and they grab at Inka who barks playfully in response. Ben giggles, which makes me feel like crying.

I kneel down and clutch at him, breathing him in.

He pats me on the back and wriggles away. 'Come on, Charlie, let's take her back into the yard.' They thunder off down the hall.

The easy natural vibe Vanessa exudes has seeped into her house. There are glass sections cut into the ceiling, swords of light criss-crossing each other along the floorboards. I can hear the tinkle of nearby wind chimes.

As we reach the end of the hallway, Vanessa pats my arm. 'I really think this is for the best, Gemma.'

'Thanks,' I say stiffly. 'But you're already doing so much. And I'm conscious that Inspector Gordon is unwell.'

'Ah, don't worry about Tommy.' She ushers me to the closest doorway. 'I thought Ben would be happy in here.'

The room is a small neat rectangle with a single bed and two navy beanbags. A giant poster of a waterfall is adhered to the far wall. Through the window I spot at least three kinds of fern.

'Do you think this will be okay?' She looks around the room critically.

I nod. 'It's great.'

'And I've got you right next door.'

The adjacent room is larger and squarer, with a tall portrait window and a glass door that opens onto the side of a deck. A cluster of dreamcatchers hang on the door handle and an over-sized canvas of tropical flowers decorates the wall. Underfoot, a multicoloured rag rug peters out to straggly threads at each corner.

'There's a bathroom next door you can both use,' says Vanessa. 'We used to run a low-key bed and breakfast here during the summer school holidays, but we haven't done that for the past few years. I don't really know why, seeing as I have more time now I'm retired . . .' She trails off pleasantly, her eyes fixed on the dreamcatchers.

'Well, thank you,' I say. 'I'm sure the hotel would have been fine but I appreciate it.'

'Rubbish.' She sniffs dismissively.

I shrug, irritated.

'Now, you need to come and meet Tommy. No doubt he'll want to talk to you about the case.' She purses her lips, her cheery tone disappearing like the sun behind a cloud. 'I still can't believe what happened to Rick. No one can. And there's still no sign of Abbey, is there? It's awful. Do you think the two things are linked?'

'It's really too early to say.'

She folds her arms and narrows her eyes. 'You're cagey, just like Tommy. Come on, why don't you talk to him while I walk Charlie back home? And then I'll sort out some dinner.'

My stomach lurches at the thought of food—no longer carsick, I am starving.

Vanessa hustles me to the rear of the house through a spacious kitchen that flows into a large lounge room. We step onto the large wooden deck running the length of the house. Beyond the deck, a neat stretch of lawn disappears into a twist of bushland. A narrow line of sand juts out between two trees and leads straight to the beach; I glimpse blue between the greenery.

Ben is playing fetch with Inka along the side fence, his giggles mixing with her playful growling. I catch sight of an older man propped up on a cane chair under the shade of a stripy umbrella. His bandaged right leg rests on a gnarled slice of tree stump. As we get closer, I realise he is snoring.

Vanessa nudges his good leg gently with her foot, then clasps his broad shoulders. 'Tommy,' she says loudly.

His weathered face squeezes together before his eyelids spring open revealing faded blue irises. A startling bruise circles his right eye and a yellow stain drifts from his eyebrow into his hairline. His eyes rake over me. 'Bloody hell, you're young.'

I blanch slightly. 'Hello, Inspector Gordon. Gemma Woodstock.'

I step toward him and hold out my hand but he coughs and shakes his head. 'Please call me Tommy.'

'How are you feeling?' I ask, feeling like an awkward child as I withdraw my hand.

He pushes against the arms of the chair to adjust his position. 'Pretty terrible. But not nearly as bad as Rick Fletcher. Poor kid.' His hand jerks down to prod at his leg just above the cast. 'Sorry, this thing is bloody itchy.' He clears the last of the sleep from his throat and folds his hands in his lap, studying me. 'There's nothing wrong with our chairs, you know.'

I gingerly lower myself into one.

'That's better.' He makes a show of looking at his watch. 'And look, it's time for a drink.' Vanessa's expression stiffens—or perhaps I imagine it, because she swiftly offers me a drink too.

'No, thank you,' I say.

I'd love a beer, but exhaustion tugs on my eyelids and I want to be clear-headed while I extract as much information as possible from Tommy. He's been the chief here for almost ten years, so his knowledge is invaluable. I'm feeling the familiar impatience I get when I first latch on to a case: the feeling that every second is putting more distance between myself and a solve. And we've already lost so much time.

'I'll bring out some water.' Vanessa lightly places her hands on her husband's shoulders and smiles at me before she walks off.

Tommy watches her go, then fixes his stare on me again. 'How long have you been in homicide?'

'Almost eight years.'

He clears his throat. 'Are there any leads from today?'

'On Fletcher? Not really. Hopefully we'll know more tomorrow after the autopsy.'

'I presume you spoke to Daniel Clark about his whereabouts?'

Tommy's unexpected interrogation has caused all the saliva to evacuate my mouth.

'We did. He insisted he was home at the time of the attack. His wife confirmed it.'

Tommy snorts. 'I wouldn't listen to a word that woman says. Dot Clark will literally lie through her teeth for that man. I mean it—a few years ago he knocked one of her teeth clean out of her mouth, and she was still covering for him as the blood poured out.'

Vanessa reappears and hands Tommy a beer, then places a pitcher of water and a glass in front of me. 'Ben's going to help me serve dinner.' She gives me an indecipherable look and disappears back into the house.

'We're obviously not ruling Daniel out,' I continue.

Tommy eyes me for a few moments before retrieving a paper bag from the folds of the tartan blanket on his lap. He rustles through it and pulls out a silver sheet of pills; he ejects several from their casing and knocks them back with a swig of beer.

'I wouldn't have thought so,' he says. 'The man's been screaming for Rick Fletcher's scalp since Sunday morning.'

Reaching down, Tommy places the bag at the foot of the chair and a strange silence falls over the yard. I can see Vanessa and Ben in the kitchen but their conversation is muted by the glass door.

The daytime animals have turned in for the night, and the second act is yet to start up their chorus.

'Well, Dot's alibi obviously makes things difficult in terms of pursuing Daniel. Plus there are no witnesses, and at this stage no weapon. Unless his prints are found at the scene, there's not a lot to go on.'

'Sounds just like the situation with the Clark girl on Saturday night. There's not a lot to go on in general, is there?'

'There's still footage to review and several people to be interviewed. Things will shake loose.'

'I'm sure you're right,' says Tommy, sounding anything but. He arranges his knobbly fingers into a triangle and presses them against his lips. 'It must be hard for you to split your focus between your kid and the job. I have to say, I've never seen it work very well.'

'It's a juggle sometimes but I manage just fine,' I say curtly.

Tommy lets out a loud sigh. 'I'm a simple man, Gemma, and I don't believe in coincidences. If you want my two cents it's that Daniel Clark is trouble, and I don't believe for a second he's not involved in this. We know he threatened his daughter and we know he threatened Rick.' Tommy separates his hands as if he's performing a magic trick to reveal a vanished coin. 'He should have been locked up a long time ago and this is probably the best chance we have to put him away. I know you're used to big budgets and whiteboard theories but just make sure you don't overlook the bleeding obvious.'

'We can't rule out the possibility that Abbey attacked Rick,' I say.

Tommy emits a bleat of laughter, which clearly causes him pain. 'This is not some bloody feminist action movie, for god's sake,' he huffs.

A buzzing surges from my feet to the top of my head as my face gets hot. 'Look, I've worked in homicide for almost ten years and

I plan to do what I always do—run an airtight investigation and get a solve.'

Tommy's blue gaze gives me one more intense blast before releasing me. He chuckles and has more beer. 'Jonesy did say you were a livewire.'

I ball my fists. I can't see Jonesy and this guy having anything in common.

Behind me, Ben struggles with the heavy glass door before calling out that dinner is ready.

'You go,' says Tommy. 'I need to wait for the boss.' His dry lips push into a childish pout.

'I appreciate you having us stay here,' I say with cool politeness as I rise. 'I know it's not ideal with you being unwell.'

He shrugs. 'Vanessa insisted. And I'm told that someone around here wasn't too happy with you making yourself at home in The Parrot.'

A shot of warm wind stirs my hair and traces finger-like strokes on my neck and arms. 'Probably just kids mucking around.'

'Yeah, probably.' He lifts his head as Vanessa emerges. 'Anyway, you won't need to worry about this for too long. I'll be back on my feet in no time.'

FOURTH DAY MISSING

FOURTH DAY MISSING

Wednesday, 13 April
5.55 am

I startle into consciousness. Dreams of bloodied bodies fade away as I register the unfamiliar surrounds. It all comes back. The butchered possum. Rick Fletcher's blank stare. Moving to the Gordons'. I stretch out my arms and legs, bumping into the softness of Ben, who'd obviously come over in the night. I briefly watch the rise and fall of his chest, the slight flaring of his nostrils.

The house is silent. I realise I still haven't called Jodie back.

'God,' I whisper to the ceiling.

I check my phone: a message from Mac apologising for missing me yesterday and asking me to call, and a polite text from Dad. There's an email from Owen; he sent some files from Jock's drug case. *Call me when you can*, he wrote, *I spoke to Jock but I don't know if it will help much*.

I lean out of the bed, grabbing my laptop from its precarious spot on top of my suitcase. I yank the screen open and click on the file of footage from Saturday night that Lane sent me yesterday. I fell asleep trying to watch it last night; I need to make sure there's nothing that indicates what happened to her after she ran off into the night.

Like most security footage, there's no audio and it's angled badly, only capturing activity at the bottom of the ramp, the wooden landing and the area directly outside the door. The internal camera captures a decent chunk of the waiting area, but unhelpfully only the reverse of anyone standing at the counter. I press play and watch Abbey step onto the base of the ramp and walk quickly up the concrete curve before she leans back slightly, arm out as she pulls open the door. There's no bike in sight and she's not looking behind her. She has a sense of purpose about her, a determination.

It doesn't seem as if she is worried about being followed, nor does she appear intoxicated.

Once she's inside I can only see a reverse view of Abbey. Lane's face is visible most of the time, though Abbey's head and hair sporadically block it. He is clearly surprised when she comes in; he reaches for his phone and presses a button, perhaps turning some music off. Then he rises from his seat and holds his hands up in a classic comfort gesture. After a minute or so he begins talking, still gesturing with his hands before he grabs the report paperwork and begins to fill it out. At 11.47 pm he answers the phone and speaks to the caller for just over one minute. He says something to Abbey and then makes a call, which I know is to Tommy, arranging to meet him at the party. While Lane is doing this, Abbey checks her own phone, shifting her weight from one foot to the other.

They walk out of the station together, and Lane locks up. They have another conversation at the base of the ramp. Abbey steps off camera while Lane is speaking calmly, his expression reassuring. He points to the car, then his head reels back a little, perhaps in surprise. This must be when Abbey rejects the offer of a lift. When he speaks again there's a swish of movement in the bottom left of the screen, which I suspect is Abbey's hair flicking out as she spins around.

Lane calls to her, holding up his hands in a slightly hopeless manner before he makes a frustrated shrugging gesture and disappears from view too.

I succumb to an intense yawn while I scroll the file back about six minutes. I pause it on Abbey's face, zooming in until the image is on the brink of total pixilation. I'm used to looking at photos of the recently dead, listening to voice messages left by the murdered or watching videos of the missing, but in that moment, from that angle, she looks so young. I wonder again if she had any sense of what was coming, whatever that was.

Ben stirs just as I hear someone slide open the back door. I watch his little face tensing as he processes the grim reality of another day without his dad. I hug him to me until he strains to extract himself.

'You can go into the kitchen,' I say. 'Vanessa is already up. I'm going for a quick run.'

He pads off down the hall, and I push my laptop aside and swing my feet onto the floor. Still yawning, I rustle through my suitcase for my running gear. The calico bag I took from Abbey's is propped next to the cupboard; I take out one of the two larger notebooks and flick through it. I read a few poems, admire a couple of her sketches, then come across a checklist. There are bullet points about homework assignments and a reminder to buy birthday presents for the twins—paint supplies? Another bullet point simply says, *Doctor appointment.*

I read through some of the passages of prose. Most are dramatic and dark, and I wonder how much of an insight they might be into Abbey's inner world.

Alone. Trapped in a square of blackness. My whole body screaming. I turned to ice as his hands burned me, poisoned me. Finger of fear choked me. I couldn't scream, I couldn't breathe. Eyes that had always been so kind were suddenly tunnels to pure evil.

A small bundle of loose papers is wedged between the back cover and the last page: a few pictures ripped from magazines, some homework sheets, a receipt for shower gel, a birthday party invite and notes from friends. I open each note but they are fairly inane—opinions on TV shows and which bathers to buy. Only one catches my eye:

I just wanted to let you know that I think you are stunning. You have the best smile. Have a great day. R.

The writing is formal, cursive. Rick? Or perhaps, more likely, another unsolicited advance from Robert Weston. Could he be the reason Abbey ended things with Rick?

In the hallway I pause to listen to Ben talking animatedly about his soccer team, blissfully oblivious to the knot of worry that has taken up residence in my core.

'Morning,' I announce myself as I step into the kitchen.

'Good morning. I hope you slept well?' Vanessa's grey hair is wild and loose, and she tosses it over her shoulder as she twists half an orange against a juicer.

'I did, thank you.'

'OJ?' she asks.

Ben nods.

'No, thanks,' I say. 'I'm going for a quick run before I head into work.'

Vanessa looks slightly alarmed. 'Are you sure that's a good idea?'

'I'll be fine.' I sit with Ben on the couch for a few minutes, the soundtrack of morning cartoons fading into the background as I plot the day ahead. Vanessa bustles around in the kitchen but there's no sign of Tommy.

'I won't be too long,' I say, giving Ben a quick hug.

'Well, there's a lovely running track along the beach,' Vanessa offers, serving Ben a glass of pulpy juice. 'It takes you right into town and then you can run south along Church Street past all the shops until you end up back here. I've never done it myself,' she laughs, 'I'm not a runner, but it's about four k's, give or take.'

Mac sends me a message as I slide the door shut.

Are you up? I can talk now if you can.

I cross the back lawn, padding down the sandy path. Parrot Bay glimmers in the early morning light. It's still cool but the sun is making a play for centre stage and the salt air reaches deep into my lungs. I drop into walking lunges when I break out onto the beach. As my leg muscles heat up, I let my mind sift through the conversation I had with Tommy last night, anger rising all over again. He's clearly irritated that I've come here. Stretching my arms over my head, I look out at the crashing waves. I think about de Luca's strange hostility too, and I feel incredibly alone.

I need to call Mac before the day starts to snowball.

After plugging in my earphones, I dial his number. My limbs feel heavy and my stomach is still unsettled. The last thing I need is to get sick.

Mac's familiar face appears on screen, catapulting me into my life in Sydney. 'Gemma! I was getting worried. Is everything okay?'

'Everything is totally fine. I'm actually squeezing in a quick run on the beach before work.'

His brow creases. 'How did yesterday pan out?'

'You know how it is. I'm mainly just trying to get my head around everything .'

He looks at me as if expecting me to elaborate. When I don't, he says, 'I still don't know about this, Gemma. A case like this feels like a lot for you to take on right now.'

'I'm fine, honestly.'

'And how is Ben? And the hotel?'

I focus on Mac's mouth rather than his eyes. 'He seems to like it here and the hotel is great. Mac, really, everything is fine.'

He sighs. 'I'm going to be sucked into this arson case for a few days but I want you to keep me across what's going on up there.' There's a pause. 'I really wish you were back in Sydney, Gem. I know it's complicated with Ben, and I shouldn't put pressure on you, but it's hard with everything feeling so up in the air.'

'I know.' My pulse races as if I've already been running. 'I gotta go,' I say, and hang up.

I lift my face to the morning sun, then get back into my warm-up. God, what a mess.

A sharp voice screeches into my ears, aided by the wind. 'Are you the new detective?'

Mid squat, I stumble slightly and spin around. A shrivelled woman is standing surprisingly close, a few metres from the opening of a sandy path that disappears into a wall of shrubbery. My immediate impression is that she looks like an ageing heroin addict. She's wrapped in a long black polyester dress that's pilling all over, her feet bare. Strands of frizzy brown hair hang down past her chest.

'Are you?' she says, eyeing me reproachfully.

I shield my gaze with my hand. 'Yes, I'm Detective Woodstock. Can I help you?'

She ignores my question and looks out at the sea. 'It's terrible what happened to that boy.'

'Did you know Rick Fletcher?'

'Very sad,' she says, clicking her tongue. She's painfully thin, and her eyes have sunken in her skull. The insides of her elbows are riddled with track marks and bruises.

'What's your name?' I ask.

'She's dead, you know.'

'I'm sorry?'

'Dead and buried.' She closes her eyes and kneads at her skull with bony nicotine-stained fingers. 'At night-time I see her,' she mutters. 'What they did to her.'

'Are you talking about Abbey Clark?' I step toward the woman, and she reels backwards, her deep-set eyes bulging open.

'No one believes me,' she says quietly, scratching her forearms. 'No one listens.'

'I'm listening,' I say. 'We can talk right now for as long as you like. Please, tell me your name?'

The wind ricochets off the water and buffets both of us, picking up pieces of her long hair. She fixes her milky stare somewhere just above my head. I consider whether she's intoxicated, though the sharpness of her movements suggests it's more likely she's high or experiencing a manic episode.

'I've lived here all my life,' she announces. 'Born on the kitchen table. They made me leave my house, you know. Said I wasn't safe on my own, but I know the real reason—they're worried what I'll say.' She starts back up the path. Her Nike backpack looks like a deflated balloon. 'Be careful, Detective,' she calls out without turning around. 'No one wants her found.'

'Hey! Please talk to me. Do you mean Abbey Clark? If you have any information about her disappearance, I need to talk to you.'

She starts to run, hunched over and frantic. Her husky high-pitched voice curls out from beyond the gnarled trees. 'Leave me alone!'

Wednesday, 13 April

7.18 am

I arrive back at the Gordons' breathing hard and drenched in sweat. The relatively easy run has highlighted just how out of shape I've become since I left Sydney.

Tommy has joined Vanessa and Ben in the kitchen, his wheelchair flush against the long wooden table. He's eating scrambled eggs on toast, the rich yellow flecked with green. The house smells of coffee and basil.

I shower, keeping the water cool. I felt shaken and emotional on my run. Even though I'm aware it's highly probable Abbey Clark is dead, I haven't allowed myself to fully believe it, but the strange woman's words hit a nerve. I know I partly took this case because of Nicki, for the chance at a tiny sliver of redemption, but it feels increasingly likely that I'm simply going to compound my grief and spiral myself into a whole other level of soul searching. I haven't worked many missing persons cases, only five over the past decade, but they are an especially brutal form of mental torment. The missing tend to take on a mythical quality; the possibility they are alive muddies the waters and weakens the practical instincts a dead body demands. It's a bizarre, drawn-out dance between hope and hopelessness. I already know that while I'll look for Abbey beyond all reason, that I will prepare to discover her corpse, the whole time I'm doing this I will pray she is the one who gives the finger to the bleak statistics. That somehow, I will cheat the odds and bring her home. More than anything, I don't want her to go to the place in my mind reserved for the long dead faces from squadroom case boards, and into the metaphorical graveyard that I rake over and over, looking for answers that will probably never be found.

I towel-dry my hair, now thinking about Mac. I try not to give any real estate to the doubts that lurk in my head as I flick him a quick upbeat message reassuring him that I really am fine.

Tommy's eyes don't leave his iPad when I enter the kitchen. I down a glass of water and say, 'I met a woman at the beach who knew me. An older woman with long brown hair. She was all dressed in black.' I pause. 'She was quite distressed and said a few things about the case.'

'I'd say you met Meg Jarvis,' says Vanessa from where she's hanging laundry on a rickety clothes horse. 'She walks along the beach most mornings. She used to live in the old place at the end of the street, but her niece arranged for her to be moved into the care home last year—only low-level care, so she's allowed to come and go as she likes.'

'She hasn't actually bothered me for a while,' says Tommy, looking thoughtful.

'Who is she?' I ask, watching Inka pad through the back door and make a beeline for Ben.

'She says she's a psychic,' says Vanessa diplomatically. 'People used to pay her to read their fortunes.'

'She's a kook,' says Tommy, rolling his eyes. 'And a junkie. She's in and out of the hospital with imaginary illnesses. It drives Eric nuts.'

'She's harmless,' adds Vanessa, swatting at her husband. 'She means well but she has a lot of crazy theories. She lost her husband and daughter in a horrible boating accident years ago, and I think she's very lonely. There's only a niece looking out for her, and she lives in Melbourne. Meg almost died a few times from overdosing on heroin. She probably heard you were here and figured you might actually listen to her. She gave up on Tommy ages ago.'

'I banned her from the station,' he says and pushes his plate away. 'I told her to keep a diary of her nutty theories and said I'd look at it once a year at Christmas. What was she on about this morning?'

'Nothing really. She was just shouting my name.' All my instincts are screaming at me to keep what Meg said to myself for now.

'I wonder whether she should be allowed to wander around by herself,' murmurs Vanessa, biting her lip. 'Maybe I'll speak to Chrissy.'

'Well, I hope you ignored her,' says Tommy, 'she's a massive time waster. She thinks there are bodies buried all over town.' He tips his head from left to right, stretching his neck. 'You said Rick's autopsy is today?'

'At midday.'

'You're going, I assume?'

'I'm sending de Luca and one of the boys.'

He raises his eyebrows. 'Wouldn't be my choice.'

I meet his gaze. 'It will be good for them. They don't have the exposure to something like this very often, and I have people I want to speak to here.'

Tommy shrugs. 'De Luca needs to be managed. She lacks initiative but I'm sure you're all over it.'

I find myself getting worked up. He grimaces and pokes his large fingers at the screen of his phone. While I found de Luca rude and standoffish, of the three of them she certainly didn't seem to lack initiative. I walk over to the couch, trying to remain calm.

'You okay?' I say to Ben.

'Yep. We're going to the beach today. Vanessa says we're allowed to bring Inka.'

'That sounds fun. Just make sure you wear your hat and have sunscreen on.' I trace my fingers across his jawline.

'I've only ever been to the beach that one time I went with you and Mac in Sydney.'

'Yes, you loved it.'

He nods but seems unsure.

'Tommy and Vanessa are pretty lucky to have a beach on the doorstep, aren't they?'

'Yeah,' he says. 'I want to learn to surf.'

I give him a squeeze. 'Well, maybe not today. One thing at a time, hey? Hopefully I'll be able to come down and meet you later. Or we can go tomorrow.'

Vanessa helps Tommy use the bathroom, then wheels him out onto the back deck. I remain inside but I hear her say, 'We'll be back soon, okay? Call me if you need me to come home.'

I grab Ben's hat and hand it to Vanessa as she enters the kitchen. 'I'll call later to check in.'

'Of course.'

She crouches down to help Ben apply sunscreen and ask whether Scott liked the beach as if it's no big deal.

I wave them off at the front door. Ben's arm flies out as Inka pulls on her lead.

On the deck, Tommy is fussing with a bag of pillboxes. I grab my things and stick my head out the back door. 'Is there anything you need?'

'No, thanks, I'm just perfect.'

As I turn to go, I decide to make a peace offering of sorts. Crossing my arms, I walk over to him. 'Actually, I wanted to ask you about the reporter, Simon Charleston. I assume you know him?'

Tommy grunts. 'Yeah, I know him alright.'

'Is he a good reporter?'

'I'm not sure I know what that means.'

I'm fast regretting this olive branch. 'Do you ever work with him? Do you rate him?'

'I wouldn't trust him as far as I can throw him. He's an overpaid gossip.' Tommy puts some tablets in his mouth and gulps back half a glass of water. My eyes land on the pillbox in front of him. Meperidine. Vanessa's name is on the prescription sticker and the date is from November last year. 'Can hardly keep track of all these bloody pills Eric has me taking,' says Tommy gruffly, shoving the medicine back into the bulging bag. 'Anyway, why are you asking about Charleston?'

'I met him yesterday.' My mind races and there's a sinking feeling in my stomach.

'Well, I'd avoid him if you can. He's *bad news.*' Tommy laughs at his joke.

'I better get going.'

Still smiling, he drops his head back against the cushion. 'Have a good day, Detective. I'm looking forward to hearing about your adventures tonight.'

Feeling increasingly uneasy, I go to my car, relieved I didn't mention what Meg Jarvis said about Abbey Clark being dead and buried somewhere in Fairhaven.

There are fewer reporters outside the station than there were yesterday. A female journalist struggles to get her hair out of her face as she grips a microphone and holds up what looks to be a map to the camera. Simon is nowhere to be seen but his car is there. His windows are tinted so it's impossible to tell if he's inside.

Grange's squad car is here but there's no sign of the others, so I keep the air con running and pull out my phone, ignoring the missed calls from Jonesy and Candy and dialling Owen instead.

'Gemma, we got him!'

'What? Who?'

'Ronson! It's all going to come out in the press this morning, but we bloody got him.'

'Shit, Owen, that's massive.'

'I know.' Owen's voice is rich with pride. 'We had a tip-off from my guy late last night and it seemed legit, so we sent a crew over, and he was just *there*. I still can't believe it.'

'Can you get him for Krystal's murder? And the other witness?'

'Looks like it. A few of his guys are talking now so we'll definitely get him for the drugs and the hit-and-run. You should have seen bloody Jock, parading around the bust.'

'Forget about him.' I pause, trying to force some saliva into my mouth, which has gone completely dry. 'Christ, Owen, well done.'

I stare at the aqua-painted brick wall of the police station and experience a strange sensation, as if a filter has been applied to the scene in front of me. The Ronson case was the first one I worked on when I got to Sydney, and even though we'd managed to nab a few of the low-level guys we could never get to Garry Ronson himself. The leads had dried up and the case had essentially gone cold. We knew he'd raped and murdered another prostitute in June last year, the third as far as we were aware, but our witness was unreliable, our evidence non-existent, and Ronson nowhere to be found. I can still picture the original case board: the crazy web of crimes and contacts, Ronson's smiling face in the centre.

'Thanks. Anyway, I'm still in bed, we didn't get in until around 3 am, but I did quickly follow up on Aiden Fletcher for you before all this exploded.'

Half my head is still working through the details of the Ronson case. I have so many questions but I can't afford to get distracted—plus, it's not my case anymore. 'Thanks, Owen.'

'No worries. I don't know if it will be very helpful. Jock said Aiden's phone number was in the call list of the guy who shot himself and that he'd tried to call him. Might be nothing. The ME ruled it suicide and the whole thing went nowhere. Anyway, I'll send you the file—it's definitely the same guy. He has a brother called Richard, and they live in Fairhaven.'

A squad vehicle turns into the car park. Lane and de Luca get out, smiling and talking as they enter the station.

'I gotta go, Owen. Thanks again. I'll let you know if I need anything else. And well done again on Ronson. Tell the team for me, yeah?'

'Thanks, Gem. Half the glory's yours, you know that.'

I get out of the car too quickly, my vision turning white as I walk up the ramp.

'Morning,' I say to Noah.

'Morning,' he replies, around a mouthful of toast.

Lane and Grange offer cheerful good mornings; de Luca gives me a subdued nod.

The leather on Tommy's desk chair is almost worn bare and I try not to think about the amount of sweat that has soaked into it over the years. I lean forward, touching my forearms to the desk, then quickly sit up straight again. The surface is a little on the sticky side.

'Right, quick check in,' I say, standing up. 'I'll go first. I know there's been barely any progress on the whereabouts of Aiden, so I want us to dig beyond the surface layer. Last year he was linked to a group involved in couriering drugs. Nothing really came of it and I have no idea whether he was involved or not, but perhaps everything we're looking at here is drug related.' I think about Tommy's bag of pills and frown. I feel so uneasy around him. He's definitely arrogant but it's more than that, there's an unpredictability and I wonder if he's always like that, or if the medication is to blame.

'It would make sense. Maybe Rick and Abbey found out about something Aiden was involved in, and someone wanted to keep them quiet. Or maybe they were directly involved—I don't know.' I turn to Grange. 'Damon, can you follow up with the forensic team today and see if anything turned up at the house that might suggest drugs.'

'Sure.'

'And you said Aiden recently left his job. What did he do?'

'He ran the hospital cafe. He set it up a few years ago when he left school. It's pretty small-scale stuff and apparently he did it all—ordering, serving, cleaning—the whole deal.'

'It's not exactly a key to the drug cupboard but it's close enough,' I say. 'Follow it up. Maybe he was working with someone higher up there and things went sour. See if you can find out if the hospital has ever had an issue with drugs going missing. I'll look further into the case from last year and see if anything shakes out.'

Grange blinks but nods.

'Any other updates?' I say, feeling a sense of progress for the first time since I arrived.

'I spoke to the petrol-tank driver,' says de Luca. 'Frank Bower, early sixties. He confirmed he arrived in Fairhaven around 7 pm on Saturday, signed in and then plugged his tank into the system. It takes about two hours for the fuel to transfer. Once it was done, he locked up and checked into The Parrot where he had dinner at the pub. That was just after 9 pm.'

'What about afterwards?'

De Luca continues as if I haven't spoken. 'He's on the security footage Cam sent through—he enters the pub then leaves about two hours later, walking in the direction of his room. He said he was on the phone to his wife at 11.30 pm for almost twenty minutes. I'll put in a request for his phone records but I doubt he's got anything to do with Abbey.'

'No, but his tank might have acted as a shield for a violent crime.' I exhale loudly. 'Okay, make sure you track down those tapes from the service station. Anyone who was in that vicinity is of interest until the blood results confirm otherwise.'

De Luca's lips form a straight line, and she directs her gaze toward the small window. 'When will that be?'

'I don't know,' I admit. 'I'll follow it up this morning.'

'That phone number for Robert Weston is a dead end,' offers Lane. 'It was his UK number and hasn't been active since he came here at the end of last year. He arrived in Australia the first week of December. He was in Sydney until he came to Fairhaven in early Feb. I dug around a bit but he doesn't have a registered phone, so he must be using a prepaid. I sent him a Facebook message asking him to contact me but nothing yet. I also got access to his accounts so I'll take a look later today.'

'We need to find him,' I say impatiently. 'This morning I found a note that might be from him in one of the notebooks I took from Abbey's bedroom. He was clearly interested in her, if not being a full-blown pest.' I turn to Grange. 'Did you hear from the caravan park manager? I really want that guest list.'

'Ah, no. Not yet,' he stammers. 'I was about to call Kate again, or I can shoot down there and speak to her in person?'

'No, I'll go,' I say. 'This is ridiculous—we need information from this woman, what's her problem?'

Grange opens his mouth but doesn't say anything.

I sigh. 'Lane will come with me this morning. We'll go to the caravan park and try to track down Robert Weston and sort out the guest lists. And then I'd like to speak to some of Abbey's workmates and school friends. I made a list from her social media accounts and phone contacts. Also, Georgina and Ian Fletcher are coming to the station at around 2 pm to make a formal statement, so we'll need to be back here for that.' I settle my gaze on Grange and de Luca. 'I want you two to attend Fletcher's autopsy today.'

They startle slightly.

'Any problems with that?'

They shake their heads.

'Good. It's at midday in the Byron Bay morgue, and Inspector Tran will be there too. Hopefully we can identify the weapon and determine how likely it is that someone of Abbey's build could have carried out the attack.'

'I arranged to speak to the school principal this morning,' says de Luca.

'Call from the car,' I reply. 'Or move it. You'll need to leave here by 11 am.'

She flicks her feathery hair and pouts slightly. 'Okay.'

'I also want to see if Abbey had a doctor's appointment recently, or even just scheduled one. We need to check here and in the local towns.'

'What's that about?' asks Lane.

'Abbey wrote a to-do list in one of her notebooks, and it has *doctor* written on it. I'm keen to understand anything about her frame of mind that might help us figure out what was going on. A pregnancy scare or some kind of illness might have been motive for a break-up or imply the existence of another relationship, or perhaps this is about mental health issues.'

Lane nods slowly. 'Makes sense.'

'I watched the station footage from Saturday,' I tell him. 'Did Abbey seem intoxicated or high on Saturday night?'

'I don't think so,' he says. 'She was emotional but I just put that down to her being upset about her bike. Plus, she mentioned she argued with her ex-boyfriend.'

'She told you about that?'

'Yeah, she definitely said something about it. I asked her if she thought he might have taken the bike, but she said she didn't think so.'

'Did she say she was on her way home?'

'No, but I assumed so. That's where I offered to drive her.'

'I didn't get the feeling she was worried she was being followed.'

'I didn't sense that either, but who knows.' He looks pained.

'Tran mentioned there was a big drug blitz in the area recently. Do you guys come across much of it these days?'

'Not really, though there's definitely a bit of weed,' says de Luca. 'And alcohol, obviously.'

'We arrested a bunch of backpackers earlier in the year,' adds Lane. 'A few kids stole a car and when they were busted there was a decent haul of pills in the boot.'

'What are we talking?'

'Amphetamines and some pharmacy stuff. None of it could be traced, and they said they'd bought it from a guy they met on the road. It looked legitimate.'

I think about Tommy taking his pills this morning. He really shouldn't be mixing Vanessa's old prescriptions with new scripts. I worked with someone in Melbourne who unwittingly slid into a prescription drug addiction and it slowly but surely destroyed their entire life.

'We don't really get the party drugs here,' adds Grange. 'It's just not that kind of place. And Tran's right, we've essentially stamped out ice for the most part.'

'Alright.' I bring my hands together. 'Let's aim for 5 pm back here. Call me if the autopsy shows up anything we need to know before then.'

Before we head off, Lane ducks to the bathroom and I call the lab to chase up the bloodwork. A distracted receptionist tells me it's been prioritised but that it's 'raining samples' so she doesn't know when it will be processed.

Sighing, I gather my things. Whether it's Abbey's blood or not, we're still looking for her with the same amount of urgency. My thoughts keep returning to Ronson. Like Nicki Mara, the man consumed so much of my time and my consciousness that it's hard to believe the hunt is over. That's the thing with detective work: even though we need to be sensitive to every shade of grey, our cases are essentially black and white. Solved, open. Found, not found. Dead, alive. Nicki Mara is a permanent black mark against my name. Ronson gets a big fat tick. I feel the urge to call Mac, to celebrate, to officially put the case to bed, but my distance continues to feel more than just geographical.

I scan the paperwork Owen sent, the case I had remembered Aiden's name from. A sizeable batch of pharmacy pills were located during a raid, and a young man was arrested. The pills had no known origin and the guy claimed he'd only been advised the pick-up location: a chemist car park in Redfern. He subsequently squealed on his housemate, Tony Foy, who admitted to buying some pills from him but denied any involvement in supply. Two weeks later Tony turned up dead in a warehouse car park, a single bullet in his head and a gun in his hand. It was ruled a suicide but I know Jock had his doubts.

'Everything okay, Gemma?' Lane says, flashing me a smile as he sails past. His casual familiarity is somehow even more jarring today than it was yesterday.

'Yep, let's go,' I say, standing as I skim the last few lines.

The day before he died, despite having no known links, Tony searched for an Aiden Fletcher on Facebook and called the mobile number listed on his page. Aiden never answered the call.

Wednesday, 13 April
8.54 am

If Lane is annoyed about not being sent to the autopsy, he doesn't show it. He talks easily, seemingly keen to give me the whistle-stop tour of his life.

'I was really good at rugby but I started having trouble with my hamstrings so that put an end to that. I was kind of interested in law—you know, just like movies set in courtrooms and whatever—but then a couple went missing from here years ago. Must have been when I was about thirteen, I guess, and it really got me thinking about being a cop. My parents knew Tommy quite well and he used to talk to me about it, you know, encouraged me to pursue it. And I really love it, so far.' Lane points to the upcoming intersection. 'Turn left here.'

He speaks with the confidence of someone with the hard-wired notion that everything will always work out just fine. In spite of myself I find him charming. He chatters on happily about his training in Yamba and his uncle, a detective I vaguely know from Melbourne.

We pass more houses and I navigate a game of street cricket before we hit a long stretch of bushland. Lane leans forward and points to a dirt driveway. 'Turn here.'

We pass under a wooden arch that reminds me of school camp, with faded block letters nailed along the curve. The squad car churns up the gravel driveway until we hit an overflowing car park. I pull up next to a ute, right outside the guest reception, blatantly ignoring the *No Parking* sign. Swinging open my door, I hear children squealing and loud splashing. An unpleasant smell permeates the air.

'This way.' Lane wrinkles his nose and walks through a door of plastic ribbons.

Inside the small cabin, the air is hot and the stench of sewage mixes with artificial eucalyptus. An unmanned desk is to our left, and hanging behind it is a huge photo board of pinned polaroids. Beaming couples, little kids and families—all guests of the park, I assume. In front of us the door to a back office is slightly ajar, and on the right wall are three rows of brochures and maps held captive behind perspex.

Lane dings the silver bell on the counter. Somewhere nearby, a mobile phone is ringing. 'Kate must be outside,' he mutters.

I push open the door and go down a wooden ramp into a communal barbecue area. The smell intensifies. I spot a huddle of rainwater tanks and a patch of high-vis: a man in a fluorescent orange vest who seems to be on his knees near the base of one of the wooden cabins.

A woman in cat's-eye sunglasses and a tight black dress hovers next to him, a mobile at her ear and a worried expression on her face.

'That's Kate,' says Lane.

I don't know what I was expecting but Kate isn't it. As I walk over to her with Lane trailing behind, she holds out her hand as if to silence me while she listens to whoever is speaking on the phone.

The man on the ground doesn't get up. Wiry hair curls from the top of his exposed arse crack.

'Well, this is very inconvenient,' Kate snaps. 'And you seem totally incompetent. I want to be contacted by your manager as soon as possible.'

She prods a bright red false nail at the screen to end the call and shoves her sunglasses onto her head, revealing dark eyes ringed with smudged mascara.

Then she stares at us witheringly. 'This is a fucking nightmare. Sorry for the language, but it is.' She leads us away from the man on the ground. 'Hi, Kai, honey,' she says, putting a hand on his shoulder and giving him a flirtatious squeeze before she looks at me coolly. 'You're the detective filling in for Tommy, right? Well, I apologise—I know that other cop said you wanted stuff from me, but this plumbing issue has taken up *all* of the past twenty-four hours. Don't get me wrong, I want to help. I couldn't believe it when I heard about the Fletcher kid.' She fondles her thick gold necklace. 'What did he do for that to happen? I've got to tell you, I'm hearing all sorts of crazy things.'

'Like what?' I ask.

'Just talk. You know, how his parents have always been a bit odd. They're hippies, I guess. Into alternative stuff. I remember the mother used to read tea leaves, though I heard rumours she might have charged for some extra services, if you get my drift. Anyway, a little bird told me the Fletchers bought some land down the coast so they could grow things they shouldn't.' Kate holds up her hands, revealing orange fake-tan stains. 'Who knows if it's true, I barely know them.' She grabs at her necklace again. 'Anyway, I care about Abbey being missing, I really do, I mean, her mother is one of my employees, but frankly this is about as bad as it gets here. People are threatening to leave and they all want discounts.' She juts her hip out dramatically.

'How often does Dot Clark work here?' I ask.

'Usually Monday to Thursday but she hasn't been in all week, so I've had to get the other girls working extra cleaning shifts.'

'Has she said when she'll be back?' interjects Lane.

'Tomorrow, apparently,' says Kate, smiling at him. 'She called last night and said she was keen to come in. Her shift starts at midday, so I guess we'll see—hopefully she turns up! I think she needs the money. She's casual, doesn't get any personal leave. To be honest she isn't the most reliable worker, but she is a *really* good cleaner. Plus, I feel sorry for her.'

'How is she unreliable?' says Lane.

Kate waves her own comment away. 'Oh, Dot calls in sick at the last minute sometimes. I don't think she's actually sick, she probably just has a black eye or whatever, but it does cause me some problems, especially over the summer. She loses things occasionally. But credit where it's due, when she is here she is good. She works hard.'

I mentally add a return caravan park visit to my schedule. If I can catch Dot away from the house, she might be candid about Daniel's abuse.

'Kate, I realise you have some issues to deal with here today but we need information from you. It's not negotiable.'

She sighs then presses her lips together in annoyance before turning back to the man on the ground. 'I gotta go into the office for a bit, okay?'

With a grunt, he lifts a hand in acknowledgement.

As Kate stalks toward the office, we rush to keep up. The smell comes in waves and is momentarily unbearable, forcing me to breathe through my mouth.

'Should be all fixed soon,' Kate trills to the crowd of guests as we pass. 'Hopefully within the next hour or so.'

There are a few murmurs of understanding among the frustrated expressions. Someone slow claps.

Inside the little wooden room, Kate rouses the computer and taps her long nails impatiently on the table. 'So you want, what, a list of all of the guests since Sunday?'

I tick our requirements off on my fingers. 'We want a complete list of every guest who checked out on the weekend. Monday too. And anyone who checked in on Saturday. We need to know if there's a man named Robert Weston staying here—he's British. We also want to know if you've noticed anything unusual lately, or had any complaints about guest behaviour.'

Her face is lit by the blue glow of the screen as she opens files and sets the printer in motion. 'I already told Damon I don't have anyone on the books called Robert Weston.'

'But you only take the names of the payees, right? So he could be here.'

Kate looks at me like she wants me to disappear. 'There's a few young British guys staying here at the moment. They arrived well over a month ago and have taken out long-term rentals in the permanent cabins. I only have the names of the two who paid.'

'Have they caused any hassle since they've been here?'

'Look,' she says, as if I'm a child, 'I run this place by myself and never have less than two hundred guests. During peak season I open the east wing and fill the whole place up to capacity. That's eight hundred people. There's about half that number here right now. I am in the business of holidaying humans, so there's always odd behaviour—but unless it's dangerous, I don't really get involved. I don't have time.'

'So there's been nothing that stands out?'

She crosses her arms defensively. 'It's just normal stuff—they're loud, boozy and messy.' Blowing her fringe out of her eyes, she says, somewhat reluctantly, 'And one of the cleaners told me a British guy was trying to film some of the girls by the pool. Younger girls.'

'When was this?' Lane pulls out his notebook with a flourish.

'Thursday, I think. Maybe Friday.'

'And you didn't report it?' I press.

'She was vague about it,' Kate snaps. 'What am I going to do, demand to see the phones? I mean, come on. If a guest complained it would have been different, but I think this guy was just mucking around. I doubt it was sinister.'

'Boys will be boys, you mean?'

She throws up her hands. 'They're adults and I'm not their mother. Plus, this town has a love-hate relationship with tourists sometimes.'

'What do you mean?' I say.

'We love their money—we're not so keen on sharing our home with them. We tend to look for bad behaviour. You'd think people would thank me for pumping tourist dollars into their businesses but no, instead I get a constant stream of bitching.'

'We do get a lot of complaints about the tourists,' ventures Lane.

Ignoring him I say, 'Kate, we'll need to talk to these guests. If they are filming underage girls in swimsuits and sharing the content, they could be up for child pornography charges. Are they definitely still here?'

Kate baulks, emitting a nervous titter. 'Porn? Come on, I think that's a bit drastic, don't you?' I don't reply and she sighs. 'They're still here. They're on some kind of gap year. They have casual employment, they listed it on their application. I demand proof of employment or upfront payment for the long-term rentals, but I think the bank of mummy and daddy is funding their Down Under adventure anyway.'

'What kind of employment?'

'I can't bloody remember. On a fishing boat, maybe? To be honest, they seem to spend most of their time surfing at the beach or drinking at the pub. I don't get the impression they're working especially hard.' She grabs the pile of paper from the printer and flicks through it. 'They're booked for another month.' Leaning forward, she highlights a few rows. Sharp tan lines cut across her cleavage. 'Oh actually, hang on.'

'What?'

'One of the boys left on Monday—I remember now, he was loading all his stuff into a taxi when I was out the front waiting for the tradesman. But the other three are definitely still here. I saw them this morning with their surfboards.'

I exchange a look with Lane. 'Did he say why he was leaving?'

'No, oddly enough he didn't share that with me. He just got in the cab and left. I figured he had to go home, but as long as his mate is still paying for the room it's not really my problem.' Kate points to the printout. 'If it helps, I think William is the one that the staff alerted me about.' She circles a name and hands me the list with a flourish.

'Very helpful,' I say sarcastically.

'Look,' she says, her tone more conciliatory, 'I understand you need to speak with them, but can you at least make sure you don't scare off the other guests? Maybe do it somewhere else? I've already got busted pipes, I don't want people thinking they've walked onto the set of *CSI* on top of that.'

A hot burn erupts inside of me while little pricks of light dot my vision. Another wave of sewage is served up by a gust of wind, and my nostrils flare.

'We'll certainly keep your concerns in mind while we investigate the suspected homicide of a teenage girl and the brutal murder of

her boyfriend,' I manage before pushing away from the desk and
through the plastic ribbons into a haze of flies, trying desperately to
contain my nausea. Mortified, I hear Lane's footsteps approaching
as I vomit violently into a flowerpot.

Wednesday, 13 April
10.39 am

Lane winds down the windows as we pull out of the caravan park. 'Fresh air.' He sticks his hand through the window slightly. 'God, that was revolting. Poor Kate.'

I lean to the left so the breeze fondles my face. I still feel new-foal shaky but the intensity of the nausea has passed.

'Sure you're okay now?' Lane is guiding the car gently through an intersection.

'Much better, thanks. I must have eaten something that didn't agree with me and then that smell just tipped me over the edge.'

He laughs. 'I won't tell Vanessa Gordon you said that.'

I smile but the panic that took over as my insides expelled the last of the coffee, the only thing I've consumed today, has not dissipated. My heart thumps in time with the faulty tick of the car motor. As my hands gripped the rim of the flowerpot, it all fell into place with a startling clarity: the exhaustion I had attributed to grief and stress, my aching limbs to a lack of exercise and unfamiliar beds.

I swallow, the lingering taste of bile repulsive. Closing my eyes, I breathe in and out a few times. I need to get my head straight.

At least this trip wasn't a waste of time; I extract Kate's list from my pocket and scan it, immediately feeling unwell again.

'There's some mints,' says Lane, pointing to the glove box.

'Thanks.' I gingerly put one in my mouth, the cool burn soothing the acid remnants.

Lane has been incredibly kind, demonstrating an unexpected maturity. Perhaps I misjudged him, assuming that his charm and confidence couldn't coexist with empathy.

I tell him about Jock's drug bust and the strange connection between Tony and Aiden.

'What Kate said about Ian and Georgina Fletcher was interesting. Had you ever heard rumours they're involved in drugs?'

'No,' says Lane thoughtfully. 'They seem like pretty simple people who mainly keep to themselves. Hippies, like Kate said. Maybe ask Tommy though? He might know more.'

I have zero interest in asking Tommy for any kind of help. 'We'll just ask them direct later today. Maybe they know more about their son's leisure activities than they've been willing to let on.'

My phone starts to ring: Mac. I switch it to silent, watching his name glow on the screen until my voicemail kicks in.

Lane glances from me to the phone but simply says, 'It's pretty strange that one of those guys from the caravan park suddenly left on Monday, don't you think?'

'Yes, I'm very keen to have a chat to all of them.' I glance at the highlighted names again, wondering if we finally have a decent lead. 'Let's head to the beach and see if we can track them down.'

My phone starts to ring again. This time it's Grange. His awkward voice comes down the line in a jumble. 'Hi, ah, Detective Woodstock. Bit of an update for you. We've just spoken to a woman called Freya Hernandez, Abbey's music teacher. We called the principal earlier, who reckoned Freya was worth talking to because Abbey often went to school early to practise music and spent a lot of time with her. Abbey plays flute, I think. Or maybe it was the clarinet.' Grange reminds me of a puppy trying to keep his legs in order. 'Anyway, I just rang Freya and she seemed pretty keen to talk to us about something that happened recently to do with Abbey, but we're about to leave for the autopsy.'

I check the time. 'Do you have her address?' When the call ends, I tell Lane, 'Slight detour. I'm going to speak to Abbey's music teacher. I assume this street is nearby?' I hold out my scrawled note, and he nods. 'Let's split up. I'll speak to Freya, and you see if you can track down the British guys at the beach.'

Lane soon pulls up at a sweet little cottage a few streets back from the shore. My nausea returns the second I get out of the car but is not nearly as brutal as it was earlier.

I bend back down to level with Lane. 'We need to escalate the search for Robert Weston. Whether he was the guy who left on Monday or not, we need to find him—or both of them, as the case may be. Maybe contact the cab company and see if you can find out where the guy went on Monday, then run a passport and credit-card check on Weston. We might need to dig into his emails and Facebook as well.'

'Done,' says Lane confidently.

'I'll call you when I'm finished here and we'll see if we've got time to chat to any of Abbey's co-workers before we meet the Fletchers.'

'Hope you're feeling okay,' he says and drives off.

I open the wooden gate, step onto the narrow porch and ring the old-fashioned bell. The wind stirs a birdcage hanging from the rafters, and a bright green parrot with beady eyes regards me solemnly, tipping his head to the left and then the right.

An elfin woman with curly black hair opens the door. 'Hello?' She's dressed in a white slip.

'Freya Hernandez? I'm Detective Sergeant Gemma Woodstock. You spoke to one of my constables earlier but he's tied up, so I thought I'd come around myself.'

'Yes!' Freya says dramatically. 'Please come in.'

She hustles me into a tiny lounge room with two large cane chairs and a puffy-looking cushion on the floor that's covered in dog hair. Dozens of photos of Freya and a dark-skinned man with a huge smile line the bookshelves.

'I am so worried about Abbey, I can't even tell you,' she says, her bird-like frame dwarfed by the huge chair. Her dark brown eyes fill with tears. 'The poor girl,' she murmurs, clutching her face. 'My mind just won't stop going to the most awful places. Especially after what happened to Rick. We were trying to arrange a memorial— you know, on behalf of the school—but apparently his parents don't want us to. They want a private funeral. I just think we need to do something.' She traces her fingers under her eyes. 'People are upset and they need closure.'

My mind serves me up an unhelpful image of Nicki Mara's face.

'We're doing everything we can to locate Abbey,' I say. 'You're her music teacher, is that right?'

'Yes, yes. She is such an amazing girl. Especially considering . . .'

'Considering what?'

She shoots me a look. 'I'm pretty sure her father is violent toward her. He came up to the school once to complain about her flute lessons costing extra. And he was just awful, so intimidating.'

'Did Abbey confide in you that Daniel was abusive?'

Freya bites her lip. 'Not exactly, though that's the impression I got. She never outright accused him of anything but you could read between the lines.'

'My colleague said you were keen to talk to us about something that happened to Abbey?'

Freya leans forward again, exposing her bony décolletage. 'Yes—I mean, I don't know anything specific, I wish I did, but a few weeks ago she came to school early to practise like she always does, and she was really upset. She walked in and just burst into tears. I've never seen her like that before and I've been thinking about it all week. I'm sure it had something to do with her disappearing.'

'Did she say what was wrong?'

'She didn't want to talk about it. I think she was embarrassed she was so upset. When she first started crying I jumped up to comfort her, and she said she was scared.'

'Scared? Of what, her dad?'

'That's what I thought. But when I asked her if that was it, she said no. I don't think she was lying—her dad had upset her in the past and she'd always been okay to talk about it. This was different. She seemed . . . spooked.' Freya's hands flutter in front of her. 'It's hard to explain but I could tell it wasn't just because of a silly argument.'

'Maybe she was having trouble with her boyfriend?'

Freya shakes her head sadly. 'No, I don't think she was upset about Rick. I taught him a few years ago, so I knew him a little. I asked Abbey if they were okay, figuring maybe they'd broken up or something, and she said it wasn't him.'

I consider Freya. Although she strikes me as someone a teenage girl might confide in, perhaps she has inflated the trust Abbey had in her. The girl might not have wanted to admit that a fight with Rick or a run-in with her dad had made her so visibly upset.

'When was this?' I ask.

'At the end of February—Wednesday the twenty-third, I just double-checked. She was absolutely fine the day before, that's why it seemed strange. Something definitely happened to make her so upset.' Freya frowns. 'I actually thought she'd been generally

happier all year. I said to my husband she'd been like a different
person since Christmas. Far more confident. And talking about her
future, asking about career options. But ever since that Wednesday
she was more reserved and nervous.'

'What do you think happened, Freya?'

She grips her hands together. 'I don't know, but when I heard
she disappeared I just kept thinking maybe someone was threatening her or had tried to hurt her.' Her jaw trembles. 'I wish I'd said
something.'

I ask Freya a few questions about Abbey's friends and whether
she noticed unwanted attention from any of the girl's classmates,
but the music teacher offers nothing helpful, unable to focus on
anything beyond her sense of guilt.

The sun is hovering directly above when I step back through her
gate. I slip on my sunglasses and head toward the shops as I dial
Lane's number. 'Any luck?'

He sounds a little puffed. 'No, I can't find them. I looked up and
down the beach and asked if anyone knew them but got nothing.
I tried to call both the phone numbers Kate had, but they went to
voicemail so I left messages. And I requested all the info on Robert
Weston, so hopefully stuff starts to roll in soon.'

'Okay, well, I guess we wait.'

I fill Lane in on my conversation with Freya.

'Maybe Abbey had a fight with Rick that night?' he says.

'Maybe, but I don't understand why she wouldn't just tell Freya
about that. It seems like they were pretty close. Plus, if she and Rick
had a falling out that night it would probably have to have been
over the phone. Based on her payslips she starts work at 4 pm on
Tuesday nights and works until 9.30 or 10 pm. I can't imagine she
was allowed to see Rick after that—surely Daniel wouldn't let her
stay out late on a school night.'

'Maybe Rick gave her a lift home after her shift and they argued then?'

'It's possible.' I sigh. 'They did break up a month later, so clearly something wasn't right between them.'

'Do you want me to come get you?'

'No, I'm almost at the supermarket. Meet me there?'

'The supermarket?'

'Yes. I'm thinking we should find out if anyone at Abbey's workplace knows why she was so upset that Wednesday morning.'

Wednesday, 13 April

11.36 am

An old man is perched on his walking frame next to the main door of the supermarket, an ancient kelpie curled up at his feet. He has a cigarette jammed between his lips, its thread of smoke trailing skyward.

The smell makes me think of Mac. He's been a smoker since he was a teenager and hasn't been able to totally kick the habit; he has one cigarette every evening with a glass of merlot. A sharp crack in his otherwise staggering self-control.

I walk ahead of Lane but the supermarket's automatic doors aren't as reactive as I expected, and much to the amusement of the smoking man I do a strange double-step before they jerk open. Directly in front of us, a blow-up doll sits in a kiddie pool full of Easter eggs; she's dressed as a lifesaver with arm floaties and an inflatable ring, and holds a sign: *Support the Fairhaven Beach Heroes!*

There are only four aisles, a small fruit and veggie section near the entry, and a modest frozen food section parallel to the checkout. A bucket of unfortunate-looking bouquets is oddly positioned in front of a fridge door, each plastic casing clumsily dotted

with a fluorescent price sticker. Ambling up and down the aisles
are a few shoppers with baskets hooked over their arms. Britney
Spears is playing softly beneath the slow repetitive *beep-beep-beep*
of items being scanned. It reminds me of the monitors in Smithson's
hospital, and for a second the shock of Scott's death is almost sharp
enough to bring me to my knees.

I pause and lean forward slightly.

Lane's eyebrows slope together. 'Do you feel sick again?'

'No, I'm fine. Can you see if the manager is here?'

'She's right over there.' Lane nods at the checkouts. 'Closest to
the door.'

Three people are on the checkouts, all facing away from us.
I head to the third one and join the queue, and within minutes I'm
standing in front of a short woman with light brown skin and black
curly hair. Her smile is wide and her name tag reads *Min*. She's
wearing Easter Bunny earrings. When Min notices Lane standing
beside me, her smile fades away.

'Hello. I'm Detective Gemma Woodstock.'

'You're here about Abbey,' she says, her expression turning serious.

'Yes. I understand she was an employee here.'

'I'm Minella Fererra, but everyone calls me Min. I run this
shop with my husband, Des. Abby has been working here for over
eighteen months now. She came here looking for a job the day she
turned fourteen.' Min smiles sadly. 'She was very prepared with a
proper résumé and references from her teachers. We were happy to
offer her a job.'

'Is your husband here today?'

'Yes, he's out the back.'

'We need to speak to both of you,' I glance at the two checkout
girls, who are robotically scanning and bagging items, 'and your
staff as well.'

'Of course. This way, please.'

We follow Min down an aisle and out into a poky tearoom. A man in his fifties is rummaging through a plastic container full of rubber bands. 'Honey, do you know where . . . Whoa, hello, sorry.' He springs to his feet. 'I'm Des.'

As Min tells him we need to speak to them about Abbey, Des's face instantly turns sombre.

She gestures to a small wooden table. 'Please sit.'

'What was Abbey like as a worker?' I ask.

'Very good,' Min replies and looks to Des, who nods. 'She never lets us down. She works three shifts every week and, apart from a few shifts in March, she never even called in sick. I had her help with the ordering sometimes, she was very mature.'

'When was the last time you saw her?' asks Lane.

Min drops her eyes and fiddles with her rings. 'On Saturday. Her shift was 8 am until 3 pm. I just waved her off and said I'd see her on Tuesday. I couldn't believe it when I heard she was missing—it's just terrible.'

Lane clears his throat and says, 'How did Abbey seem on Saturday?'

'A little quiet. Not that I thought anything of it at the time, but I don't think she seemed like herself. Earlier in the year she was so happy, then these past few weeks she's been a bit flat. Last Tuesday I asked her to run some supplies over to the cafes and the pub, but she said she'd hurt her leg. She seemed quite upset about it.'

I exchange a look with Lane, confirming this is the first he's heard of the injury as well. Surely Abbey couldn't have ridden her bike to the party if her leg was sore.

'Could you see an injury?' I ask.

'No, and when I asked her about it—after I sent one of the others off to deliver the stock—she definitely didn't want to talk about it. I just assumed it was her dad again.'

'Again?'

'Yes. Abbey often had bruises. She always said they were from sport, but I've long suspected her father. We used to be friendly with Dot, that's partly why I was so keen to hire Abbey.' Min fusses with her hands before she looks at me imploringly. 'It was our way of helping.'

Getting Abbey out of that hellhole of a house would have been a much better way to help her, but Min was hardly alone in doling out the metaphorical bandaids.

'Abbey worked a shift here every Tuesday afternoon into the evening, is that right?'

Min's gaze drifts to the roster hanging on the wall. 'Yep, she works Tuesdays and Thursdays after school until close, and Saturdays plus extra shifts in the holidays.'

'Do you recall anything that took place during one of her Tuesday shifts about five weeks ago?'

Min's faint eyebrows draw together. 'Like what?'

'Unfortunately I can't be more specific, we're just keen to know if anything happened that seemed out of the ordinary.'

'Do you know the date?' She strains to get to her feet as she shuffles over to the roster.

'Tuesday twenty-second February.'

After flipping a few pages, Min trails her finger along the paper. 'Abbey worked that day with Erin. You were here too, Desi.'

He shrugs. 'Nothing stands out. I'm normally out the back checking the stock on Tuesdays. We get most of our deliveries that day and we despatch orders too, so there's generally a fair bit to work through.'

'Apparently Abbey was quite upset the next morning, so we wondered if something might have gone awry at work.'

Min and Des continue to look bewildered, and I smother a sigh. 'What time was her shift that day?'

'Same as always, 4 to 9 pm,' says Min.

'So, straight after school?'

'Yes, we structured the shifts so the younger kids could work here. We have a few part-timers, local mums mainly, to support us during the day, then the girls come here straight from school and get changed into their uniforms. For a five-hour shift they each get a twenty-minute break either at 6 pm or 6.20 pm.'

'How does she get to work?'

'Sometimes her boyfriend drives her. Lately she's been coming on her bike.'

'And so she rides home?' says Lane.

Min and Des exchange a look. 'Yes. It's not far, and to be honest I've never thought about it. I guess I think of Fairhaven as a safe place.'

'Do you have internal security cameras?'

Nodding, Min draws herself upright, clearly pleased at finally being able to answer something in the affirmative. 'We have them on the main doors and the check-out area, and we have one over the safe.' She points. 'Just there.'

We all turn to look at the black shiny eye of the lens.

'How long do you keep the footage?' asks Lane.

She deflates slightly. 'Only a week.'

No one speaks for a moment, and I glance around the small room. Through the door next to the fridge I see a stockroom area with boxes piled high in rows. I look at Des; his head is bent forward revealing the early stages of baldness, and his knee bobs up and down involuntarily. My instincts tell me he is a good man.

But he was here that night—did he do something to upset Abbey?

'Did you speak to Abbey much, Mr Fererra?'

His eyebrows bounce upward. 'No, not really. I was nice to her, of course, but I left all the staff management to Min. I don't understand teenage girls. But we've been lucky, really. All our staff are very reliable, never give us any trouble, so I just let them do their thing. It's a small town,' he adds. 'We know most of our customers, and everyone is very nice. And then on the holidays it's so busy that there's no time to talk anyway.'

'We really hope you find her,' says Min, her hand back at her throat.

'Yes, we hope so too.' I battle a wave of frustration: *I'm trying.* 'If you remember anything, especially about that Tuesday shift in February, please let us know.'

'Yes, of course. We'll do whatever we can to help. Des joined the search last Sunday.' Min's chin wobbles as she looks at her husband. 'I kept thinking, *My god, what if they find her out there somewhere?* And then I heard about her boyfriend and, well, it's just awful. I don't really know what to think. I mean, who would do something like that? It can't be a local.' She begins to cry. 'I know everyone is saying it was her dad but I can't bear the thought he would hurt her.' Min looks at me and then at Lane. 'Like that,' she adds.

I let a silence settle over the room for a few beats before I say, 'We need to talk to the rest of your staff, especially anyone who regularly worked shifts with Abbey.'

Min's face pulls tight, and her eyes dart around the room nervously. 'It's mainly Erin who works with her. They're pretty friendly, I think. Taylor sometimes works Saturdays with her. You can talk to them now if it's one at a time. We can easily manage the tills with two people.'

'Thanks.'

Taylor's heavy make-up weighs down her thin face. She enters the room as if she's walking the plank. I give her a reassuring smile when she takes a seat opposite.

Initially I let Lane take the lead. He's good with Taylor, lulling her into easy conversation and explaining we need to gather as much information as we can. She noticeably relaxes and even cracks a smile. Then he gently asks her about Abbey.

No, she doesn't know her very well even though she's known her since—well, forever. Yes, they chatted occasionally but they barely had shifts together. Taylor has mainly worked during the day since she left school two years ago, so their paths only cross on Saturdays and it's usually too busy to chat. Taylor thought that Abbey seemed nice enough. Taylor's younger brother is friendly with the Clark twins, but her parents never let him go to their house because everyone knows Daniel is crazy. Taylor last saw Abbey just over two weeks ago and thought she seemed a bit down but nothing especially stood out.

I stay in the tearoom while Lane walks Taylor out and fetches Erin. In contrast to Taylor, she is fresh-faced with womanly curves I imagine she oscillates between loving and hating. She is far more insightful than Taylor but also much more upset.

'Me and Abbey are pretty good friends,' she says. 'I left school last year but I still do the afternoon shifts on Tuesday and Wednesday 'cause Min already had people during the day. I didn't really know Abbey at school but we chat here. Sometimes it's not that busy, especially in winter, so there's a lot of time to kill.'

'Who else is she friendly with?' Lane asks.

Erin picks at the quick of her fingernails. 'Some of the other girls at school, I guess. And obviously she was with Rick.' She pulls a piece of skin away from her nail, bright red blood pooling in her cuticle. 'I can't believe he's dead.'

'Yes,' I say. 'We are still in the very early stages of that investigation.'

Erin nods and starts combing through her thick hair with her fingers.

'Were you at the party on Saturday?' I ask.

'My brother and I went together—he's friends with Beth Kinlon, whose house it was.'

'Did you speak to Abbey that night?' says Lane.

'A bit. My brother and I got there late, 'cause we were watching a movie at home with Mum and Dad first. It was pretty wild by the time we turned up. Everyone was off their faces, and there were heaps of people I didn't know. I saw Abbey in the backyard, I said hi, but she was talking to Rick.' Erin's eyes flicker to the floor.

'You didn't like Rick?' I ask.

She lifts her head, but I notice her jaw is shaking. 'I'm sad he died, but he was a bully. Not, like, physically or anything. More emotionally.' She presses her hands against her knees. 'That probably sounds dumb.'

'It doesn't sound dumb at all,' says Lane kindly.

The corners of her mouth turn up. 'Yeah, well, he used to be a real jerk to my brother when they were at school together.'

Lane makes a few notes, sympathy on his face.

'Did you notice anything at the party that seemed odd?' says Lane. 'Was Abbey talking to people you didn't know or acting differently from usual?'

Erin makes a frustrated whimper. 'I'm trying to remember but I just don't know. I guess I wasn't really paying attention. Like I said, I saw her talking to Rick outside. And later in the night I saw her talking to some backpackers, they've been into the shop a few times. One of them kept asking her out, but I think he was just, like, mucking around. Abbey and I were laughing about it the other day.'

Lane and I exchange glances at this.

'Do you know his name?' asks Lane.

Erin begins to look worried. 'No, sorry. I know they were English but I didn't really talk to them.'

'When did they come into the shop?'

'A few times over the past few weeks. I think they came in last Tuesday afternoon.'

'And it was definitely the same guys you saw her talking to at the party?'

'I'm pretty sure.' Erin sneaks a look up at me through her long lashes. '*I* was a bit of mess, to be honest though. We drank on the way and my brother pretty much had to carry me home. I think we got in just after eleven.'

'Did Abbey like the guy who kept asking her out?'

Erin shrugs. 'I don't think so. She just thought it was funny how full on he was. He picked her a flower the other day, which she thought was sweet.'

'Did she seem like she wanted to talk to him at the party?'

'I don't know. I just figured she was trying to make Rick jealous.'

'Was that what their relationship was like? Making each other jealous?'

'I don't know. I guess I always thought Abbey would get out of Fairhaven and move to the city. I don't think she was as serious about Rick as he was about her.'

'Did she ever say anything to you about breaking up with him?' I ask.

'No, not to me.' Her eyes fill with tears. 'Do you think someone at the party hurt her?' Erin's voice drops to a whisper. 'Or that Rick did? My mum reckons Daniel killed him because he found out he hurt Abbey.'

'We can't comment on that,' I say gently. 'But, Erin, I'm wondering whether anything ever happened at work to upset Abbey?'

'No, I can't think of anything.'

'What about on Tuesday the twenty-second of February? Was that maybe when the backpackers came into the shop?'

'Um, it might have been. I'm really not sure, but they weren't, like, mean to her or anything. They were just being funny and flirting with her.' Erin's smooth forehead wrinkles. 'That was about a week after Valentine's Day. Me and my boyfriend broke up in early Feb, so we didn't go out like we were supposed to, but then we got back together and he wanted to see me that night. I had to be home straight after work, but Abbey said I could leave early so I could see him for a bit. She said she didn't mind.'

'So she was left alone to close the shop?'

'Yes,' says Erin meekly, 'but that wasn't weird. One of us would usually do a final clean and close once the money was in the safe.'

'What time did Mr Fererra leave that night?'

'He normally leaves at 7.25 pm so he can get home to watch the *7.30 Report*. He and Min live one street back from the shop so it only takes them a few minutes to get home.'

'So Mr Gordon left at 7.25 pm that night?'

Erin lifts her shoulders. 'He was definitely gone when I left at nine-thirty. I don't know the exact time.'

'Where did you and your boyfriend go?'

She flushes deeply. 'Just for a drive up to one of the lookouts. You know, we talked and stuff. Then he dropped me home.'

'Okay. And before you left nothing happened that upset Abbey? She didn't say anything?'

'No, she seemed fine.'

'She and Rick were fine?'

'Yeah, though maybe he'd been, like, coming in a bit less than he used to, but Abbey didn't say anything was wrong.' Erin leans forward slightly, her face slowly returning to its normal colour.

'Do you know if she met him after her shift that night?' I ask.

'No idea, but I doubt it—during the week she just rides her bike straight home.'

'And what about since then? She never mentioned anything was upsetting her?'

For a few moments Erin doesn't reply. 'She didn't *say* anything but she did seem a bit weird.'

'How do you mean?'

'It's hard to explain. Like, she just seemed on edge.'

'Did you ask her about it?' says Lane.

'I tried. About two weeks ago we were closing up and I said she seemed out of it but she just fobbed me off.' Erin chews the inside of her cheek. Her eyes dart around as if she's looking for the answers on the shelves above us. 'I just figured she'd had a run-in with her dad or something. Or Rick maybe.' Erin takes a deep shuddery breath. 'And she seemed a bit . . . I dunno.'

My phone buzzes in my pocket. Ignoring it, I let a hint of impatience into my voice. 'Erin, if there's anything you know that will help us find her, you need to tell us. It's really important.'

Tears bud in Erin's eyes and run down her cheeks when she blinks. 'I don't know anything, I really don't. It's just, something happened last week that seemed strange but maybe I'm just being stupid.'

Lane is sitting on the edge of his seat, looking intently at Erin. 'It doesn't matter if it seems silly. Little details can end up being really important.'

Erin takes a tissue from the box on the table. 'Well, it wasn't anything she said, it's just that I saw her last weekend.'

'The one before she went missing?' I say.

'Yeah. Mum was driving me home after netball on Saturday night, and I saw Abbey standing next to a tree near the police station, at the start of the driveway.'

'What was she doing?' I say.

'I don't know. She was just, like, standing there staring at the station. I don't think she saw me.'

Lane leans forward, his elbows on his knees. 'She was just standing there?' he echoes.

Erin tucks her hair behind her ears, then repeats the motion a few times. 'It was just, she looked really nervous. Maybe she was even crying.' A pained expression washes over Erin's own tear-stained face. 'It looked like she wanted to go into the station and ask for help.'

Wednesday, 13 April
1.28 pm

I grab a plastic cup of fruit salad from the supermarket's Fresh 2 Go section and join Lane on the park bench across the road. He wolfs down a sweaty sausage roll smeared with sauce from the petrol station, following this up with swigs of chocolate milk. He's gone very quiet and I suspect the intensity of our investigations is starting to take its toll. I pick unenthusiastically at the cubes of fruit before replacing the lid and returning the missed call from the station.

Noah answers. 'Hi, Detective Woodstock. I was just passing on a message. Someone from the forensics team in Byron called to say nothing turned up on the possum. Does that make sense?'

I had all but forgotten about the possum but now I picture someone placing the bloody carcass outside our door, metres from my sleeping son, and feel a surge of anger. 'Yes, and thanks for passing on the message. Is everything else going okay?'

'All good here. There have been quite a few calls about the Fletcher murder but I don't think there's much that'll be useful for you. Most callers have just wanted to talk about when they last saw Rick or how scared they are that something like this might happen again. None of the callers so far have information about the attack.'

'Okay, well, thanks for holding the fort. I'll see you later.'

I stretch out my legs as I try to pin down the theory that's been rattling around in my mind following our conversation with Erin and my interview with Freya.

Lane's phone rings and he wanders off, standing under the shade of a huge gum. I call Tran. Her greeting is frosty but I just launch into my updates, trying to paper over the awkwardness I feel after hanging up on her yesterday.

'The thing is, if Rick and Aiden were dealing, I would have expected to find something at the house. Anyway, we're seeing their parents shortly, so we'll question them about it too. If the caravan park owner is right about them being involved in drugs, maybe they know more than they're letting on.'

'Make sure you're very careful, Gemma,' says Tran curtly. 'They have just lost their son.'

'Of course.'

'How did you go with Daniel's car?'

'He had no issue with it being searched,' I say. 'We won't get anything official back until next week but the techs say there wasn't any obvious blood residue or evidence of a recent clean.'

'I guess that would have been asking too much,' says Tran with a sigh.

'Nothing came back on the possum either,' I say.

'I guess it would have been a long shot. Either way, I'm glad we have you at the Gordons' house.' She pauses. 'Gemma?' she says finally, surprising me by sounding a little nervous.

'Yes?'

'Are you sure you're okay?'

'Yes, I'm fine. Why?'

'I spoke to Tommy earlier. He said he thought you were a bit overwhelmed.'

'I'm not,' I say, my chest compressing. 'I work cases like this all the time.'

'I know how experienced you are, of course, but we need real focus on this. I've been made aware of your recent circumstances, and I have to say it has me a bit worried about your current ability to lead something like this properly.'

I grip the phone so hard my knuckles crack. 'Tommy needs to mind his own business. He's dosed up on so many painkillers he wouldn't have a clue what's going on.' I know I sound petulant but I can't help it, the fury pouring from my mouth like lava. 'How dare he come running to you like a schoolkid. That is such bullshit.'

'He's just concerned,' says Tran, without a hint of emotion.

'Concerned my arse,' I retort. 'I can't believe you're not seeing this for what it is.'

'I can only go on what I'm being told, Gemma, and Tommy's concerned.' Tran sounds almost evangelical. 'And he obviously has a vested interest in his squad. I have no doubt he's a bit put out with you replacing him on two of the biggest cases to hit the town in years, but he's well respected and has a lot of local knowledge. I'd be using him as much as you can.'

It's all I can do not to throw my phone onto the road.

Lane returns, plonking himself back down on the bench. I tell Tran that I will speak to her later and end the call. I turn to Lane, seething while trying to hide it. 'Is everything alright?' I ask, noticing his expression.

'I got a text back from one of the Brits, William Mayne. I guess he's the one the caravan park staff reported to Kate for taking those videos. He said he and his mates are out on one of the fishing trawlers and barely have reception. They are back late tonight.

He confirmed that Robert Weston is their mate and that he was staying with them, but he left for Sydney on Monday, so at least we know it's the same person. I said they need to be at the caravan park at nine tomorrow morning to meet with us. That will work, won't it?'

I sigh. 'I guess it will have to.' I press my fingers into my temples. 'Actually, that's good. I'll try to speak to Dot before that. Her shift at the caravan park starts at 8 am.'

'Do you give much weight to what Erin said?' Lane ventures. 'You know, about seeing Abbey near the police station? It's not very conclusive—she could have been doing anything.'

'It's certainly not hard evidence, but maybe that's what Saturday night was actually about. Maybe Abbey was planning on coming to you for help and then chickened out at the last minute and made up the story about the stolen bike?'

Lane looks doubtful. 'I guess it's possible but she seemed pretty genuine to me.'

I sigh again. 'She probably was. It's just, that bloody bike really bothers me. It doesn't make sense. Plus, if Freya's right and something did upset Abbey recently, she might have had a reason to go to the police. I wonder what it was.' I look back over at the supermarket. 'Maybe a customer said something, or Weston was hassling her.' I shake my head. 'But then why would she write back to him? That was only last week.'

Lane exhales heavily. 'I reckon it was probably just her dad. He was definitely getting worse and maybe she didn't want to go home after the fight they had. I'm starting to think she just hitchhiked out of town or something.'

'That's possible.'

Lane's hands have curled into fists but I don't think he's noticed.

We all find this hard, our inability to protect the most vulnerable against such a blatant abuse of power. The betrayal the victims feel is extended to many cops, they end up feeling betrayed by the whole system. I certainly know I have felt this way over the years.

I clear my throat. 'You attended the last two calls out there, didn't you?'

'Yeah. It's such bullshit. How he can act like that and no one can do anything about it.'

'I know,' I say with a grimace. 'Did Abbey ever try to talk to you about what was going on?'

His eyes go to his shoes. 'Not really. It was obvious she was worried about her mum and her brothers. I think that's why she never said anything—she was terrified of what Daniel might do to Dot and the kids. She basically had to be the adult. It was such a mess.'

'Situations like that are never easy.'

We sit in silence for a few moments. On the nearby phone booth the poster with Abbey's smiling face flaps in the breeze, and we both stare at it.

I check the time and heave myself to my feet. 'Let's go. We need to get back to the station to meet the Fletchers.'

Georgina and Ian Fletcher are much younger than I expected and very stylish in a casual homemade way. Ian's blond hair is long like Rick's, and Georgina wouldn't look out of place at Woodstock. Under different circumstances I suspect they'd be an exceptionally attractive couple, but their grief has zapped their tans and reduced them to barely coherent mumbling and bouts of sobbing.

'We blame ourselves,' says Georgina, one hand clutching her husband's and the other gripped around her throat. 'We shouldn't have let them live by themselves but, well . . .' She trails off and looks at Ian.

'Aiden's twenty,' he says, 'and Rick was almost eighteen.' His voice cracks. 'We trust our boys but I guess we never thought about anyone hurting them, not like this.'

The Fletchers both start sobbing, and I wait for them to calm before I coax out more details about Rick and Aiden.

'We last saw both boys two Sundays ago—all the kids come to lunch on Sunday,' says Georgina. 'Sometimes they bring a friend or a girlfriend or whatever but they rarely miss it.' She tugs on the hem of her skirt. 'Aiden has been making it less lately because of work, but the other two always come.'

'We didn't meet last Sunday,' adds Ian, 'because of Abbey.'

'Was Rick the one to inform you about that?' I ask.

'Yes,' says Georgina, 'Rick called us after her father came to his house. He was very worried about her but I think he hoped she'd just gone to stay at a friend's for a while.'

'Did Abbey ever come to your family lunches?'

Georgina blinks and they both nod.

'Sometimes,' she says. 'Daniel hated her spending time with Rick, which really upset him.'

'I knew Daniel in high school,' Ian says. 'I never liked him.' He presses a fist to his eye. 'If I'm honest I didn't like Rick having anything to do with him—but Abbey was a lovely girl. Rick was wild about her.'

'I felt sorry for Abbey,' says Georgina, starting to cry again, 'and I know people are saying Rick did something to her, and that's why she's missing, but it's not true. He adored her.'

I can already tell that Rick's parents aren't going to provide us with a breakthrough. They clearly loved their son and saw him frequently, but their relationship existed at a surface level; their view of him seems naive and slightly romanticised. At least they acknowledge that despite Rick being bright, he struggled with school.

'We were so pleased when he decided to start the landscaping business,' Georgina tells us. 'He was so entrepreneurial, we knew he would do so well.'

'Do you have any idea where Aiden is, Mr Fletcher?'

'No idea,' says Ian. 'It's so unlike him to take off like that, but he and Rick were so close. He's in shock.'

'Mrs Fletcher?'

'No.' She pulls her left earring down, stretching her earlobe grotesquely. 'I'm so worried about him.' Her face collapses. 'Both my boys are gone.'

'Aiden sleeps in his van sometimes,' adds Ian. 'You know, on camping trips and things like that. He can be a bit of a free spirit. I never used to worry about it, and now everything seems so dangerous.'

'We're doing all we can to track him down, but if you think of anywhere he might be or someone he might be with, please let us know. We think he might have information that will help us find out who attacked Rick.'

'I'm sure he would have said if he knew anything,' whispers Georgina, then navigates another bout of grief. They are clearly devastated but I detect a caution that I can't quite place. It reminds me of what Kate said about them.

'We'd like to conduct a search of your property,' I say bluntly.

They both visibly tense.

'Why?' says Ian.

'Just to rule a few things out. We've searched Rick and Aiden's place but there might be other clues at your property. I'm sure you're happy to do anything you can to help us find Abbey and get justice for Rick.'

'When?' asks Georgina, an edge to her voice.

'Straight away. A team will most likely be sent out there this afternoon, if that's okay.'

Still gripping each other's hands, they fall into silence.

'That's fine,' says Ian softly.

I exchange a glance with Lane. 'We have everything we need for now,' I say. 'We'll be in touch.'

They stagger to their feet, Ian's arm around Georgina's waifish waist. She doesn't look much older than her sons. 'The other cop,' she pauses to swallow, 'said they are doing the autopsy today.'

'Yes, that's right,' I say gently.

'Oh god. I can't bear it. When you have a baby, you just never think . . . I mean, you *worry* of course, but you never think *this*.'

'No.' Suddenly her agony is unbearable to me. 'I'm so sorry about Rick.'

Lane walks them out and I sink into my chair, utterly drained. Georgina is right: you never associate that kind of pain with your child, but from the moment of their birth, sometimes from their conception, you are exposed—vulnerable to the soul-destroying grief that only their absence can create.

Lane returns, frowning. 'They're hiding something.'

'I agree. And so is Aiden, wherever he is.'

'I'll organise the search of their property.' Lane trots off to his desk. I can hear Noah on the phone in the front room and, underneath that, the cicadas. The beige fan in the corner circles drunkenly, ruffling the plastic bin liner every time it reaches its left rotation.

I watch the recording of Rick's interview again. Then, tipping my head from side to side, I stretch my aching neck. All my instincts tell me Rick lied about not seeing Abbey again after the party.

'Hey,' says Lane, eyes on his screen, 'I'm going through all of Robert Weston's Facebook messages. Last year it looks like he messaged two girls he didn't know, just like he did with Abbey.'

I read over Lane's shoulder. The messages are almost identical to the ones I read the other night: light-hearted declarations of attraction based on a chance meeting.

'He seems to have quite the script,' I say. 'Keep going through his accounts. See if you can work out where he is.'

Lane nods. 'It's a bit creepy, isn't it?'

I press my lips together. 'I'm not sure yet, but considering he left town on Monday, it doesn't look good.'

'And then Aiden bailed on Tuesday.'

'I know.' I rub my eyes. 'I'm starting to wonder about Aiden's alibi.'

'It's pretty solid,' says Lane doubtfully.

'The alibi for his van certainly is—we know it went in and out of Sydney because of the toll points, but what if he wasn't driving it? What if he was in Fairhaven the whole time?'

'Then who was driving his van?'

'No idea,' I say, 'but I think we need to dig into it a bit further. Maybe the brothers weren't as close as they seemed.' I think back to the Nicki Mara case and my calls with her father, Lucas. His grief was real but it hid the truth, the biggest clue of all: his role in her disappearance. Maybe Aiden Fletcher is the same?

'And if he wasn't in Sydney, there's a chance he was here on Saturday night too,' I add.

'His credit card was used to buy some food in Sydney,' Lane reminds me. 'And petrol.'

'I know, and this might go nowhere, but see if you can pull any CCTV from the purchase times. I'd much rather be sure he wasn't here than assume he wasn't.'

Lane nods and turns back to his computer.

I have a quick look at Aiden Fletcher's Facebook and Instagram pages as well as his emails. He is barely active online; occasionally he posts surfing shots and sporadic news articles about climate change. As I relisten to the voice message Rick left the police on Sunday night, I remember Aiden saying he spoke to Rick that afternoon after Daniel had paid him a visit.

I pull up Aiden's phone records. 'Was there a landline at the brothers' house?' I ask Lane. 'Maybe a number registered in the parents' name?'

'What?' says Lane, eyes glued to Robert Weston's online world. 'Ah, no—no landline.'

'Well, then Aiden lied.'

'About what?'

'Aiden said he spoke to Rick on Sunday about Daniel Clark, but there was no call between the two of them.' I glance back down at the rows of calls and texts. 'At least not on their mobiles. According to this, they hadn't spoken for over a week.'

Lane turns around. 'That's weird.'

It all comes together in my mind. 'I think they were using burner phones. It's the only thing that makes sense. Their official call logs are too lean and too inconsistent. For brothers who were allegedly so close, they weren't in touch much based on these records.' I drum my fingers on the desk, thinking out loud. 'So why be off the grid? Drugs? Theft? Something else? Rick and Aiden might have got in over their heads on some scheme. Abbey might have been collateral damage.'

Lane nods slowly. 'Tommy reckons Daniel was the one who attacked Rick.'

'You've been talking to Tommy about the case?' I say, trying to keep my voice light.

'Not really,' Lane stammers. 'I just wanted to check in on him, you know, make sure he was doing okay, and we had a quick chat about it then.'

Frustration ripples through me but I can't berate Lane without seeming completely childish. I look back at the constellation of information on the case board. 'Maybe Rick knew his drug contacts had taken Abbey's bike from the party, and that's why he lied about seeing her leave on it.'

Lane stops to think about it. 'Yeah, that works. They could have been following her when she went to the station.' He pauses again. 'And when she left.'

I prod my foot at the carpet as panic seizes me. God, I just want to find her. The thought of another horrible ending is unbearable. Worse again is the thought of leaving here with no answers.

'I still don't get why she'd turn down a lift home in the middle of the night,' I say. 'She must have been planning to go somewhere she didn't want you to know about.'

The office door swings open, and de Luca and Grange walk in. They bring death with them: the harsh scent of chemicals and the indefinable fragrance that's unique to a morgue.

I point to the meeting room. 'Great, you're back. Let's all meet in, say, five minutes? We've got a bit to fill you in on.'

They don't move.

'What's going on? Did something happen at the autopsy?'

'The footage from the council came in while we were driving back,' says de Luca.

'Finally,' I say. 'Have you looked at any of it yet?'

'Yes.' Grange's Adam's apple bulges from his neck. 'She's on it. Abbey.'

Wednesday, 13 April

4.58 pm

'Abbey is on the footage?'

'Yeah,' says Grange.

Lane's eyes widen. 'Where?'

'In the main street.'

I point to the meeting room. 'Load it up, let's all watch it now.'

We file into the stuffy meeting room and wait impatiently while Grange fiddles with his laptop and connects cords to the dated TV unit on wheels in the corner. Fairhaven's main street appears on the screen. Grange drags the file to the footage that was captured at 12.14 am—and Abbey appears. Her long hair is thick and loose, making it hard to see her face, but even on the grainy footage she's clearly agitated. Her eyes are large and her movements jerky, adrenaline charging through her system. She dashes across the middle of the road to the top of the beach path where Lane and I sat and ate this afternoon before she disappears from view.

'Play it again.' I squint at the vision as the tape rolls again. Everything about Abbey's body language is primal and urgent, but there's certainly no one chasing her.

Grange looks nervous. De Luca seems thoughtful. Lane is as white as a ghost.

'Are you okay?' I ask him.

'I'm fine. I'm just kicking myself again for not driving her home.' He grips the back of his head. 'Fuck,' he mutters.

'How much more footage is there?' I say to Grange.

'The council sent everything they have from the timeframe we requested, but there's only one other camera and it's much further along the street—near the church outside the public toilet—so probably only one or two hours are going to be useful to us.'

I turn to Lane. 'Can you start reviewing it all now? I obviously want to know if Abbey appears again but I also want to timecode and ID every single car and individual that appears. We need to speak to anyone who was in the vicinity that night.'

I feel completely wired. Fairhaven seems infinite: ocean on one side, endless bushland on the other. She could be anywhere. Meg Jarvis's bizarre rantings on the beach ring in my ears. If Abbey really is buried out there somewhere, we'll probably never find her.

Grange hands Lane his laptop and another memory stick, along with a bunch of cords. He marches out to the main room, his face grim.

'So, how was the autopsy?' I say to the others, my heart still pounding.

'Pretty confronting,' replies Grange earnestly.

'What did Lamb say?'

'Apparently Fletcher was in perfect health when he died,' begins Grange.

'Mick reckons the weapon was a gardening tool, probably a mallet,' says de Luca bluntly. 'Or an axe used side-on.'

'Jesus.'

'Yeah.' She swallows.

'Does Lamb still think Abbey could have done it?' I ask.

De Luca nods slowly. 'He can't rule it out but thinks it's unlikely. The initial blow required significant force,' she pauses, 'and accuracy. Mick wants to do some further analysis and tests. He said he'll contact the Fletchers personally because it will delay the funeral.'

The idea of Abbey bringing a mallet down on Rick's head remains jarring, but I've seen too many unfathomable things in my career to discount this, no matter how counterintuitive it feels.

'The weapon definitely wasn't at the scene,' de Luca continues, 'but it does look like one of Rick's tools was missing. The killer could have taken it with them.'

'That would suggest the killer came unarmed, which is at odds with the planned nature of the attack,' I say.

'Or, it could just mean the killer knew Rick well enough to know he had a lot of tools,' says de Luca. 'That was probably less risky than carrying something over.'

'Good point,' I say. 'Though the killer still had to carry it out of there.'

De Luca shrugs. 'True. Mick confirmed Rick had no defence wounds. Our attacker wasn't mucking around. One quick blow to the back of the head, then three to the temple. Rick was almost certainly unconscious after the second hit and would have been clinically dead within minutes.'

I try to imagine the fleeting moment of shock before he sank into eternal oblivion. Would he even have registered anything at all?

'Aiden knows the house backwards,' I say. 'Abbey too.'

De Luca crosses her arms. 'You think they were working together?'

'I don't know. I'm starting to wonder if Aiden's appearance at the house on Monday was an act. Maybe he thought putting in some face time as the grieving brother would count him out of the investigation and give more weight to the notion he left town because he couldn't cope.'

'But doesn't he have an airtight alibi? I thought he was in Sydney.'

'Lane and I have been wondering about that,' I say. 'We're going to dig a bit more and see what shakes out.'

Pursing her lips, de Luca glances back at the TV. 'Do you think Aiden and Abbey might have been involved with each other?'

'Well, they would have seen each other regularly. It wouldn't be the first time someone fell for the partner of their sibling.'

'Surely Aiden didn't knock off his brother over a high school romance?' says Grange.

De Luca lifts an eyebrow but doesn't bother to respond. She looks at me with unfocused eyes, and I can tell she's working through various theories. 'Maybe Rick discovered that Abbey ran away and that Aiden helped her.'

'Could be.' I explain the anomaly regarding Aiden's claim he spoke to Rick on Sunday. 'Perhaps they did speak then but had some kind of falling out. Maybe there's no phone call on the record because the conversation was in person. Or maybe that's what Rick's call to the station was about. He might have been planning to dob in his brother—and Abbey.'

We fall into silence, and I know we're all thinking about Rick's lost phone message and how different everything would have played out if he'd spoken to Tran that night.

'Alright,' I say, ending the speculation loop. 'What about his tox? Any initial findings?'

'Mick is aiming to get it to us tomorrow,' says de Luca. 'He said Rick's stomach contents were consistent with him drinking whisky the night before.'

Grange scrunches up his face. 'You could smell it.'

'He also said he suspected some drug use—something about the condition of Rick's blood vessels and teeth,' says de Luca.

'Where are the bloody drugs then?'

They both look at me blankly.

'Were there any prints on Rick's body? Anything?'

'Not so far. They reckon the murderer might have been in the bedroom and the kitchen. The tech I spoke to said a few of the surfaces looked like they'd been wiped.'

'Great,' I say, exasperated. For some reason I'm surprised: I assumed a sleepy small-time killer wouldn't have the foresight to do something like that. 'What about on Rick's phone? Anything turn up?'

'Nothing,' says de Luca. 'But I did notice something strange about the records. Until a month ago Rick barely used his phone on Tuesdays.'

'What do you mean?'

She shrugs. 'It's like he just goes off the grid. Sometimes he would text Abbey in the morning and tell her he'd come pick her up, but that was pretty much it.'

'Maybe he was just at work? Or maybe he was using another phone during those times. Find out what shifts he used to work at the pub.'

De Luca leans back in her chair with an arrogant tilt to her mouth. 'Sure, but it won't be relevant. He obviously worked more than one shift a week, and there are no other black spots in his usage like this.'

'Well,' I say with exaggerated patience, 'it must be linked to his job at the pub if you say it was happening until a month ago. That's the only thing that changed in his life at that time, right? Let's workshop some other theories.'

'Guys!' Lane calls out from the other room. 'Come look at this.'

The three of us crowd around his computer screen, which shows a recording paused on the same stretch of the main street as the footage we watched earlier. The time stamp is 12.31 am.

Lane presses play and the trees start to move in the wind. After a few seconds a man dressed in dark jeans and a white T-shirt appears. His hands in his pockets, he walks briskly along the edge of the road from the direction we just saw Abbey come from. The footage is grainy and his facial features aren't clear, but he looks over his shoulder several times as if he's agitated. After a moment he begins to run.

'Go back,' I say, and Lane does.

We watch again as the man walks along the street then runs off screen.

'Zoom in,' I bark.

We all stare at the blurry profile. I scan his bare arms for tattoos but see nothing.

'Anyone know who he is?'

They shake their heads.

'Well, find out. Send it off for analysis. See if they can work on the file so we can get a proper shot of his face. I don't care if we have to crossmatch him with every person in town—we need to find out who that guy is.'

I grab my bag and shove my water bottle inside, spilling it all over the desk in the process.

'I have to go. Can you send me the screen grabs before you head off?'

I'm halfway across the room when I hear the front door swing open.

Georgina and Ian Fletcher are back.

'There's something we need to tell you,' says Ian.

Wednesday, 13 April
5.49 pm

The Fletchers have quite the set-up. Moving to the larger property last year meant they could scale up their marijuana production and make about five times as much.

'We'd been growing plants in the bush for years,' says Ian quietly. 'It was easy when the kids were little but it got harder to manage as they grew older. We figured if we bought some land we could run it from home, do it properly and keep it completely separate from the kids.' He looks up at me, desperate. 'They have no idea about any of it. We monitor it all very carefully. That's why we moved and let the boys stay in the house. Belinda was already living with her boyfriend. We didn't want them involved, and it was the best chance we had at making a good living.'

'We want a better life for them than we had,' says Georgina, tears dripping into her hands. 'Neither of us finished school, that's why we were so disappointed when Rick dropped out and was working at the pub. That's what we didn't want for him, a life of struggle and odd jobs.'

'If people don't buy it from us, they'll just buy it from someone else,' adds Ian. 'We can barely keep up with the demand.'

'Please,' says Georgina, 'we would never hurt anybody. We never sell to anyone underage. And it's only pot, we've never been involved in anything else.'

Feeling weary, I question the Fletchers for another forty-five minutes. I leave them in the meeting room, holding hands like schoolkids, while I fill Lane in so he can upgrade the search of their property to involve the drug squad.

'Well, you said you wanted to shake something out,' he says. 'This is definitely something.'

'Yeah.'

In the meeting room I explain to the Fletchers what will happen next. Then I stand in the doorway and watch them leave. They pause at the end of the driveway; Ian takes his wife in his arms, and she sobs into his chest.

I swallow past the lump in my throat and head out to get into my own car.

The universe is clearly messing with me because Mac calls just as I pull up outside the chemist. I let it ring out; the panic I felt this morning roaring back. I know I'm being immature but I just can't talk to him right now. I have no idea what to say.

I slam the car door shut and step into the warm evening. Despite a slow start, the temperature ended up hitting thirty degrees.

A noisy bell announces my arrival in the chemist. I tentatively make my way up the aisle closest to the door, trying to work out how the products are arranged. Half the shelves seem to house various types of sunscreen.

'Hello!' The shop assistant singsongs at me. She moves her head from side to side, peering at me past all the signage. 'Do you need a hand?'

'Hi,' I call out as I duck behind one of the displays. 'No, thanks.' My pulse starts to fly and I am sixteen again, working out how to buy condoms without Dad's friend Mary Curtis noticing. I apply the same strategy now as I did back then, grabbing a basket and plucking random things I don't need from the shelves. Hopefully the offending item will be lost in the jumble.

Finally I am standing in front of the row of pregnancy tests. I grab the most expensive one.

I don't even know why I'm bothering with the test—I already know what the result will be. I've been pregnant twice before, so I recognise the sluggishness, the certain flavour of all-consuming tiredness. But the sickness, the sickness is new.

'Just these?' The lady beams at me as she begins to scan my collection of items. 'You have lots of goodies in here. How long are you staying in Fairhaven?'

'I'm not sure yet.'

'Lovely. It's nice this time of year. Not as crowded as the summer. You must get out on one of the boats.'

She scans the pregnancy test but continues a steady stream of babble about a sea adventure she has booked later in the year.

'Thanks, thanks,' I mumble when she hands me my bag.

I virtually run out of the shop, fishing around in my handbag for my keys. Head down, I push my hand further into its depths, feeling around all the old receipts and business cards until my hand closes on the keys and I beep open the car. Straightening, I almost crash into someone who is standing next to my driver's-side door, partly hidden by the giant four-wheel drive next to it. 'Oh!'

'Whoa, steady on.' Simon Charleston takes me gently by the elbows, his grey eyes on my chemist bag.

I wrench myself out of his grasp and swing the bag behind my legs, hoping like hell he can't see the pregnancy test through the flimsy white plastic.

'You scared me,' I say angrily.

He looks apologetic. 'Sorry, I didn't mean to. I actually wanted to know if you have time for a quick drink? We need to talk.'

———

I message Vanessa, explaining I'll be late, as Simon grabs us a table.

Cam flashes me a big smile when I make my way to the bar. 'What can I get you, Gemma Woodstock?'

'A pint and a lemon squash, thanks.'

His expression drops and he scans the room, trying to identify my drinking partner.

'How are you?' he asks sincerely. 'You doing okay?'

I brush away his concern with a question. 'Hey, this is a long shot, but do you know this guy? You must see pretty much everyone who comes in and out of town.' I hold out my phone and show him a grab from the security footage.

He squints at the screen. 'It's pretty hard to tell . . . I can't really make out his face, but I recognise those shoes.' He points to the mystery man's runners. 'They're limited-edition Adidas. We had a chat about them one night—I kind of have a thing for shoes, and I commented on them. If it's the same guy then he's English. His mate worked on the bar for a few weeks. I think they were staying at the caravan park.'

'You can't remember his name?'

'Sorry,' Cam says with a shrug, 'I couldn't say.'

'Could it have been Robert?'

Cam places the drinks in front of me and leans forward, resting his muscular arms on the bar. Dark auburn hair curls from the top of his shirt. 'Maybe. I think it was something boring like that. Why, what's he done?'

'Sorry, I really can't go into it.' I hand him my credit card, which he waves away.

'These are on the house, Gemma.'

'Thanks, Cam.'

'No worries. Enjoy your drink.'

I feel his eyes follow me as I carry the drinks over to Simon and I find myself adding a slight sway to my hips.

'Hang on,' I say, sliding the beer toward him and pulling out my phone. 'I need to make a quick call.'

'I'm not going anywhere.'

I fire off a message letting the team know the guy on the tape might be Robert Weston. We need to confirm it and issue an alert for him. Glancing over at Simon, I quickly call Candy.

'Candy, what do you know about Simon Charleston? The journo.'

'Hello, Gemma,' she says drily. 'I'm fine, thanks for asking.'

'Sorry, but I'm kind of in a rush. I'm about to meet with him.'

'For a date?'

'*Candy.*'

'Simon is a good guy. He's a great writer and he's done some decent investigative stuff. He's not entirely by the book, a bit of a maverick. You guys would make a good pair actually.'

'I'll keep it in mind.'

'You should. I hear he's worked his way through most of the women at Channel 7 and moved on to 9. He may very well be keen to add a detective to his list.'

'But you rate him?' I confirm.

'I rate him,' she agrees, snapping her gum. 'Just keep your legs crossed.'

We hang up and I head back to the table. 'Right,' I say, 'this needs to be quick.'

'Well, cheers to you too,' says Simon, tapping his beer against my lemon squash glass. 'Don't worry, I know you have to get home to your kid. I won't keep you long.'

'You can leave my kid out of it, thanks.'

'I was just trying to be friendly, you know, build rapport.'

I roll my eyes. 'Okay, well, I'm here, so spit it out.'

Simon sits up straight. 'You're staying at Tommy Gordon's now, right?'

My eyes wander to the bar. Cam is mixing drinks but I catch him looking over at us.

'I can't see how that's your business.'

'Did you know him before you came here?'

'Not at all. An old colleague of mine knows Chief Inspector Gordon, but I'd never met him before.'

Simon seems to relax at this. 'Why are you staying there? Surely the force could have picked up the tab for a mediocre hotel. You were here on Monday night—why did you move?'

'At the risk of repeating myself, that's none of your business.'

'It seems odd.'

'I know *you* stayed here on Monday night.'

He opens his mouth to reply then pauses, looking puzzled. 'I always stay here. But, Gemma, come on, tell me why you ended up at the Gordons.'

'Next question.'

He holds up his hands. A fuzz of beer froth lines his top lip. 'I'm not trying to pry, honestly.'

I give him a withering look. 'Oh, come on.'

When he smiles, I can't help smiling back. 'Okay, I *always* pry, but that's not what this is about.'

'Fine. What is this about?'

'I think there's something weird about Tommy Gordon's car accident.'

I put my glass down, surprised. 'What do you mean?'

'A few things just don't add up.'

'Like?'

'Well, for starters it wasn't investigated properly. By the time it was called in, Abbey Clark had already been reported missing so all the resources were allocated to that. Tommy called his wife from the crash scene, and she drove out and got him.'

'Vanessa took him to the hospital?'

'Vanessa took him *home*. And the car didn't get towed until Monday arvo.' Simon takes a nervous sip of beer and looks at me expectantly.

'Okay. So there was a delay in clearing the scene, which isn't ideal, but it was a non-fatal single vehicle accident so there was no need to gather witness statements. Tommy probably just called Vanessa because he's a stubborn old man who hates to ask for help.'

'Maybe. But I went out to the scene myself.'

I cross my arms. 'Doing some detective work, were you?'

He shrugs. 'No one else was.'

'And what did you find, Sherlock?'

'Not much,' he admits, 'but from what I heard, Tommy said the sun was in his eyes and a kangaroo jumped out in front of the car, making him swerve off the road. But I went back there the following day at the exact time he said he crashed. There's no way the sun would have been in his eyes.'

In spite of myself I feel a prickle of unease. 'Sometimes people remember accidents differently to how they happened. Maybe he just meant it was sunny.'

'Maybe. But I've also never known roos to be there before, and I drive that road all the time.' A slightly sullen note creeps into his voice. 'I'm telling you, something is off.'

I take a deep breath and study him. He's good-looking in a rumpled way. There's a coffee stain on his shirt collar, and his fingers are tinged with ink. The soft skin under his right eye pulses with a tic. In spite of my misgivings about him, he seems genuine.

'I asked Tommy about you,' I say. 'I didn't get the feeling there is much love lost.'

He scowls. 'Tommy doesn't deal well with criticism.' Simon pauses, seemingly deciding whether to elaborate or not. 'I wrote a piece a decade ago about the handling of a suspected homicide case. It wasn't complimentary to the police. Tommy's predecessor was furious about it, and so was he. I wrote another article last year criticising his ostrich approach to some issues in the area—that didn't go down so well either.'

I poke my straw into an ice cube and try to think of what to say. In the end I attempt to avoid the whole issue. 'Yes, I've read your old articles,' I say dismissively. 'Hard to believe you were a journo back then. I would have assumed you were still in nappies ten years ago.'

'I'm older and uglier than I look. Same as you.'

'I have to go,' I say, pushing my half-finished drink toward him. 'I appreciate your concern, but as you know we are working at least one homicide investigation, possibly two, and that is obviously my priority.'

Simon's face softens. 'I know. It's awful, both of them just kids.' He downs his beer and slides off his stool. 'But there have been rumours about Tommy cutting corners for a while now, and this just doesn't add up.'

I lean forward; he mirrors my action. I can see the faint freckles on his cheeks, a faint scar through his eyebrow.

'I have to go,' I repeat.

I wave at Cam, who watches Simon follow me to the car park. 'Gemma,' he says insistently, 'at the very least, you should ask

Vanessa why she didn't take Tommy to the hospital straight away. Four hours is a long time.'

Tran rings me and I make a show of answering it, shooing Simon away with my hand.

'Gemma,' Tran's voice stops me mid-gesture, and I lock eyes with Simon. 'We've found a body.'

Wednesday, 13 April

8.32 pm

'What is it?' Simon's eyes seem to glow in the darkness.

'Nothing,' I say. 'I have to go.'

I tear out of the car park leaving him with his hands in the air, yelling my name.

I call Tran back using bluetooth. Just after 8 pm, a bushwalker's blue heeler found a partially buried body about twenty k's from Fairhaven. One of the victim's arms was severed and the face was partly missing, blown off by a suspected shotgun injury. A forensic team is heading there now and will stay into the night.

'I think it's unlikely to be Abbey.' Tran's voice is uncharacteristically high-pitched. 'Too decomposed, by the sounds of it, but I'll keep you posted.'

As I drive to the Gordons', my emotions swing wildly from wanting it to be Abbey to wanting it to be anyone but her. Finding her body will make our job easier but all hope will be gone. We'll simply be dragging ourselves toward the booby prize of justice. No Abbey means we are still in limbo, nothing certain but a sliver of hope that things can be put right.

Vanessa offers me dinner but my appetite is non-existent, so I help her transfer the leftovers into Tupperware containers. She pours herself a fresh glass of wine. In the lounge room Ben is watching a movie with Charlie, something with talking dinosaurs.

I hear the toilet flush down the corridor and the slow shuffling of Tommy making his way to the bedroom with the walking frame. 'Night, ladies,' he calls and I bristle involuntarily. He's behaved oddly since I came home, vague and distracted, grilling me about the case before seeming to lose interest. I didn't mention the body and neither did he, even though I'm certain he's seen the alert.

Vanessa walks to the top of the hallway and calls, 'Do you need me to help you get settled?'

'No,' he says, 'I'm fine, Ness. I need to get back to doing things for myself again.'

She crosses her arms. 'No, you need to take it easy.'

'Enjoy your wine, honey,' he singsongs.

Turning back to me, she rolls her eyes but there's a pinch of worry in her expression. 'That man just can't be told. Come on.'

I follow her outside. The temperature has dropped but it's still mild. A possum makes a dash along the side fence and scrambles noisily into a tree. Vanessa ducks under the table to light a citronella candle. 'The mozzies can be fierce this time of year,' she says, tucking her hair behind her ears. 'Do you want some spray?'

'I'm okay.' I tug my denim jacket sleeves to my wrists and curl my legs onto the chair.

After sinking into the seat opposite, she savours a sip of wine. 'Gosh, I'm so tired!' She yawns and covers her mouth, then laughs. 'Sorry.'

Her warmth gives an impression of openness, but I'm starting to detect a guardedness. I wonder if Simon is right. Maybe she's holding something back—hiding something.

I say, 'I hope you've been finding Ben okay? Looking after a boy that age can be a bit of a shock to the system.'

'They are little balls of energy, aren't they?' She laughs again. 'It's a good shock,' she insists. 'I know it's not an easy time for either of you, but I love having him here. I'm enjoying having you both here. It's a nice change from just the two of us.'

'Ben seems to be liking it here.' I pause. 'But maybe I'm just telling myself that.'

'Gemma . . .' Vanessa begins before biting her lip.

I tilt my head questioningly.

'Ben asked if he could call Jodie today. His stepmother?' Vanessa looks at me with concern. 'He knew the number off by heart and I said it was fine. I assume you're okay he called her?'

My heart thunders in my chest. 'Yes, of course it's fine. He's lived with her for the past two years.' I drink water too quickly and it goes down the wrong way. 'She's really nice,' I croak.

'They didn't speak for long but I got the feeling he didn't want me to tell you. I just don't think it's right to keep things from you.'

I glance inside. Ben is pointing at the screen and saying something to Charlie.

'I don't *not* want him talking to Jodie,' I say slowly. 'I should probably be talking more to her myself.'

'Unfortunately, there are no hard and fast rules when it comes to the things that really matter.'

I think about the pregnancy test buried at the bottom of my suitcase. 'That's true.' Rearranging my legs, I fix my gaze on her. 'Tommy's accident must have been pretty scary. Someone mentioned you drove him to the hospital?'

She has another sip of wine. 'Yes, it was terrifying. When he called, he made out like it wasn't that serious, but then when I got there I totally freaked out. There was so much blood.'

'But you didn't call an ambulance?'

'Oh well, I wanted to—but you know what Tommy's like. He insisted he was okay, and of course the wait time for an ambulance around here isn't like it is in the city. People are encouraged to be resourceful.' She says this primly, as if she feels I'm judging her.

'But in the end you took him to the Fairhaven hospital and not Byron?'

She gives a strange little laugh. 'Well, like I said, Tommy didn't even think he needed to go to hospital! There was no way he would have let me drive him to Byron. He said it looked much worse than it was, and he was worried about pulling people away from the search for Abbey. So we came back here. I cleaned him up as well as I could. Eventually I insisted he needed to be checked out—I didn't want him sleeping that night without medical advice.'

'Right.'

She uncrosses her legs and fusses with her shirt. 'Anyway, I'm just glad he's alright.'

'Yes, sounds like it could have been much worse. It was a kangaroo that caused him to swerve?'

With a laugh, she taps her hands on her thighs. 'Yes, of all things. Tommy bloody hates them.'

We sit in silence for a few moments, listening to the insects.

'Have you always lived in Fairhaven?' I ask her.

'Tommy has. I was born in Brisbane and lived there until I was twenty. We met when Tommy was up there doing some training, and that was it.'

'He swept you off your feet?'

She laughs again, the colour returning to her face. 'I guess he did. I was living here within a year.'

Aware I've slipped into interview mode, I try to soften my tone a little. 'Did you ever think about living anywhere else?'

'Not really. Tommy always wanted to run the local station. He doesn't like all the fuss in the bigger offices. Then about nine years ago the previous chief inspector left unexpectedly, and Tommy was given the chance to step up. We won't leave now. If you haven't noticed already, Tommy is pretty set in his ways.'

'Was that the missing teenagers case? I read up about it online.'

'Yes.' She sighs. 'Greg and Sally. I taught Sally for two years, she was divine. Her parents still live here, rattling around the town like ghosts. I don't think they feel like they can leave—you know, in case she comes back. They used to come over here all the time talking to Tommy, it was awful for him.'

'Not knowing is always worse,' I say. 'It destroys people. That's what I don't want for Abbey.'

'No,' Vanessa murmurs.

'I read the inquest ruling. That Greg most likely killed Sally and fled town.'

'Tommy never believed that,' says Vanessa. 'He argued with the chief inspector about it a lot. They couldn't see eye to eye on the case at all.'

'Tommy thought something happened to both of them?'

Vanessa gives an uncertain nod. 'No trace of them was ever found and Greg's car was gone, which is why so many people said they skipped town together. A few sightings were reported months later in places like Broome and even Adelaide, but Tommy thought they were bogus. None of their stuff was missing, and Sally was supposed to be a bridesmaid in her sister's wedding the following week. Her family were always adamant she would never have missed that voluntarily.'

'What do you think happened?'

'Surely something happened to both of them. There were rumours of a serial killer hiding out in the bush.' Vanessa looks up at the tiny wedge of moon. 'That seemed more plausible, somehow, than Sally missing her sister's big day.'

'Did Tommy have a suspect in mind?'

'The case almost tore the squad apart. They copped a lot of heat in the press. Tommy fell out with the former chief, and by the time he was in charge the case was cold. The whole thing hit him really hard—he suffered a fair bit of self-doubt. He had some health issues at the time and there was a lot of pressure. Those first few years running the station were very tough on him.' Something in her voice makes it clear those years were tough on her as well.

'Why did the other chief leave?'

'He never said, but I think he just got sick of Fairhaven. Plus he came from a wealthy family who ran property development projects. Last I heard he went to work with them interstate.' Vanessa swirls the dregs of her wine around in her glass. 'Do you think Abbey is dead?'

'I'm not sure. I think there's a strong chance she was killed on Saturday night.'

Vanessa nods, her mouth set in a grim line. 'I know it's silly to say, but it's like the poor girl was cursed from the beginning.'

'Did you ever teach Abbey?'

'No, but she served me in the supermarket every Saturday. She seemed like a nice girl, lovely manners. And she was so pretty with that beautiful skin and long dark hair.' Vanessa curls her lip. 'Probably the only good thing she got from her father.' With her fingertips, Vanessa pushes her empty wineglass across the wooden slats of the tabletop. 'Tommy would always tell me if they'd had a call-out to the Clarks', and I would always check on her at the supermarket the following week. You know, trying to let her know there were people around here looking out for her.' Vanessa pulls her cardigan tighter around her body. 'A lot of people write Daniel off as stupid,' she says. 'But really he's just dangerous. He's rude in public, sure, and angry, but it's funny how he's only violent when no one else is there to see it. He's no fool. I know Tommy would like nothing more than to see him put away, and hopefully this situation with Rick leads to that.'

Vanessa looks so vulnerable. It's on the tip of my tongue to ask her if there's more to Tommy's accident than she has let on, but the moment passes. The whine of a mosquito triggers itchiness, and I can't relax. Through the window I see the kids' movie credits rolling.

'Do we need to get Charlie home?' I ask Vanessa. I get to my feet, suddenly desperate to be behind the glass with the curtains drawn.

Vanessa leans forward, peering at the two boys sprawled on the couch. 'I told Charlie's mum he could stay. They get along really well, don't they? I thought they might. Charlie has a much older sister but she's moved to Sydney for uni so he's pretty much an only child.'

'You're really great with kids,' I say tentatively, wondering if she once wanted to have children of her own.

She looks pleased. 'That's what almost thirty years of teaching does to you.'

I smile. 'Maybe more people should be teachers before they become parents.'

'You'll figure it out, Gemma. Or you'll muddle through. People raise kids in a thousand different ways, and I tend to find that most of them are doing their best. You and your ex have done a good job with Ben so far. He's an amazing kid.'

'I know,' I reply, squaring my shoulders. I look past my reflection in the window to see Ben laughing sleepily at something Charlie said. 'That's sort of what I'm afraid of. It's just me now and I don't want to be the one who stuffs him up.'

I finally call Jonesy back after I put Ben to bed.

'You can't go off the grid like that, Gemma,' he says gruffly. 'I worry.'

'I'm fine, honestly.'

'You're not fine, you're working a bloody homicide investigation *and* a missing persons case.'

'You know that's generally when I achieve peak happiness,' I quip.

Jonesy clears his throat, signalling something sensitive. 'Gemma, Tommy told me about the possum. I suppose you weren't planning on letting me know about that?'

'I wasn't, actually,' I say stiffly. 'I was sort of hoping we could avoid a conversation like this.'

He grumbles under his breath. 'I should have talked you out of going.'

'We both know that would never have worked. Plus, I think Ben likes it here.'

'I'm glad the little fella is doing okay, but I'm worried about you as well.'

'How well do you know Tommy?'

'Not that well. We did a course together, hit it off and stayed in touch afterwards. Lucy and I went to Fairhaven for a holiday since then, but that was years ago. I haven't seen him—oh, well, it must be at least five years. How are you finding him? I hope the old bugger's not being too territorial?'

'He's a bit hard to read,' I say, evading the question.

'I imagine he'd be pretty tough. He's pretty old school. I know he had some health problems a while back. He's lucky to have Vanessa, she's a saint.'

'Yeah, she's been great with Ben.'

'We should both get some shut-eye,' says Jonesy with a yawn. 'Just remember you've had a tough time lately, Gemma, and even though you at half speed is still most people at turbo, there's nothing wrong with admitting you have a limit. So if you reach yours, you need to promise you'll let me know.'

I look at the crumpled chemist bag on my nightstand, the two blue lines glowing behind the plastic window.

'I promise.'

FIFTH DAY MISSING

Thursday, 14 April

6.16 am

I wake with a sense of anticipation, picturing the forensic team hard at work under their portable lamps as they trawl over the rotting human remains in the bush.

I reach past Ben to pick up my phone.

The text from Tran reads: *It's not her. It's a kid from Evans Head who was reported missing two weeks ago. Dale Marx. We're working through possible links but there's nothing so far.*

I drop the phone to my chest and stare at the ceiling, exhaling a breath I didn't know I'd been holding. It's not Abbey. We still have nothing but at least there's a chance she might be out there somewhere.

I have breakfast with Ben and Vanessa. Tommy is up early too but declined breakfast and simply sits at the end of the table, staring with glassy eyes at his iPad.

As I drive to the station, parts of my conversation with Vanessa keep bubbling up. Clearly there were issues in the way the cold missing person case was handled, and Tommy is hard to read, but I'm not convinced anything warrants the conspiracy theory categorisation that Simon has given it.

I say good morning to Tim and Kylie, the junior stand-in constables who are in the middle of their shift handover.

De Luca arrives fresh faced and with an impressive dossier on Robert Weston. Aged nineteen, he's on a gap year from uni where he is enrolled to study law. He has no priors, though she tracked down a detective in the UK who informed her of something interesting: Robert is due in court in November to give evidence against a man who attacked him outside a pub and broke his arm. The detective de Luca spoke to seems to think the attack came about because Robert had been harassing the assailant's girlfriend. The girlfriend is apparently giving evidence and will be documenting the unwelcome messages she received from Robert.

'The UK cops reckon Weston is a real pest. A borderline stalker.' De Luca hands me several printouts: a copy of his passport, a few grabs from social media, and photos of the three men he was travelling with.

'Good work,' I say.

'You were the one who ID'd him,' she says dismissively.

We lock eyes, and again I try to understand the battle I seem to have unwittingly stepped into.

'We're a team,' I say, and sense the slightest roll of her eyes.

I take the three young cops through the schedule I've mapped out for the day: Grange is going to the hospital to speak to Doctor Eric Sheffield and try to find out whether Abbey made or attended a doctor appointment recently, while Lane and de Luca are interviewing more kids from the party. I'm heading to the caravan park to catch Dot before I meet with William, James and Miles at 9 am.

I call out goodbye as the others file from the meeting room, then I log into the system and look up the authors of the Gregory Ng/ Sally Luther case file.

As per Vanessa's run-down, Stuart Klein was the chief inspector who led the case. I google him and find a piece written by Simon detailing his retirement from the force. The article says he was planning a move for family reasons and looking forward to a new career in Sydney.

Janet Rixon, the only constable in Fairhaven back then, reported to Tommy, who was the senior sergeant. According to a Google search, Janet currently runs a small scuba-diving operation with her husband in Evans Head. Their website includes her short bio and a photo. She looks around forty, with a friendly moon face and a short blonde bob. I scroll through the website gobsmacked at the cost of the diving packages.

Knowing it's probably too early, I call Janet's office number. A cheery recorded voice explains that the daily dive sessions start at 6 am and the best time to make a phone inquiry is between 4 pm and 7 pm.

'Dammit,' I say to the empty room.

I catch a ghost version of my reflection on the whiteboard and give myself an exasperated look. What was I expecting, anyway? That Janet would feed me a clue from a nine-year-old cold case that somehow helps me find Abbey? I can feel myself fixating on the past, distracted by the stale clues. It's a tendency I've always had because it's often easier to tackle than what is right in front of me. After plugging Janet's number into my phone I grab my things, conscious of my sluggish limbs.

After getting into the car I quickly fire off another text to Mac, blaming my lack of contact on my workload and a mild virus. I turn off my personal phone, putting it in the glove box.

My body is tense during the short drive. Ben was quiet this morning, more withdrawn than he had been all week, and I fought tears as I kissed him goodbye. I have another sip of water and try to be grateful that at least I don't feel like hurling my guts up today.

The birds converse excitedly in the gums that tower above the caravan park while I'm walking into reception. Kate Morse is on the phone and looks at me witheringly, but I simply wave at her and step through to the communal area. The sewage stench is gone, replaced by the smell of bacon. Katy Perry blasts from a portable radio hooked onto the pool fence. A little girl squeals in delight as a scrawny teenager threatens to drop her into the water. A few older women are propped up on deckchairs, their leathery skin glistening. Two men in novelty sombreros are attacking the barbecue with metal tools, scraping black muck into a bucket.

I make my way down the path, noting the neat garden beds and the communal laundry and bathrooms. On the other side of the bathrooms is a row of permanent caravans with elaborate annexes, and beyond them is a huge stretch of grass dotted with tents and campervans, sporadic power poles indicating where new guests should drop anchor.

A mother and a boy around Ben's age come out of the bathrooms. His hair is so fair it's almost white and his face is mottled with sunburn, prompting me to think I must double-check with Vanessa that Ben is reapplying sunscreen during the day. The mother and I exchange polite smiles before I fall into step behind them, watching the boy's narrow shoulderblades press out against his skin as his mum lectures him about wearing his rashie.

I veer off toward the west-wing cabins. I encounter six closed doors and one that's ajar, though it's quickly apparent that no cleaning is going on inside but rather a heated argument between a couple about money suddenly not being in a bank account.

The door to the next cabin is propped open by a cleaning cart, but the woman bustling around inside is not Dot. She's a cheerful redhead who tells me her name is Joy and informs me that Dot should be in the laundry room. 'It's terrible about her daughter,' says Joy, whipping a fitted sheet into submission. 'And that boy too. It reminds me of when that young couple disappeared—it was the same terrible feeling around town. Like evil had come to visit. Is there any word on where the poor girl is?'

'I can't really discuss it,' I say apologetically. 'Have you spoken to Dot today?'

Joy bends her elbows, placing her hands on ample hips. 'Oh, just the usual. A hello, and of course I said I was sorry to hear about her girl. Dot's not a big talker though, which is fair enough.' She picks up a pile of discarded linen and bundles it into a hamper. 'Plus, what do you say about something like that? You can really only pray.'

I thank Joy and make my way to the laundry. A lone light globe is trying its best to illuminate the dark room, which is thick with artificial fragrance and lint. The solemn faces of the whirring washing machines stare out at me as I call Dot's name and poke my head into the side rooms trying to find her. I turn to go back outside just as she appears in the doorway, her hunched form silhouetted, bucket in one hand, mop in the other.

'Oh!' Her hand flies to her throat.

'Hi, Dot. You remember me from the other day? Detective Woodstock. Sorry to turn up at your work like this, but I'm keen to talk to you alone.'

She recovers from her surprise and shuffles over to the sink, placing all the cleaning tools down before she faces me. Her chest heaves with a steady wheeze.

'This is your first day back?' I ask, trying to ease her into conversation. I'm desperate to be the one who can help her find the courage to admit the truth. I never quite managed to connect with Nicki's mum, Deirdre. Ultimately she didn't trust me enough to confide in me, to tell me she suspected her husband knew more than he was letting on.

Dot's head moves up and down as she fusses with the hem of her oversized T-shirt. 'Yeah. We need the money.'

'Remind me what Daniel does for work?'

She blinks. 'He's a mechanic but the shop closed down so he's just doing odd jobs at the moment. We get the dole too.'

'Must be tough,' I say, wondering why she hasn't asked me about her daughter.

She sighs heavily, and shrugs. She looks exhausted.

'Dot, I'm sorry but there's still no sign of Abbey.'

'Yeah.' Her hands are trembling.

'We're obviously doing everything we can to find your daughter.'

'Yeah.' Her eyes go to the floor.

'I want to ask you some questions.'

'Thought you already did.'

'Sometimes it's worth going over things again. Sometimes people remember things differently.'

She juts her chin out in a non-committal gesture but she won't look me in the eye.

'You and Daniel stayed home with your sons on Saturday evening after Abbey went out?'

'Yes.'

'And Daniel was definitely home all night?'

'Where else would he be?'

'It's just important for us to be sure.'

'He was up early in the morning,' she says, after a moment. 'He was the one who realised Abbey was missing. He saw she wasn't in her room and her bed was still made.'

'And you're certain she didn't come home during the night?'

'I was asleep,' says Dot stiffly. 'But I didn't hear anything.'

'And Daniel was definitely home on Monday morning?' I ask more firmly. 'At around six?'

'Yes,' she says, her voice wavering.

'Daniel and Abbey argued on Saturday night, didn't they?'

Dot wipes her nose and scratches at her shoulder, her eyes anywhere but on me. 'They always argued, it was no big deal.'

'I think it was a big deal. A few people told us it was really heated, that maybe it was a bit worse than normal.'

Her head jerks up, eyes gleaming. 'I don't know what's got into her lately. She was angry, talking back to him, and I begged her to leave it alone but she wouldn't listen.' Tears spill from her eyes. 'She hit him.'

'Abbey hit Daniel?'

Dot nods as her jaw clenches furiously and tears run down her face. 'She knows better than to wind him up like that.'

'What did Daniel do?'

She falters a little before saying, 'He got really mad and she just left.' Her voice shakes and she wipes the tears from her face. 'He started drinking.'

'Dot, is there a chance your husband did something to Abbey later that night? He might have thought she deserved it after lashing out like that.'

Straightening her back, Dot sniffs loudly; confession time is clearly over. 'I don't see how. He was at home with me all night.' She puts the bucket in the sink and turns on the tap. 'I have to get back to the cabins,' she says over the running water. 'Kate won't pay me past two, and I have lots of rooms to get through.'

'Dot, let me help you. If Daniel has done something I can help protect you and your children. You will be safe.'

She looks at me with a mix of disdain and fury, her hands repeatedly gripping the mop, her knuckles bone-white. 'My husband has a temper, everyone knows that, but he loves his family.'

'Sometimes that's not enough. I just want you to know you have options. I want you to feel safe.'

'Yeah? Maybe I don't want your options. Everyone thinks they know what's best for me.' She pauses before saying firmly, 'Daniel was home with me on Saturday night and on Monday morning.' Her voice drops to a whisper and her lips tremble. 'We just want our daughter back.'

'I've read the reports, Dot. Even if Abbey comes home, I know what happens when Daniel loses his temper. You don't have to put up with that.'

'Leave me alone,' she hisses, her hands hovering around her ears. 'I don't want your help.'

'Okay,' I say, backing away. 'Okay, Dot. I'm going.' I feel hollowed out as I watch her shadowed against the wall in the dim light, struggling with the heavy bucket. 'Just one more quick question and then I'll go.'

'What is it?' she says wearily, an eyebrow raised, and I get a glimpse of the woman she could be if given half a chance.

'Abbey's bike. She said it was a gift from Daniel. Was that something she asked for? I understand it was quite expensive.'

Dot looks confused. 'Daniel hated her having that bike. He didn't buy it, she did.'

Thursday, 14 April
9.08 am

I wait for William Mayne and his mates in the communal area just before 9 am, calling the two mobile numbers from Kate's sheet several times. Frustrated, I call Lane. 'They're not here,' I say, stepping into the shade of a tree.

'I told them to meet you there at nine,' he confirms. 'Maybe they're still asleep?'

'Maybe.' I sigh. 'I'll check with Kate. Hey, also, I just spoke to Dot Clark. She said Abbey bought that bike herself. Daniel apparently had nothing to do with it.'

'That's weird,' says Lane.

'I wonder why she told you Daniel bought it?'

'No idea.' He sounds mystified.

'They're not here,' says Kate, charging past as I hang up. 'I saw them leave for the beach about half an hour ago. They had their boards. I don't blame them, there's great surf today.'

Furious, I storm back to the car trying William's number again. I direct the car toward the beach when Grange calls. 'Yes?' I snap, having zero patience for his dithering today.

'I'm at the hospital but the doctor, Eric, says he is very uncomfortable about giving out patient information.'

'For god's sake,' I exclaim. 'Rick's dead and Abbey is missing.'

'Yes, I know, but he's saying there is still a level of professional—'

'I'll be there in ten minutes,' I snap. 'I want to speak to Doctor Sheffield anyway.' I hang up.

———

The automatic doors of the hospital open, and Meg Jarvis steps out.

'Hello,' I say.

Her gaze sharpens and she steps back, her strange robe-like clothes flowing, panic all over her face.

'Meg? I'm glad I bumped into you.'

The doors strain to close around us, jerking strangely. Meg simply looks at me, her cloudy gaze extremely disconcerting.

'I'd like to talk to you about what you said to me on the beach the other morning. Do you want to come to the station? Or I can meet you somewhere.'

'Sorry, I don't know you,' she mutters.

'Wait,' I call out as she pushes past me. 'Meg, please!'

She rushes away from me in the direction of the Gordons'.

'Detective Woodstock.'

I spin around to see Doctor Eric Sheffield holding his hand out toward me.

'Do you treat Meg Jarvis?' I say. 'Is she your patient?'

'I know Meg,' he replies diplomatically, rocking back on the balls of his feet. He's in tailored shorts and a formal shirt, his tanned calves bulging.

'What was she doing here?'

He smiles, revealing teeth so white they are almost blue. 'I see we're launching into the patient confidentiality conversation right off the bat.' He takes my arm. 'Come this way—Damon is in here.' Eric walks quickly and applies more pressure to his grip than I think is necessary. I tug myself free and follow him past the reception, where a petite nurse with glittery green eyeshadow is on the phone, and into a small office. Grange is perched on the edge of an armless beige padded chair.

Eric rounds the desk and sits heavily in a plush leather office chair, wheeling it forward. He makes a pyramid with his tanned fingers. 'It's good to meet you properly, Detective Woodstock. I meant to introduce myself earlier this week but it's been busy here, and I had to help my wife, Tara, deal with some issues at the salon. Plus, I'm about,' he checks his watch, 'seven hours away from two days off. I'm taking my eldest son camping before the madness of Easter.'

'You run the hospital?'

'Yes. I had my own practice here for about five years, but I was the only GP and I was always keen to develop something more substantial. For some time there was talk of a public hospital being built, but I don't know how likely it ever was to be greenlit. My mother died about ten years ago and suddenly I had the means, so the pipedream became a reality. It was a huge outlay, so I hope it will be worth it.'

'How many beds do you have?'

'Only ten but we can accommodate more. Our business is all about summer and school holidays, as you can imagine, and we churn through a lot of out-patients. I have three GPs on staff. We don't do maternity or high-risk surgery, but who knows? I have big dreams.' He smiles. 'The tourist population is growing, which helps.'

'It all sounds very positive—and expensive,' I say. 'But as I know Constable Grange already explained, we need your help. We believe Abbey Clark either made or attended a doctor's appointment before she disappeared, and we think it might be helpful to understand what it was about. We'd appreciate anything you can tell us.'

He folds his hands and places them on the desk. 'Yes, and as I already explained, I am absolutely not going to comment on that. It's confidential and I'm almost certain you don't have a warrant.'

'Can you confirm she was a patient here?'

'Most Fairhaven residents are,' Eric replies evenly. 'The nearest GP is over thirty kilometres away.'

'What about Rick Fletcher?'

He seems to hesitate. 'Rick was never treated here. I feel comfortable to confirm that. Fit, healthy young men tend to avoid me like the plague.'

'But not fit, healthy young women?'

'No comment.'

I meet his gaze, his dark eyes steady behind his glasses. 'I assume you never treated Abbey Clark for an injury you suspected may have been the result of abuse?'

He sighs. 'I have heard the rumours like everyone else—but no, I never felt compelled to report anything.'

'Young girls tend to seek medical advice for only a handful of reasons.' I list them on my fingers: pregnancy, contraception, sexual disease or mental health. 'It would be helpful if we could narrow down what was going on with Abbey around the time she went missing.'

He looks at me and then at Grange. 'I'm sorry, Detective Woodstock, I want nothing more than for Abbey to be located and I appreciate it's frustrating, but I have been tangled up in a situation like this before. As I told Damon, I'm simply not willing to go there again. It's critical that this community trust me and trust my staff. If you get a warrant or there is an inquest down the road, I may reconsider my position.'

We lock eyes for several moments. I know he won't budge and, as irritated as I am, I know if I were in his position I would behave in exactly the same way.

'Aiden Fletcher works for you,' I say, changing tack.

'He did. He said he wanted to do some other work—with his brother, I think, and some job he mentioned in Sydney.'

'Did that bother you?'

Eric shrugs. 'No, not at all. After three years it makes sense. Plus, Aiden organised a replacement so we haven't really missed a beat.'

'What's his name?'

'Zach Dickson.'

'And what is the role, exactly?'

'Well, with Aiden it evolved over time. He started out manning the canteen. It's only open during visiting hours, 4 pm to 6 pm, and now some schoolkids do that. He managed a lot of the general logistics. He liaised with council about waste disposal, and even helped me out with some of our utility and insurance contracts. He's a smart kid. I guess his role could be described as operational.'

'Did he have access to drugs?'

Eric leans back like I've slapped him. Grange clears his throat nervously. 'No, of course not. Aiden managed the pharma deliveries on Tuesdays, and now Zach does it. But I check off the inventory and we scan it in. It's a very rigid system for obvious reasons.'

'So you sign it all in and out?'

'Yes, I sign in every drug for the hospital and the pharmacy, and I make sure it matches our original order. My signature of receipt is then faxed back to the drug company.' Eric's phone buzzes in his pocket and he glances at his watch. 'Look, Detective Woodstock, why don't you come here after the long weekend and I can take you through the process?'

'We just might do that,' I say. 'And in the meantime, if you think of any way that drugs might be being taken from your hospital without your knowledge, you'll let me know.'

Eric eyes me stonily. 'Will do.'

He comes around to open the door, and Grange looks relieved to be ushered out.

'Tara tells me you're staying at the Gordons',' Eric says conversationally.

'That's right,' I say quietly, aware that Grange is within earshot.

'How is Tommy getting on?' Eric asks.

'He seems better. You treated him after his accident?'

To my surprise, Eric laughs. 'A genuine nightmare patient.'

'What do you mean?'

'He's very stubborn, as I'm sure you've picked up.'

I smile, glad to break the ice a little. 'I'm told he wasn't going to come in at all.'

'No.' Eric seems to hesitate, then says, 'Good thing he did though. He wasn't in great shape. Anyway, I really need to push on. Sorry I couldn't be more help.'

I step to the door and hold out my hand.

'Good luck with your investigation.' He shakes it firmly and then pauses.

'What?'

'Have you had your iron levels checked recently?' His eyes rake over me, dissecting. 'Sorry, it's a bad habit, diagnosing people on the run.' He holds his hands up. 'Just look after yourself, Detective, okay?'

My chest tightens at his patronising tone. 'I also need to check your whereabouts on Monday morning. Can anyone confirm where you were?'

He exhales through pursed lips and crosses his arms, biceps bulging. 'Really?'

'Yes, please.'

Sighing, he says, 'I was at home with my family, then I came in to catch up on some paperwork. Tara can confirm it.'

'What time did you leave the house?'

'Around 6 am.'

'And did anyone see you here?'

'I'm not sure. But I'll be on the security cameras—I can arrange for footage to be sent to you if you need it.'

'That would be good, thanks. Do you know what else would be helpful?' I ask, stepping away from him. 'Copies of all your drug orders, along with the hospital's latest financial statements.'

Eric bristles, his jaw hardening. 'Is that really necessary? I don't see what our business has to do with your investigation.'

I stalk across the reception area, Grange trailing behind me, and call out to Eric over my shoulder. 'Well, I guess that's what we'll find out.'

Thursday, 14 April

11.46 am

Grange and I get several odd looks as we make our way along the beach, just above the rows of sunbakers. The scent of sunscreen mixes with the smell of fish guts wafting from the pier. I can hear the tinkle of an ice-cream truck approaching, and several kids lift their heads in response. Grange struggles along behind me in his standard-issue police boots but I don't slow down. The scene at the hospital has fired me up—I need to direct my rage somewhere.

A young mother with two chubby toddlers wearing head-to-toe lycra fixes her gaze on us, and I try to give her a reassuring smile. There are about a hundred people on the stretch of beach in front of the shops. Under different circumstances I'd be tempted to take a photo. Even I know that this is about as good as it gets: the white sand unblemished, the sky a bold blue, the glow of the sun locking the perfection in place. An old-school boombox is wedged in the sand, a breezy pop song swirling through the air. The waves reach for the sunbakers, crashing about twenty metres from the shore before lapping in giant semicircles on the lower stretch of sand.

Holding a hand above my brow, I scan past a trio of girls in gravity-defying bikinis to where a crew of young men are playing cricket. The redhead comically bowls, and his mate holding the bat swings wide and misses to a chorus of jeers. Three surfboards lie on the sand near a pile of towels. I detect English accents and recognise one of men from de Luca's sleuthing.

'Bingo,' I mutter. I make my way around the girls, Grange still trailing behind. 'William Mayne?' I call out as the cricket ball smacks the ground near my foot.

'Argh!' The batsman collapses to the ground. Thick lines of white zinc cover his nose and cheeks. 'You're such a dickhead,' he calls to his friend.

I toss the ball to him. 'Are you William Mayne?'

'Nope, sorry. Will's over there.' He points to two guys wrestling a few metres away. Their muscled backs are glowing red with sunburn, and I wince as one of them is thrown hard against the rough sand.

'And you are?' I ask.

He smirks, then notices Grange in his uniform and falters, turning even whiter. 'Oh. Right. Will got that message yesterday. Fuck, sorry—we were supposed to meet, weren't we?'

'Your name, please,' I snap as he stands up.

'I'm James.'

'James Peacock?' I ask, recalling one of the highlighted names on the sheet.

'Yeah,' he says warily. 'What's going on?'

Another young man ambles over. 'Sorry we bailed on our meeting with you this morning.' He slaps Grange on the back. 'We thought it was at eight, but no one showed and everyone said the surf was brilliant today. But it was nine, wasn't it? I should have double-checked my messages earlier.' He's either drunk or stoned.

'And you are?'

'Oh sorry, how rude of me. I'm William Mayne.'

Beads of sweat have erupted all over Grange's bald scalp. I feel moisture collecting in the small of my back.

'Grab your other mate, then let's get out of the sun,' I say, walking off toward a picnic table under the trees at the top of the beach. A subdued James rushes to fetch Miles Procter.

The three of them sit opposite us, looking ridiculous with their zinc stripes and sunburned shoulders. William bites his lip; I can tell he's trying not to laugh.

I hold out my phone with the image pulled from the town's security footage. 'Do you know who this is?'

'It's Robbie!' exclaims William, laughing. 'What's he doing?'

'Robbie who?' I press.

'Robert Weston,' says James. 'One of our mates.'

'Where is Robert now?'

'In Sydney,' replies James, but he sounds uncertain.

'He left on Monday, is that right?'

William grunts and rolls his eyes. 'I hate how coppers do this, ask questions even though they know the answers.'

'Shut up, Will,' says James, elbowing him in the ribs.

'Why did Robert leave?' Grange asks.

'He's a whiny bitch,' says William, giggling.

I want to grab him by the shoulders and shake him. 'What do you mean?'

James gives William another scathing look. 'He hurt himself surfing so he figured there was no point being here. He reckoned he'd go get a job in a call centre or something.'

'Oh, come off it, he'd cocked up with the birds around here,' adds William. 'And he kept whingeing about it.'

'Which "birds"?' I say, failing to hold back the sarcasm.

'All of them,' William quips. He adjusts his fluorescent visor and water from his drink bottle sloshes over his head. 'Whoops,' he says, then giggles again.

The little patience I have is rapidly diminishing. 'Mr Mayne, this is really important. Do you need to come to the station and sober up?'

'Nah, nah. I'm alright. Sorry.' He closes his eyes, inhales deeply through his nose and slowly releases the air via his mouth. I can tell he's fighting another bout of giggles.

I look at James. 'When did Robert hurt himself?'

'Last week. Wednesday, I think.'

'Are you sure?'

James looks slightly bewildered. 'Yes. He went to hospital on Wednesday night. He got some painkillers, and the doctor said his wrist was sprained and he shouldn't put any pressure on it for at least a month.'

'And what about Saturday night? What did you guys do?'

'Partied,' says William obnoxiously.

'Where?' I say.

'It was a house party,' says James. 'Two sisters.'

'Robert came?'

They all nod.

'How did you end up there?' I say. 'You're not in high school.'

'We heard it on the grapevine,' sings William to the tune of the popular song.

'We got chatting to some birds at the pub, and they said we should come,' adds James.

'Do you know a girl called Abbey Clark?'

'The missing one,' says Miles.

'Did you speak to her on Saturday night?' I say.

'I'm sorry she's missing, but she was a stuck-up cow,' says William, the lightness in his voice gone. 'Robbie was just trying to chat to her—he does have a habit of coming on a bit strong, but he doesn't mean any harm. She was a real cock-tease though. I think she was having a tiff with her boyfriend or something. Whatever.'

'You do realise she is only fifteen?' Grange interjects, sounding outraged.

William doesn't miss a beat. 'No way! She looked way older. Robbie'll be disappointed.'

'What do you mean?' Grange says.

'He fell for her pretty hard. We had to walk past the supermarket all the time just so he could look at her. That's Robbie though, he tends to get a bit obsessed.'

'Did Robert speak to her at the party?'

James nods, while William guffaws. 'He tried to. She told him where to go.'

'Alright,' I say, keen to get to the point so I don't have to talk to William anymore, 'how late did you all stay at the party?'

He smothers another chuckle. 'Well, Robert was trying his luck with some other bird after that Abbey bird burned him, so we left his bitch-slapped arse at the house.'

'Around what time was that?'

For the first time, William looks thoughtful. 'I have no idea.'

'It was just before midnight,' says Miles. 'I remember thinking the pub would definitely be closed.'

'Where did you go?'

William kicks at the sand under the table and hooks his arms around the others' necks. 'We went back to the caravan park to drink beers in the pool until some old bat went off at us for making too much noise. Apparently you're not supposed to swim after 10 pm, which seems kind of stupid.'

'Did Robert come back there too?' I ask.

'Yeah, but later,' says James.

'What time?' I press.

'Around one in the morning, I think, but I was half asleep.'

'Was he alone?'

William slaps his thighs at this, completely losing it. 'He was *beyond* alone. He was all depressed the next day.'

I look at James. 'What do you mean?'

James shrugs and looks uncomfortable. 'Will's right. He was acting weird. We were giving him shit about having a bad run with girls—you know, just mucking around—but he cracked it. We figured he'd cool off, but on Monday he said he was leaving.' James's thick eyebrows knit together. 'We thought he was joking till he grabbed his stuff and cleared out.'

Thursday, 14 April
2.51 pm

I assemble the team in the stuffy meeting room and stand at the head of the table, leaning forward on my hands. 'Grange, get onto that footage from Sheffield, okay? If that goes nowhere, follow up his alibi. And the financial info for the hospital too.'

'Um, yes, sure.' Grange presses the tip of a pen into his notebook. 'Who do I speak to about that?'

'I don't know but find out,' I say sharply.

'You're talking about Eric Sheffield?' says Lane, looking puzzled.

I nod. 'I'm still concerned there's illegal drug activity running through the hospital.'

De Luca raises an eyebrow but simply says, 'I followed up with the airline company about Weston. He flew from Byron to Sydney on Monday. He withdrew a few hundred dollars from the airport ATM and hasn't used his bank cards since.'

'Good work.'

She shrugs, her gaze stony. 'Doesn't really help if we can't find him.'

'We will. Let's get in touch with backpacker hostels and other accomm around the beach areas. Even if he's injured I bet he'll still stay near the sea, and most places will demand to sight a passport. I'll put you in touch with some of my old colleagues.'

'Okay,' she says flatly, her fingers flying across her laptop.

I frown. Her ice queen routine is so maddening.

'The thing with Weston,' I say, 'is that his mates confirmed he was at the caravan park on Monday morning, so it seems he had nothing to do with Rick's murder. Which takes us back to the question around whether or not Abbey's disappearance and Rick's death are linked.'

We sink into silence, the puzzle pieces shifting around us.

'We need to follow up a few other people on the council footage,' says Lane. 'I don't think it will go anywhere, I know them all by sight. It's mostly families and couples. Oh, and Meg Jarvis was in the church for two hours and left just after eleven.'

'Meg Jarvis?'

'Yeah. My mum used to say she spends half her life in there lighting candles and praying.'

'Let me know how you get on with her,' I say. 'She tried to talk to me the other morning, but I couldn't work out exactly what she was trying to say. She might know something.'

'That's just Meg,' says Lane. 'She's always hassling Tommy about random stuff but never actually knows anything useful. She's not exactly the most stable person.'

'I understand she has health issues, but I want you to take her seriously. That goes for all the people on your list, whether you know them or not. That footage is so patchy, they might have seen something really relevant and just not realise it. I want their alibis confirmed too.'

Lane opens his mouth as if to protest, then snaps it shut.

'How did you go with your interviews?' I ask him and de Luca, moving over to the whiteboard.

'It was like pulling teeth,' de Luca says, 'and the kids are all pretty shell-shocked, which isn't helping. But a few of them admitted that drugs were at the party, so that's further than we got on Sunday.'

'What kind of drugs?'

'Non-specific pills,' she says drily. 'They seem to be all the rage these days.'

'Where were they getting them from?'

'The backpackers, of course,' says Lane. 'It's always the mysterious backpackers around here.'

'What about pot?' I say, thinking of the Fletchers.

'No one really mentioned it.'

'Yeah,' I say with a sigh. 'Apparently most of Georgina and Ian's customers are from up north. They wanted to keep their business away from Fairhaven, which makes sense. That was one of the main reasons they wanted to avoid a memorial for Rick—they were worried about the media attention and being recognised.'

We're all quiet for a minute. Right or wrong, I think we feel a degree of sympathy in regard to the catastrophic way Georgina and Ian's world has fallen apart over the past few days.

'Did anyone mention if Robert Weston or his mates were selling drugs?' I ask.

'They weren't specific with names,' says de Luca. 'We asked about male attendees with accents or identifying tattoos but got nowhere with that.'

'Did anyone say Abbey was taking drugs?'

De Luca shakes her head. 'The general consensus seems to be that she was pretty straight. She wasn't much of a drinker and didn't smoke.'

'What about Rick?' I ask.

'It seems it's a bit easier to throw the definitely dead under the bus,' says de Luca. 'Rick was known as someone you could go to for drugs. One girl mentioned he sold her ex-boyfriend some Stilnox tablets last year.'

'But we found nothing at his house,' I say, frustrated.

'I know.' She sits back in her chair. 'Maybe that was a one-off. It doesn't seem like he had a rep for being the town's drug dealer or anything, just that he knew the people you could go to. He was definitely rougher than his girlfriend—boozing and smoking weed, that kind of thing.'

Just like Gregory Ng.

'I wonder if that's part of the reason they broke up,' I say. 'Wasn't there a text Abbey sent him about not stopping something?'

'Yeah.' De Luca flicks through the papers in her folder. 'Here it is. About a month ago Abbey wrote a message to Rick that said: *This is really important to me. I don't like it, especially not after what I told you.*'

'That could have been in reference to drugs, but it also could have been a sex thing,' I say. 'Or just a certain kind of behaviour? Working at the pub?' I reach across the table. 'Show me.'

She hands me the transcript and I scan the rows of words, the mostly inane back and forth between two teenagers who were oblivious to the fact that one day their communication would be analysed by a roomful of police officers.

Abbey's texts to Rick since the start of the year are increasingly vague and disinterested; when I read them, I could almost see her slipping away. I scan the messages again, flipping the pages. Rick suspected she was seeing someone else, but nothing on her phone suggests that was the case. However, if even I can see the distance growing between them, this shows something was going on. And if the suspicion only existed in his head, it wasn't any less powerful.

I say, 'No one mentioned Rick being violent at the party?'

'No, not violent,' says Lane. 'His fight with Abbey was heated but everyone who witnessed it seems to agree she was just as angry as him. All his mates say he adored her. I get the feeling it kind of annoyed them, you know, that he'd found someone he was so into when they just wanted to have a good time.'

'Yeah.' I think back to my high school romance with Jacob. It had been completely consuming; it certainly felt as real as anything I've experienced since. Some of our peers were irritated by our interest in each other. They had the sudden realisation there was a binary developmental milestone no one had told us about: those teenagers who experienced this intoxicating madness of love versus those who didn't. I remember how I felt when Jacob started to slip away. I lost my mind. Had it made Rick crazy too? Crazy enough to destroy it?

'A lot of the kids reckon Abbey's run away,' says Lane, interrupting my trip down memory lane.

I frown. 'Why?'

'Because of her dad, mainly, and breaking up with Rick.'

'It was mostly the boys we spoke to saying that,' de Luca corrects. 'The girls are all pretty worried—they don't think she would have left in the middle of the night.'

'Me neither,' I say, 'but maybe she was desperate. The fact she lied to you about the bike being a gift from her dad is strange,' I say to Lane. 'I just can't work out what that was all about. I wonder if she reported the bike stolen so we'd be less likely to assume she ran away, but then why bring her dad into it?'

Lane makes a frustrated noise. 'I don't know.'

I think about Abbey arguing with her dad before the party. Maybe she figured going home after that was akin to a death sentence, and she just freaked out and fled.

'Did anyone you spoke to say anything about Abbey being violent? Threatening Rick?'

'No,' says de Luca. 'A few of the guys said there were rumours that maybe Abbey killed Rick, but none of them believed it.'

I squeeze my eyes shut; when I open them, little white dots are scattered across the scene in front of me. 'Any luck with our theory about Aiden and Abbey being involved with each other? Or Aiden's alibi.'

De Luca shakes her head. 'None of Aiden's friends reckoned he was seeing anyone. They all said he's a bit of a loner and that his brother was his closest mate.'

Lane says, 'I'm still tracking down CCTV of Aiden in Sydney on Monday morning. I spoke to the servo where his credit card pinged, and I'm waiting for the manager to call me back.'

'Okay.' I lean against the table again. 'We've got lots to follow up. Let's keep pushing.' I give them a pointed look. 'I'm just going to stay in here while I make a phone call.' Once they're gone, I sink into a chair and rest my head on the table.

My call to Mac goes straight to voicemail.

I slam my phone on the table and start shaking. Things feel like they're slipping further and further out of my control.

I get to my feet. I'm so thirsty.

There's a knock at the door, and Grange sticks his bald head in. 'Lab on the phone for you.'

Forgetting about getting a drink, I walk slowly to my desk and take the call.

When I hang up, I turn to find the others all looking at me expectantly.

'The blood from the ground is Abbey's,' I tell them.

Thursday, 14 April
6.32 pm

The confirmation on the blood changes everything and nothing. We go over the possible scenarios for a few minutes, but we're only slightly less in the dark than we were before. I call the Clarks and endure a ten-minute rant from Daniel about my incompetence while Dot cries in the background.

As I leave the station, I realise I didn't try to contact Janet Rixon again and decide I'll call her from the car. But when I hit the bottom of the ramp I see Simon Charleston waiting for me. He looks like a uni student in faded jeans and a T-shirt that reads, *OUT OF OFFICE. LEAVE A MESSAGE.* A pen sticks out of his unruly hair and there's a smudge of blue ink on his face.

'I can't talk now, Simon,' I say wearily.

'Did you speak to Vanessa about the accident?'

'It all checks out.'

He rolls his eyes. 'That's bullshit and you know it. Something stinks and it all comes back to Tommy.' Lowering his voice, he steps closer. 'I know you've just landed here but I've been sniffing around for a long time. I think something happened with the suspected homicides from years ago. Witnesses were dropping like flies,

retracting their statements left, right and centre, and refusing interviews with me. And then suddenly Tommy was promoted and no
one could explain it to me. And now there's the bizarre behaviour at
the car accident scene.' He tenses his jaw and grips it with his hand.
'Come on, Gemma. I need your help with this. I know you don't
just toe the standard line. Don't let me down.'

He's aimed where it hurts and landed the shot. 'Look, I don't
need your guilt trip. I'm here to do two things: solve Rick Fletcher's
homicide and find Abbey Clark. I suggest if you have something
concrete and it's bothering you then you take it to the minister.
There's no way I'm doing your job for you.'

'Thanks for nothing,' he says, stalking off.

Shaking slightly, I get in the car and stare blankly at the steering
wheel. If I wasn't so angry I could fall asleep right here. I blink a few
times and rub my eyes, trying to wake up before I start the car and
head toward the Gordons'.

My phone rings, a number I don't recognise. I answer on the
hands free and the sound of a woman crying fills the car.

'Hello?'

'Detective, he called—Aiden called.'

'That's good news, Georgina,' I say, guiding the car off the road
and stopping it under a giant gum tree. 'At least we know he's okay.'

'But something's wrong! He was being so strange. Oh my god,
I don't understand. He wants us to leave the house and stay somewhere else! What's going on?'

'Okay, Georgina, I'm really glad you called me. Tell me exactly
what happened.'

Her loud breathing becomes more even.

'Did he call your mobile?' I ask.

'Um, yes, but not on his phone. It came up as a private number.'

'Okay, and what exactly did he say?'

Her voice lifts an octave and veers out of control again. 'He was so upset! He didn't sound like himself—he kept saying he's sorry and this is all his fault. He said he's worried that Ian and I are in danger, and that we should take Belinda and go. He's worried that what happened to Rick might happen to us. I really just don't understand.'

'Okay, Georgina, it's okay. That must have been really frightening. Listen to me, where are you right now?'

She emits a long shuddery breath, and I think I can hear her teeth chatter. 'At home. The cops were here all day but they've left. I'm with our lawyer.'

'Where's Ian?'

'He took Belinda to see his mother at the nursing home. She's not well.'

'Alright. This is what I'm going to do—I'm going to organise a constable to come to your house now and stay with you for a while.'

'Do you think Aiden is right? Does someone want to hurt us?'

'I don't think so, but it doesn't hurt to be careful.'

'We were going to stay with my sister in Sydney next week.' Georgina sniffs. 'They're not letting us ... have Rick until next week anyway, and she is going to help us arrange the funeral ... Maybe we can go earlier?'

'I think that's a good idea.'

'What about Aiden? What if he's not safe?' Her loud sob pierces my ear.

'Georgina, did anything about the call give you an idea of where he might be?'

'No, I don't think so.'

'And you're sure you can't think of anyone Aiden would trust enough to stay with?'

'Maybe his ex-girlfriend,' she murmurs. 'They are still close. She lives in Sydney somewhere.'

'Do you know her name?'

'Um, yes. Elise Craven. I think she lives in Newtown.'

'Okay. Georgina, I'll arrange for someone to come to your house now, okay? And we're going to keep looking for Aiden.'

I call Tran and talk her through my call with Georgina.

'I can get someone from my team to go up there for a few hours,' she says distractedly. 'But I can't spare them for very long. Our overtime is through the roof.'

'Is everything alright?'

'Yes and no. We've spent all day interviewing the family of Dale Marx but we're not really getting anywhere. All his mates said he'd gone to ground in the few months before he disappeared. His parents haven't got a clue what he was up to. His father is very unwell and I think they've been pretty consumed by that.'

'But you're thinking drugs.'

'I'm not *thinking* drugs. The team found a decent haul in his bedroom—a whole cupboard of pharmacy grade stuff. And his car is gone. I'd say whoever knocked him off took it and whatever was in it.'

'Does he have any links to Aiden or Rick?'

'We're checking, obviously, but nothing has turned up yet. They weren't in contact and didn't go to the same school.'

'What did this guy do?'

'He worked at a vet clinic—cleaning and helping to manage the kennels.'

'Kind of like Aiden at the hospital,' I say.

Tran sighs. 'I know.'

I update her on our leads then steer the car back onto the road as I try to think. Are we looking at a love triangle or a drug triangle or both? If it was drugs, maybe Abbey dumping Rick prompted him to threaten dobbing her in. Would that be reason enough for her to fake her disappearance and attack him? For the hundredth time

I try to imagine her creeping up behind Rick and striking him, but my brain struggles, desperately searching for other scenarios.

A long email from Jodie lands in my personal inbox with a sharp ping just as I pull up at the Gordons'. She has bolded certain words for emphasis and divided the text into sections. I feel exhausted as I scroll through sentence after sentence. Ben has a school camp in four weeks' time—does he want to go? What should we do about his birthday this year? Will he want to have a party? Is it okay with me if Jodie takes him to her sister's fortieth birthday in late June? Does he want to keep playing soccer next term? Do I want my name added to his emergency contacts? Do I want to transfer him onto my health insurance policy now?

When are we coming home?

Anxiety grabs at me in exactly the same way it does every time I speak to Mac. I toss my phone onto the passenger seat where it clips the corner of my laptop.

It immediately starts to ring: Mac.

My temple throbs and I moan, pushing my fingers into my hair and gripping my head.

I can't do this.

My phone stops ringing and buzzes with his voice message.

Less than a minute later, it rings again. This time it's Cam.

I take a deep breath and answer, trying to keep my voice light. 'Hi, Cam. I'm glad you called. I need to ask you more questions about Rick. Do you know if him leaving the pub was a sudden thing or something he'd been thinking about for a while?'

'Whoa, whoa, Gemma.' Cam laughs nervously and I can tell he's running a hand through his thick hair. 'Um, I actually have someone here at the hotel who's been trying to get onto you. I'll just put him on.'

'Gemma, it's me.' Mac's voice simmers before it erupts. 'What the *hell* is going on?'

Thursday, 14 April
8.21 pm

As I put Ben to bed, I can hear the low rumble of Mac and Tommy's voices in the kitchen.

'Is Mac going to stay here now?' asks Ben.

'No, baby, he's just saying a quick hello to us and then he's going back to Sydney.'

Ben nods and closes his eyes; I smooth the sheet over him and kiss his cheek.

Then I return to the kitchen. 'Ben was out like a light,' I say brightly.

'I'm not surprised,' says Vanessa. 'He doesn't stop.'

There's an awkward pause as everyone looks at me.

'Well, Mac and I are just going to grab a quick drink and chat about some work stuff,' I say. 'I won't be long.'

Mac says goodbye to the Gordons and follows me out the front door.

'Are we really getting a drink?' he says stiffly as I walk ahead of him down the driveway.

I whirl around, my fists clenched. Since I picked him up from the hotel we've barely spoken. Looking at him, it's all I can do not to scream.

'I don't know, Mac, you tell me.'

'No way, no way.' He holds his hand up, eyes on fire. 'You don't get to be angry at me. I came here because you were ignoring me. Because I *care*, Gemma.'

We're locked in stalemate, blood surging hot and fast. My heart hurts.

I break the stare. 'This way.' I walk across the road to the beach.

Silvery clouds block the moon, only the faintest glow reaching around their edges. The gums dust peppermint through the warm air, but there's a layer of something heavy as well. Something nearby is starting to decay.

Halfway up the shore I sink to the ground, crossing my legs like a child. Mac folds down next to me.

'Look, I'm sorry,' I say, with as much calm as I can muster. 'I told you I need time to think.'

Mac is staring out at the sea. 'And don't you think that terrifies me?'

'Mac.'

'What, Gemma? Come on, be fair. I know everything is upside down for you and for Ben right now, but it's not much better for me. You left, and right now I have no idea whether or not you're coming back.' He sifts a handful of sand through his fingers. 'But the worst part is, you won't talk to me. You're shutting me out, and when I get here I find out you've lied to me about where you're staying. It's not okay.'

I wedge my head between my knees, blocking my ears so I can barely hear myself say, 'I'm sorry. I just don't know what to do.' Tears spill from my eyes and drip straight onto the sand.

'Let me help you, Gemma. Don't shut me out.'

His hand circles my back while I cry, and I don't fight it. A series of shivers run up my neck to my scalp and I breathe out. It feels good to relax, to not be on alert for a moment.

'What happened at the hotel?' Mac asks. 'The owner was cagey when I asked him.'

I tell Mac about the possum, and about Tran's insistence that I stay with the Gordons. He doesn't react; he just keeps stroking my back, his movements in time with the waves.

'I would have been happy to stay there,' I say, 'but in the end it was just easier. And I thought being close to Tommy might help with the case.' I huff a laugh.

'But it hasn't?'

'Not really. He isn't very happy I'm here.'

Mac smiles. 'No, I wouldn't have thought so.' He gathers my hair into a mane down the centre of my back. 'I remember Tommy from that inquest for the missing couple. He's such a man's man.'

'Is that code for "prick"?'

Mac laughs, and I smile.

'What did you think of the inquest?' I ask.

'God, you're incorrigible,' says Mac, yawning. 'It was a mess. Evidence was misplaced, witnesses refused to talk, and other statements were deemed inadmissible because the proper procedures hadn't been followed. The ruling was probably right in the end but it certainly wasn't helped by the way the case was put together.'

I look out at the ocean, its silvery tips like fishtails.

'One of the witnesses was the father of the missing girl,' Mac says.

'What?'

'Daniel Clark. He was drinking at the pub that night and apparently had a run-in with the missing Ng boy—he kicked Clark out. Originally Clark said he was so drunk he just stumbled to the beach and passed out there.'

My mind is cranking into gear, frantically joining the dots. 'Originally?'

'Yeah.' Mac adjusts his position and edges closer to me. 'He said he passed out on the beach and when he came around he saw Gregory driving off in his car with another person.'

'Did he see who it was?'

'He just said it was a man.'

'Definitely not Sally?'

'No, Clark insisted it was a man. But it didn't matter anyway because later he claimed to have no memory of the night after Gregory asked him to leave the pub. He said his original statement must have been a false memory.'

'Someone scared Daniel off?'

'That's what I wondered,' says Mac, 'but I'm not sure. I remember entertaining the possibility that he was in with the cops at one point, but I think the general consensus around here was that he was just a drunk who couldn't get his story straight. I chalked it up as one of those messy cases.' Having edged close enough to me, Mac leans forward for a quick kiss. 'I just thought you should know. Maybe Clark has friends in the force. It often happens in places like this where everyone has known each other for a long time.'

'Maybe,' I say, leaning back on my elbows.

Mac exhales and stretches out his legs. 'I'm worried about you, Gemma. Obviously I don't like the idea of someone threatening you. You should have told me.'

'I'm fine. I didn't want to worry you.'

Mac lifts his gaze to mine. 'I am worried. I'm worried about us.'

'Kiss me.' I move my head so it's level with his.

He makes an exasperated sound but presses his lips to mine. Peppermint, and a hint of beer. I try to meld into him but he's being too careful with me. I can almost feel his worry.

'Properly,' I say, pushing against him. I feel myself merging into him as my body relaxes. But it still isn't enough. 'Get up.' I scramble to my feet and try to pull him with me. He doesn't fight back and I edge him toward the wall of trees.

'Gemma, stop. We need to talk.'

'I don't want to.' I cover my mouth with his, satisfied when I feel him respond. 'Come to the car.' I keep pulling him along the beach and up the sandy path.

'Gemma, stop. You're crazy—what are you doing?'

'I want you,' I say, hustling us across the road, stopping to kiss him every few seconds. I'm desperate, dizzy. He's half laughing as if he thinks I'm joking but it's all I want. I unlock the car and open the back door, turning off the interior light. 'Get in.'

'Are you serious?'

'I want you,' I say again. 'Now.'

He opens his mouth then snaps it shut, shuffling into the middle of the back seat.

'I want you too Gem but—'

'Shhh.'

I glance at the Gordons': the lamp next to the front door casts a dim semicircle of light across the lawn, but aside from that the house is dark.

I pull the car door shut and straddle him. 'I want you so bad.'

'Gemma,' Mac murmurs, as I start kissing him again. 'I know what you're doing. It's just like after we found Nicki—you know, you shut me out then too.'

'Does it look like I'm shutting you out?'

'You know what I mean. You're ignoring the issues. You're pretending everything is fine.'

I almost laugh. I feel such a long way from fine. Instead I hike up my skirt and loosen his belt.

My knees press into the leather on either side of his body. Mac draws a sharp breath, his firm hands circling my thighs. 'Gemma, are you sure?'

I nod and clutch at his face, hooking my hands around the back of his neck, covering his mouth with mine.

'Well, you have to promise to talk to me afterwards.'

'I promise,' I whisper.

The past few months disappear. It's exactly like the first time we slept together; the whole universe is reduced to just him and me.

'God, I love you,' he says breathlessly, as I move on top of him, just as I think the words.

He holds me close when I shudder in pleasure, the exquisite agony of the moment giving way to our bleak reality. The windows are cloudy, and all I can hear is our ragged breathing. Sweat cools on my skin and I shift sideways, tugging my clothes back on.

'Don't be in such a hurry to get away from me,' he jokes, fumbling with his pants and handing me some tissues as he tries to keep an arm around me. He looks at me huddled against the car seat and bursts out laughing. 'Well, I guess that's one way to apologise.' He wipes his sleeve across the side of his head, then his expression turns serious. 'I miss you, Gemma. Not just this but all of it.'

I let him pull me close again and his heartbeat pounds against my ear. 'I miss you too.'

He smooths hair from my face. 'Come home. Finish this thing here if you need to, but after that come home to Sydney and be with me.'

'I can't promise you that,' I say, the words catching in my throat. 'Everything is different now.'

He moves away from me, his beautiful full lips firming into a hard line. He tilts his head, looking hurt. 'Why are you shutting me out? I don't understand.'

'It's not as simple as you think.' Panic is squeezing me.

'But what if it is?'

'I'm pregnant,' I whisper.

Mac's jaw drops open just as a blinding light beams into the windscreen. A nearby car has sprung to life and speeds off into the night. Mac scrambles to neaten his clothes as I scan the dark street, my pulse racing even more than it did before. Everything is eerily still; not even the tree branches are moving. I whip my head in the other direction, feeling vulnerable and exposed. Then, without meaning to, I start to laugh, the giggles quickly turning manic.

Mac looks uncertain. 'Gemma?'

'I have to go,' I say, straightening my legs and adjusting my skirt.

'Gemma!'

'No, not now. I don't want to talk about it now. I can't.'

Mac smacks his palms into the felt ceiling and moans. 'Fuck, you're unbelievable. You drop something like that on me and refuse to talk about it? Be fair.'

I push open the door, feeling a bizarre mixture of chaos and calm. I lean back into the car and kiss him hard on the mouth, half wanting to climb inside and do it all again. 'I'm sorry but you can't stay here, and I have to go. I need sleep. Let's meet in the morning— early. There's a cafe on the main street near the hotel. I'll be there at seven-thirty.'

SIXTH DAY MISSING

Friday, 15 April
5.24 am

Mac and I are in the case room. It's late and we're arguing.

'You're not listening to me,' I repeat. 'Everything still points to Nicki running away. Her parents swear it's her writing on the postcard. Owen and I have spoken to over twenty of her friends. She had talked about running away for months. She broke up with her boyfriend and her dog died. I can't explain the thing with Susie, but maybe it was just someone out there wanting to jerk us around. Even if Susie was paid to say she'd seen Nicki, it doesn't mean she isn't out there somewhere.' My voice drops. 'She was messed-up, Mac. Her relationship with sex was problematic—you've seen the photos, the messages. I think she made a snap decision to run away and now she's proving a point by sticking to it. What more do you want?'

Mac holds my stare for a few seconds, then pushes away from the desk and stands up, hands on his hips. He's facing a board covered with information about a girl neither of us has ever met. 'That doesn't explain the CCTV. If she caught that bus, why isn't she on the tape? It doesn't add up, Gemma. Anyone could have bought that ticket. And the dog dying bothers me too.'

'What do you mean?'

'It was three years old and just dropped dead in the backyard.'

I fold my arms. 'Maybe it had a heart attack.'

'Maybe, but when I spoke to Lucas something felt wrong. There was something he wasn't saying, I'm sure of it.'

We've both found Lucas hard to read. He flips from grieving to numb in a moment and is desperate to know every step of our progress.

'Mac,' I say, as calmly as I can, 'I want to find her as much as you do, but I don't see what a dead dog has to do with a teenage girl going missing. My bet is that she took off and has probably convinced some poor guy to put her up for a while. We're wasting our time.'

Mac leans forward, fists on the table. 'Can't you see, Gemma? There are too *many* red herrings. Someone is setting us up, trying to make it look like she ran away.'

I sigh. All I want is to grab his face and kiss him. We first slept together a month ago, barely making it from the pub to his house. I was glued to him in the taxi, knowing that everything was about to change between us, that the thing I wanted so badly was finally going to happen. I wrapped my arms around him as he fumbled with the keys to his door. As the door slammed shut behind us, he pushed me gently against the wall. We had sex right there, next to the hatstand in his hallway, our clothes puddled around us. I couldn't get close enough to him.

Since then I've stayed at his place almost every night. I'm in a blissful bubble of intensity that I thought only existed in films and illicit relationships. I'm still getting my head around the idea that this could be real, that we can actually be together.

But Nicki Mara is a thorn in my side, the only thing Mac and I can't seem to agree on. I notice that Owen is often leaving us to fight it out, perhaps sensing our relationship has transcended a professional partnership.

'I've got to be honest with you, Mac, I feel like I'm being dicked around by this girl. If it wasn't for the media coverage we would have dropped this a long time ago. I don't disagree there are red herrings. Maybe she bought that ticket on her credit card and then paid cash for a train trip out of here. She probably sent that postcard but that doesn't mean it isn't full of lies.'

'But what if we're wrong, Gem? What then?'

His words echo around me as I stare in horror at Nicki's bruised face, her broken fingers nestled on her lap in the empty bath.

What if we're wrong?

I blink awake, Mac and the case room retreating into the shadows. All of my frustration is gone, and I lie in bed feeling hollow and numb, my nerve endings muted. I reach my hands up to the ceiling as if to prove to myself that I'm real.

I slide out of bed and pull on the wetsuit I found in the guest-room cupboard. Standing in front of the mirror, I smooth my hands down the front of the suit. Last night with Mac feels like it happened a million years ago. I creep down the corridor and out of the house.

The air is cool. All traces of the moon are gone but the sun is yet to make an appearance. I consider the ocean. It ripples prettily. I step into the water, my feet smarting from the cold. No one else is in sight. I know I shouldn't go into the water alone but the desire to be cleansed, to be reset by the shock, is overwhelming. I take another step. My thighs are swallowed by the chill. Another step and the sandy floor disappears, and I kick frantically to keep my head above water. My teeth rattle as the cold overcomes me. My muscles, my skin, my organs are all screaming; in my mind their cries blend with the crashing cycle of the sea. I tip forward to frog kick.

The suit chafes around my pelvis but it feels good to be suspended, to be weightless and free. I move past the breaking waves to the eerie calm of the swell. After a few minutes I roll myself onto my back and stare at the sky with my ears underwater.

Is Scott watching me right now? Is he looking down at me as I bob around and thinking how unfair it is that he was the one who died? Is Mum watching me and attributing her unexpected death to my failings as a mother?

I push my hands out in front of me and wing them back to my sides as if I'm flying. I think about Mac and how much I want to fuse my life with his, to finally let someone look after me, but now I just can't see a path toward that anymore. I start to cry, tears streaming into the sea. Ashes to ashes.

I have people who care about me, who I love in return, but right now I feel completely alone.

The shore is already a surprisingly long way away. I can see the mouth of the path that leads to the Gordons' house beyond the thick strip of sand. I cycle my legs and hear my breathing in my head like an echo. Is this how Abbey felt that night, raw and alone? I want so badly to find her. I can't give up on her yet; I have to keep trying to bring her home, one way or another.

A wave slaps against my face, shoving me under the swell. I cry out and my mouth promptly fills with water. I kick harder and come up for air but am struck down by another wave. Bubbles tickle my nose, and my eyes sting. I snatch a breath before another wave hits. I drift sideways; the sea is playing games with me. The wave bears down and I am under again. I'm being tossed around like a piece of seaweed; my limbs are splayed and my head snaps back. Once again I am thrust from the water, gasping above the surface. Another wave. This time I kick, my thighs burning. I need to get out of here.

I kick again with as much force as I can muster, but suddenly I'm not sure which way is up. All I can see is navy-blue. My chest tightens and panic rips through me. Am I in real danger? The thought is oddly numbing. My mind empties; I let the ocean toss me from left to right as I hold my breath.

Moments later I am spat out into the air again. The sky is lighter now, the clouds preparing for the arrival of the sun. The angry waves have vanished, replaced by innocent-looking peaks. My breathing is crazed, desperate, and a bizarre energy pulses in my veins. I enjoy the ache in my muscles as I push my limbs through the water and torpedo myself toward the sand. I've been kicked but I'm not down.

My legs shake as I stagger onto the shore. I unzip and peel off my artificial skin. Feeling the strangest combination of dazed and intensely alert, I make my way slowly up the path, squeezing water out of my hair.

'Mum!' Ben runs from the porch where he has clearly been waiting for me. He's still in his pyjamas. 'I didn't know where you went! What were you doing?'

Fading goose bumps bristle on my arms. Through chattering teeth I stammer, 'I just went for a swim.'

Ben blinks. 'In the sea?'

I nod, pulling a towel from the railing.

'I didn't know you did that,' he says.

Wrapping him into the fold of the towel, I kiss the top of his head. 'I do now.'

Friday, 15 April
7.28 am

I wait at one of the tables outside the Bird of Paradise cafe, feeling the same panic that tore through me after Scott's fateful phone call.

At a table inside, a woman with Bali braids is trying to bribe two boisterous children to behave with offers of cake and hot chocolates, but the street is virtually empty, with only the occasional jogger plodding past.

Pushing a spoon around in a jar of sugar, I try to force the dread deep down into my core but it just keeps bubbling up again.

A cheerful young woman in extremely short denim cut-offs sticks her head out. 'Sure I can't get you anything, love?' Her skimpy tank top reveals a generous wedge of her large breasts. 'We're not really supposed to be open today seeing as it's Good Friday but the owners aren't religious and they figured we could see how we go and close early.' She clamps her hands on her hips and looks at me expectantly. 'So. Coffee?'

'Thanks, but I'm waiting for someone.' I check the time on my phone and wonder if what I just said is true.

One of Abbey's missing person posters has been taped to the inside of the cafe window. It already looks slightly faded and the bottom corners have ripped. I wonder who put the posters up.

An older woman in a visor is power-walking past and smiles at me. 'Hello.'

A guy carrying a surfboard jogs across the road in front of me. I'm pretty sure I saw him on the beach yesterday.

Even the dog tied to the leg of the park bench looks familiar.

On the other side of the intersection, Tara Sheffield sidles out of an Audi four-wheel drive and beeps it shut with a flourish. A few moments later she struggles to manoeuvre an A-frame sign from the narrow entrance to the beauty salon. I can see her bright pink nails from here. She tugs the signage straight, its metal legs screeching along the concrete.

The nerves in my spine contract just as two hands grip my shoulders from behind. I gasp and release my hold on the spoon, which clatters noisily against the table.

'It's just me,' says Mac, brushing his lips against my cheek and taking a seat opposite.

The waitress appears instantly, seemingly as relieved as I am that my date actually showed up.

We order coffees and spend an excruciating minute struggling to make eye contact.

'I'm sorry about last night,' I begin.

Mac smiles wryly. 'It wasn't all bad.'

I stare at the table. Snapshots from the car flit through my mind but it's like they happened years ago. 'No,' I say, fighting tears. 'But I am sorry about everything else.'

Our coffees arrive and Mac stirs a teaspoon of sugar into his. I soak up his face, the way his watch sits on his wrist, the faint spray of silver on either side of his sandy hair.

'I'm not going to lie,' he says. 'I was awake for quite some time last night.'

'Are you mad?'

'Well, it doesn't strike me as something to be mad about.' He keeps his voice neutral. 'At this point I'm mainly interested to know how you feel about it.'

My rib cage contracts. 'That's the thing, I don't know how I feel about it. I don't have time to feel anything about it.'

'Are you sure you're pregnant?'

I nod. I try to force a smile but can only manage a grimace.

Mac has more coffee and starts to laugh. 'Well, fuck, hey?'

'I honestly don't know how it happened—I mean, you know I have an IUD. It must have stopped working. Or maybe I did something wrong? I don't know.'

'I don't think the "how" matters too much right now, Gemma.'

'No,' I murmur. 'I suppose not.' I bite my lip. 'I thought about not saying anything to you, just sorting it out and pretending it never happened, but I—'

'I'm glad you told me,' Mac says quickly. 'Very glad. And I'm even more glad I came here now and that we're having this conversation in person.'

'Yeah.' I pick up the spoon and prod at the sugar again.

'So, back to your feelings . . . Gemma?'

A car swings into a park outside the beauty salon. Lane's girlfriend with the dreadlocks gets out and fetches a large canvas from the boot. Tara teeters down the front steps and waves her arms, clearly praising the artwork.

I take a deep breath and try to keep the panic at bay, but my voice becomes increasingly shrill. 'I don't want this, Mac, you know that. Ben is nine and I haven't lived with him since he was five. Your children are adults and you're almost fifty. I miscarried the last time

I was pregnant, and there's every chance it will happen again. Scott is dead and I'm worried about Ben.' My voice cracks. 'I'm not even good with kids.'

'Everything you just said might be true,' replies Mac calmly, 'except the last bit.'

'I'm just really sorry.'

'This is definitely one of those fifty-fifty situations—we each take half the blame.' He reaches across the table and holds my hand. 'Did you really mean it when you said you don't want this?' His voice is uncharacteristically tentative.

'I don't know,' I say softly, feeling a surge of intense affection for him. A whirring sound starts to fill my brain. The relentless crash of the waves this morning. Sheets of glass breaking. 'I'm sorry but I really don't! I feel so overwhelmed right now, about everything.'

Mac squeezes my hand and nods. As I struggle not to cry, I wonder what he's really thinking. No matter what he says, I know none of this was on his mind when we started seeing each other.

'He wants a dog,' I blurt.

'Who does?' says Mac, puzzled.

'Ben.'

Mac laughs. 'So get him a dog!'

'Just like that?'

'Why not? Dogs are good. I like dogs. You like dogs.'

I make a frustrated sound.

'What, Gemma?'

'I just want to know it will all work out, whatever "it" is.'

'Oh, Gem. That's way above my paygrade, I'm afraid.'

I glance over at the salon again. The pink of the exterior is the same colour as Tara's nails.

I pan back to Mac's concerned face. 'I need time to think. You shouldn't have come here, and I shouldn't have said anything yet.

I need you to leave.' I'm whispering as I struggle to keep myself in check. I don't want to hurt him but his feelings are suffocating me. 'I'm sorry but I can't do this right now. I can't afford to fall apart. You need to leave me alone for a while.'

'Are you kidding me?' Mac looks incredulous. He pulls his hand away and sits back in his chair. 'You can't keep shutting me out. Have a baby or don't, stay in Smithson or don't, I'll try to support you either way. Buy Ben a bloody dog. It doesn't mean you're putting down roots. I know you're scared but you're not alone.'

'This isn't what you want, though, is it? This isn't what you signed up for. None of it is.'

Mac's jaw clenches. 'I'm not going to pretend any of this has been easy. It has made one thing clear to me, though, and that's how much I care about you. Obviously a lot of stuff is up in the air, but that's the one thing I do know. I can't make you guarantees—no one can. You need to stop looking for them.'

I push myself to my feet. 'I'm sorry, Mac. I need to finish what I started here. And I need to talk to Ben about what he wants. Just give me some more time.'

'I'll just wait to hear from you then, shall I?' His jaw tenses.

There's nothing more to say. I wrench my eyes from him and head shakily over to my car. Through the windscreen I watch him leave a ten-dollar note on the table and walk away. I let my stare get lost in the pattern of the dash, taking deep breaths, and after a few minutes the ringing begins to fade. As the beauty salon comes into focus, a niggling realisation lands solidly in my consciousness.

I get out of the car and jog across the road.

Tara must see me coming—she emerges from the shop and waves to me with a friendly smile. 'Morning, Detective!' she trills. 'I'm so glad you finally stopped by but we're actually not open today. I'm just here catching up on a few things. It's relentless running a small business, always so much to do.' She plucks a brochure from the plastic pocket on the sign and hands it to me. 'All our treatments are listed in here.'

'Tara,' I begin, frantically pulling on threads that are knotted in my head, 'your front window was broken, right? I'm pretty sure I saw it being fixed. You said you had a break-in?'

Her smile disappears. 'Yes, someone threw a brick through the window.' She pouts. 'It completely ruined the painting on the display wall. I have to say,' she continues, 'I felt really bad about that. Windows are replaceable but artwork obviously isn't. Elsha, she's the artist, was pretty upset about it and I don't know if the insurance company will pay for it.'

'When did it happen? Was it on Saturday night?'

'Yes, well,' says Tara, looking slightly put out, 'I *called* the station on Sunday morning and I spoke to that girl cop, and she said I had to call back. I could hear someone yelling in the background, but I didn't know about Abbey then. Of course later on we heard about the search, so we just cleaned up the glass and got the salon sorted as best we could. There was a full week of bookings—I didn't have much choice. And then Tommy had his accident as well, so the whole thing didn't really get sorted out for a few days. Eric put some plastic sheeting he had at the hospital across the windows, which was the best we could do in the meantime. It was a bloody nightmare actually.'

'But it definitely happened overnight on Saturday?'

Tara steps back and says slowly, 'Yes, I assume so. We had family dinner at the pub on Saturday night like we always do. There was a fundraiser on, a bingo night for the hospital. It finished early, probably about nine-thirty, and we walked home past the salon. Everything was fine then. But by seven o'clock on Sunday morning it certainly wasn't.' She points along the street. 'Mary from the cafe called to tell me. She noticed it when she was opening up. We don't keep any cash on the premises so we don't have an alarm.' Tara gazes at her building. 'Maybe we should get one. What do you think?'

I'm barely listening to her as I step sideways and run my eyes up the length of the window. 'What did you do with the brick? Do you still have it?'

She looks at me blankly. 'I have no idea, but Eric might know. I can call him . . .?'

'Tara, has anything like this ever happened before? Has anyone ever vandalised your house?'

'Of course not.' She falters, looking horrified. Her arched eyebrows struggle to penetrate her rigid forehead. Then she squares her shoulders and says, 'Eric's a *doctor*. We are highly respected members of this community. Do you know how much we do for—'

But I am already heading back to my car.

Friday, 15 April
9.14 am

On the way to the station I realise I left my work phone at the Gordons'. Vanessa's car isn't in the driveway, and I vaguely remember her asking me if Ben could come with her to take Tommy to an appointment at the hospital today.

Except for the hum of the dishwasher, the house is silent. Inka stares at me mournfully from the back door and whines sharply. My pulse picks up and I become aware of a faint ringing. Is it coming from the fridge? Inexplicably jumpy, I grab my phone from my bedroom and turn to go. I pause in the sunlit hallway, knowing what I'm about to do before I've even processed it properly.

The door to Vanessa and Tommy's ensuite is slightly ajar and I push on it, exposing the mirrored cabinet unit. I open the cupboards and scan an array of bathroom products before yanking open each drawer. The middle drawer is full of prescription boxes. There must be at least fifteen of them. The bottom drawer is the same: valium, oxycodone, alprazolam.

Bending down, I carefully pick up one of the boxes—prescribed by Doctor Eric Sheffield and dated November last year. Way before Tommy's accident. I pick up another; this one has Vanessa's name on it and the date stamp reads January. Another of the boxes is prescribed to a Kevin Gordon by a doctor in Byron Bay, while one box of valium has Kai Lane's details on it and was prescribed by Eric.

A little montage quickly forms and plays in my mind. Tommy's glassy-eyed stare. His vagueness. His constant pill-popping. Simon Charleston's knitted brows, and Eric's cryptic inquiry into Tommy's health at the hospital.

The walls seem to close in as I stare at the contents of the drawer. What the hell is going on?

Is Tommy involved in some kind of drug dealing? Is he stock-piling drugs and selling them? Is Eric somehow connected to this? I look back at the pillboxes. Is Lane?

I stand up and feel the blood lurch around my body. As the dizziness dissipates, I consider my reflection in the mirror. I look terrible. I wonder what it would be like to just throw back a couple of the little white pills. Would they take away the throbbing pain that has consumed me since Scott fell ill? Would they block out all the noise? The ringing in my head?

I shove the box back in with the others. No. It might make things easier for me but it certainly won't make things easier for Ben.

'Fuck this,' I say, kicking the drawer shut and storming out of the house.

I work myself into a lather of anger as I drive back into town. Everyone I encounter in this place seems to be hiding something, and I'm jack of it.

Mac's face bubbles up in my mind. And I swiftly force it down again.

I park outside the supermarket, where I purchase a packet of cigarettes and a lighter from Roxy without making eye contact. A few hundred metres from the police station, I pull over at the end of the bush path and fumble with the plastic wrap as I get out of the car.

I picture Abbey here on Saturday night. Was Rick with her? Were they tangled up in drugs and working together until something went bad? Had they threatened to blow the lid off the whole thing? I light the cigarette and stare up at the sky. And what about Lane? What's his role in all this?

My memories begin as a trickle and then flood in: Nicki Mara's battered body, her sightless eyes. Mac holding me back as I tried to get closer to her. Owen's crushed expression.

The notion that Abbey is somewhere close by, broken and rotting, taunts me relentlessly. Finding Nicki was bad—never finding her would have been worse. The smoke sticks to my skin and blood rushes to my head. I retch and toss the cigarette onto the ground, burying it in the dust. What the hell am I doing? I need to get it together.

I get back in the car and gulp water from my drink bottle before I drive to the station.

As I stride in, I eyeball my three constables. 'Who was responsible for the report about the beauty salon break-in?' I bark.

No one moves. After a few beats, de Luca gets to her feet. 'I was.'

Music is playing from someone's computer. 'Turn that off,' I snap.

Grange fumbles with his speakers, knocking one over.

'Why didn't you tell me about it?' I ask de Luca.

Although my eyes are on her, I'm aware that Lane is close by; I picture the pillbox with his name on it in Tommy's bathroom drawer and ride another surge of frustration.

De Luca turns an unflattering red and looks bewildered. 'I just didn't think it was relevant,' she stammers. 'I mentioned it to Tommy on Sunday morning when Tara called, but by then we'd already received the call from Daniel about Abbey being missing. Tara said nothing had been taken from the salon, then Tommy asked me to go to Rick's with him.' De Luca looks uncharacteristically flustered. 'With the search and then Tommy's accident, I didn't follow it up until Monday after we'd been to the Fletchers' and I had Noah do the paperwork on Tuesday.'

I close my eyes, well aware I'm angry about a lot more than this oversight but still finding it hard to control my rage. 'Did you not think,' I say quietly, 'that an act of vandalism taking place in close proximity to a suspected homicide might be worth considering?'

She swallows and looks to her colleagues; they're no help, their eyes trained to the floor. 'I'm sorry,' she says, her cropped hair falling around her face as she drops her head.

'"Sorry" is not going to solve this case. Everything is a potential clue and I need to rely on you not to miss critical information. It should have been part of the timeline. It's not like we have an abundance of leads.'

'I can appreciate it was an oversight,' says de Luca formally, getting to her feet. 'Excuse me.'

I think I hear a faint sob as she pushes the office door open.

Lane and Grange glance up at me before fixing their gaze on the faded carpet again.

'I need to talk to you too,' I tell Lane. I stalk past him and hear him fall into step beside me. Still tingling with rage, I shut the meeting-room door and cross my arms.

Lane sits gingerly on the edge of a chair, swallowing noisily. 'What's up?'

'Have you ever given Tommy Gordon drugs?'

The muscles in his face harden into incredulity. 'What?'

'I found some medication at the Gordons' and it was prescribed to you. Explain that to me.'

Lane looks at me blankly then snaps back to life. 'Oh, valium, right? Yeah, last year I was prescribed some for an old sports injury but I didn't really need it in the end. Tommy hurt his back here at the station one day, and I gave him the packet and said to keep it. No big deal.' He stands up, his confidence restored, and lifts his eyebrows. 'Is that it?'

We lock eyes. 'That's it,' I say, yanking open the door. My gaze is trained to him as he walks out before I follow. 'Right,' I say briskly. 'Grange, you've still got Eric to follow up. Lane, I want you to focus on Aiden. First, I want to confirm that Georgina really did receive a call from him yesterday. Assuming she did, see if you can trace its origin. Then get in touch with his ex-girlfriend and see what shakes out.'

'I've also got those alibis to follow up, the people on the footage,' says Lane. 'And some footage through from the locations Aiden's credit card was used in Sydney.'

'Good, get busy,' I say as I head outside.

I hear de Luca before I see her. I walk around the side of the building where she's talking on her phone, shading her eyes and flexing each foot in turn. When she sees me coming, she mutters something into the phone before hanging up, quickly wiping a finger under her left eye. The delicate curves of her nostrils are a little red but she projects her usual reserved demeanour. 'I'm sorry I walked out before,' she says curtly. 'That was unprofessional.'

'I'm sorry I dressed you down like that,' I say. 'It was unnecessary and, if I'm honest, not wholly directed at you. I was frustrated.'

She looks surprised but simply nods and then lifts her chin, squinting into the sun. She is at least a foot taller than me, but I recognise a vulnerability, a simmering frustration. I remember what Tommy said about her at the house the other morning and feel a sudden sense of kinship with her, despite her prickliness.

'How long have you been on the squad?' I ask.

'Four years.'

'What's your plan? Are you keen to become a senior constable? Or are you keen to push for sergeant?'

Her fists clench. 'There's no chance of me becoming a sergeant if I stay here.'

I cross my arms and lean against the wall. 'Why not?'

'It just won't happen.'

'I don't understand.'

'I've spoken to Tommy about it but he doesn't think I'm ready.' Her upper lip flares.

'Well,' I say diplomatically, 'it's not really my place to comment but perhaps you can speak to him about any specifics and agree to a career plan.'

She rolls her eyes. 'I know what the specifics are. He thinks my "lifestyle" is an issue and, on top of that, I'm simply not his type.' She scoffs. 'I have no interest in his stupid jokes and archaic attitude. So it's pretty obvious I'm not getting anywhere here.'

'It's not easy, is it?' I say, after a pause.

'It's easier for some,' she says sullenly. 'You wouldn't understand.'

I laugh, surprised. 'What do you mean?'

She shrugs. 'You're so senior, and people like Tommy trust you to come in here and run two major investigations.'

I blink. 'I barely know Tommy but he certainly didn't ask me to lead the investigation—Tran did.'

'No,' de Luca stammers, 'that's not right. I suggested I could lead the investigation with Tran's help, and apparently she was considering it until Tommy kicked up a fuss and said I wasn't capable of running anything. Lane said he wanted to bring in someone he could rely on.' She tips her head to the side. 'I have to admit, I was surprised you're a woman. Obviously he doesn't have the same problems with you as he does with me.'

I hold up my hands. 'I don't know where any of this is coming from but I am here by chance only. Tran contacted my old boss initially, and I stepped in instead. I don't care what was or wasn't said, but I'm here now and I would like us to work a lot better together, if that's okay with you?'

De Luca looks at the ground and nods stiffly.

'Good. I think we've got enough on our plates as it is without the extra drama. Agreed?'

She wipes her nose and straightens to her full height so she's looking down at me. 'Agreed. I didn't get the chance to tell you before but I think I've found Robert Weston.'

Friday, 15 April
3.06 pm

De Luca made contact with a Bondi hostel that said Robert Weston checked in on Monday night. 'He wasn't there last night, and the girl I spoke to this morning said she couldn't leave the desk to check his room but when she called through he wasn't answering.'

De Luca logs on to her email and shows me the booking confirmation the hostel sent through. Robert's plain face stares out at me from the scan of his passport.

I glance at the board: Robert, Aiden, Rick, Abbey. Daniel Clark. Eric. The Fletchers.

'This is great work,' I say, putting my hand on her shoulder. 'Let me make some calls. We'll send some uniforms over there and see if they can track him down.'

I call Owen, who assures me he'll send a constable to the hostel as soon as he can.

After the brief frenzy of excitement, the four of us sit at our desks surrounded by sheets of paper. It's so quiet I can hear the press of tyres on asphalt every time a car drives past. The lingering smell of a toasted sandwich triggers nausea and I take another sip of water, eyeing the others. De Luca alternates between making notes and typing on her laptop. The tip of Grange's tongue pokes out; he could hide a toothpick in the ridge between his eyes it's so deep. Lane's resting face is serene, but his eyes don't seem to be moving across the piece of paper in front of him, and he keeps clutching at the back of his neck and massaging it aggressively. I cross my legs the opposite way to deter the cramp that's threatening to set in.

Closing my eyes, I think back to Aiden coming to his house on Monday and breaking down. I'm certain his grief was real, but it remains unclear if he was involved in Rick's death.

I startle when I realise Grange is standing next to me. 'Detective Woodstock,' he says tentatively, 'I'm having trouble getting my hands on the hospital's financial details. It's complicated—there are holding company names, and it's tied up with the beauty salon finance. Their accountants are based in Sydney. The guy I spoke to said he needs both Eric and Tara's permission, but Eric is away camping with his kid. He did mention that at the hospital.'

'Fuck's sake,' I mutter.

'Yeah, I know. But I did confirm Eric is in the hospital security tapes on Monday morning.'

'What time?'

'Um . . . 6.33 am.'

De Luca looks up. 'That doesn't rule him out from being at Rick's place.'

'No, it doesn't,' I say. 'Speak to Tara about what time he left the house that morning and keep digging into the finance stuff. If we have to get a warrant, we'll get one eventually, though I don't like our luck over Easter.'

'Bingo,' says Lane, looking at his computer.

'What?'

'Aiden's van at the Penrith servo.'

'And?'

'He's not driving it. It's some other kid I don't recognise.'

'Shit, alright. See how you go trying to ID him. It doesn't mean Aiden wasn't in Sydney last week, it just means we have no idea where he was. They must be using burner phones. Were there any prints on the phones found at the house?'

'Yeah, just Rick's and Aiden's.'

'Were they old models?'

Lane refers to the case file. 'No, but they were low-end models. Not like the ones on their contracts.'

'Maybe Abbey had another phone too,' I say. 'It seems like she paid for everything in cash. If she had a second phone, she might have contacted someone after she left the station and we don't know about it. She could even have called someone to pick her up. Or maybe she and Rick were in contact on Saturday night after all.'

Lane nods slowly.

'We need to speak to anyone in town who sells phones and plans. Maybe they will remember selling Rick, Aiden or Abbey a prepaid phone during the last few months.'

'Just in Fairhaven?' asks Lane, shoving his wallet in his pocket.

'Whatever you can manage,' I say. 'Take copies of their photos—they probably won't have paid by card but maybe someone will remember them.'

He's scrambling to grab his things.

'Ask about Daniel Clark while you're at it,' I say.

He pauses, meeting my gaze, and nods.

'There's something else,' says de Luca as Lane leaves. She comes over to my desk and lays some documents on the table. 'See here?' she asks, pointing to some rows of numbers at the top. 'This is when Rick started working at the pub last year. You can see his salary coming in every week, between one and two hundred dollars.'

I trail my index finger along the paper. 'Yep.'

'And then he left school and obviously started working more, right? So you can see the increase from November. It jumps to a few hundred dollars a week.'

'Sure,' I say.

'Okay, so we know he quit the pub in late February, right? You can see when the payments stop coming in. Anyway, I pulled all his business info—he set up the ABN on the twenty-sixth of Feb and opened a business banking account on the same day. He started pitching for jobs straight away. We've pulled a few emails he sent to the parents of friends.'

I nod. 'This all makes sense.'

She takes out another piece of paper. 'It does, except for his spending. Unlike Abbey, Rick had a credit card—he'd had it since he was sixteen.' She leans across me and points a pen down a series of transactions. 'He spent a lot of money, on food, cigarettes, clothes, surfboards and music. I'm talking way more than he ever earned at the pub.' She flips back to the bank statement. 'And see here? Unexplained cash deposits, up to six hundred dollars sometimes.'

'Were his parents giving him money? He was only seventeen.'

'As far as I can tell he paid no rent and his parents paid all the utilities. He definitely wasn't receiving any transfers from them.'

'Maybe they were giving him cash? That makes sense based on their own business activities.'

'Maybe.' She frowns. 'It just seems like a lot.'

'Hang on,' I say, pulling out the crime-scene photos. The blood on Rick's face is bright red against the darker colours around him. 'What about his car? It looks fairly new.' I point to the garage wall. 'And the tools? They all look new to me as well. And we still don't know the story about the cash in the biscuit tin.'

De Luca picks up the photos. 'There's nothing in his bank statements about purchasing tools and nothing about the car either.'

We look at each other in realisation. 'Speak to the Fletchers,' I say. 'And check all of Aiden's statements as well.' I think about Abbey's supermarket earnings; was she giving money to Rick?

'No problem.' De Luca purses her lips, gathers all the papers and heads back to her desk.

I check in with Tran.

'The coroner still won't release Rick's body,' she tells me. 'He wants to get a weapons expert across it, a guy who can't be here until Monday.'

'Well, I guess until we know what's going on with Aiden, the Fletchers won't want to have the funeral anyway.'

I fill Tran in on the discrepancy around Rick's income and Aiden not being the one to drive the van at the petrol station.

'It doesn't look good, does it?' She sighs. 'I must say I feel for the Fletchers despite what they have been doing. Anyway, keep me posted. I'm off after today for the weekend, but just call. I'll probably need a break from my family by this time tomorrow anyway.'

'Hang on a tic,' I say, dashing into the meeting room and easing the door shut. 'I also want to suggest that once this is all settled, perhaps Edwina de Luca might be put in touch with a senior woman in your squad. It doesn't have to be you,' I add quickly, 'but I think she would benefit from a mentor. She's very ambitious and performing well, but I don't think she's going to get the support she needs here.'

'She has Tommy,' says Tran.

'I know. I just don't think he's great for her confidence levels. It isn't urgent, I just wanted to mention it to you, seeing as I won't be here for long.'

'Okay, yep, noted. But I think de Luca needs to get better at working within her environment. She can't expect special treatment.'

I blink in surprise. 'She doesn't expect special treatment but I'm not sure Tommy is as supportive of her as he could be. You know what it's like.'

'Gemma, let me be clear, Tommy has never put so much as a fingernail out of line. But he has indicated issues with de Luca. He thinks she has a problem with men.'

'That's not true. I think she has an issue with unimaginative dinosaurs in senior roles.'

'Gemma, I know you and Tommy haven't exactly hit it off, but I don't appreciate your tone. I suggest you focus on the case and stay out of the squad politics, okay?'

Tran rings off, and I stay in the meeting room fuming. Her obsession with toeing the company line is blinding her to the obvious. Either that or she's choosing to ignore it.

Realising the time, I stick my head into the main office. 'You guys should go,' I say. 'We've hit overtime again. Grange, can you text Lane?'

He nods.

My phone rings and I jump at it, but it's Owen, not Mac.

'We've tracked down Robert Weston.'

Friday, 15 April
5.02 pm

I speak to one of the constables in my old team and arrange a video-link call.

'It'll be set up in about twenty minutes,' she tells me. 'Does that work?'

'Yep, I'll be ready,' I say, grabbing my laptop with my spare hand.

Lane is back at his desk staring at the far wall. In the fluorescent light the mauve crescents under his eyes are pronounced.

'Did you have any luck with the phones?' I say.

He turns to me blankly. 'Oh, yes. Sort of. A guy at the post office reckoned Aiden came in to buy two handsets and prepaid SIMs late last year. He said it was for mates visiting from overseas.'

'An unlikely story.'

'Yeah.'

'Any luck ID'ing the guy on the Penrith servo's CCTV?'

'No, but I was thinking I'll get it in front of the high school principal, make sure it's not someone from here, and then send the image out in Sydney.'

'Good idea.' It's on the tip of my tongue to ask him to join me on the call to Weston but he looks like he needs a good nap. 'I've got to jump on a call. Nine am here tomorrow, okay?'

He nods. 'Sure.'

I connect to the video portal and make a cup of tea while I wait. Lane is gone by the time I come out of the kitchen.

In the meeting room, an electronic sound alerts me to the call and I accept. Two men appear on the screen: Robert is seated on the right, in baggy shorts and a white T-shirt, and a young constable I don't recognise sits opposite him. He aims a remote at me and the sound comes on. 'Right, Detective Woodstock, can you hear me?'

'Yes, I can.'

The constable states the date and times, then introduces himself. He explains to Robert that I'm going to ask him a few questions and that our interview will be recorded but that he is not under arrest. When the constable swivels the camera to face Robert, I introduce myself and ask him to do the same.

'Robert Phillip Weston,' he says softly. 'I'm nineteen, and I'm from Brighton in the UK.'

'Robert, do you know why I want to speak with you?'

He taps his fingers on the table. 'I think so. About that girl.'

'Which girl?'

'The girl who went missing. Abbey Clark.'

'Did you know her, Robert?'

'I met her a few times. At the shops and then at the party.'

'You spoke to her?'

He nods. 'At the shops only a bit. But I spoke to her at the party. I didn't know she was fifteen, honestly. I only saw it after, on the news.'

'Would her age have been a problem?'

'Well, I wouldn't have, you know, flirted with her if I'd known.' He leans forward and wipes at his nose. 'I just thought she was really pretty and all that.'

'Did you have contact with her apart from at the shops and the party?'

He twists in his chair. 'I sent her a few Facebook messages. I don't know why I did that—I just liked her, I guess.'

'Did she reply?'

He nods eagerly. 'She wrote me back a really nice message.'

'How did she respond to your advances at the party?'

Suddenly he looks crestfallen. 'She was *right* angry. I don't know why, I was just being friendly but she was really moody and kind of rude. Another girl told me she'd had a fight with her boyfriend, so I guessed it was something to do with that.'

'What happened after you spoke to her?'

'Nothing, really.' He shrugs. 'I kept trying to talk to her. I figured if she'd just speak to me, she'd realise how good a match we were but she kept shutting me down. My mates went back to the caravan park but I stayed. They'd kind of been getting on my nerves anyway, to be honest, giving me grief about Abbey.'

'Right, so you stayed at the party. Who were you talking to?'

'This other girl. Beth. The party was at her house—well, her family's anyway.'

'And how long did you stay talking to her?'

Robert sighs. 'Not long. We hooked up for a bit, just like kissing and whatever, she seemed great, but then she went all funny and said she kind of had a boyfriend. So I left.'

'Where did you go?'

He's scratching at his wrist but his eye line remains steady. 'Back to the caravan park. Then I wanted to buy some smokes.'

'Did you see anyone on the way?'

He pauses and lets out a big breath. 'Yeah. I saw her. The girl. Abbey.'

I feel myself pitching forward and hold on to the desk. 'What time was this?'

He shrugs. 'Just after midnight, I think. I left the party at maybe quarter to. A neighbour started going crazy about the noise when I was leaving.'

'Where did you see Abbey?'

Running his fingers through his short hair, he says, 'I was walking down the road, the one that cuts into the main street.'

'Felton Way?'

'Yes, I think that's it. Anyway, I was going along on the edge of the road. When I was maybe fifty metres from the corner, something came out of the trees on the other side of the road. After a bit I realised it was her.' He clasps his hands together and his eyes are averted. 'She was running—and she was holding something.'

'What was it?'

'I couldn't tell from that far off, but it seemed like something heavy.'

'Did you call out to her?'

Robert shakes his head. 'No, I wasn't that close and I didn't want to scare her.'

'Are you sure? This was a girl you'd been chatting up at a party, and then all of a sudden you're alone with her and you don't want to try it on?'

'It wasn't like that, really it wasn't. It's like she was in the middle of something . . . She was running along the road really fast. It's hard to explain.'

'But you definitely didn't speak to her?'

'No, but I did follow her—I mean, that's the direction I was heading in anyway.'

'Okay, what happened next?'

Robert picks up the pace. 'She reached the corner, you know, where that pink beauty spa place is. I was kind of watching from the other side of the street a little further along.'

I'm pretty sure I know what happened next, but I ask anyway. 'What was she doing, Robert?'

'She stood there for a bit, just staring at the shop. It was creepy, like she was possessed or something.' He swallows. 'And then it's like she snapped out of it, she kind of jumped up, and then she stepped backwards and sort of ran at the window.' He looks directly down the camera, his dark eyes bright and bewildered. 'She threw the brick right into the glass.'

Friday, 15 April

5.47 pm

I can see it. Feel it. A moment of pure, unadulterated rage. The slowing of time as the brick sailed through the air, then the blissful release as the glass rained down. It would have been violent and exquisite and then terrifying. I wonder if, as the glass settled, Abbey's anger was sated, or had the act of violence rallied and empowered her? Convinced her that she could fight back?

'What did she do after that?' I ask Robert quietly.

He coughs. 'She just stood there for a second looking at it, and then she ran. She took off back into the bush away from the shops.'

'Did you follow her?'

'No! I swear. The whole thing just totally freaked me out. I was a witness in a fight last year and the guy died—and, I don't know, it probably sounds stupid but the whole thing just made me think of that. I just wanted to get out of there.'

'So what did you do?'

'I stood there for a while and then no one came and there was no alarm, and so I went back to the caravan park. I didn't even bother getting smokes in the end.'

'What made you leave Fairhaven on Monday?'

'I don't know,' says Robert, looking confused. 'I guess I just didn't want to be there. I saw the news . . . I knew she'd disappeared and I knew it would look bad that I'd been messaging her and trying to talk to her. And the girls at the supermarket knew I'd been coming in.' He grips his head. 'I do that sometimes, get really invested. I don't know why. Abbey seemed like a cool chick and I wanted to talk to her. There's nothing wrong with that.'

I don't say anything, and Robert's jerky breathing fills the room.

'Plus, my mates were giving me shit and just dicking around . . .' He drops his head into his hands. 'I know it was bloody stupid not to say anything. As soon as the cops called today I was like, yeah, I need to tell someone what I saw. But on Monday, I don't know, I just needed to get out of there.'

'You didn't know her boyfriend, Rick Fletcher?'

'No, never met him. But Beth told me he was the guy Abbey argued with at the party.' Robert looks down the camera wide-eyed. 'I saw that someone killed him. Was it because of what happened to Abbey?'

I ask Robert a few more questions. Apparently he didn't see anyone else on his late-night stroll last Saturday. Advising him we'll need to speak to him again sometime soon, I disconnect the video and rest my head in my hands. Everything about Robert's body language and demeanour seemed genuine but I make a note to check with Kate about whether she somehow records what time customers come back to the caravan park after hours.

I stand up and stretch out my back, looking at my phone. Nothing from Mac.

Feeling anxious, I call Vanessa. 'I'm still at the station,' I say. 'Can you pop Ben on for me?'

'Of course.'

He seems perky again, chatting about some new game Charlie taught him. I swallow back tears as I listen to him explain it to me. He asks, 'Do you have to work late tonight, Mum?'

'There's just a few more things I have to do, okay? I won't be too late. Maybe you can show me how to play Charlie's game then.'

———

I make an instant coffee in the squad tearoom and drink it as I drive to the pub. The caffeine charges through my bloodstream and I feel a renewed sense of energy. Robert's description of Abbey rolls into my mind. Why would she attack the salon? A random act of violence to release rage? Revenge on the Sheffields? Had Tara or Eric done something to her, or to Rick?

I get out of the car and do a double take, my heart rate picking up: a man is walking along the beach path and for a minute I think it's Mac. Feeling wired, I head into the pub and am immediately engulfed by the fug of beer.

It's already busy, with groups of young people crowding the pool tables. I spot Simon Charleston at the bar and give him a curt nod, then make my way over and order a light beer.

Cam lights up when he sees me. 'Gemma! Hi.' He leans across the bar, startlingly close to my face. 'I hope I didn't get you into trouble the other night? With that guy?'

'Ah, no, it was totally fine. There was just a bit of a mis-understanding.'

He rolls his eyes. 'I know how those go—I seem to make a habit of them.' He expertly pours three beers and passes them to a petite blonde. 'So everything is cool between you guys now?'

'Yep, all good.' I sip my beer and notice that Simon is eyeing me broodily from a table in the corner as he drinks his. I throw him an exasperated look and turn my back to him. 'Hey, Cam, I know it's busy but do you have time for a couple of questions?'

'I'm not in the habit of saying no to police officers.' He laughs. 'Give me a sec and then I'll join you, okay?'

Five minutes later he hands me a water. He straddles the bar stool next to me and sips the froth from the top of his beer.

I take a breath to talk but he beats me to it. 'How are you holding up?' he asks sympathetically.

'I'm okay,' I say. 'A bit tired.'

'I don't know how you do it. Especially with a kid.' He takes another sip. 'I heard about the Fletchers being arrested—I can't believe they were dealing pot. It's crazy.'

'Are a lot of the kids around here drug users?'

'Not that I see. I mean, I'm sure there's a bit of it, but I certainly wouldn't tolerate it in here.'

'You never noticed Rick being involved in anything like that?'

Cam shakes his head. 'No, he seemed like a pretty average kid.'

'Was Rick's decision to leave sudden?'

'I think he'd been considering what he was going to do for a while. I remember him saying that Abbey encouraged him to have more of a life plan, but I guess he didn't want to talk to me about it until he was sure. I'd talked about moving him into a more senior role here, managing shifts and helping to order stock. When he quit he told me he just really wanted to run his own business, which I obviously understood.'

'And was Aiden in here much?'

'Not really. He was more introverted than Rick. Seemed like kind of a loner. I never saw him hanging out with mates or a girlfriend.'

'What time did you close up on Saturday night?'

'About eleven, I think. We'd had a charity bingo night for the hospital, and that was really family friendly so it wrapped up early.'

'You didn't see anyone hanging around on your way home?'

He scratches his head. 'Not that I noticed. By the time I went upstairs to go to bed there wasn't really anyone around.'

We sip our drinks while the madness rolls around us.

'Still no word on Abbey?' he asks.

'I can't really discuss it. But it's certainly not an easy one.'

Cam sighs. 'No. I have to say, I don't feel much sympathy for Daniel Cark but I feel terrible for Dot—the not knowing must be torture.'

I nod. 'Hey, Cam, you know those kids who went missing years ago?'

He rubs his eyes. 'Sure, the whole thing turned my life upside down for months. What happened with Rick brought a lot of it back. That feeling like maybe you didn't know someone as well as you thought you did. It's pretty shitty.'

'You worked with Gregory Ng that last night, right?' I ask, remembering this from the online news article.

'Yep. I must have replayed our conversations a hundred times in my head. The whole thing is so bloody weird, I can't work it out for the life of me.'

'What was Greg like?'

'Had a bit of a chip on his shoulder. His family were bad news, and I think his childhood was pretty rough—but he really loved Sally, she was pretty much all he talked about. You know, how smart she was, how proud he was of her, how pretty she was. It could be a bit sickening, to be honest.' Cam chuckles, then falls silent for a moment. 'But he was a good worker. Occasionally patrons were a bit rowdy, so he'd have little tussles from time to time but nothing serious. He did have a run-in with Daniel that night, which came up during the investigation. I've always wondered about that, you know—if Daniel was looking for payback.' Cam wrinkles his nose. 'But because of the cash Greg nicked from the till, I guess I figured everyone was probably right, that he had stuff going on I just didn't know about.' He tips his head. 'I still can't believe he'd hurt Sally, but who knows?' Raising an eyebrow at me, he asks, 'Why?'

'I was just curious.'

'One case not enough for you?' he teases.

I smile ruefully. 'It's more than enough.'

When I finish my beer I say goodnight to Cam, giving Simon a wide berth as I leave the pub.

'Wait, Gemma!'

'Go away, Simon,' I say.

'I need to talk to you.' He's wearing a black T-shirt and faded jeans. His face looks sunburned.

'Five minutes.'

'You're always giving me time limits,' he grumbles, shoving his fingers through his hair. His smile fades. 'Gemma, I'm writing a story that I think will go live tomorrow. It's about you.'

'What?'

'I don't have much of a choice—we got a tip-off and my editor creamed her pants over it.'

I throw my hands out in front of me. 'What's the story, Simon?'

'Visiting homicide detective run out of town after being threatened by dead animal carcass.'

I lean back against my car. 'That's ridiculous.'

'Well, someone called my editor about it.'

I cross my arms, trying not to shake. 'Who?'

'She said it was a woman, that's all I know.' He shifts his weight to the other foot. 'Do you want to provide a quote?'

I look over at the pub. Maybe Cam said something to a staff member and they called the press? A dead possum is hardly good

PR for The Parrot, but one of the juniors might have just wanted to be part of the story.

Or would Tommy go this far to undermine me? My throat constricts and my insides sink. Then I think about my argument with de Luca today, remembering when she quickly hung up the phone as I went outside. I have no doubt Tommy told Lane about the possum; he might have mentioned it to her. Was she so frustrated by my being here and so pissed off by my criticism that she tried to sabotage me? Surely not, based on our subsequent conversation.

Perhaps Tommy coerced Vanessa into calling the paper.

'No comment,' I snap at Simon. I feel almost weak with loneliness. 'And clearly I haven't been run out of town—I'm bloody well standing in front of you.'

'Gemma, I know it's true about the possum. I saw Cam outside your hotel room that first morning, you both bending down and covering something with a garbage bag. That's what it was, right? Someone was threatening you? As soon as my editor told me about the tip-off, I put two and two together.'

'How did you know which room was mine?'

Simon falters. 'I saw you and your son arrive on Monday. I was staying upstairs and your door was in my line of sight from the window.' He presses his lips together as if unsure if he should continue. 'The caller said you were spooked. She mentioned the case you worked on with the missing girl in Sydney and said that people in the senior ranks are worried about your mental health.'

'For fuck's sake, Simon,' I hiss. 'What, so an unfounded source calls up your editor, doles out a bunch of lies, and you print it? I thought you were a better journalist than that.'

He looks hurt. 'Gemma,' he says quietly, 'the case isn't officially progressing. The body in the bush wasn't Abbey. You guys either know nothing or you're giving us nothing. Either way, that doesn't lead to a lot of column inches. Then this lands in my lap. Someone is clearly threatened by you being here, and the similarities to your previous case . . . Well, it's a good story. I'm really sorry but I'd be crazy not to write it.'

'I didn't realise you were such a fucking puppet.' I open the car door with such force that my shoulder almost leaves its socket. 'Write what you want, Simon.' I slam the door and don't look at him as I throw the car into reverse and speed off.

———

Vanessa is serving dinner when I reach the house. I decline wine but devour the lamb cutlets and salad, listening to Ben chat about his day while engaging with Vanessa and Tommy as little as possible. I can't stop glancing every so often at the two pill packets in the middle of the table. Tommy is quiet tonight and Vanessa seems jumpy, getting up and down to let Inka in and out the back door.

Feeling uneasy I offer to clean up, and they retire to the couch to watch TV. Ben stays at the table doing a crossword, and I help him in between clearing the table and rinsing the dishes. I love him so much it hurts.

Once the dishwasher is full and humming, I say goodnight to Vanessa and Tommy, then lead Ben down the hallway. 'Tell me about the game Charlie taught you,' I say, and we spend the next hour playing before I help him through his bedtime routine. 'Why don't you just sleep in my bed tonight?' I suggest, not acknowledging he's going to end up there anyway.

He shrugs. 'Sure.'

I read to him until he falls asleep, then I lie there staring at his face. I think about Abbey hurling the brick through the wall of glass.

SEVENTH DAY MISSING

Saturday, 16 April

7.01 am

Pulling the Gordons' front door shut, I slide my sunglasses on. The sky is clear of clouds and the sun glows yellow through the trees. For the first time in weeks I slept well, only waking once, and though my face is a little puffy I feel reasonably refreshed.

I checked Simon's paper online but there's no sign of the article yet. Then I spot a note on my windshield and feel a flash of anger toward him, though it's not as intense as it was yesterday. He's just doing his job; no doubt if I were a reporter I would be just as dogged, if not more so. And maybe he's not going to run the piece.

I free the folded note from the grip of the windscreen wipers and open it.

I drop it onto the bonnet like it's on fire. Automatically I glance around, but there's no one on the street, no faces in the windows.

I look back at the note and carefully pull open its corner. It's a photocopy of Scott's obituary from the local Smithson paper, a small rectangle in the middle of the otherwise blank page.

To the right of the text someone has written: *Leave now. Your son doesn't deserve to be an orphan.*

I drop my bag on the desk so forcefully that Grange jumps.

After I read the note for a second time, the acid that charged up my throat brought some coffee with it. I fish a mint from the depths of my bag and toss it in my mouth. 'Right, sorry for calling you all in early, but there's been a development.'

Lane, de Luca and Grange all look at me expectantly. De Luca's short hair is gathered into a wispy ponytail, accentuating her thin face. More than ever, they seem like strangers and I have no idea what they think of me. Could one of them want me gone so badly they would try to scare me out of town?

'I managed to connect with Robert Weston last night. He admitted to seeing Abbey after she left the police station on Saturday.'

I notice de Luca grimace, and I kick myself for not having her present at the interview. It was her lead.

I point to the photo of the broken salon window, which I've pinned up on the case board, and take them through my conversation with Robert.

'That does back up what the UK cop emailed me,' says de Luca.

'He could be lying,' says Lane. 'Not about seeing her, but it could have been him who broke the window. Maybe he did it to scare her. He could have hurt her too.'

Robert's face looms large in my mind. 'I'm inclined to think he's telling the truth, but yes, we can't write him off just yet. He has an alibi for Monday morning, though, so he didn't kill Rick.' My legs are aching and I take a seat. But I can't relax; my nerve endings are buzzing. I glance at Lane, realising he looks about as good as I feel. 'Are you alright?' I ask him.

'Um, yeah.' He shakes his head and rubs his eyes. 'Sorry, I just didn't sleep well last night.'

Grange picks up his pen and chews the end, looking perplexed. 'Why would Abbey do that?'

'I'm wondering about the Sheffields,' I say. 'Could she have had some kind of beef with them?'

'Maybe she did have an appointment with Eric and he upset her?' suggests de Luca.

'Maybe,' I murmur. 'Regardless, it suggests she wasn't in the most stable frame of mind.'

'You're wondering about suicide?' says de Luca.

I purse my lips and nod slowly. 'This certainly makes it seem more likely. We know she had arguments with both her father and Rick that evening, and that she seemed upset about her bike being stolen.'

No one says anything, and I hear the sharp trill of the reception desk phone. Lane squeezes his eyes shut; he looks completely wiped.

Noah sticks his head into the main office. 'Sorry to interrupt, but Tim's called in sick for tonight's shift. He's got gastro and says there's no way he'll be back on his feet by this evening. I checked with Kylie but you've already got her on tomorrow. I obviously can't stay more than an hour or so longer tonight and I can't work tomorrow, it's my mum's seventieth and she's not well.'

'Great,' I mutter. I was already on edge and that note has tipped me over it, so a tiny challenge seems like an insurmountable obstacle.

'I'm happy to do the night shift,' says Lane quickly. 'If I get some sleep this afternoon, I should be fine. To be honest, I think I'll be more effective—I barely slept last night. You can always leave me any desk research to follow up with.'

I don't really have another option, plus I'm keen to keep Lane away from the possible connection with Eric Sheffield. His explanation about the valium prescription rang true, but I still feel uneasy about it. 'Okay, that would be good. Give us your hit list for today and we'll do what we can. Then be back here tonight at six for a handover with Noah.'

'No problem.' Lane makes a few notes and passes them to de Luca. 'Call me if you need to,' he says, looking relieved as he heads off.

The door clicks shut behind him, and I look at de Luca and Grange. 'I want you to speak to those kids from the party about the drugs again. I want to know exactly what they're taking and where they get it from. Mention Doctor Eric Sheffield as I think there's a chance he was doing a little bit of dealing on the side.'

Eric is still uncontactable, and the perky receptionist tells me he's not expected back until this afternoon. 'It's been crazy today,' she trills down the phone. 'Easter is always busy, but honestly I just have not stopped.'

Easter. *God.* I haven't even thought about that. I write a note on the back of my hand, hoping I'll get to the supermarket before the end of the day.

I haven't heard from Mac since I left him at the cafe yesterday morning, and despite what I said about wanting to be left alone, it's chewing me up inside.

I can't afford to think about it. I piano my fingers on the desk and try to untangle my thoughts. If there really is a link between Rick and some sort of drug ring, how far does it go? Was Abbey involved? Daniel? Or am I struggling to make connections where there are none?

My desk phone bleats loudly and I snatch it from its cradle. 'Detective Sergeant Woodstock.'

'I thought I recognised the number,' says a friendly female voice. 'It's Janet Rixon—I used to be a cop in Fairhaven. I had a missed call a couple of days ago. I assume Tommy Gordon wants to speak with me?'

'Yes, Janet, hi. Thanks for calling back. It's actually me who wants to talk with you.'

'Oh, well. Hello. Sorry, what was your name?'

'Detective Sergeant Gemma Woodstock. I'm with the Fairhaven team, temporarily working on both a homicide and a missing person case.'

'Rick Fletcher and Abbey Clark—yes, I saw the news. Bloody sad business, though I can't say I'm surprised about Abbey. She never had much of a chance with a father like Daniel.'

I glance around. De Luca and Grange are talking in the tearoom.

'Janet, can I call you back on this number?'

'Sure. I've got a cold so I'm not diving today. I've got all the time in the world.'

'Okay, hang on a tic.' I grab my mobile and step outside into the heat, walking around to the back of the building in between the two storage sheds where there is a strip of shade. 'Sorry about that,' I say when Janet picks up.

Her laugh is warm and contagious. 'No worries. I'm betting you're outside trying to get some privacy?'

I scan my eyes up the wall of the closest shed. A scribble of graffiti. Peeling paint. A spray of bird shit. The tangy salt taste of the ocean. 'Affirmative,' I quip.

Janet's voice has a fond, whimsical tone as she says, 'Fairhaven's a funny little place, isn't it? Anyway, sorry!' She pulls herself up. 'I'm sure you have something serious you want to talk to me about.'

'Yes, I do.' A wave of apprehension hits me. Once I unlock this box, I may not be able to close it again, even if it's all in my head. I square my jaw. 'Janet, I understand you helped investigate the disappearance of Sally Luther and Gregory Ng. You were a constable in Fairhaven at the time, is that right?'

'Yes, that's right.' She breathes out heavily.

'I have a few questions for you, if that's okay.'

'My memory might be a bit rusty but I'm happy to help. Mind you, I haven't thought much about this in years—I spend all my time these days with my face in coral.' Her laugh turns nervous. 'You don't think Abbey's disappearance is linked to Sally and Greg, do you?'

I pause, not sure what to say that won't sound crazy. In the end I opt for 'no'. 'What did you think of the inquest verdict?'

Janet hums. 'I'm starting to remember why I stopped thinking about this case. Look, I really don't know. We all talked ourselves round in so many circles, by the time we put the case on ice we were back where we started.'

'Which was?'

'Well, everyone thought Greg did it.'

'Why was everyone so quick to assume Greg hurt her?'

Janet sighs. 'All the obvious reasons. He stole cash from the pub that night. His father had an extensive criminal record. He was Asian. There were rumours he had a drug problem, though we could never confirm that. I think his star just didn't shine as brightly as Sally's in town, and deep down no one in Fairhaven liked that she picked him.'

'Was there any sign that he'd been abusive toward her?'

'No, nothing like that. If anything, he seemed absolutely besotted. And I have to tell you, the theory that they ran away together? I just didn't buy it. I could never see a reason why Sally would need to run. Her parents were super supportive of her—they had accepted Greg—and she had a new job working as a receptionist for the local GP, and freedom to do whatever she wanted. It just didn't make sense.'

'Maybe Greg convinced her they had to clear out? I mean, he was desperate enough to steal money, so maybe something happened suddenly and he needed to jump town. Sally might have made a split-second decision.'

'Maybe, but Cam and the other hotel staff said he seemed absolutely fine that night, chatting about Sally and her sister's wedding. Yes, his family situation wasn't great, but he was working and he had Sally. His stock was rising. And even if he asked her to go with him, I just can't believe she'd miss her sister's wedding. Even though they cancelled it in the end of course. That's the thing that really has her family convinced something happened to her.'

Neither of us speak for a moment.

'Gosh, I can hear those Fairhaven cicadas,' Janet says with a laugh.

'I've been digging up the files on the case,' I admit.

'Can I ask why?'

'I've been led to believe that a few things perhaps weren't documented properly.'

'You've been speaking to Simon Charleston,' she says, and I feel a twinge of embarrassment.

'I have met Simon, but I also spoke to someone else and—'

'Look, Gemma.' She sighs. 'I never made it very far in the force, it just wasn't for me. And nothing made me realise that more than the Luther/Ng case.'

'What do you mean?'

'I can't even explain it to you properly—all of a sudden, there was just so much tension in the squad.' She pauses, then says, 'The former CI, Stuart Klein, wasn't a very nice man. I never liked him, but during the case his behaviour was bizarre.'

'In what way?'

'He was aggressive and inconsistent. I'm the first to admit the case was all over the place during those initial few weeks, but I was very junior so just kept my head down and tried to stay out of the way. Some of the witnesses retracted statements, and as I'm sure Simon has told you there were whispers of backdoor payments. But nothing was ever proven. And to be honest, I don't know who would have been paying who. Then, just as the case was going cold, Stuart moved interstate. I can't explain it to you but the whole thing left a bad taste in my mouth. I stayed on for a while, but I had issues with Tommy too, and in the end my heart wasn't in it.'

'What kind of issues did you have with Tommy?'

'Oh, we just weren't on the same page. I wanted more balance in my life, and ultimately he didn't think I had the right level of commitment. He doesn't think much of women in the force—that's not a secret.'

Even though it's hot outside, all my hairs are raised. I lean against the shed, trying to think.

'Do you believe Stuart was bent?' I ask.

Janet sighs. 'I don't know. I'm not going to tell you it didn't cross my mind, but my issue with him was more his arrogance than anything else. He came from wealth and was used to getting his way. He treated me like dirt. Tommy was actually quite good in comparison. Then as soon as the new junior constable started, a young man, I was chopped liver.'

'That's awful,' I say sympathetically, then get the conversation back on track. 'Daniel Clark changed his mind about making a statement on seeing Greg that night. Why?'

'Because he was an alcoholic? I really don't know—I was pretty far down the pecking order and not privy to conversations.'

'Was Daniel a suspect?'

'Not officially, but I always got the feeling Tommy thought Daniel was involved somehow.'

'What did Stuart think?'

'He thought Daniel was a drunk who beat his wife. Full stop. He didn't think Daniel had anything to do with it, and essentially forbade us from investigating him. After Daniel refused to make an official statement, there wasn't much to link him to the case anyway.'

'But Greg kicked him out of the pub that night, and he's prone to violence, so he had motive. I can see why Tommy wanted him in the mix.'

Janet sighs. 'Yeah, I know, but for some reason Tommy's and Stuart's relationship soured over the whole thing. It was all over my head but clearly something was going on.'

'Could anyone alibi Daniel?'

'Dot said he was home by 11 pm.'

'That doesn't leave enough time. If he did something to Sally and Greg that night, he couldn't have done it and covered his tracks so comprehensively in thirty minutes.'

'I know, but Tommy was convinced Dot was lying for him.'

'Same as now,' I murmur.

'It's just the way it is, I guess,' says Janet diplomatically. 'Partner alibis are always fraught. The other thing that complicated matters was that Daniel also said he saw Greg's car being driven later when he was walking home.'

'What do you mean?'

'He reckoned he saw Greg driving it. He said it was speeding, nearly out of control.'

'Did you think he was telling the truth?'

'I'm not sure. By that stage everyone knew Sally and Gregory were missing, so it's hard to know if Daniel was mucking us around.'

I breathe out through clenched teeth, trying to make sense of it all. 'I'd better let you go. Thanks for your time, Janet. I appreciate it.'

'No problem, Gemma. Can I ask why you didn't just speak to Tommy about this?'

I nudge a tuft of grass with my shoe. 'He's not well. He was in a car accident last week, so he's taking some time out. I don't want to bother him with anything unless I have to.'

'Oh, well, that's no good. I wasn't a Tommy fan but his wife is lovely. I always felt like she was overcompensating for him.'

I'm about to agree about this when something strikes me. 'Hey, Janet, you said "witnesses" before. Who else retracted their initial statement in the case?'

'Oh, well, that was even trickier because mental health issues were involved. Megan Jarvis claimed she saw two men carrying a body across the car park.'

'Meg Jarvis said that?'

To my surprise, Janet chuckles. 'Yes.'

'I don't understand, what's so funny?'

Janet's voice becomes serious again. 'It wasn't funny—the whole thing was actually really frustrating. One minute Meg was telling anyone who'd listen what she saw that night, and I even had to give her a warning because she was creating such a racket outside the supermarket the next morning. But when we gave her the chance to make a formal statement a few days later, she was suddenly swearing black and blue that she didn't even leave her house that night.' She sighs. 'Honestly? I didn't know what to believe.'

Saturday, 16 April
10.02 am

I linger outside and walk a lap around the station, thinking about everything Janet said. The ringing in my head returns as the threads of that fateful evening ten years ago merge with what I know about last Saturday night. I begin another lap, wanting to keep moving. White sunlight bounces off the windows, the cars and the tin roofs of the sheds.

Sally, Greg, Tommy, Abbey, Rick. Is Daniel the clue to this whole thing? The animosity between he and Rick could have been an act. Daniel went to his house the morning after Abbey disappeared—maybe they nutted out a plan, then Rick got cold feet and Daniel attacked him. Aiden might have been involved.

I think about Tommy and the drawer full of pills. Is his behaviour toward me territorial, or is he afraid of what I might uncover? In all of our conversations he has abhorred Daniel's domestic violence, suggesting that the man should be locked up, but maybe he's been covering a mutually beneficial relationship. What did Daniel see the night Sally and Greg went missing? Is it possible that Tommy forced him to pull his statement? And maybe got to Meg too?

Or maybe I'm just chasing my own tail as I grow increasingly desperate.

Think, think. Was Abbey just a troubled girl who decided it was all too much, or does her attack on the salon prove she was violent enough to kill Rick? Had Daniel's relentless abuse finally broken her, causing a primal darkness to erupt? Perhaps Rick had done something that reminded her of her father and caused her to snap.

I think back to the footage of Abbey arriving at the police station last Saturday night: her desperate movements before she disappeared into the night. I look over to the front of the station. It's set back from the road, and several trees line the gravel driveway. I remember what Erin said about seeing Abbey here that Sunday, her bike propped against the tree as she stared at the station.

My gaze drifts from the security camera positioned over the door to the parked cars, as I trace its line of sight with my eyes.

An icy thought splinters into my chest. The timeline—it always comes back to the timeline. How had Tommy beaten Lane to the party on Firestone Drive? I remember watching the footage remaining after Abbey had gone: the shadow moving in the bottom left of the screen, the delay in the glow of Lane's headlights appearing before he drove the squad car to meet Tommy at the house party. What was Lane doing? Had he used the bathroom before he went? No, if he had he would appear on the footage in the station again. I reel around, looking between the station and the sheds.

I think of Lane's keenness to work a night shift, his supposed guilt about not driving Abbey home. The artwork in the salon window. The girl with the blonde dreadlocks wrestling the canvas out of her boot yesterday morning. Lane's hand down her skirt at the pub. His girlfriend.

I rush back into the station. My sun-drunk eyes reduce Grange and de Luca to blurry outlines.

'Where are the keys to the sheds?'

They both stand.

'In the safe,' stammers Grange.

'Get them. Now!'

I don't wait for their reaction but go into the tearoom and pull the roster off the wall, flicking back to the week before last. My heartbeat pounds through every part of my body: Lane worked that Sunday shift.

His hand, held out to her on that video—calming, authoritarian, but not for the reason I suspected. Oh my god. I flick forward to last week's roster. He was scheduled on at 6 am Monday. I close my eyes. I never asked who picked up Rick's voice message first.

Grange is talking on the phone. As I return to the main room, he says, 'That was weird.'

'What's weird?' I demand.

'The shed keys aren't in the safe, so I called Lane to see if he knows where they are.' Grange blinks, his long eyelashes fluttering. 'And he hung up on me.'

The crunch of metal makes me wince. The three of us stand back as Xander the locksmith yanks a severed metal hook from the holder of the second shed.

He turns to us, grinning. 'Nothing else you need busted open?'

'Thanks, Xander,' I say, 'you've been a massive help.'

I wait for him to get back into his truck before I pull the door open. It creaks ominously and a cloud of hot air swirls out. De Luca and Grange peer around me into the darkness, as I stare past the shelves lined with plastic crates full of papers, an old fan and two broken chairs.

A bike is propped against the back wall of the shed, covered by a plastic tarp.

'I don't understand,' says Grange.

'Lane,' de Luca murmurs, her face white.

'Yes,' I say.

'But why would he lie about the bike?' asks Grange. 'Why would Abbey?'

The piercing ringing in my mind has become a sharp headache that settles behind my eyes.

'It was a cover,' I say, walking back to the station. 'Grange, secure this scene. Take photos and call Tran. We need to get a forensic team here asap, so we'll need her muscle.' I run up the front ramp, calling out behind me, 'De Luca, come with me.'

'We're going to his house?' she asks.

I nod. 'I'll drive. Can you get a trace put on his phone? And check if his squad car can be tracked.' Something else briefly surfaces in my whirlpool of thoughts, but I can't catch it. I simply grab my bag and race out the front.

Saturday, 16 April

11.44 am

Lane's car isn't at his home and neither is he, or at least he isn't responding to our aggressive knocking. We circle the house, a single-storey detached unit with a garden of native grasses. The blinds are drawn; I peer through a crack in the kitchen blind but can't see anything.

'I know it's legally iffy, but I'm going to break in,' I say to de Luca, who swallows and nods. 'I don't want to run all over town if it turns out he's been here the whole time.'

'Do you actually think he's dangerous? Maybe this is just a misunderstanding. He might have found the bike.'

'Edwina,' I say.

She nods again, her face all hard lines. 'I'll go around the front.'

I pull out my gun and double-check the carport door is locked, aiming my right boot at the door, I kick it hard. The lock caves after three kicks, and the door swings open.

I quickly search the main bedroom, lounge, kitchen, bathroom. A second bedroom door remains shut, and I twist the knob and nudge it open with my elbow. It hits something with a *thud* and I spring forward.

The curtains are a garish red, bathing the room in orange light. A corduroy beanbag, an old desk and a half-filled bookcase. He's not here.

I turn to go and stop in my tracks.

Behind the open door is a large wire cage. An animal trap.

I back away, my hand on my throat. Faint tufts of brown and grey fur line the base of the cage. I think about Lane's hand on my back after I was sick at the caravan park. His happy chatter in the car. His baby face.

I cry out with frustration and fold forward, his betrayal hitting me square in the gut. How could I have missed it? How did we all miss it?

'Detective!' De Luca calls from the front lawn.

A strange numbness comes over me. Throwing one last look at the cage, I unlock the front door and stalk out, my gun still in my hand. 'Do you know where his girlfriend lives?'

De Luca glances back at the house, then falls into step beside me. 'Elsha? I'm not sure. I know she works at the salon.'

'I thought she was an artist?' I say, holstering my gun.

'She's also a masseuse,' says de Luca.

'Right. Let's go.'

De Luca calls Lane's parents on the way, pretending to be an old schoolfriend.

'Nope, they haven't heard from him since last week,' she says, hanging up.

'He has siblings, right?'

'I think they live in Melbourne,' she says distractedly, her brow creasing. 'I'm just wondering . . .'

'What?'

She turns to me, her eyes twitching as she talks. 'It's just that the last call-out we got for the Clarks, back in early Feb, Lane insisted on going. The call came in just as he was about to finish his shift. I said I'd go but he said he would do it and write up the report the next day.'

I feel her gaze on me as I circle the roundabout that leads into the main street.

'He wanted to see her,' she says. 'Abbey.'

'Yes,' I say. 'I think so.'

'They were together?'

'Something was going on between them.'

De Luca cups a hand over her mouth, her long fingers reaching to the edge of her face. 'She was only fifteen. Do you think they were . . . ?'

'I don't know,' I say, pulling the handbrake into position. 'Come on.'

The sickly-sweet scent of vanilla envelops us as we step into the salon. Tara is blow-drying a brand-new bob and jiggles her elbow in greeting, though annoyance flashes in her eyes. 'Give me a tick!' she calls out.

De Luca and I shift over to the little waiting area, and I scan the rows of shiny products lining the wall and wonder what the hell they're all for.

Next to me, de Luca is kneading her forehead with her hands. 'Maybe he was just trying to help her somehow?' Her voice is thick with emotion and her expression is one I'm familiar with: denial mixed with the knowledge that something is very wrong. 'Should we call Tommy? He might be able to explain all this.'

I shake my head. 'No. I'm sure he'll hear the alerts but I don't want to engage him in this.'

The buzz of the hairdryer ceases and other sounds come to the fore: the snip of scissors, the rip as wax is wrenched from skin, and the low hum of a neon light being held over a woman's foil-wrapped fingernails. Tara applies a liberal dose of spray to the dried hair before grabbing a mirror to display the reverse view.

After waving her customer off at the counter, she comes over to us. 'Sorry!' she says, her arms folded. 'It's been a bit busy today, which is a good thing 'cause earlier in the week was so quiet. Kate Morse was saying that a few caravan park bookings pulled out.' Tara's face puckers slightly and she glares at me. 'I guess some of the recent events have scared people off.' She looks past us to the mirror and adjusts her hair before smoothing her fingers along her jawbone to blend in a line of make-up.

'Tara, have you seen Constable Lane today?'

'No, but he did call earlier. He was looking for Elsha and I told him she was with a client.'

'What time did he call?'

'Just before nine, I think.'

The bell above the door tinkles, announcing the arrival of a sunburned woman. Tara flashes her a smile then strains her neck into the salon, directing one of the girls to the front counter with her eyes.

'And you haven't heard from him since?' I ask.

'No,' says Tara, getting increasingly frustrated. The bell above the door sounds again, and she whips her head around. 'But this lovely lady might have.'

The girl who was at the pub with Lane on Monday night is standing next to the counter. Today her dreadlocks are wrapped around her head like a turban, and silver chains circle both ankles and hang at various lengths around her neck. When she sees me she stops short and looks wary. Then she props a small canvas against the front counter; the painting is a burst of colour, an abstract flower set against a magenta background, its loose silver seeds trailing off the side.

'Elsha,' I say, 'have you spoken to Kai Lane this morning?'

A sharp chemical scent now fills the salon, making my eyes start to water.

'Not since he left my house,' says Elsha. 'He tried to call me but I was with clients. I tried to call him back but his phone is off.'

'He's your boyfriend, right?' I say.

She nods uncertainly. 'Yes. Only for a few months—we met in November.'

'You said you saw him this morning?'

'Yes, he stayed at my place last night. Went straight to work.' She pulls a filigree ring off her finger before sliding it on again, and tilts her chin at me defiantly. 'He woke up when you called him to come in early again. He didn't sleep well last night—he was very tired. Why do you ask?' Elsha's disdain for me is obvious, and I wonder what kind of picture Lane has been painting for her.

'How has Kai seemed lately?'

'He's been pretty stressed. I haven't actually seen him that much this week. He hasn't been sleeping well, and I get up early to paint, so . . .'

'Were you together last Saturday night?'

'Um, no. He was working a late shift and he went back to his place.'

'What about on Monday morning? Was he with you before he went to work?'

She crosses her arms defensively. 'I'm not sure. I think so.' Her eyes widen suddenly. 'Yes, yes, he was. He stayed at my place on Sunday after the search for that missing girl.'

'What time did he leave on Monday morning?'

'It was early,' she says, wary again. 'But I'm not sure exactly. I went to the beach to paint.' She takes a deep breath and turns to de Luca. 'Can you please tell me what's going on?'

I go to the front desk and scribble my number and email address on the back of a price menu. 'We're trying to find him,' I say. 'Do you live alone?'

She nods.

'Don't go home after work. Go to the pub or a restaurant, okay? Maybe stay with a friend tonight—can you do that?'

She nods again. 'Why, what's he done?' she says sharply, her voice rising.

'I'm not sure yet,' I say gently. 'We're just a bit worried—he didn't seem well today, and we need to ask him about something important.'

She blinks, Bambi-like. 'Elsha. I think Kai might contact you, and it's really important you call me the second you hear from him.'

Saturday, 16 April
1.23 pm

De Luca and I arrive back at the station and are immediately accosted by Noah. 'Dot Clark just called,' he says. 'She says she needs to talk to you.'

I lean my weight on the counter, trying to relieve my aching legs. 'Okay, I'll call her back.'

He shakes his head, looking a little anxious. 'She said she'll call you back. She specifically said she doesn't want you to call the house.'

'Did she say what it was about?'

'No, but it sounded important. She seemed quite worked up.'

I go to my desk with de Luca trailing behind. 'What now?' she says.

'We pull all of Lane's records.'

She swallows but keeps her face impassive. 'No problem.'

I call Owen.

'Still nothing on Aiden Fletcher's whereabouts, I'm afraid, Gemma, but I have something you might be interested in. Jock and I just pulled in a delivery guy for a food company. He says he was approached online about a month ago about doing extra deliveries.'

'What do you mean?'

'The email said if he wanted to earn some extra cash, he simply needed to pick up some boxes from an address that would be confirmed at a later date, then deliver the items as part of his usual run.'

'How much cash?'

'He reckoned five hundred bucks,' says Owen.

'Per delivery?'

'Yeah.'

'So, he did it?'

'Yeah, he says he replied that he was interested, then a burner phone turned up three days later. The day he was leaving he got a text about the pick-up address, and sure enough there were fifteen boxes and an envelope full of cash on the front porch.'

'What was the address?'

'Just residential. We think the house was unoccupied at the time—the guy says it had a rental sign out the front.'

'Right. So, what kind of deliveries does he make?'

'Canteen supplies to schools and hospitals.'

I breathe out. 'Where?'

'The western suburbs.'

'But you can't trace the origins?'

'No, it all leads nowhere. It's smart. They keep it low-key and rely on the delivery guys thinking it's an easy way to supplement their income.'

'I think the hospital here is being used in the same way. I've been trying to get my hands on the finances, but we haven't had much luck.'

'We're looking into a hospital here too. I'll let you know what shakes out.'

'See if he knows the doctor up here, Eric Sheffield.'

'Will do.' Owen clears his throat. 'How is everything else?' he asks softly, and I know he's been talking to Mac.

'Everything's fine, Owen.'

The station phone rings and Noah sticks his head into the office, eyeballing me.

'I've gotta go, Owen, call me later.' I hang up. 'Dot?' I ask Noah, getting to my feet.

He nods.

'Put it through to the meeting room.' I turn to de Luca. 'Come on.'

'Me?' she says, surprised.

'Yep.'

When the phone rings, I put it on speaker. Dot's voice stumbles into the room. 'Detective Woodstock?'

'Yes, Dot, I'm listening.'

'What you said the other day . . . well, I've been thinking about it. I, um, I want to do the right thing.'

De Luca's eyes are fixed on the phone, and she leans forward.

'Okay, well, I'm really glad you called, Dot.'

'Yeah. It's about Daniel. He did go out the other morning.'

'Which morning?'

'Monday,' she wheezes.

'What time?' I say, as De Luca leans even closer to the speaker, her eyes intense. She seems to be holding her breath and I remember the marks on her arms. This is personal for her somehow.

'Before sunrise.'

'Do you know the exact time?'

Dot falters. 'I'm not sure. I think maybe five-thirty, or a little bit later? I was half asleep.'

I can feel de Luca's eyes on me but I keep mine on the speaker. 'Did your husband leave the house by car?'

'Yes,' Dot whispers. 'I heard the car start outside, which I thought was strange because he never goes out in the morning since he lost his job. But then I figured maybe he wanted some smokes because he ran out the night before. He wasn't gone long, I think I fell asleep again, but I heard him come back. That was at about six-thirty.'

All my muscles are straining; the tendons on my hands have turned to ropes.

'Did he come back to bed? Or speak to you?'

'No, no. That was the thing.' She pauses.

'Dot?'

'He turned the shower on.'

'He had a shower?'

'Yes.' She says it so quietly that de Luca and I lean forward even further.

'He was in there for ages.' Dot's voice trembles. 'And the thing is, he never has a shower in the morning.'

Saturday, 16 April
7.22 pm

Ben is off his food at dinner, pushing meat and vegetables list-lessly around his plate. Tommy is withdrawn, his skin a soft grey. My nausea is back with a vengeance and though I don't think I'll actually be sick, my stomach churns ominously.

Vanessa talks for all of us, a desperate edge to her voice. 'There's a bad storm coming,' she says to no one in particular. 'Inka will need to sleep inside tonight.'

Tommy grunts. He presses two tablets from a silver sheet and downs them with a glass of water. 'You're too soft on that animal.'

I smile at Ben but he doesn't notice.

Dot's phone call and Lane's betrayal circle in my head. Dot refused to come in to the station to make a formal statement because Daniel was at the house, but she agreed to meet me there tomorrow after her shift at the caravan park. Something seemed different about her this afternoon—maybe despair over her missing daughter has forced her to find the courage she didn't know she had.

'Daniel blamed that poor boy for Abbey going missing,' she told us flatly. 'He gets so angry sometimes, it's like he loses his mind. I'm sure he did something to him.'

I explained that her statement would be enough for us to bring Daniel in, though there were no guarantees we'd be able to make an arrest.

'I want to make a statement about the other things too,' she said then. 'About what he's done to Abbey these past few years.'

'And to you?' I asked.

'Yes,' she murmured, starting to cry.

There is still no sign of Lane, or his car. I rake over our interactions, replay conversations and analyse his demeanour, wondering how I could have missed his deception. I think of what de Luca said about Lane attending the most recent DV to the Clark house. It's easy to imagine a vulnerable teenage girl watching a handsome young constable stand up to her violent father and mistake his duty for affection. Had playing the hero tempted Lane to take things further? As I try to force down some salad, I wonder how far he was willing to go to protect himself. Is that what happened? Did Abbey threaten to expose him?

Oh god, what have you done? I think, an unexpected wave of grief washing over me.

I haven't always made the best judgement calls in the past. I've acted against orders, I've failed to disclose things I should have, and there's no doubt my personal involvement and emotions have, at times, led me astray. But I've survived: through a bit of luck, supportive managers, and the fact I only strayed very slightly from the hard line of the law. But this is different. No matter what happened that Saturday night, I can't see a way out of this for Lane. A moment of rage, an accident, a cover-up—it doesn't matter.

At the very least he's lied on record and botched a major criminal investigation. At worst, he's a rapist and a killer. His career is over and it will just come down to a sliding scale of gaol time.

Tommy is gulping down his beer, his gaze glassy. I'm not sure what he knows about Lane, as it hasn't hit the news, but there have been a few alerts this afternoon. I'm not sure if he's been checking his work messages.

There's a clatter: Vanessa is clearing the dishes, and I jump up to help.

'Dessert?' she says with false cheer. We all murmur 'no, thanks' and panic ruffles her features. 'Not even you, Ben?' she asks in mock horror.

'No, thank you,' he repeats. He puts his plate on the bench and glides over to the couch where he starts to play with a Lego set.

Once everything is in the dishwasher, I join Tommy back at the table and quietly tell him about Dot's call this afternoon.

'Well,' he says, blinking, 'I have to admit, I didn't think she had it in her. Do you reckon she'll go through with the statement?'

'I hope so but I'm not banking on it. She's very scared.'

He nods slowly. 'Surely you have to admit this means it's possible Daniel was involved in Abbey's disappearance too? I hope you grilled her about Saturday night. Maybe she'll magically remember something else.' Before I can speak, he holds his paw-like hands up in the air. 'Yes, yes, I know about Lane. I saw the alerts. But just because he's MIA doesn't mean he has anything to do with Rick's death.'

'Tommy,' I say, leaning closer and tilting my head until he looks me in the eye, 'Daniel might have attacked Rick, I'm not sure yet, but I think there's a strong likelihood Lane was involved in whatever happened to Abbey. He lied about her bike being stolen and god knows what else. As soon as he knew I was going to find the bike he took off. It's pretty bloody obvious he's involved, Tommy.'

Tommy's mouth pinches. He picks up a salt shaker and tips it as far as it can go before the granules fall out. 'I can't see it. Not Lane. Something else must be going on with him.'

I feel hot all over. 'We can't account for his movements from when you last saw him and when he met you at the station at ten on Sunday morning.'

'I thought you always keep an open mind,' Tommy says stiffly.

'I am.' I try to keep the heat out of my voice. 'But we've got deception, motive and opportunity. That would be bad enough, but then he disappeared. So you tell me what I'm keeping an open mind about.'

Tommy stares moodily at his dirty plate. 'I'm not saying he didn't do the wrong thing—I don't know what the hell is going on with that bike. But I'm not willing to write him off just yet. He's a good kid.'

I stand up, on fire now, picturing the possum trap in Lane's spare room. 'There was nothing good about the way he lied to everyone,' I hiss. 'But maybe that's the kind of behaviour you reward.'

We're locked in a silent stand-off, his dislike for me so palpable I feel it push me backwards.

Ben suddenly rises from the couch and slinks down the hallway. I call out to him, but he keeps walking.

'Sort your kid out, go on.' Tommy waves his hand and says sarcastically, 'Priorities.'

Fuming, I stomp down the hallway until my toes touch the line of light that runs under Ben's bedroom door. Holding my breath, I hear a burst of muffled crying. I twist the handle open and launch myself at the bed, gathering him up in a clumsy hug. 'Baby, baby, what is it? It's okay, Ben. I'm here.'

He doesn't fight me off but doesn't hug me back either. He keeps his grip on the pillow strong, his face buried in the cover as more sobs come. I let him cry, his tears neutralising my own sadness and turning me numb. I feel shamefully neglectful and utterly foolish. Of course Ben isn't okay. He's stronger than I ever was, but he is not okay. I trace my fingers across his face, smudging the tears. My son is broken and I don't know how to put him back together.

I wriggle forward so he's spooned up against my chest. Our heartbeats fall into sync, his staccato sobs forming the melody to my steady bass. After a few moments he stops shaking quite as intensely, and I have to forcibly release my grip on him. My eyes seem to have forgotten how to blink.

I start to ask him what's wrong, then mentally kick myself. I know what's wrong: he lost the person he was closest to in the world, and his part-time, emotionally challenged mother took him to a strange place where he knows no one.

I'm sorry, I mouth into his hair as my eyes fill.

'Are you thinking about Dad?' I say quietly.

'Is your job really dangerous?' he replies.

'What?'

'Charlie said that police officers die all the time. He showed me a news story about one who died yesterday in Sydney.'

'Oh, Ben,' I say. I'd seen the news and got the alerts—a domestic violence call-out had proven more serious than initially thought. A female officer had been restraining the perpetrator when he threw her against a brick wall. She died in hospital from head injuries a few hours later. 'That was a terrible incident, but that kind of thing is really rare.'

'But it could happen to you,' he presses. 'You could die.'

'I won't.' I swallow around my swollen throat.

He gives me a withering look, an adult look. 'You can't promise me that. If you do it will be a lie.'

I sigh. 'Hey.' I sit up and pull him with me. 'You're right, I can't promise you, but I'm very careful. And you are so important to me, I can promise you I will fight like crazy to always be here for you.'

I find his hand and squeeze it. He clenches his jaw into the start of a smile, but we both know all too well that my best intentions will never be enough if the universe has other plans. I wonder if this is my destiny: telling Ben things I hope like hell will prove to be true.

I gently lift his chin. 'Do you want to go home now? Back to Smithson?'

He shrugs. 'Sort of. I want to see Annabel.'

'Of course you do, baby,' I say.

'And Grandad and Rebecca.'

'And Jodie,' I add.

'Yeah,' he says quickly. 'But I still feel funny about going to school. When I think about it I feel sick.'

'Your dad loves you so much, Ben. He always will.'

He looks at me, confused. 'I know.'

'I'm not good with this stuff,' I say, stumbling over the words. 'But I want to talk about him more. We should both talk about him more, don't you think?'

Ben nods, then his face twists in grief.

'Ben, Ben, hey . . .'

Just hold him, Gemma, I hear Scott say. *Just hold him.*

And so I do. I shut up and hold on.

Saturday, 16 April
11.02 pm

I turn over my pillow for the third time, trying to get comfortable. I feel like I've been hit by a truck. In a desperate attempt to find sleep I run through the names of people in my Sydney squad, but I'm still half-awake when my phone rings, lighting up the water-colour on the wall and turning it an eerie blue. I lean out of bed and place my hands on the floor, walking them over to where my phone is attached to the charger.

It's a number I don't recognise. With my legs still in the bed, I answer as formally as I can manage.

'Oh yes, hello.' A female voice with a strong accent. 'Is that the detective I met today?'

I side onto the floor and scramble into a sitting position. 'Yes, this is Detective Woodstock.'

'This is Elsha. Kai's girlfriend.'

I push my hair out of my eyes and try to concentrate. 'Have you heard from him?'

'He called me.' Her voice wobbles. 'He's very upset. I'm so worried about him.'

'You've done the right thing in letting me know. Did he call you on his usual phone?'

'Ah, no, it was a blocked number.'

'And did he just call you?'

'Yes, he hung up and I called you right away like you said.' When she starts to cry, it crosses my mind that this might be a ploy.

'Okay, Elsha, you're doing great. What did he say?'

'He wanted me to meet with him. He said we needed to talk because a whole lot of stuff has been blown out of proportion.'

'What did you say?'

'I said he was scaring me. And then he started yelling about whether I'd spoken to the police! He said whatever you were saying, it wasn't true, and that I had to trust him.'

'Okay, Elsha, this is important—did he say anything about where he was going?'

She sniffs loudly and her voice is muffled for a moment. 'No, he just said I shouldn't believe what anyone's saying, and he's going to prove to me that he didn't do it.' Her voice breaks open. 'But he sounded crazy, and I think that you're right. I'm so sorry. Tell me, what has he done? Did he . . . Is it to do with that missing girl? Oh my god!' she wails.

'Elsha, listen.' I start to pull my jeans on. 'Are you safe?'

'Yes. I'm with my friend at her parents' house.'

'Okay, good. Text me the address of where you're staying. If you hear from Kai again, call me straight away. Can you do that?'

'Please don't hurt him,' she whispers.

I hang up, throw some chewing gum into my mouth, and scribble a note for Tommy and Vanessa that I leave on the kitchen bench. I slip out the front door, already dialling de Luca.

'Is it Lane?' she answers, sounding wide awake.

'Yeah, I just spoke to Elsha.' I'm battling through the wind to get to the car. 'Lane just called her. She said he wanted to meet with her. If they're both telling the truth, he must be close by.'

'Do you think she is? Telling the truth, I mean?'

'She sounded terrified, but who knows? It's all we've got right now. I'll send Grange to her friend's place just in case Lane goes there.'

'Right. Do you want to pick me up from the pub? It'll be quicker if I drive there and meet you.'

'Yep, I'm coming now. We'll work out a plan then, and I should let Tran know what's going on. Can you see if the guys can trace Elsha's call? I doubt they can but it's worth a shot.'

It starts to spit with rain and I flick on the windscreen wipers, smudging a fine layer of dust into the glass. Before I start the car Elsha's text comes through with the address, so I forward it to Grange and ask him to get there as soon as he can. My nerves are going haywire, the full weight of Lane's betrayal bearing down on me with renewed force.

I pull out onto the road and flick on the headlights—just in time to swerve and narrowly miss running over Meg Jarvis.

———

Meg mutters under her breath and clicks her tongue, her eyes squeezed tightly shut. This seems to be the equivalent of a kid sticking his fingers in his ears and singing to block out requests to tidy his room. Large droplets of rain begin to fall on us as we stand in the glow of my car headlights. I feel even more wired than before, the wind churning around us.

'Meg, will you let me drive you home?'

She opens her eyes and makes a low angry noise. 'I saw them with her, you know. She was already gone.'

'Who, Meg?' Rain runs down my face. I want to grab her by the shoulders and shake it out of her, but of course that would only make things worse. 'Please tell me.'

'They paid for my sins,' Meg says sadly. 'My sister was sick, I had no choice.' She shakes her head.

I wipe my wet face on my jumper sleeve. My phone is lighting up the centre console.

'Gemma, we just got an emergency call.' De Luca's voice is an octave higher than normal. 'It was from the Clark house—one of the kids called triple zero. Lane's there and apparently he's going crazy.'

Saturday, 16 April
11.23 pm

I grip the wheel so hard my hands hurt.

Theories fly around my head, matching the mad dance of the trees.

What the hell is Lane doing at the Clarks'?

Meg's warnings are like a chant in my brain. Did she really see something? I remember what Janet said about Meg retracting her statement all those years ago, and something suddenly clicks. *They paid for my sins.* Could she have been talking about Sally?

Up ahead, de Luca's car hurtles into the pub car park. She darts across the asphalt in the drizzle, sliding inside my car just as Grange calls me.

'Elsha's here at her friend's place,' he says, sounding like he's been hyperventilating.

'Okay, great. Stay there until you hear from me. If Lane calls her, call me.'

'What's going on—?' he says as I hang up.

De Luca and I don't speak. I press on the accelerator and launch the car back onto the road, racing toward the Clarks' house.

'The kid left the phone on at the house after the emergency call. Lane has totally lost it, yelling and screaming at Daniel Clark.' De Luca gazes out into the darkness. 'I just can't believe it.'

'How long until back-up arrives?' I say.

'They said thirty to forty minutes.'

'We'll have to go in without them.'

She nods. 'I know.'

The rain becomes a sheet of silver as we hit the dirt road. The sky lights up then plummets us back into darkness, the wind pulling the car from my control.

Out of the corner of my eye I see a movement, and I swerve just in time to avoid the crush of a falling tree.

The back wheels slide out and we slam hard to the right. Holding on to the steering wheel, I feel the air leave my body as I throw my weight to the left. The night sucks us in like a whirlpool. I can't see anything except for the two white discs of the headlights.

All sound evaporates. De Luca is pressed back against the seat, her chin almost touching her chest, eyes bulging. One hand is pressed to the dash while the other clutches her phone. She leans toward me; her lips are moving but I can't hear a thing.

The absolute silence shifts into a soft but urgent sting before exploding into a horrific blaring.

My forehead is on the horn and the sound stabs my eardrums.

'Oh!' I exclaim, reeling back to stop it. Silence again. 'Are you okay?'

She nods. 'Are you?'

'I'm okay.'

'You did well to avoid that.' She looks at me in astonishment as if only just realising we didn't hit the tree. Even in the dim light I can see that her irises have completely succumbed to her pupils.

I nod, taking in the carnage around us: the carcass of the tree, the road turning to water. I right the car and keep going. She gestures to the upcoming turn-off, and the car shakes wildly again as I veer into the shallow court and switch off my headlights.

Something shines against the dark matt of the bush. Lane's squad car is parked outside Jacqui Cobb's house.

As I step into the rain, my legs buckle and I steady myself against the car. We press our doors shut and approach the house. I notice de Luca check her gun and I do the same, praying like hell we're not going to need them.

Branches brush the edges of the house; the sharp scratching creates an angry symphony.

I plug my earphones into my phone and push in the right bud, then wrap the cord around my ear and fix it in place. 'Call me and I'll stay on the line.'

Panic flashes across de Luca's face. 'We're separating?'

'Yes. I'm going to go in first.' I set my jaw. 'You're on standby if things escalate. I don't want Lane to feel ambushed—I'm hoping we can talk him down.' The wind surges again, my hair flying skyward. I frantically pull it into an elastic; it's dripping wet. 'You go around that way. See if the side door is open. Keep your phone on and enter if you need to.'

She nods sharply and disappears into the darkness. I step onto the broken tiles and place my hand on the doorknob, pausing to listen.

Nothing. Maybe the faint murmur of voices, but I can't be sure. I twist my hand. It's open.

'I'm going in,' I say, for de Luca's benefit.

A gust of wind masks a tiny creak as I ease the door shut behind me.

My hand flies to my throat when I come face to face with a shadowy version of myself: the bathroom door is open and I'm looking straight into a mirror.

'Inside,' I murmur.

I hear a male voice, sharp and high, and follow it up the passage. Another voice. A thick line of light runs under the lounge-room door; it's slightly open.

I press my hand to the door and push it gently, widening the gap by a few centimetres.

Lane stands a few metres from me, facing the other way. From the angle of his arm I can tell he is holding a gun. An odd sense of calm covers me. It's all come down to this.

Peering into the room, I see the twins on the couch on the other side of the room, their terrified eyes blinking in the dim light. Dot is standing in front of them, shoulders squared, chest heaving. The TV blares in the corner of the room, an oblivious game-show host leaning toward the camera and winking exaggeratedly.

Outside, the wind scratches to be let in.

'I'm not leaving till you admit what you did.' Lane's voice is a low growl.

I widen the gap a bit more and look around his bulk to see Daniel standing in front of a cluttered coffee table. His chin is set in an arrogant tilt, but I can see a pulse in his neck and the tautness in his calves.

'I need you to confess,' says Lane flatly. 'You've wasted our time from the start.'

'You're mad,' spits Daniel.

'I'm not going down for this. I need you to come forward, Daniel.'

He snarls, 'I told you to *get out*.'

Lane shuffles in an odd little semi-circle, turning the gun on Dot and the kids. 'You killed Rick,' he says to Daniel, 'because you found out he did something to Abbey.'

Dot whimpers; her gaze darts from the gun to her sons. 'Please.'

Daniel is glowering. 'Don't you *dare* threaten my wife. Get out of here or I'll fucking kill you!'

Lane thrusts his free hand into his hair. 'No way. Not until you tell me what happened!'

'Get the fuck out of my house!' Daniel roars.

On the couch, one of the boys begins to cry. Lane's head jerks toward the sound and he grunts, holding his hands on either side of his face as if in pain. The gun points to the ceiling. Wind rushes into the crevasses of the house; false echoes bounce from the walls.

Lane steadies himself and points the gun back at Dot. 'Tell me what you did or I shoot her!'

I step forward, my gun trained on Lane. When Dot sees me, hope washes over her expression. Daniel sees me too, but his face remains blank.

'Kai,' I say firmly.

He spins around. All traces of boyish charm are gone. 'I didn't hurt her! Or Rick. You have to believe me.'

'I'm not saying you did.' I take another step. 'But we need to talk about this properly. Not here.'

He has the rabid energy of a junkie. The glow from the TV catches in the black of his pupils, and my heart skips a beat. He is capable of anything right now.

'I know how it looks,' he says. 'I know you found the bike, but I didn't see her after she left the station, I swear!'

I picture him hustling the bike into the storage shed, Abbey racing off into the darkness. The bush was warm and still that night, nothing like the raging beast it is now.

It's hard to control my anger. 'Okay, Kai, I believe you. But this is between us—we don't need anyone here to be involved. How about you come with me and we can talk it through?' I inch closer.

'No! I know how it works. I don't have an alibi. Shit will get pinned on me and I'll be screwed.'

The boys blink. Dot bleats a tiny sob.

'Kai, you know a confession can't work like this.' I gesture to the room. 'We need to do it properly or it will be worth nothing.'

'He must have done something to her,' Lane chokes out, 'when I went to the party.' He brushes tears from his eyes with the sleeve of his jacket. 'He must have been waiting for her at home, or Rick was. Or that backpacker. But none of it was me, I swear.'

On the TV, the audience begins to clap and cheer.

'Did you see Abbey after she left the station?'

Lane's movements are jerky and he won't look at me. The eye of the gun is fixed firmly on me. 'She ran off, like I said, and I went to meet Tommy. But then I came here later, and . . .' He shakes his head.

'Why did you come here that night, Kai?'

'Because! I was worried about her. Abbey . . . she was angry at me. I just wanted to make sure she was okay.'

No, I think, disgusted, *you were just terrified Abbey was going to say something about what you'd been doing to her.*

'And how were you going to check that she was okay?'

'I was just going to look in on her, you know.'

'How?' I press. 'Were you going to call her?'

His shoulders sink in defeat. He knows I know. 'There's a tree outside her room. She never closes the blind to the window.'

Daniel stiffens.

'And was she there?' I say softly.

'No. I don't know if he came out looking for her or if he lost it when she got home or what. Or maybe Rick hurt her and that's why he killed him.' Lane's face crumples again. 'I don't know what happened—but he does,' he says, gesturing wildly at Daniel. 'He needs to stop fucking us around.'

Jacqui Cobb's high-pitched voice worms into my ear. *A car stopped at the end of the street at some point. I got up to go to the loo and heard it, just idling. It only had its parkers on, which I thought was weird.*

Lane, parking the squad car at the end of the street.

'Okay, okay,' I say quietly, still hoping I can calm him down enough to cuff him and get him out of here unharmed. 'Why was Abbey angry with you, Kai?'

His face folds up like a piece of paper. 'I guess I let her down. She wouldn't come with me after that, she wouldn't let me take her home. She ran off. And then you killed her!' He stabs the gun clumsily toward Daniel. 'The next morning I could tell you knew what happened to her. You *knew*! What did you do to her?' Lane retches, mopping at his mouth. He's out of control, muscles pulsing in his face and veins jutting from his neck, but the anguish in his voice seems real.

'Kai,' I say as calmly as possible, 'you know we need to go. Why don't you come with me?'

'I'm not leaving until he comes clean.' He looks at me pleadingly. 'Don't you get it? I'm fucked otherwise.'

In spite of myself I feel a tug of empathy. He seems so lost. I can't work out if he's a sociopath or simply desperate.

'I didn't bloody touch Abbey or her piece-of-shit boyfriend!' says Daniel.

'You're lying.' Lane narrows his eyes and firms his grip on the gun.

Daniel's face contorts in rage; he still seems completely unperturbed by the gun. 'She was my daughter! I told you, Rick did something to her and I wanted to beat the living shit out of him for it, but someone got to him before I had the chance. I have no idea who it was.' The words hiss from his teeth.

Chris and Wayne are statues on the couch. Dot's eyes slide briefly to the other side of the room. I can't see around the dividing wall, but I can picture the small dining room that leads to the staircase and the bedrooms upstairs. I hope de Luca has managed to get into the house.

'What did you do?' Lane yells.

'Get out,' sneers Daniel. 'You're a complete joke of a cop. You're a bloody rock spider and I hope they put you away.'

Lane stumbles back, edging along the wall toward the door, his right arm still outstretched, the gun still trained on Daniel. His fingers tighten and he adjusts his aim.

'No, Kai, don't!' I scream.

A door slams somewhere deep in the house and the walls shake.

Lane throws one final mad look around the room, the gun swirling in a wild arc, before he slips into the dimness of the dining room and disappears.

Currents of electricity burn through me as I point my gun to the space where Lane was standing a second ago. 'Everyone stay here,' I yell. 'Don't move!'

As I pass the dining table, the house shudders with another almighty crash, followed by a gunshot. And a scream.

Saturday, 16 April
11.59 pm

I hurl myself into the hallway. I don't breathe as my eyes adjust to the darkness.

A horrible moan fills the long passage.

My heart presses into my throat, and I rush forward just as a spray of bullets rattles above me. I drop to the ground, balanced on my hands and feet.

Not gunfire but rain, smacking against the tin roof at the front of the house. All I can see is a square of light at the end of the blackness as I scramble to my feet again, pitching myself toward it. A gruesome montage plays in my mind's eye: scenes from the past week: the possum's gaping throat, Rick's bloody skull, Abbey's blacked out face in the photographs. My brain attempts to whir into overdrive but the rain is making it impossible to hear anything, impossible to think. Is that crying? Talking? Is someone calling for help? Are there two voices? Please let there be two voices. I point my gun forward and step through the doorway.

It's a spare room, dimly lit by the moonlight through the window.

A dark puddle is spreading on the dirty cream carpet. Limbs folded into limbs. Two guns lie discarded on the floor.

I drop to the floor and crawl forward. My knees are sticky with blood and I want to weep at the sight. Even though I gave up bargaining with a higher power a long time ago, I find myself praying as I yank a sheet from the bed and add to the pressure a sobbing Lane has applied to de Luca's torso. It's a desperate attempt to stop the flow of blood from her body.

That underwater sensation returns to me. I frame de Luca's face with my hands and feel her pulse thrumming against my fingers as I stare into her eyes, saying her name. A tiny bead of light dances across her pupils. Someone is screaming for help; it takes me a moment to realise it's me. I push through the surface of the water and greedily pull air into my lungs.

Daniel appears in the doorway, his face unreadable. I'm hyper-aware of the guns on the floor. *We might all be dead in a minute*, I think, cradling de Luca and pressing down on the wetness.

And then Daniel is gone. Was he even there to begin with? Time shifts around us, fast then slow, and suddenly Daniel is back, armed with bandages, his jaw a hard line, hands wresting de Luca's neck to the side as he checks her pulse. 'You're going to be fine,' he says.

Lane stands less than a metre away, his face almost as slack and bloodless as de Luca's.

Our eyes meet with crippling intensity. The guns seem to glow on the floor.

I keep my eyes on Lane as I lurch to the right. He moves at the same time.

Closing a hand around each gun, I scramble to my feet, stumbling into the wall. Breathing hard I watch Daniel hovering over de Luca. I hear the roar of an engine and reach the front door only to see the taillights of Lane's squad car burning holes through the fuzz of rain.

EIGHTH DAY MISSING

EIGHTH DAY MISSING

Sunday, 17 April
12.24 am

The wind continues to thrash at the house, wild and furious.

I am frozen in the doorway, chaos behind me, chaos before me.

The cul-de-sac explodes with blue and red light. The hazy dots firm into thick shapes, and they dance drunkenly across the road, the lawn, my face.

Car doors snap shut. Strangers march through the rain toward the house, armed with the energy and tools that will hopefully mean this nightmare is over.

'Gemma?' Tran's worried features appear in front of me.

'It's de Luca,' I splutter, gesturing to the bedroom. 'He shot her.'

The ambulance officers enter the house. They talk to Daniel. They talk to de Luca.

I'm still holding the guns. Tran and I look down at them.

'Gemma?' she asks again.

'Lane's gone. He took his car. Dot and the twins are in the lounge. They're fine.'

'Lane shot de Luca?'

I nod. 'I don't even know if he knew it was her. I didn't see it.'

'Are you injured?'

'No.'

Daniel stands back as de Luca's face is covered with a plastic mask. The ambos decide it's too risky to move her and needles are inserted into her veins as she lies on the floor; her torso is bound like a mummy's.

Daniel's face is stained with blood, his hands are slick with it.

Tran is on the phone now; her sharp orders echo up the hallway.

I go to the lounge. Dot has a child under each arm, her face as hard as stone.

'Are you all okay?' I ask.

She nods.

'Daniel's fine,' I tell her.

Another nod.

Tran is off the phone. She gives the twins a reassuring smile and calmly explains to Dot what is going to happen next.

An ambulance officer enters the room. 'We'll get her to the hospital while she's stable.'

I lean on the wall and let their voices swirl around me.

My phone vibrates with a text. I pull it from my pocket and see that the call with de Luca is still going. I yank out my earbud and end the call.

I open the text and stumble back against the wall.

My legs shake uncontrollably as adrenaline oozes from my pores, air evacuating my lungs.

I stumble to the bathroom just in time to retch and vomit repeatedly into the toilet, Lane's message slamming through me over and over.

I swear I didn't hurt her but I know I've ruined everything. Tell my parents and Elsha I'm sorry.

Sunday, 17 April
5.13 am

Small broken branches crisscross the Gordons' front lawn, and a wattle is slumped against the front veranda, yellow flowers like confetti on the porch.

I ease my key into the front door and pull it shut behind me, resting my forehead on the timber. I still feel shaky but I'm no longer tired; I'm way beyond that now. A grim determination has taken over, propelling me to get to the bottom of this stinking mess, to shut it down so Ben and I can get the hell out of here. I push away from the door and let the anger rinse through me, liking the way my fists ball and my jaw tightens.

Ben is in my bed now, curled in sleep. Did he panic when he discovered I was gone? Did he cry into the dark wondering if I'd come back? What would have happened if I hadn't come back? I smooth a curl of his hair and trace my fingers across his freckles. I know that face better than my own, but he still remains a mystery. He is both mine and completely separate. The joy he brings me only just outweighs the dread he evokes deep in my bones.

I slink out and pull the door closed.

In the living room a soft line of light edges across the floor, the new day sneaking past its predecessor. Tommy and Vanessa sit side by side at the table, empty mugs in front of them. There is a basket of Easter eggs on the kitchen bench.

'Are you alright, Gemma?' Vanessa's voice is unsure.

I sit down heavily in front of them.

'I spoke to Tran,' says Tommy. 'I can't believe it.'

'Yeah,' I say.

'Ben came into our room last night,' says Vanessa, 'when he couldn't find you. I told him you were fine and would be back soon.' She twists her wedding ring around her finger. 'He settled very quickly in your bed.'

'Thanks.' I fight a flurry of feelings as I look at them, these strangers in front of me.

Their faces are lined with worry but there is a caution there too, a tinge of defensiveness.

'How's de Luca?' Tommy asks.

'She's stable,' I reply, 'but critical. That's all I know. Her mum refused to come—apparently they're estranged—but her girlfriend is with her.'

Tommy's fat fingers grip the mug. 'I just can't believe Lane could do that,' he mutters, his eyes wet. Vanessa takes his hand and pulls it into her lap.

My resolve falters. 'They are trying to get to his body now the rain has stopped.'

Vanessa squeezes her eyes shut. 'God.'

'I don't think he could see another way out.'

Tommy nods but I can sense that, like me, he's stuck on playing out the scene: Lane driving to the cliffs, stumbling out of his car, throwing himself into the void. Tommy bends his neck and presses his fingers into the ridge of his eyebrows. 'He was a good kid.'

'He probably raped a teenage girl,' I snap. 'And he lied to all of us. He threatened the Clarks and shot a cop.'

Tommy baulks at my outburst.

'We all misread him,' I continue. My hands are shaking so I clasp them together. Put them in my lap.

'We're allowed to be sad, Gemma,' says Vanessa.

'Sure, and I'm allowed to be angry.'

Finally Tommy says, 'How long was something going on between them?'

'I don't know.'

'And the bike?'

'I'm guessing he panicked when she turned up that night. He knew she'd be on the security tapes. Once he saw she'd left her bike on the street, he must have figured a fake robbery report would be a good cover for her visit. If anyone ever asked about it, Abbey could just claim it turned up the next day and he could mention it casually to you but let you know it was all resolved. No loose ends.'

'So what went wrong?' asks Tommy.

'I think she told him she broke up with Rick and that she wanted to be with him, and he shut her down. She got upset, refused his offer of a lift and ran off. Lane had already received the call about the party and called you. So he stashed the bike in the shed. He knew no one ever used it, and he thought he'd sort everything out when Abbey calmed down.'

'That's why I beat him to the party.'

'Yes.'

'But Lane wasn't the one who—'

'I don't think so. My guess is that Abbey met up with Rick that night—she knew he was meeting friends on the beach. I think she confessed what had been going on between her and Lane, and that Rick lost it. Lane was just hell-bent on clearing his name because he knew that after everything else, he'd be the prime suspect.'

'And Daniel killed Rick?'

'If Dot is telling the truth about him leaving the house on Monday morning, then it makes the most sense.'

Tommy mumbles something under his breath.

'Will Daniel be charged?' asks Vanessa.

I picture the spread of red on the dirty cream carpet. Daniel's arms around de Luca, his mouth moving as he spoke to her.

'If Dot goes through with her statement, including the historical abuse, then I think he will.'

A neighbour opens their back door and a cheerful 80s song rolls into the Gordons' yard.

Vanessa glances at her watch and eases herself to her feet. 'I'll make some tea. Tommy, you need to take your pills.'

He and I lock eyes across the table.

'Tommy,' I say, 'I know you have a problem.'

'I don't know what you're talking about,' he says gruffly.

'The pills, Tommy. The doctor shopping. Your accident. Were you covering the fact you were high?'

'Don't be ridiculous.'

'Did you contact the newspaper about me? Try to scare me out of town?'

'What? No. You're clearly exhausted. Take a nap.'

Leaning forward, I bare my teeth. 'Don't tell me what I need, Tommy. I'm not sure I even know the half of it, but I swear to god I will find out.' I narrow my eyes to slits. 'Are you running some kind of scheme with Eric Sheffield? How far does this thing go, Tommy?'

He pushes his chair back from the table in a flourish. 'You're mad,' he hisses. 'Clearly the strain of this case has gotten to you.'

'Ben's awake,' Vanessa warns, cocking her head to the hallway. I hear the toilet flush.

I give Tommy another sharp look and go to see Ben. He's pulling on clothes in his bedroom. He looks tired, a dark smudge under each eye.

'I got called out last night,' I say into his hair. 'I'm sorry I wasn't there when you woke up.'

'Gemma.' Vanessa is standing in the doorway, a sharp line between her brows.

I pull away from Ben. Draw myself tall.

'Give Tommy a break,' she says. 'He's very upset about Lane.'

'That doesn't excuse his involvement in something illegal.'

Hurt cuts across her face. 'Tommy wouldn't do anything like that.'

'Please,' I say, rolling my eyes, 'don't you get sick of blindly supporting him?'

Her eyes flash as her arms fold. 'We've done a lot for you.'

I snort. 'Stop protecting him, Vanessa.' I give my son a stiff smile. 'Come on, Ben, we have to go.'

'Now?' He raises his right eyebrow and looks worriedly back and forth between us.

'Yes. Get your jumper on and brush your teeth.'

I push past Vanessa and go into my room, where I swap my filthy shirt for a clean orange T-shirt, blast my underarms with deodorant and shove some things into a backpack.

'Come on, Ben!'

Vanessa tugs on my arm, the skin around her neck strained as she says, 'Gemma, don't you think he's been through enough?'

'Let go of me.' I open the front door and usher Ben outside.

'This is ridiculous, Gemma,' Vanessa calls after us, 'you need to get some sleep! It's driving me mad watching you run yourself into the ground in your condition.'

I gape at her. 'What?'

'I know about the baby,' she blurts. 'I saw the test in the rubbish.'

Sunday, 17 April

7.11 am

Ben's head jerks, his eyes wide.

We stand in a strange little triangle on the porch. I feel like I'm going to explode.

'How dare you!' I snap.

Vanessa doesn't let up. 'I don't understand what you're doing, putting yourself in danger. It's like you don't even care. What's wrong with you?'

'Shut up.' The words slice out of my mouth, and I'm worried I will slap her if I don't leave.

'Mum?' Ben's little face tilts upward, solemn between us.

I rush down the veranda stairs, my boots sliding on the storm debris, tugging Ben along behind me. The sun tentatively prods at the night's carnage as if trying to work out what's salvageable. A cherry picker is parked in the street a few houses along from the Gordons', and two men in high-vis vests are wrestling a fallen tree off a car.

Ben and I walk along the beach amid an eerie calm. Today the ocean looks as innocent as a child. My son seems deep in thought and I wonder if, by some miracle, he didn't hear what Vanessa said.

I call Tran but there's no update on de Luca's condition. Critical but stable.

'Daniel Clark probably saved her life, you know.'

'Yes,' she says. 'I know. Apparently he was a surf lifesaver years ago.'

'God,' I say, watching Ben bend down to examine a shell.

'We've recovered Lane's body from the rocks. I've just left his parents' place. The autopsy will be tomorrow.' She pauses. 'Dot is going ahead with her statement about Daniel this morning.' Tran sounds just as exhausted as me.

'Where is Daniel now?'

'Still at the house with Dot and the kids. We're taking their statements about last night in an hour. Dot will go last. The plan is to detain him then.'

'When will Rick's body be released?' I ask her.

'Wednesday, I think. The weapons expert is scheduled to examine the body tomorrow. I spoke to Georgina Fletcher earlier—they're now staying with her sister. I think they'll have the funeral on Friday.'

'Still no word on Aiden?'

'Apparently not. Maybe he'll come out of the woodwork when he hears that Daniel has been put away.'

'Right. If he and Rick were involved in trafficking drugs, Aiden probably assumed his brother's death was caused by that, but Daniel's arrest might make him think otherwise.' I struggle through a bracing yawn. 'Please keep me posted about de Luca. And Daniel's arrest.'

'Will do.'

I call out to Ben, who is picking up pieces of seaweed from the shoreline and chucking them in the water.

'Did you find the missing girl yet?' he asks me, squinting into the sun.

'Not yet.' I nudge a piece of driftwood with my foot. 'But no matter what, we're going home soon. To Smithson. I think we should leave tomorrow. Does that sound good?'

'Yeah.' He's staring out at the ocean.

More than anything I want to read his mind, to sift through his thoughts and check that he really is okay.

'Why are you and Vanessa fighting?' he asks.

'It's complicated. I lost my temper and I shouldn't have.'

'Are you having a baby like she said?'

The world tips one way and then another.

'I don't know,' I say finally.

'With Mac?'

'I don't know.' My mouth feels full of wool. I lick my lips. Salt. 'Maybe.'

'I like Mac.'

'Me too,' I whisper.

'Mum, can I ask you another question?'

My throat constricts. 'Of course.'

'Is "Mac" Mac's real name?'

I let out the breath I've been holding, stroke his hair. 'It's "Cormac", but I don't think anyone ever calls him that.'

Ben smiles and darts off, grabbing a fallen tree branch and dragging it along the sand to join another one.

'Be careful,' I say automatically.

'I am,' he replies just as swiftly.

For a few minutes I watch him wrangle the branches into a rough tepee, the crease of concentration between his eyes an exact replica of Scott's.

I sit on a flat shelf of rock and draw my knees to my chest, folding my arms and resting my chin on them. I'm drained. Lane's broken body looms in my mind; I squeeze my eyes shut trying to make it go away. The loose threads of his guilt taunt me. What exactly did he do?

'Mac!' Ben shouts.

I turn to the right and open my eyes. Ben has run off in the direction we came from. I gaze past him down the beach to see Mac rushing along the sand toward him, a worried look on his face.

I get to my feet. Maybe I'm dreaming.

He approaches with Ben jogging happily beside him.

'Ben, can you go back to finishing what you were building before, please?'

He rolls his eyes but trots off.

'What the hell are you doing here?' I hiss at Mac.

He falters. Flushed red and out of breath, he holds up a hand. 'I heard what happened last night. You didn't answer my calls so I went straight to the Gordons—they said you came this way.' He pauses, still huffing. 'Gemma, are you alright?'

My face scrunches up as I try to understand. 'You flew here this morning? How?'

'I never left,' he says, eyes pleading.

'*What?*'

'I couldn't, Gem! Not after what you told me. I couldn't just go back to Sydney and pretend everything was fine. I've been working from here and keeping a low profile.'

'And keeping tabs on me?' I snap.

'It wasn't like that. You know I care about you. You have to stop acting like it's a bad thing.'

I fold my arms and fight another wave of exhaustion. 'So, what, you're staying at The Parrot?'

'Yeah. I asked Cam not to say anything.' Mac steps closer. 'Please, don't be angry. I was worried. Your dad was worried too, and so was Jonesy. Candy too.'

'Great,' I mutter, furious at the idea of everyone talking about me.

'Gemma—'

'Take me to the hotel? Please. I need to sleep.'

Sunday, 17 April

11.32 am

It's light when I wake up. A TV is on nearby, the volume low. I'm at the Parrot Hotel; I recognise the décor from our first night in Fairhaven. I roll over and stretch out my legs, relishing the pull of my tired muscles. Then I remember everything and feel sick again.

I check my phone: a missed call from Owen. I sit up and call him back.

'Shit, Gemma.' His swearing is uncharacteristic. 'Are you alright? I heard—'

'I'm okay, but the whole situation is pretty terrible. And I doubt we'll ever find the girl now. At this point, I don't even know what happened.'

Owen murmurs his sympathies. We all understand the pain of a missing body, the horror of the eternal limbo.

I rest my hands lightly on my gut—I need to eat. 'I have to go, Owen. Thanks for checking in.'

'Of course. Hey, look, I just wanted to let you know that the team on the drug thing are closing in on a few doctors they reckon might be involved. One has a link to a guy who runs a packaging company, and the team think that's how they're getting the stock to fly under the radar. We're not sure if the stock is stolen—we think it might be manufactured from scratch and being cut with a lot of cheap stuff to get the margins up. But bottom line is that it looks totally legitimate when it's all packed in barcoded boxes. It could easily be sitting in a warehouse or even on a pharmacy shelf somewhere, and nobody would ever know.'

'God, we're in trouble when the drug dealers are worried about bloody graphic design and the quality of their cardboard boxes.'

Owen laughs. 'I know, it's a whole new breed of dealers. Drugs masquerading as drugs.' He sighs. 'Please take care of yourself, Gem. Let me know when you're coming back.'

I shuffle into the lounge and give Ben a kiss. On the TV a cute rabbit is wrestling with a giant egg.

In the kitchen, Mac looks up from his laptop. 'Hey. How are you feeling?'

'Better. I'm going to get myself some cereal.'

'Good idea.'

I feel him watching me as I shake the cornflakes into the bowl, pour in the milk. I check my phone. An email from Tran confirms that Dot has made a formal statement about Daniel's whereabouts on Monday morning; he will be detained and arrested shortly. I scroll through my other emails and see that Grange has finally sent through the hospital finance records.

Switching to my laptop, I scroll through the statements. There's a recurring monthly payment of one thousand dollars to Parrot Bay Holdings Pty Ltd listed under 'freight'.

I google the company: it's the registered name of Tara's beauty salon. I sit heavily back against the chair. The ringing sound returns.

'How many weeks are you?' Mac asks quietly.

'What? Um, I think about seven. From when you came to Smithson.'

He nods.

'I just spoke to Owen about a drug investigation in Sydney. The team thinks it might be linked to prescription drugs being sold around here and other regional centres.'

'And is it also linked to your case?'

'I'm not sure,' I say, my mind whirring. I remember Janet saying that Sally Luther had worked with the local GP and Eric had mentioned this was what he did before he opened the hospital. 'And Aiden worked at the hospital,' I murmur.

'What?' Mac leans forward and takes my hand.

Although I'm looking into his eyes, I can't focus on him. Is Eric the key to all of this? I replay seeing the note on my windshield. The shock of it. But Elsha said Lane stayed with her that night, and that he woke up when I called him to come in early. He didn't have time to come past the Gordons'.

'Lane didn't leave me the note about Scott,' I say.

'What?' says Mac.

'I just . . .' I swallow, trying to think. 'It doesn't make sense.'

Drugs masquerading as drugs. Hiding in plain sight.

'This isn't finished,' I say, pushing my chair back.

Mac looks alarmed. 'Gemma, you don't need to think about this case anymore. You've done enough.'

'Please don't do that, don't tell me what I need.' My head spins. 'Can you mind Ben for me? I need to follow something up. It's not to do with Rick or Abbey—I think there's something else going on.'

Mac breathes out through his teeth. 'I said I'd help Cam. The pub flooded last night, and it's a mess. He came past before, when you were asleep, and I think Ben is keen to help anyway. But, Gem, at some point we really do need to work everything out.'

I retie my hair and straighten my clothes. 'I know, but there's something else I need to do first.'

I say goodbye to Ben and step outside. It feels a lot longer than a week ago that I discovered the dead possum. Realising my car is at the Gordons', I stand in the sunshine trying to decide what to do.

'Gemma!'

I whip around.

'Don't worry,' says Simon, his hands already raised in defence. 'I'm just walking past, I don't want another serve.' He steps around me and unlocks the door to his room.

'Actually, Simon,' I say, 'is there any chance you can give me a lift?'

Simon parks his car outside the main entrance of the hospital. 'I didn't run that article.'

'I noticed.'

'I had a big fight with my editor about it.'

'Lucky you're tough.'

He flexes his arm. 'True. She did tell me that the woman who called had an accent—possibly Dutch or Scandinavian. Anyway, I convinced her it was part of a smear campaign and that it would bite us in the arse if we published it.'

'Thank you,' I say vaguely.

An accent. Elsha. Lane's betrayal continues beyond the grave.

I turn to Simon. 'I have to go.'

'Sure. Good chat.'

'I might only be a second.'

'I can wait,' he says. 'I brought a book.' He hooks his thumb toward a dog-eared Tom Clancy novel in the back seat. 'Plus, I'm obviously hoping there's going to be a story in this for me. It would be good to get your exclusive take on the events of last night.'

'You have a one-track mind,' I say, rolling my eyes.

'That's what my ex-girlfriends say,' he quips as I get out of the car.

I burst into the hospital foyer. The receptionist eyes me nervously but chirps, 'Happy Easter!'

'I need to see Doctor Sheffield,' I snap.

'We-*ell*, he's on the ward. Do you know, he ended up assisting with the delivery of a baby last night? It was so amazing—the ambulance couldn't get through to the house because of the storm, so they called him instead.'

'Through here?' I say, already pushing the double doors.

'Um, hang on, I'll page him . . . Wait, please!'

The doors swing shut behind me. Eric is at the other end of the corridor and looks up in surprise.

'Hello, Detective.'

'Doctor Sheffield, I need to speak with you. Right now.'

'Okay, no problem.' He smiles reassuringly at a nurse and moves at an excruciatingly slow pace, handing her some paperwork and scribbling on a notepad. 'My office?'

I nod and we walk down the corridor together.

'I heard about Edwina,' he says as I close the door. 'How terrible.'

'What's going on with Tommy Gordon?'

'What about him?'

'You have been prescribing him bogus medication for years.'

'Yes,' Eric says calmly. 'Tommy is an addict, and it has manifested into pseudo chronic pain. I didn't realise he was doctor shopping until about a year ago when Vanessa started coming in with various ailments, all of them very vague. After a while I twigged that it was all for Tommy.' He rubs his eyes. 'You have to understand, these situations are difficult—I can't ignore what a patient is telling me even if I'm almost a hundred per cent certain it's false or in their head. I confronted her about it, but of course she kept mum. I told her I wouldn't be giving her any more prescriptions.'

'Tommy was high when he had his accident,' I say. 'That's why Vanessa went and got him. It meant he could go home and claim to have taken medication after the fact, which would muddy any bloodwork done.'

'I suspect you're right,' says Eric wearily. 'I tried to talk to him, but you know what Tommy's like.' He hesitates. 'I have considered reporting him, but I admit I feel conflicted about it. I don't know exactly how bad it is, and due to his position it does feel somewhat complicated.'

Everything Eric is saying rings true. His voice is calm and kind, and for a second I lose my bearings. He crosses his arms and looks at me expectantly.

'But are you selling prescription drugs off the books?' I say.

'What? No.'

'Is the hospital being used as a delivery point for illegal drugs coming from the city?' I press.

He laughs, seemingly bewildered. 'Not as far as I know. Why don't you sit down?' He gestures to a chair.

I remain standing. 'Other hospitals in the area have been used as a hub. Schools and vet clinics too. It looks like the standard deliveries have been supplemented with extra stock, prescription medication that is packaged and then sold illegally within regional communities. We're not talking small-scale stuff.'

Eric's eyes widen. 'I don't know anything about that.'

'I've gone through your financial records. There's a significant monthly freight payment to a holding company in your wife's name. What are you hiding?'

Eric looks bewildered. 'Nothing.'

'Explain it to me then. Why do you pay your wife's salon for freight?'

'It's for tax purposes. A few years ago we all got together and agreed we could pool our funds to create some efficiencies.'

'Who's we?' I ask impatiently.

'Me, Tara and some of the other small-business owners in the area. It makes sense. We all receive regular supplies from Sydney, so rather than each paying separately for freight, we figured we could save some money. Tara already had the company set up for the salon, and it made sense that her business would pay the freight for tax purposes, and then the hospital and the others transfer her our percentage of the costs. My accountant can probably explain it better. I'm not trying to hide anything, but I don't really understand what you're getting at.'

'What other businesses?'

'Well, the salon like I said. That's Tara's baby and I don't get too involved in it. And Des and Min at the supermarket, and Cam at the pub.'

'So, what, the one delivery comes into town for all of you?'

'Yes,' says Eric. 'It's all run through the one company. Everything comes in on Tuesdays, like I told you.'

'Who organises the delivery company? Is it Tara?'

'She pays for it, but Cam manages it all. He's always been very entrepreneurial. It's great, actually, like a relay system. The delivery comes to us first because of the sensitivity of our orders. We cross-check all of the pharma stock and any new equipment, then the driver drops off the supplies to the supermarket, the salon and lastly the pub. After Cam takes his stock allocation, he loads up the truck with any catering we need for the week, and the driver comes back to drop it off here. It runs like clockwork, a lot better than the system we used to have. Plus having it all contained to Tuesdays means the truck can be leased out for the rest of the week, and Cam has some of the kids at the pub using it for regional delivery work to earn some extra money until it goes back to Sydney on Sunday. That's what Aiden has been doing lately, long-haul freight deliveries. Cam is always looking for ways to support the local kids, offering them flexible work. We've talked about the brain drain that happens here—it's one way business owners can encourage people to stay on.'

The room feels like a vice closing in on me.

'Sally Luther used to work for you,' I blurt, 'when you had the GP rooms.'

Eric brings his hands together and looks bewildered. 'Yes, she did. She was a great girl, an excellent receptionist. She had decided to stay here because of her boyfriend and do university by correspondence, but she was keen to earn some money. It was devastating to lose her.' Eric stretches out his back. 'It does feel a little like déjà vu with Abbey and now Aiden disappearing. Cam called me yesterday, checking to see if I'd heard from Aiden. He sounded quite worried.'

'Fuck!' I exclaim.

Eric jumps at my outburst.

I fumble to open the door and am vaguely aware of it slamming against the wall as I race out to the car park.

I jump back in Simon's car and jab my finger toward the road. 'We need to get back to the pub! Now!'

He nods, snapping his laptop shut and tossing it into the back seat like a frisbee.

I call Tran and shout a message for her to send back-up to the pub.

Cam's at the centre of everything. Rick, Aiden, Sally, Greg. Abbey. Maybe Dale Marx. He is the access point into Fairhaven, blinding his young disciples with the promise of money they had only dreamed of. Dread and bile churn in my stomach.

'Going to tell me what's happening?' Simon asks.

'My little boy is there,' I take a shaky breath, 'and I think he murdered Rick Fletcher.' I fold my lips together. 'And maybe Abbey too.'

Simon glances at me. '*What? Who* murdered them?'

'Cam O'Donnell!'

Simon is shaking his head. 'O'Donnell? But I thought Daniel Clark killed Rick Fletcher. Dot's going to make a statement, right?'

'How do you know that?'

'Police radio.'

I throw him a look. 'Just hurry.'

Fairhaven flies past. My knees are pressed to the glove box. Simon weaves around storm debris, and my organs lurch as if I'm on a rollercoaster on the cusp of the biggest drop.

The pub looms large up ahead, gold letters glittering, the hard angles of the roof offset against the vivid blue sky and steady stream of wispy white clouds.

'Cam was friendly with the former chief inspector,' says Simon. 'There were heaps of times when his liquor licence should have been pulled for serving underage kids, but he never even got a slap on the wrist. I think he's had a tougher time with Tommy but, you know, if you run the local pub in a place like this, I guess you're kind of untouchable.'

I nod but think only of Ben. The past few weeks of confusion have faded away and sharpened to the clearest of points: he is everything.

Through this moment of clarity, Simon's comment eventually reaches my brain.

'Was Cam questioned over the disappearances?' I ask.

'Abbey's?'

'No,' I say, exasperated, 'Greg and Sally's.'

'I assume so. I mean, he was the last person to see Greg. And obviously he reported the money stolen from the takings that night, which played into the theory they ran away.'

We turn too fast into the car park and hit the kerb. I fall hard against the door.

Greg was working for Cam. Rick was working for Cam. It all comes back to Cam. Not Eric.

'Sorry,' says Simon, swinging into a park, 'I don't understand what's—'

My feet hit the ground before the car has come to a complete stop. 'Just wait here,' I bark. Simon's hands are still glued to the wheel. 'Back-up is coming.'

A group of people stand in a circle near the main entrance, regaling each other with storm damage stories as I run over.

'Our entire front yard is a disaster zone,' says a woman, pulling hard at her dog's leash.

'Our cubbyhouse is toast,' says another.

'I had to get out the chainsaw this morning,' says one of the men, rocking back on his heels and pushing up his shirtsleeves. 'The yard was a bloody nightmare.'

'It's not open yet, love.' The lady with the dog is smiling at me, orange lipstick on her teeth. 'Apparently it's flooded.'

I ignore her and push on the door. It swings shut behind me with a dull thud.

Inside, the lights aren't on and the absence of music gives the place a sinister feel, like an abandoned theme park. My pupils dilate as my nose tunes into a nasty medley of smells: beer fumes, garbage, stale aftershave and damp carpet. Water drips from one of the light fittings above where the band usually plays; a bucket has been placed underneath.

I cross the floor, every nerve firing. What if I'm too late?

The last time I was too late—Nicki Mara was dead, her face frozen in a scream for help that no one heard.

A metallic bang comes from the kitchen. I cut through the bar and push open the door.

Ben. Ben is here, carefully emptying a bucket into a big stainless-steel sink. My relief is almost painful. 'Ben, baby, I'm so glad you're here. I need you to come with me.'

'We're helping Cam clean,' he says, his eyes on the water pouring from the bucket. 'It flooded last night and everything is wet.'

'Come on,' I say. 'Where's Mac?'

'He's upstairs—he's trying to fix one of the pipes.'

'Quickly, Ben!' I hiss.

He looks up, confused. 'But, Mum, we're not finished.'

'*Now*.' I gesture wildly and Ben sighs, putting the bucket down just as Cam enters the kitchen from the storeroom next to the fridge. His T-shirt rides up his lean torso, and his arm muscles strain as he struggles with a large plastic tub full of cleaning items. 'Gemma! What a nice surprise.' His eyes lack their usual warmth. 'Might just shut this.'

He ducks behind me and closes the door to the bar. Everything goes quiet.

When Cam spins around, he flashes me a giant smile. 'What a bloody disaster, hey? The roof leaked and the electrics have shorted.' He hoists the big tub onto the stove and wrenches his hands free. 'Cripes, that's heavy,' he says, out of breath, leaning against the oven and stretching his fingers.

His eyes don't leave mine as he picks up an industrial lighter with a long red handle, his index finger resting on the trigger.

'We need to leave, actually,' I say. 'I was just coming to get Ben. Family business.'

Cam rocks slowly back on his heels. 'That's a shame, I could use a friend right now. I've just had some bad news about my brother.'

It swirls through the room. A hostility. A recklessness. I pray like mad he can't smell my fear.

'I'm sorry to hear that, but we have to go. Come on, Ben.' I gesture to him and try to smile. 'We'll grab Mac and get out of your hair.'

Cam's mouth twists into a horrible boyish grin. 'Mac's good with a task, isn't he? He's surprisingly handy. I think he'll be busy upstairs for some time.'

My heart starts to punch out of my chest.

'What's the rush anyway, Gemma? An important lead? A new case?'

'We just really need to go,' I say, my voice firm as I hold my hand out to Ben.

Cam eyes me coolly and steps over to where Ben is standing. My fingers twitch at my sides. If I pull my gun on him now, there will be no other way out of this but a showdown—I can't let that happen.

Cam's left hand rests on Ben's shoulders. The tip of the lighter touches the bottom of his T-shirt.

My spine is a steel blade.

'Why don't you go, Gemma, and sort things out? Ben can stay here with me. We can't have him getting tangled up in something dangerous.' Cam bends down so he's level with Ben. 'Right, buddy?' he says, squeezing him affectionately.

Ben nods, his small frame tense under Cam's grip.

'Please, Cam,' I beg. 'Don't.'

'I don't like the way you're looking at me,' he tells me with mock sadness. 'What's changed, Gemma? I was nice to your boyfriend this week, hiding him away in your old room.' He juts out his hip. 'I thought we were friends.'

'Stop it, Cam, you're scaring him!'

The last traces of lightness fall from his face and it hardens into a mask.

'Let him go,' I hiss.

'Sorry, I can't do that.'

Ben's eyes are slits. Lips pressed together, nostrils flaring.

I feel dizzy, pale spots swirling through my vision.

Our nightmare blooms in front of me like a bloodstain.

'The police are coming,' I say.

Cam laughs as a mottled flush creeps up his neck. 'I think the police are pretty busy following up last night's events. I've managed to get a few updates of my own this morning. It's handy having friends in high places.'

I have no idea if he's bluffing, but surely Tran has picked up my message by now and Simon has called for help. *Please, please.*

'The note on my car, that was you,' I blurt out.

He smirks, pulling Ben backwards against him. Ben flinches. 'Yes. I did some research. I have to say, I was delighted when someone left that possum for you. It's not my style but I thought it was very effective. And then instead of bailing, you just moved in with the local plod.' He tips his head at me as if we're in on the same joke. 'Based on where we're standing right now, I think we can all agree you should have left.'

'What did you do to Abbey?'

He rolls his eyes. 'I didn't touch that silly bitch.'

Alone. Trapped in a square of blackness. My whole body screaming. I turned to ice as his hands burned me, poisoned me. Finger of fear choked me. I couldn't scream, I couldn't breathe. Eyes that had always been so kind were suddenly tunnels to pure evil.

'Yes you did,' I say. 'That's why she started calling in sick at work and avoided coming here. She was scared of you.'

'Bullshit.' Spittle flies out of his mouth.

Ben blinks.

'She wrote about you in her diary.'

'Abbey was nuts. I mean, who wouldn't be, growing up in that family? But she's gone now anyway, so who cares?'

'You came onto her at the supermarket that Tuesday night in February when you realised she was alone in the shop. She told Rick about it. That's why he quit working with you.'

'Abbey flirted with me all the time,' Cam snaps. 'She was a bloody Lolita. If she wrote about me, it was because she was obsessed with me. I was just playing along with what she wanted. But I'm telling you, she was trouble. Rick was better off without her—I told him that.'

The air is thick; I'm panting.

'She's fifteen years old,' I say.

'She was a total cocktease,' Cam snaps. 'And everyone around here knows it.' He widens his stance and shuffles Ben back toward the stockroom doorway. 'Anyway, it's her word against mine and, well, she's not here. I'm not worried about some schoolgirl ramblings in a diary.'

I try to harness my rage, to focus it. I need to bring this monster down. I need to keep Ben safe.

'You saw her that night. You and Rick. What happened?'

A little tic pulses under Cam's eye, and his fists curl. 'The stupid slut stumbled up to us, and I said hello to her but she lost the plot. Apparently Rick had promised her he'd have nothing to do with me. I chased her for a bit, just mucking around. Rick was so cut up about it. I reckon she either topped herself or she went home and Danny beat the shit out of her. Truth is, I have absolutely no fucking idea. And as long as she doesn't come back, I don't care.'

'Come on, Cam. If you didn't hurt Abbey we can sort this out. It doesn't have to be like this.'

He sighs. 'But it does, because you stayed here when you should have just gone home. And you've figured it all out. I could tell you wouldn't let anything slide that first night I met you.' He tugs Ben further away from me.

A red mist explodes in my vision, and I draw my gun in a flourish, aiming at his temple.

He hesitates.

'Let Ben go, he's just a kid.'

When my son looks at me, I start to shake. The room comes in and out of focus.

'I'm not going to gaol,' says Cam. 'No way.'

'It might not come to that.' My voice is blurry, words running into each other.

'Oh, I think it will definitely come to that, thanks to you, Miss Gemma.' He adjusts his hand on the wand of the lighter resting near Ben's hair.

A new kind of fear grips me. He's insane.

'What happened to Rick?' I ask.

He shrugs lazily. His lips curl away from his teeth, exposing his gums. 'Poor Rick.' Perspiration shines on his skin, and I feel my own sweat run along the curve of my eye socket. 'That stupid little shit thought I'd offed his pathetic girlfriend. Can you believe it? He wanted to go to you lot about it. He should have just run away like his piss-weak brother. Cowardly, but much safer.' Cam's face is bright red now, the whites of his eyes gleaming an odd yellow.

'So you killed Rick?'

Cam laughs flatly. 'What's with these idiots who fall for stuck-up girls so badly they can't see straight? It drives me mad. Rick was great, you know, a really nice kid—he was making decent money and we had a good thing going, but he threw it all away for a girl.'

'Just like Greg,' I murmur.

'Yeah,' Cam spits. His face ripples under its mask of skin. 'Do you know how much I've done for this fucking town? How many kids I've helped?'

Ben seems to have fallen into a trance. His eyes are wide; he barely blinks. My thoughts are wild and slippery. I pray in time to the beat of my heart.

'Tell me about Sally and Greg.' My words come out in gasps.

Cam's voice is huskier now, fleshy. 'I didn't kill her—it was an accident. But it happened when she was sticking her nose into things that didn't concern her.'

'What things?'

He stares past me but I don't take my eyes off him. 'Greg and I had a good thing going too. He was so desperate to impress Sally and make something of himself, and I offered him a way to do it.'

'You had him dealing drugs just like Rick.'

He laughs. 'It's not like I'm running a meth lab. It's all prescription stuff. No one's going to die unless they're too stupid to live.' His eyes narrow. 'It was Greg's fault—he let his emotions get the better of him.'

'Just like Rick?'

'It's easy to forget they're only kids,' Cam muses. 'They have no self-control.'

'What happened to Sally?'

'After closing time, the stupid girl snuck in here to surprise Greg. She interrupted us doing some business and was not a happy camper.'

'She saw the drugs?'

Cam shrugs. 'Greg's father was in trouble with the cops again, and Sally's snobby parents had been none too pleased about it. So when she came out the back and saw us sorting out some stock, she just went hysterical. The business wasn't even that big back then, but she started ranting and raving about breaking up with Greg and going to the cops. Little did she know I had them in my back pocket.' Cam's stare goes glassy; I realise he's looking beyond me to the main bar. 'Greg was pleading with her—it was sad, really—but she wouldn't have a bar of it. She ran out of the kitchen and through the bar, and she slipped on the floor that Greg had just mopped. The sound was terrible—her head cracked the side of the counter.' Cam shudders. 'I can still hear it.'

I can see it. Sally lying there, her neck at an odd angle. Greg's panic. Cam's calm.

'The two of you got rid of her.' Feeling faint, I force my shoulders apart to keep from slumping.

'We had to. Even Greg could see we had no other option.'

'So you snuck her out of there and dumped her body in the bush,' I say, 'but someone saw you. A couple of people, actually.'

Cam's gaze is cool, focused back on me now. 'Greg had his car outside, so we put her in the boot and cleaned up the mess here.'

The amount of information Cam is volunteering is terrifying, and even though I know the more he tells us, the more danger we're probably in, keeping him talking still feels like the safest option. 'You drove her car home?' I prompt.

He nods. 'Yeah. Greg followed me to her place, then we drove to the edge of town. It was a Sunday night with no one around. Everything would have been okay, but Greg couldn't keep it together. Once we buried her, he just lost it. I couldn't get through to him. I was telling him it was done now anyway, we couldn't go to the cops once we buried her. It was done.'

'Then what happened?'

Ben is limp in Cam's arms, his eyes closed, and I taste salt. I hadn't realised I was crying.

'We got in the car, and Greg was bawling and rambling about not being able to live without her. I was trying to settle him down, but he jumped out and ran back to where we'd buried her. I went after him—I had to. But he wouldn't listen. He even tried to dig her up.' Cam raises an eyebrow at me as though this is a joke. 'It was bizarre, honestly.'

'You killed him?'

'I fired a couple of warning shots so he knew I wasn't mucking around. But he just started screaming. He turned on me, saying it was all my idea. He said we had to go to the cops.'

'You shot him and buried him with Sally.'

Cam smiles slightly. 'I figured that's what Greg would have wanted.'

The red of my anger washes over the scene in front of me. 'Where are they?'

'A little way off the road near the town sign. I had to get rid of Greg's car too, so I drove it into a lake and had to walk all the way back into town. Took me hours.'

'Daniel Clark saw you driving that night.'

'Bastard should have stayed right out of it,' says Cam, scowling. 'Same as that junkie hag.'

'But you and Stuart Klein paid them off.'

Cam laughs. 'I don't think they know what they saw, but in the end it wasn't that hard to get them to forget about it. It seems everyone talks the language of money.'

'What was Klein's role in all this?'

'He was just happy to get a bit of pocket money to stay out of my way. I find it always pays to have friends in high places, Gemma. It's a shame I never really cracked Tommy, but you can't win 'em all.'

I'm so dizzy, finding it hard to stay upright. Gas, I finally realise. The air around us is thick with gas. I remember Cam stumbling against the stove as he set down that tub. I glance at the lighter in his hand.

He could blow us all to pieces. I have to keep him talking.

'What did you do to Abbey, Cam? She knew about the drugs too.'

'I told you, I didn't touch her. I don't think he told her about our side business.'

'Yet you murdered Rick.'

'He couldn't leave it alone!' Cam's veins stand to attention as he clutches Ben. 'He was just like Greg. Threatening me, saying he'd tell the cops I knew what happened to Abbey. I never wanted any of this. I'm not a killer, I just had no choice.'

My knees buckle and I waver on the spot, the gun dipping up and down in the direction of Cam and Ben. 'Cam, let's just get out of here and talk about it all properly.'

He holds the lighter in front of him, the innocuous piece of plastic bright in his hand. 'No, I'm not going to gaol, Detective. No fucking way. I can start over. Disappear just like Abbey. I've done it before.'

His pupils dance. The room is hazy with poison.

'No!' I yell. 'Mac!'

'The storm must have caused the equipment to fault,' Cam says. 'It will be a terrible accident, just another of those Fairhaven tragedies.'

The only movement in the room is Cam lifting his finger. Our eyes lock.

'Let me leave quietly and I'll give you your kid.' He smiles at me, warm and friendly. 'There's a little passage from the stockroom to the side of the building. I'll just slip away.'

He steps back, his hand still on Ben's shoulder.

Either way, Ben and I are going to die, trapped in Cam's inferno. Once he's outside, he'll burn this place to the ground.

I hear Scott's voice. I see Ben's face.

Bang.

A rush of air. Movement. Cam lurches into the stockroom, one hand on the metal door, the other poised on the lighter trigger. Ben tumbles forward.

A clear shot.

A moment. A million thoughts. Then nothing.

My shoulder jerks and a hot burn leaks from my arm into the rest of my body. My legs cramp in a series of spasms. The lighter hits the ground with a tinny rattle. My knees press hard against concrete.

Someone is calling my name over and over.

'Ben,' I gasp, 'help Ben.'

Hands grip my underarms. Cam stares at me as I'm dragged away, his blue eyes like marbles. A large red patch darkens his T-shirt.

'Ben.' I claw at the air, trying to see him. I'm back in the main room now; I recognise the exposed beams on the ceiling.

Simon's worried face hovers above me, his hands clutching my shoulders. 'We've got him, Gemma. It's okay now.'

Tears are slick on my face and run into my hair. 'Ben.'

Through my half-closed eyes I see Mac, ghostly white, holding Ben in his arms. He drops to his knees and lowers my son next to me, gripping his face between his hands, saying his name over and over.

Figures in blue surge around us. Simon disappears. I can't see Mac either. Someone eases my arm back down to my side and gently extracts the gun from my fingers. My hand aches from gripping the weapon; the bones feel broken.

I killed a man. The thought is suspended in front of me, strange and impossible.

'Is Cam . . .?' I ask.

'I'm afraid so,' says a voice next to me.

I turn to see a young uniform with curly hair and a healthy serve of freckles. He glances toward the kitchen and lets out a breath as an ambulance officer appears by my side, the friendly man who watched over Ben last Monday at Rick Fletcher's house.

'Help my son, please.'

'Try to relax. Ben is being looked after.'

I hear familiar medical sounds, pressure on my arm. A bright light cuts into each eye.

'There's a gravesite, on the edge of town. That's where they're buried,' I say, though no one seems to be listening.

'Gemma!' It's Tran. 'Are you alright?'

'Cam killed them all,' I mumble. 'And he was planning to burn the hotel.'

'Will she be alright?' Tran's voice is fading. 'Is the little boy going to be alright?'

My eyes close and I don't hear a response.

Sunday, 17 April
5.32 pm

Nicki Mara was a statistical anomaly: a missing teenager who was actually a kidnap victim. I entertained many theories but never suspected the truth.

A year earlier, Lucas Mara had fallen out with his fellow partners in a law firm. Unbeknown to us, he'd helped himself to considerable wealth on the way out, which he hid in old dummy accounts. His former business partners had been blatantly disobeying the law; they were involved in drug trafficking, bribery and violent hits. Lucas had broken their pact and gone rogue, so he needed to be punished. They threatened him and killed his dog, but he held firm: he refused to give the money back.

After Nicki went missing he feared the worst, but he heard nothing for weeks. So he said nothing to us, praying she really had run away. And then the threats came. Never traceable, and nothing overt but enough for Lucas to know some bad people had Nicki and she was in danger. He felt trapped. He couldn't give them what they wanted without revealing his role in their crimes and going to gaol. Plus, I suspect deep down he didn't believe they would hurt her.

After Deirdre told us he was sneaking out of the house at night we questioned him, grilled him, until he finally admitted to us he thought she'd been abducted and that he was trying to find her. Unbeknownst to us the stupid fool also contacted his old co-workers and said he would turn them all in unless they returned Nicki.

It backfired badly. They ordered their hit men to kill Nicki. To make her go away. They pumped her full of heroin and strangled her.

———

I wake groggy and bloated but feel no pain. The hospital bed is surrounded by a light blue curtain, and I close my eyes and see Nicki slumped in the grimy bathtub, her skin mottled and bruised. I immediately jerk my eyes open again.

Cam appears on the blue curtain screen. He's holding the lighter, leering at me as he moves his thumb. I grimace when I hear the gunshot reverberate through the pub kitchen. A strange rasp escapes my mouth.

The curtain shifts and Mac's face appears. He pushes past the material and lowers himself into a hard plastic chair next to the bed.

'Where's Ben?' I croak.

'In the next room, sound asleep,' says Mac. 'He's going to be fine. Same as you.'

I relax, my limbs melting back into the bed.

'The baby is fine as well,' Mac says softly. He leans forward and rests his elbows on his knees. 'Earlier today, after you left, Ben mentioned that you said we might have a baby. I didn't quite know what to say.'

'It's a long story.'

'Yeah.' He sighs. 'I'm sure it is.'

'Lucas Mara called me,' I say quietly. 'A few days before we found Nicki.'

Mac pauses, frowning. 'I know, you told me.'

'No, I didn't.' I start to cry. 'I didn't tell you what he said to me.'

'I thought you said he was just rambling. You called Deirdre and suggested she make sure he saw a counsellor.'

I try to sit up but my wrists buckle. 'I should have listened to what he was trying to tell me. He told me he had a dream. That some men had taken Nicki. That he had a feeling she was in a house in Mosman. And I just thought he was losing his mind. He was babbling and manic, and I didn't take it seriously—I was distracted with the Ronson case and still thought Nicki was a time-wasting runaway.' I groan and put my face in my hands. 'I gave up on her. But we could have found her, Mac. We could have saved her.' My voice dips to a whisper. 'She must have been so scared.'

He strokes my cheek. 'Gem, don't. Don't torture yourself. You know better than that.'

'I really wanted to find Abbey. That's why I came here.'

'I know,' says Mac. 'But it wouldn't have brought Nicki back. You're a good cop, you care, and you do the best you can with what you've got.'

'It's not always enough,' I say.

'No, it's not, but you've known that for a long time. Nicki's case was complicated. We all got things wrong. Even if you had taken Lucas seriously, what would you have done? Searched every house in Mosman?'

'I just wish I'd made Lucas tell me what he knew. Now they're both dead.'

Lucas hanged himself in custody a fortnight after Nicki was killed.

'Yeah.' Mac slumps back against the chair. He looks awful.

'Are you alright?' I say feebly.

For a second I think he is going to cry. A strange ripple shudders across his face before he straightens and grabs my hand, saying, 'Yes, but I never want to go through anything like what happened today ever again.'

I soak up his touch. 'Me neither.'

'Gemma, I'm going to go.'

'What do you mean?'

'I'm flying back to Sydney tonight.' He extracts his hand and checks his watch. 'In about two hours.'

A surge of emotion renders me mute.

'It's Molly's birthday tomorrow, and I should be there,' he continues.

'I forgot about that,' I murmur.

'I shouldn't have stayed here,' Mac continues, thrusting his fingers through his hair. 'Not only would none of this have happened but I should have given us both the space we need to think.' He looks so lost.

'I'm so sorry, Mac.'

He nods. 'Me too. There's a lot I admire about you, Gemma, but I need you to let me in if this is going to work.' His hands curl and his jaw tenses. 'No matter what we decide. That's non-negotiable for me.'

'I know,' I whisper.

'You need to think about what you want.' He gets up. He presses his lips against my forehead. 'All of it. Today scared me, Gem. I need to go home. I need to think too.'

In the huge hospital bed, Ben looks heartbreakingly small. He is washed-out but surprisingly animated. I sit on the edge of his narrow bed and hold his hand, trying to answer his questions about Cam. He traces the freckles on the back of my hand as he considers my answers and I'm relieved he doesn't seem to remember a lot of what happened.

'We can organise some counselling for him,' says Tran to me later as we sit in the tiny hospital cafeteria, steaming mugs of hot chocolate in front of us.

'I need to find someone in Smithson for him to see anyway. He needs to deal with a lot more than just what happened today.'

Tran looks at me steadily. 'You'll be cleared, Gemma, no question. You had no choice.'

'How's de Luca?' I ask.

'She's doing okay.' Tran shakes her head. 'They're going to start digging at the site Cam mentioned tomorrow. It's unbelievable—I've driven past that bloody *Welcome to Fairhaven* sign a million times. Sally's mother fainted when we told her.'

'My colleague Owen Thurston called me,' I say. 'He and his team have brought Cam's brother in for questioning. He's a doctor in Sydney and his wife is a pharmacist.'

Tran takes a sip from her mug. 'Yes, it's bigger than we realised. We're looking into what the former CI knew. Back then the drug network wasn't as widespread, but at the very least he turned a blind eye. At worst he was taking a cut. Cam has made some serious money through all this, especially over the past two years.'

I nod. 'He had a steady pipeline of impressionable boys who were desperate for extra money and looking for some kind of purpose. And he had the perfect transient market of backpackers and wealthy holidaymakers to sell to. As far as he was concerned, everybody was a winner. I think he even convinced himself that because the drugs weren't illegal the whole set-up was somehow above reproach.'

'I still find it hard to believe no one ever said anything. I mean, especially these days.'

I dip a spoon into the froth and feel the bubbles dissolve in my mouth. 'Cam ran everything off the grid. He used existing delivery networks, paid people just enough for the risk to be worthwhile. And once they were involved, they were complicit. I'm guessing he sold half the stuff straight from the pub, yet he was never the frontman. I don't think he let many people into his inner circle— Rick and Aiden were exceptions.'

'And Greg,' Tran murmurs.

'Yes, though I have no idea if that night played out the way Cam described. Whether Sally's death was really an accident, for instance. I hope forensics can settle that.' Lane's pleading face rears up in my thoughts, and I think of his insistence that Rick or Daniel killed Abbey. 'Cam also wouldn't tell me what he did to Abbey. I wonder if perhaps because she was so young, he couldn't even admit it to himself.' I picture him blacking out Abbey's face in Rick's ruined bedroom, the teenage boy's blood-soaked body lying metres away, and shiver.

'Well, the team found nothing about Abbey at the pub today,' says Tran, 'but we'll see how we go around the Fairhaven sign.'

I hold air deep in my lungs before I slowly exhale. At the end of the corridor I see Vanessa, her long hair streaming behind her as she hurries toward me.

'When do you want me to give my statement?' I say to Tran.

She yawns. 'Let's do it tomorrow, then you can take your little boy home.'

I don't let Vanessa see Ben until she has stopped crying.

'I just can't believe any of this,' she says, walking back to my room with me. 'Though, do you know what, Tommy never liked Cam. One of those gut feelings, I guess.' Her face crumples. 'But I did. He had me fooled.'

'He had all of us fooled,' I say. 'And I'm pretty sure Stuart Klein was involved in Cam's scheme. I think he paid off witnesses before the inquest.'

'Was he involved in the drugs as well?'

'I don't know. Maybe.'

Vanessa bites her lip until it turns white. 'God, Gemma, I'm so glad Ben is okay. When I heard he was there today, I just—well, it doesn't bear thinking about.'

I shake my head. I can't let myself go to the dark place, the alternate version of reality where Ben is not okay.

'Tommy's very upset about everything, not just Lane,' she says cautiously. 'He's so glad Sally's parents might finally get some closure, but he's distressed about what happened today.'

I pull off my robe and throw it over the chair before I climb back into my hospital bed. 'Vanessa,' I say once I'm settled.

'I know,' she whispers, her hands almost covering her entire face. 'He needs help.'

'Yes.' I try to look stern. 'And if he doesn't come clean, I will report him.'

'He's very old-fashioned, Gemma. He hates asking for help. But I know you're right.'

'It's not just the addiction issues,' I say, and she winces. 'He's lied to a lot of people. He needs to think about whether being a cop is the right thing for him now.'

Her eyes widen. 'What else would he do? That's all he knows.'

I pause as I pull the covers up to my waist. 'I'm sorry, Vanessa. I understand this isn't easy.'

Her gaze drifts to the side of my bed where there is a glass of water and a tablet.

'He hurt his back. That's how this all started, you know. He'd given up smoking the year before but he wasn't dealing well with that. He kept relapsing. And then he landed in hospital with his back—he'd got knocked over breaking up a fight at the hotel.' She picks at the hem of her purple skirt and worries her fingers against it. 'He was in so much pain, and the medication was a godsend. In the end, though, well . . .' She clears her throat. 'I could see what was happening but he wouldn't listen to me. So I left a few years ago, you know. I moved out of the house for almost three weeks. No one knew. I was so angry because we'd talked about adopting a child, and then he went cold on the idea and I knew it was the drugs. It was like his whole personality changed.' She gives me a strained smile. 'He had me getting them for him until after Christmas this year when I refused to be a part of it anymore. I don't know where he's getting them now.' Her face crumples. 'He even had a kid from the station making doctor appointments at one point. God, it might have been Lane.' Straightening her spine, she forces another smile. 'But in the end I was weak. I moved back home.' She looks at me imploringly. 'The thing is, I love him, Gemma. He has his flaws but he's a good man. I just told him I didn't want to know. I do my thing and stay out of his business. We don't have children but I guess I see him as my responsibility. I look after him.'

'Ben loved spending time with you, Vanessa,' I say quietly. 'Thank you for looking after him. Both of us.'

Her eyes brim with tears and she nods, sniffing. 'When are you going home?'

'I'll probably have to give my statement tomorrow, so sometime after that.'

'I can look after Ben while you do that, if you like?' She dabs at her eye with the sleeve of her ruffled blouse.

'I'm sure he'd love that, thanks. I also want to see Dot. I need to apologise for not being able to find her daughter.'

NINTH DAY MISSING

Monday, 18 April

3.17 pm

A fallen branch rests on the roof of the Clark house and the lawn is littered with decaying leaves. But the fresh smell of rain has succumbed to the musky scent of the ocean. Walking down the path to the back door, I almost smack into one of the twins as he barrels around the corner. 'Mum's inside,' he yells, without stopping.

The door is unlocked. I step inside. 'Hello?' I call out softly.

Dot's voice echoes in the dark hallway, and I realise she's on the phone. 'Not yet,' she says, sounding anxious. 'We need to wait.' She makes a fretting noise. 'How would I know?'

There's a long pause. I can hear the boys yelling at each other outside.

'I hate this,' says Dot, followed by a heavy silence. The boys keep yelling.

'Dot?' I call out.

There's some low mumbling before she appears in the hallway. 'Detective. I didn't know you were coming.'

'I just wanted to say goodbye,' I tell her, after a few beats.

She pulls at a loose thread on her sundress. Her chest rises and falls as if she's been running. 'You're leaving?'

'Yes.'

'I heard about what happened. At the pub.' She looks at the floor. 'I'm glad your son is okay.'

I nod. More and more, the whole incident seems like a dream. I can't seem to picture Cam's face, just his broad shoulders, auburn hair, sparking blue eyes. 'Me too,' I say.

'It's funny, you know,' Dot murmurs, 'I remember Daniel coming home that night, ten years ago now. He was so insistent he saw two men in Greg's car. I should have known something was up when he suddenly said he must have been too drunk to know what he saw. And then he said he won some money, enough to put a second storey on the house. I don't think I even asked him where it came from.' She seems to snap out of her reverie. 'Do you want a drink?'

I follow her into the kitchen. It seems lighter; I think a curtain has been removed from the window.

'I can make you a tea?' she asks.

'No, thank you.' I watch her fuss at the sink, plates and utensils clanging against the steel. 'Will you stay in Fairhaven, Dot?'

She puts her hands on her hips as her lip begins to tremble. 'Oh well, I don't know. I guess it depends on what happens with Daniel. I don't really understand it all yet.'

'It's okay to be scared, Dot. What you've done isn't easy.'

She stares out the window. 'It's strange, him not being here. Both of them not being here.'

I look at her hunched stance and the bags beneath her eyes, and think that despite everything that's happened, the hardest days might still be ahead of her.

'You know, there's a lot of support you can tap into. People who can help.'

'Yes, I know.' She grips the corner of the bench, her eyes averted. 'Thank you.'

'Dot, I'm so sorry we haven't found Abbey. Her case is still a priority. I certainly haven't given up hope that you will get some answers.'

Dot traces a fingertip along the grain of the wood. 'I know she's out there.'

Nicki Mara's mother, Deirdre, had stood in her marble kitchen and said the same thing.

I had made the mistake of agreeing with her. I say nothing to Dot.

The silence stretches out between us. I wonder what her life will be in six months. Or a year. Longer. I can't picture it, and I suspect that she can't either.

A small wave of nausea ripples through me, reminding me I have my own future to navigate.

'Well, I need to get going,' I say. 'Please look after yourself.'

She nods and glances around the small room, almost as if surprised to find herself there. 'Yes.'

I get back in the car feeling strangely rattled. Maybe coming back here was a bad idea. I can picture Lane's face, tinted blue in the moonlight, watching the blood pool around de Luca's body. I close my eyes. I feel beaten. Through half-lidded eyes I study the house: the tangled mess of the fallen branch, the stringy grass choking the garden beds, the discarded toys on the lawn.

I start the car and turn onto the dirt road that leads to the main street. Suddenly I'm struggling to breathe. I'm back at work in Sydney, hanging up the phone after Lucas Mara called me babbling incoherently about Nicki.

'I think that's where she is!' he yelled. 'I saw her in my dream. She's still alive.' He wasn't crying but his voice wobbled as he choked back sobs. 'Please, Detective.'

'Lucas, I know this is difficult, but we haven't given up on your daughter. Can you think of any reason why she would be in Mosman? Does she know someone there?'

'No. No, I don't think so.' His voice shook. 'But what if she's there?'

After I calmed him down we hung up, and I went to the bathroom and studied my face in the mirror as I washed my hands. *He's finally lost it*, I thought. The decline of Nicki's grieving father had been obvious to me, and his call simply proved it. Surely there was no truth to his vision. I leaned forward and checked my teeth, smoothed my brows. No, he was just exhausted and desperate to give me anything he thought might help find his daughter, even if it had come to him in a dream.

I allowed myself one more moment of internal debate. *I'll call Deirdre*, I decided, *make sure she keeps an eye on Lucas. Perhaps suggest he see the psychologist again.*

But deep down I knew, I knew. It niggled at me: the pleading note in his voice, the desperation. He was trying to tell me. I could have found her. I could have saved her.

Not again, no way.

A black bird swoops low, dipping in front of the windshield.

I slow the car and pull over, fumbling for my phone. 'Grange, it's me, Gemma.'

'Oh, Detective Woodstock, hi. Hello. God, how are you?'

'I'm fine. I need you to run a check on a phone number for me. I want to know who Dot Clark was speaking to just now.'

––––––––

'They left!' Kate Morse holds up her fake-tan orange hands as I walk into the caravan park office. 'They left yesterday and I don't know where they went.'

'I'm not here about the Brits,' I say.

A few minutes later, Kate leads me down a winding path on the east side of the park. She fusses with a set of keys. 'We shut this whole section down at the end of March—it's easier to manage one section than have people all over the place.' We arrive at a row of permanent cabins, and she scans the numbers and stops in front of number seventeen. 'This is the one.' Flustered, she searches for the right key. 'The cabins are all on the same line, then each room is simply an extension. We had to offer the land-lines because the mobile reception is so bad here. I have been at the council about it for *years*, but do you think they give a shit? No, of course not. Right, here we are.' She slides a key into the lock.

I sense the faint rumble of movement, or it might just be the blood surging through my veins.

'What are you expecting to find?' asks Kate. 'No one has been in here since February.'

She pushes the door open, revealing a small square space. The air inside is cool and the curtains are drawn. My eyes adjust to the darkness and I see the bed is unmade. There are a few packets of chips on the small glass table near the door. A bulging calico bag hangs from the side of a chair.

'What the . . .' murmurs Kate.

The room I found Nicki in was just like this: a dark, musty granny flat in the backyard of a suburban home. Signs of life everywhere, except for on her decaying corpse.

'Is there a bathroom?' I whisper.

Kate looks around, her eyebrows sloping together. 'Over there.' She points to a sliding door in the corner of the room.

The floor falls out from under me but I stay on my feet. I breathe in the stale cigarette smoke, my gun in my hand, as I make my way toward the bathroom door, praying, pleading, hoping against hope that somehow, miraculously, Nicki will be behind it, that she will be alive.

The roar in my head is deafening.

I gently ease the door to the left.

Little explosions pinball around my body.

The girl is curled up at one end of the bath.

I forget to breathe.

It's Nicki.

But this time she blinks.

'What the hell?' Kate murmurs behind me.

I tip my head against the wooden doorframe and exhale until my lungs are empty.

'Hello, Abbey.'

Monday, 18 April
5.41 pm

Tran bursts into the hospital foyer. She's tied her hair back since I gave my statement this morning and a few loose wisps fall across her eyes.

'Over here,' I call out. I'm sitting in the small waiting room nook, keeping an eye on the Clark twins who are working their way steadily through a crate of toys.

'Gemma, you found her? I can't believe it.' Tran's incredulous gaze lands on the boys.

'Abbey is in there with Eric now. Dot's with them too. Abbey's going to be fine but the cut on her leg is badly infected.'

Tran sinks down on a chair. 'Did Lane have sex with her?'

I nod. 'Abbey says they slept together at least a dozen times and that Lane instigated it. When he attended the DV call-out late last year, he apparently pulled her aside and said she should come talk to him away from her dad. She met him on the beach the next day and they ended up at his place. After that, he would pass her a note at the supermarket telling her times he could meet. She says he even left one in her school locker once.'

'Jesus Christ.'

'I know. He swore her to secrecy.' I can tell Tran is thinking about how this could play out in the media. Even dead, Lane is going to cause the force a lot of trouble.

'How on earth did he think he'd get away with it?'

'He trusted that Abbey was infatuated enough to keep his secret. She wasn't close to her parents, and because of Rick she was hardly going to tell her friends. All of their contact was on Lane's terms. She was the perfect girl to prey on.'

'Until she turned up at the police station,' says Tran.

'Exactly. Lane reacted badly, and once she told him she'd broken up with Rick so they could be together, he realised he had to shut it down. So he told her about Elsha.'

Tran is wide-eyed.

'Abbey says that destroying the painting wasn't planned. She glimpsed it through the salon window and acted on impulse. She was heading to the beach to try to make amends with Rick.'

'But she ended up seeing Cam and Rick together.'

'Yes, and Rick had promised her he'd have nothing to do with Cam after he assaulted Abbey in the supermarket stockroom.'

'How much did she know about the drugs?'

'I don't think she knew anything—I think she just freaked out. Lane had just betrayed her, then she found Rick going behind her back with Cam.'

'So how did she escape?'

'When Cam started chasing her, she ran around the side of the petrol tanker and threw her shoe into the bushland, hoping he'd look for her in there—which he did. She climbed in between the truck and the fuel tank to hide. That's when she cut her leg. She heard Rick yelling out her name for a few minutes. She doesn't know where he went after that, but he must have made his way to the beach to meet his sister.'

'I wonder what he wanted to tell us when he called,' murmurs Tran.

'I think we can assume he figured Cam had done something to Abbey, so I'm guessing he was planning to dob him in. Whether he was going to tell us about the drugs too, I have no idea.'

'How long did Abbey hide there for?'

'Almost two hours. She was terrified Cam would come back.' I look over at the twins, who are spraying each other with water from the drink tap. 'She thinks she got back to the house at about 3 am.'

'What made her go to the caravan park?'

I shrug. 'Access. She took her mother's work keys and all the cash she had in her room.' In my mind's eye I see Abbey, frantic and exhausted. Her leg throbbing, her heart broken. 'She wasn't thinking long-term. She managed to steal some food from the rubbish bins on Monday night, but by Tuesday she was getting pretty desperate. She saw Dot when she turned up to work and took the risk of calling out to her when she walked past the west wing.'

'And that's when they formed the plan to implicate Daniel in Rick's murder?'

'Dot told her about Rick, and I think Abbey genuinely believed her father was responsible. Even though Dot was almost sure he hadn't left the house, I think she allowed herself to get swept up in Abbey's conviction. Abbey probably coached her on what to say, although obviously all the historical abuse is true.'

'God,' says Tran. 'From one mess to another.'

'I know.' I sigh. 'They're both still determined to press charges against Daniel. I think he'll serve time.'

'Yeah, well, they all might,' says Tran, glancing at the twins. 'I just can't believe she was so close the whole time.'

'I know. It's surreal.' I try to suppress the conflicting emotions that flare in my chest. 'She has a tough road ahead. She's lost a lot of people she cared about.'

'And she's only a kid,' adds Tran. She rubs her eyes and gives her head a little shake.

There's a swishing sound behind us as the double doors through to the consulting rooms swing open. Abbey walks out flanked by Dot and Eric. He says something to Abbey and she nods. There's a bandage looped around her thigh. It's obvious she has been crying. Eric gestures to me and mouths that he'll send through the report before disappearing back through the doors.

Tran and I stand up and walk over to them, the twins chattering noisily behind us.

Abbey hooks her hair behind her ears and stares at us from beneath her dark lashes. 'What happens now?'

Tuesday, 19 April

11.55 am

'Phones off, please.' The flight attendant eyes me pointedly.

'Yep.' I send a quick reply to Tran telling her I'll call her later.

Sally and Greg have been found. Their skeletal remains will be exhumed today, then submitted to a post-mortem and forensic testing tomorrow. Despite what Cam said about Sally's accidental death at the pub, Mick Lamb's initial assessment of her body suggests that she was shot in the head, just like Greg.

Meanwhile, Tran's team have linked Cam to the body found in the bush last week. Dale Marx, twenty-three, had worked at the same Sydney hospital as Cam's brother; no doubt he was collateral damage in their elaborate network.

I arch my back and check my messages again before I switch my phone to flight mode. Still no word from Mac. I have been trying to call him since last night; I left him a message this morning about Ben and I returning to Smithson, but he hasn't replied.

Dread prowls my stomach. I fuss with the contents of the seat pocket in front of me, trying to ignore it.

We came straight to the airport from the hospital in Byron. De Luca is pale and weak, but she's through the worst of it.

The doctor has told her she'll probably be able to go home in a fortnight.

Her girlfriend, Louise, took Ben to look at the fish pond in the garden while we talked.

'I can barely remember anything once we got to the house,' she told me, her face creasing with frustration. Even without make-up, her features were striking.

'I don't think that's such a bad thing,' I said. 'There's a lot I wish I couldn't remember.'

'I still can't believe what Lane did.' Her voice was uneven but her eyes were dry. 'Preying on Abbey and lying to us all. But also that he jumped.'

'And he shot you,' I added.

'You know, it's funny, I've barely even thought about that. I just keep picturing him jumping off the cliffs.'

'Me too,' I admitted.

We sat in silence for a few moments. It felt oddly peaceful. I barely knew her, but we would be forever bound by what happened at the Clark house that night.

'Aiden Fletcher turned up this morning,' I told her. 'He's fine.'

'What? Where?'

'Hiding out in the house. Apparently he snuck in there on Tuesday night after the forensics cleared out. I guess he figured Cam wouldn't return.'

'And is he talking?'

'Like a canary,' I said with a smile. 'He's not holding back on Cam, or his own involvement for that matter. He'll be charged. Same as his parents.'

'Wow.' For the first time since I met her, de Luca seemed genuinely shocked.

'So, do you think you'll go back to the squad?' I asked her, just as Louise and Ben returned.

Louise looked at her witheringly, tossing her long blonde ponytail over her shoulder. 'Yeah, Eddie, what are you going to do?'

De Luca sighed. 'I'm a cop. What happened hasn't changed that, but Lou's worried about me going back to the Fairhaven squad. A change of scene might be good anyway, so I was thinking I'll look into a transfer. We've talked about moving—Lou's work is flexible.' She glanced back at Louise, whose arms were crossed at her chest. But her expression was full of love as she looked at her girlfriend.

'Do you have family around here?' I asked de Luca.

'Dad's dead,' she replied bluntly. 'Mum lives close by but we're not really in contact. It's a long story, but she sided with my father over a whole lot of stuff. Even once he died, we couldn't seem to get on the same page.'

I recalled her outburst the day I met the Clarks and what Tran said about her mother refusing to come to the hospital the night she was admitted. And the scars I'd noticed on her arm.

'What's Tommy going to do?' she asked me.

'Well, he's extended his leave, and Tran said she organised a full-time CI for the next few months. Tommy's got some stuff to work through.'

A hint of steel crept into her gaze. 'I wouldn't work for him again,' she said. 'That's for sure.' She gestured to her bandages. 'It's weird—I feel like I've been hit by a truck, but I also feel strong. Lots of things suddenly seem really clear.'

'I'm so glad you are okay,' I said as I hugged her goodbye. 'Stay in touch. I mean it.'

As the plane peels off from the runway, I glance at Ben's profile. He astounds me; I am so in awe of his strength. He leans forward to see the wing through the little window. His hair is wild and curly like mine, and his eyes are the same light green, but the shape of his face, the curve of his lips are all Scott. My heart cramps cruelly. I feel so guilty that Scott won't be able to see Ben grow up. I remember what Scott said to me just before he died, about looking after myself for Ben's sake, and briefly consider how badly the last fortnight could have turned out for both of us. Overwhelmed, I find Ben's hand and squeeze it, making a silent promise to Scott in my head. Better late than never.

'God, I'm starving,' I say, swallowing back tears.

'Vanessa put some muesli bars in my backpack before we left. You can have one. You probably should—you didn't have any breakfast.'

'Thanks.' I bend over to get one out of his bag, and I smile at him as I chew.

I already know our relationship is going to be a little unusual, that we will take turns looking after each other. If I'm honest, he's been doing it for years.

'I spoke to Jodie,' I say. 'Do you want to hang out with her and Annabel tomorrow?'

'At Dad's house?'

'Um, yeah.'

'Sure. I bet Annabel's grown heaps since we've been away. Babies grow really fast, you know.'

I swallow past a huge lump in my throat and circle my hand around his. Outside, the world is a blur of green and blue. The past two weeks feel completely surreal. I wonder whether I will ever come to Fairhaven again, whether I will ever see any of those people again.

I kiss Ben on the top of his head. 'You're right,' I say. 'They do grow fast.'

Thursday, 21 April

10.52 am

'Jesus Christ, Woodstock,' booms Jonesy, 'trust you to solve three murders for the price of one.'

I blush as several officers spin around to gawk at me, standing in the doorway of Smithson Police Station.

'I haven't submitted my paperwork yet, so at this point I won't be getting paid at all,' I quip awkwardly. 'Plus, it's actually four murders if you count the other teen Cam killed.'

'Well, bloody good work anyway.' Jonesy clamps his giant hand around my shoulder and glares at his staff, implying their lack of miraculous case breakthroughs is a sackable offence.

'In you come,' he tells me, guiding me toward his office. 'This way, this way.'

Nostalgia hits me as we walk down the corridor. It feels like yesterday. It feels like a million years ago. I spy a portable fan in the corner that I'm pretty sure was on its last legs when I first made detective.

Jonesy directs me to the couch and closes the door, easing himself into his worn leather chair.

He hinges forward and peers at my face. 'Seriously, Gemma, I couldn't believe it when I heard what happened. Is the constable going to be alright?'

'Yes, but she has a long road in front of her. Fortunately she's extremely tough.'

'And what about you? How are you holding up?'

'I'm fine.'

'You shot and killed someone, Gemma. Ben was threatened. I doubt you're fine.'

I look at him in surprise. No one has described what happened in Fairhaven like that, and Cam's death feels dirty and horrible, exposed in the air between us.

'I wish that wasn't how it played out,' I say slowly. 'But I had no choice. I had to shoot him.'

'I'm bloody glad you did,' agrees Jonesy, 'but these things can be mysterious in the way they sneak up on you. See a shrink—god knows there's enough of them floating around in the force—and make sure you get your head straight.' He narrows his eyes at me. 'You should be doing that anyway.'

'I see someone in Sydney all the time. I have for ages.'

'Sure. But you're not in Sydney right now, so get a new person.'

My chin lifts automatically before I force it down. 'You're right, I will.'

'Good.' He leans back in his chair again. 'You look tired, Gemma.'

'I am. It's been a pretty intense couple of days.'

Dad and I stayed up late last night talking. Rebecca had gone out with a friend, and Ben was at Jodie's, so it was just the two of us. Dad was still angry at me for going to Fairhaven. He felt betrayed and rejected. I apologised and tried to explain the suffocating feeling I often get in Smithson. How I'm worried that if I live here again, the horrible restlessness I battled for years will return and I'll slowly go mad. We talked about Mum and Ben, Scott and Mac. We talked about Rebecca. About Dad getting old. He told me all the things he worries about. I don't think either of us have ever been so honest with each other before.

'You don't understand how much you and Ben mean to me, Gem,' he said, his voice rough. 'You are everything to me, both of you.'

'I know, Dad,' I said, letting him hug me like I was a little girl.

I didn't tell him about my pregnancy—I didn't want him to feel invested in something that might simply fade away.

'How is Ben?' asks Jonesy, jerking me back to the present.

I breathe out through puffed cheeks. 'He's okay. He's a pretty amazing kid.'

'Well of course he bloody is. Never a doubt.'

'How are things here?' I say, noticing his desk is uncharacteristically neat.

'Not bad.' He clears his throat. 'A few issues keeping me on my toes as per usual, but nothing we can't handle.' He pauses. 'I spoke to Tommy earlier. He wouldn't go into detail but he mentioned some ongoing medical issues. He's considering calling it a day, I think.'

'That's good to hear. I know he's your friend but I'm definitely not his biggest fan.'

Jonesy's nod is slow and thoughtful. 'I feel pretty bad about how it all panned out,' he says gruffly. 'I keep thinking it would've been better if I had gone.'

'It wasn't your fault—I wanted to get out of here. I think I needed to.'

'How do you feel about being back?'

I twist my hands together and notice how long my fingernails have grown. 'I don't know,' I reply honestly. 'Ben needs stability, that's all I am sure of right now.' I look into Jonesy's concerned eyes but find no answers there.

'Will you be staying in Smithson for a while?' he asks tentatively.

'For a while,' I say with a small smile.

'How does your boyfriend in Sydney feel about that?'

A laugh bubbles in my throat. 'I think I'm a bit old to have a boyfriend. And Mac's closer to your age than mine.'

'Well, whatever you bloody well call him,' says Jonesy, looking embarrassed.

I sigh. 'I don't know. Things between us are a bit up in the air right now.'

Mac still hasn't responded to my message from Tuesday; his radio silence is killing me.

Shifting awkwardly, Jonesy folds his arms across his chest and changes the subject. 'And what about work?'

'I don't know.'

There's a silence. He twitches a pen between his fingers, tapping the tip against the wood. I fight an urge to grab the pen and throw it in the bin.

'I don't know,' I repeat. 'The internal investigation will go for another few weeks. Assuming it's fairly straightforward and I'm cleared, I'll extend my leave.' I look past Jonesy to the main room. A brunette constable lifts the top of the photocopier, briefly illuminating her face. 'After that, we'll see.'

Jonesy looks like he's about to say something else, and I tense up, hoping he won't present me with an offer I'll have to consider. Something that will complicate things even further and force a decision—yet another one.

'Anyway, I really should go,' I say. 'I just wanted to say hi, but I've got heaps to do, you know, getting stuff organised for the next few weeks. There's a lot I need to work out with Jodie.'

'Of course.' Jonesy shoots up from his chair surprisingly quickly. 'But if you're going to be hanging around here for a while, I expect you to pop in occasionally. I want to stay across your plans. There might be, ah, options for you closer to home.'

'Definitely.' I get to my feet and stamp them gently, shifting some mild pins and needles. 'I'll be in touch.'

I lift my hand in a series of awkward waves as I make my way through the office to the car park. I picture a former version of myself at the desk in the corner: a young woman in uniform with long tangled dark hair, her jaw angled in a stubborn tilt, eyes narrowed at the world.

Sliding into Scott's car, I lean back and stare at the underside of the sun visor. I actually don't have anywhere to be. Ben is still at Jodie's; Dad and Rebecca have gone shopping in Gowran. It's still a few hours until my call with Simon, who's writing a special feature about the murders and Abbey's reappearance.

I shake my head so hard my brain rattles, feeling oddly restless and at a loss. Maybe I should just drive back to Dad's and try to nap. I turn on the car just as my phone rings.

'Hey, Candy.'

'Gemma, come have a coffee with me.'

'Now?'

'Yeah, I'm at Reggie's. Are you free?'

'I'm just leaving the police station. Be there in a sec.'

I drive around the block and park next to Candy's bright red Fiat. The cafe is packed and noisy. Candy sits in a booth along the back wall, her huge belly encased in a stretchy lime dress. A half-finished chocolate milkshake is in front of her, and she's talking animatedly to someone seated opposite.

Her face lights up when she sees me, then she wriggles out from the bench seat.

'Yes, I'll give you an interview about Rick's murder,' I say, hugging her tight and feeling the firmness of her belly between us. 'But not about finding Abbey. I've already promised an exclusive to Simon.'

'Typical.' She rolls her eyes. 'As if I would ask you for that, anyway.'

I swat at her. 'As if you wouldn't.'

Candy's dark eyes bore into mine and she squeezes my hand. 'I'm really glad you're okay, Gem. I was worried.' She looks back toward the booth and bites her lip.

'What's wrong?'

'Mac's here.'

'Where?'

'Over there.'

My heart rate picks up. 'I thought he was in Sydney. Does he know I'm here?'

'Not *here* here.' She smiles with her trademark sass but I sense some nervousness. 'He's finding you hard to navigate and wanted my advice, but I don't know what to tell him. You're a total nightmare.'

I glance over and can see the side of his leg and his Italian leather boot.

'You need to talk to him, Gemma.'

I try to smile. 'Candy, he obviously wants to talk to *you* right now, not me.'

'Get over there now or I'll go into labour and make you deliver this baby with your bare hands.'

She gives me a little shove.

Mac holds his Breitling watch taut between his hands, turning it in a slow circle.

He looks up.

'Gemma!' He half stands, then realises he's wedged behind the table. Eyebrows raised, he turns to Candy.

'What a coincidence!' She grabs her bag and wiggles her fingers at us. 'I guess I'll be off. Bye, kids!' She manoeuvres her belly around a group of women at the front counter.

I slide in opposite Mac, adrenaline wrestling with my weary limbs. 'Hi.'

He looks flustered; he's buttoned his shirt wrong and the collar is lopsided. I'm making him crazy. I stare into his familiar eyes, trace his full lips with my gaze and let the sounds around me blur into a steady buzz while I simply focus on breathing in and out.

'I know I need to stop showing up like this,' he says, 'but I'm finding it hard to stay away from you.'

Tears fill my eyes. 'I don't think anyone has ever shown up like this for me before.'

'Gemma?'

Mac takes my hand. After a few seconds, I grip his back.

'Okay,' I say. 'Let's talk.'

Acknowledgements

When I started writing *The Dark Lake*, my goal was to finish it and maybe, just maybe, pitch it to a publisher. Now there are three published books. Suffice to say the whole thing still feels completely surreal most of the time, and I appreciate I'm fortunate to have had the opportunity to develop such a wildly complicated character as Gemma.

It turns out, however, that this writing business does not get easier, so it's lucky I have people on hand to keep me on the straight and narrow, or rather, the twisty and layered.

Particular thanks to my agent, Lyn Tranter, my publisher, Jane Palfreyman, and my editor, Kate Goldsworthy, who did all but pull the words out of my head. This book would not exist without you, or, if it did, it would be a shadowy version of its current self.

Thank you for all of your ideas, advice, encouragement and patience.

Whether via practical help or lofty esoteric conversations about narrative and characters, my personal support team all contribute to my writing getting done. The key members are: my kids, Oxford and Linus, Tom, my parents, my sister, my work colleagues and my friends. It is a pretty special bunch of people and I know I am incredibly fortunate to have them in my corner.

To my ever-growing gang of writerly friends, thanks for the support, the hilarious stories, the empathy and the inspiration. I am jealous and proud of you all, and making such wonderful friends has by far been the unexpected bonus of this crazy ride.

I want to thank the police officers and GPs who assisted me with making this book as plausible as possible. I know my 'but what if' questions are tedious and I appreciate your willingness to make my fictional desires work in with the rhythm of policing and the law. It goes without saying that all mistakes are mine.

A huge shout-out must go to the entire Allen & Unwin crew, who approach publishing my books with contagious passion and who are always so wonderful to deal with. Likewise to the bookselling community—you are all legends.

This book is dedicated to my parents, Susan and Kevin Bailey, who not only taught me to read and write but who have always encouraged me to aim high and finish what I start. It turns out that all of these skills came in really handy when writing this book so thank you for having the foresight to instill them in me (and for a whole lot of other things, too).

And finally, thank you for reading.